the
Templar's
garden

Catherine Clover completed her doctoral degree from Trinity College, Oxford, and her research about the end of the Hundred Years War informs the Maid of Gascony series. She has a particular professional interest in one of the great surviving English medieval treasures, the two-panel painting known as the Wilton Diptych, which plays a key role in the trilogy. Catherine is also producing a series of choral music albums that connect with the characters in the series. Visit www.catherineclover.com to learn more.

CATHERINE CLOVER

the Templar's garden

The Maid of Gascony Series, Book 1

DUCKWORTH

This edition published in 2020 by Duckworth,
an imprint of Duckworth Books Ltd
1 Golden Court, Richmond, TW9 1EU, United Kingdom
www.duckworthbooks.co.uk

Illustrations on pages 14, 94, 189, 223, 264, 313, 318, 338, 349
by Grace Ironside

Print ISBN: 9780715653890
Ebook ISBN: 9780715653906

Printed in the UK by Clays Ltd

For RC

The Unity

The lily white, its purity refined,
All that, for love remains fully tied.

To the sacred soul the Lord blesses bright,
He bestows no darkness to hinder the sight
Of His presence so near; His glory in the light;
That spills forth, its warmth and might.

Always sheltering us, and protecting from on high,
His Son's mercy given so that no man might die,
Without knowing His grace sent from above:
Our Father's greatest gift, our one pure love.

In the shadow of Heaven's glorious gates,
Our souls are left to contemplate:
The earthly love we shared as one,
A perfect vision of what is given by His Son.

O Holy Father, receive us as we are:
Mere mortal men who wish never to stray far
From Your blessed Trinity, Your perfect family,
You guard and protect us for all eternity.

For it is Your divine love that provides us peace,
When in forsaking all others we cannot cease,
The disruptive doubts that cloud our thoughts,
And create such unwieldy knots.

Help us to break free and live without
The strains and burdens that cause us to shout
In fear and pain; our loved ones seek refuge near
Out of such unhappiness that shall cost us dear.

Provide us Your wisdom, call us to You:
For only Your divine mercy can make us anew.
It is Your presence that we seek,
In times of trouble, when we are so weak.

By Your redemption and grace,
Eternal love shall fill this place;
For if we unite our souls through You,
Our love will be renewed.

Prologue:
Abbaye de Saint Nicolas de Blâmont, France

*A*s I face the final years of my life here in the care of the Benedictine nuns at the Abbey of St Nicolas of Blâmont, I have begun compiling my journals into a narrative of my life, for the path God granted me has had many joys and sorrows. The people I met, the places I visited, the intrigues that I faced: I observed and chronicled them all. In recalling the details of these encounters and with the end of my years growing ever closer, I offer my story as a means of preserving it for future generations.

I grew up in the southwest of the country that has today become part of France. But when I was a young girl it was still called Gascony. We were able to communicate in French, Latin and Gascon, the last of which combined parts of both languages.

As Gascons we lived by customs and traditions more than written laws, and as such enjoyed more liberties and freedoms than our neighbours in countries to the north and south.

Our landscape was dotted with the silhouettes of sturdy fortifications, though our nobility lacked the great wealth of their counterparts in France and Spain.

Until the final battle was lost to the French in 1453, Gascony remained an appendage of the kings of England. Throughout the period of their administration, the English benefited from the allegiances of the main ruling Gascon families, including the Counts of Armagnac, the Counts of Bigorre and Foix, the Viscounts of Bearn and our noble house, the Seigneurie of Albret. Members of our house turned their fealty to the French in the 1400s, even serving in the French king's army. Yet our separate branch, the Albret Courteault family, remained aligned with the English. In acknowledgement of our loyalty we were granted financial advantages in the running of our estate.

My mother was a descendant of Edward, the Black Prince of Bordeaux. Marie Claire Margaux, or simply Maman, as she was known to us, was born on 10 June 1410 to Philippa Margaux, the Black Prince's illegitimate daughter and half-sister to King Richard II of England.

Maman's features were clearly those of her Plantagenet English ancestors; her hair and skin were both fair and she would grow tall and slim in shape. Her mother Philippa was quite old at the time of her pregnancy and she died in childbirth, leaving our mother abandoned. Were it not for the attentive kindness of the midwife who delivered her, our mother's fate would have been the same. Knowing our mother's ancestry, the midwife decided it best to place her as an orphan with the Sisters of Charity from Saint Jacques-de-Compostelle. The nuns agreed to care for and bring up our mother, whom they referred to as "la princesita," in their convent according to their ways. Being surrounded from infancy by such pious Christian women, it is little wonder that Maman showed the compassion she did toward others throughout her life.

A Gascon descendant of noble birth, our father, Lord Philippe d'Albret Courteault, was born in 1405, the youngest of seven children. His facial features bore the hallmark of nobility in the region, both in his round face and his Gascon nose. It was slightly long and pointed, not wholly dissimilar from that of the Roman noses we children saw on ancient coins portraying the faces of great emperors from antiquity. He was kind and pious; fair in heart and mind with all whom he encountered.

Because of our father's decision to marry a woman of low social standing and English ancestry, he was given the poorest share of inheritance in the Seigneurie d'Albret lands. Our family demesne included the forested area between the towns of Roquefort in the south and the cathedral town of Bazas in the north. Though he was considered an outcast by the rest of his family, as a tradition, every year he and his brothers would spend many days in the autumn hunting for wild boar that inhabited the vast wooded acreage of our lands.

I was the middle oldest of five children, two boys and three girls. At the time I begin this story in 1450, the oldest was Margaret at seventeen years old, then fifteen-year-old Johan, next me being fourteen years old, followed by nine-year-old Christophe and finally eight-year-old Sarah.

With long fair hair and a rosy pink complexion, Margaret resembled our mother. She did not take much interest in potential suitors, that is, not until she met Count Alfonse de Nérac. A quiet lord, Count Alfonse was kind and thoughtful, and his commitment to our sister was evident very early on in their courtship. He composed beautiful poems to Margaret in which he described the chivalrous activities of the Knights Templar. My mother and I would sit by the fire in my parents' solar, listening to Margaret read his words, giggling and swooning over every verse he so lovingly composed. From what Count Alfonse described, I knew in my heart at a very young age that the only man I should ever wish to marry would be one who had served as a Templar Knight, for in my mind their saintly piety and kind acts of charity set them apart from all other men of rank and nobility.

Johan was a hearty fellow. In his adolescence, my father began teaching him about the administration of our farms, and in the autumn took him on the annual hunt for wild boar. Johan loved being outside: he was quite an accomplished equestrian, his skill no doubt inherited from our father. He was of medium build, with a soft, ruddy complexion and thick reddish-brown hair. My brother did well in his studies but no scholar was he, for he preferred to hunt and to ride. When Johan reached the age of twelve, our father asked him to assist our family chaplain, Père Charles, in the management of the farms on our demesne. Johan thrived with this new responsibility and he seemed to mature overnight.

Little Sarah and Christophe were barely a year apart and, as such, practically grew up together as twins. They were both big-boned and dark-haired, and their hearts were full of sweetness and joy. My younger brother and sister adored our chaplain and tutor, Père Charles; they took to their studies and learning the Bible from him with great purpose. I can remember telling them stories from the Old Testament at night to help them fall asleep. At bedtime we would gather in my brothers' bedchamber where Sarah and Christophe would lie down together. As I related the tales, I watched as first one and then the other closed their heavy eyelids and drifted off into peaceful rest. Leaving Christophe to sleep in his bed, I would then carry my sister back to our room and gently tuck her in for the night.

While enduring heavy labour at my birth, my mother had a vision from God that in turn directed my purpose in life. He revealed himself in glory to my mother just as she made her final pushes to free me from her womb, telling her as I came into this world that I was his messenger and, as such, I was to be allowed to spread the word of his love amongst those whose lives were touched by devastating loss and feelings of unworthiness. Such a calling from our Lord suited me perfectly. I grew up bearing a divine love in my soul for Christ and his great suffering upon the Cross; for his mercy and forgiveness for our sins.

Since I was born into a noble Gascon family, I did not face the same social constraints as I would have, had my family been closely tied to a royal court. The liberties I experienced in my youth were not common to ladies of noble birth in England or France. But my parents, being devout Christians, respected and feared the word of the Lord, and his message foretelling my purpose, which was to be revealed one day.

Of all my siblings, this air of inherited independence affected me the most. I grew up feeling an entitlement to being treated on an equal level as the men in my family and our household, and indeed, because of my calling by the Lord, which those around me knew I had been granted, I was left to pursue a life following the teachings of my faith. Because our Gascon customs and norms were so vastly different to those of neighbouring countries, my independent spirit was never questioned by those with whom I associated.

It was my father who taught me to ride, and on my tenth birthday in 1446, he gave me my first horse, a Spanish breed from an area called Andalusia, whom I named Peyriac. He was a gentle giant; his coat was dapple grey in colour and his four legs, mane and tail a rich shade of ebony. Spending time with Peyriac became my escape from the world around me. I would take him out on long rides as we explored the countryside and forest near our home. I rode so much and so well from an early age that my father lovingly called me his little hussar after the famous Hungarian knights.

From my childhood, I always wore a long woollen surcoat with a fitted bodice over my britches when riding; the bottom half could be spread out behind me, giving the appearance of a gown, helping to disguise my manner of riding astride. This special outer garment made it possible for me to ride and care for my horse without being encumbered by a dress with its heavy folds of cloth draping about my feet. Though we had a groom, after pleading with my parents to allow me to do so, I was permitted to care for Peyriac myself. My horse became the centre of my world; with him and on him I felt a loving bond unsurpassed by that of any human connection.

As much as Father wished for me to have a certain degree of free-dom for exploration, Maman always believed I was to be her little scholar. She took great care that I should be fully literate. When I expressed an interest in architecture, on my twelfth birthday it was she who gave me my first bound book, a copy of a treatise on the architec-ture of Rome, written around the time of Christ's birth. I studied the heavy tome with great determination, committing the architectural vocabulary to memory. The detailed drawings captured my imagin-ation; nothing in Gascony resembled the buildings that illustrated the text. In my youth I wished to one day visit the places filled with such perfectly proportioned buildings. I could only imagine seeing in person the engineering and mechanical marvels of God's wisdom that seemed to mysteriously allow the great cathedrals and palaces to stand.

Our home, the castle of Rosete, was a small square fortification with four round corner towers and a moat. One entered Rosete through massive wooden doors set in the portal of a barbican, though access to the inner ward was only possible upon the raising of the portcul-lis. Within that complex resided our porter, Pey LeFevre. His small narrow room housed a fireplace and private latrine. Two additional rooms were located in the barbican on the first and second floors. One of the rooms was shared by our cook, Jeanne Chastel, and a servant. The largest room was given to my Aunt Christine, my father's sister, who lived with us after my mother's death.

A childless widow and staunch supporter of the French king, our aunt would remain with us, acting as our governess after Margaret's marriage and departure from Rosete, though I was never fond of her, nor did I trust her; her true purpose for living with us would become clear over the course of time. Additional servants and household attendants could be called upon to serve on special occasions such as the feast after the Great Hunt. Similar to other noble Gascon families of similar rank and means, we did not require a large household of servants to maintain our home.

On the other side of the barbican sat a square building of two levels housing the wardrobe on the ground floor and the private chamber of our chaplain, Père Charles, on the first floor. His fair hair was the colour of freshly crushed wheat; his strident voice commanded our attention whether in our lessons or chapel services. With his tall, sturdy build one might mistake him for being a Crusader knight, rather than a country priest. On his face he always wore a gracious and welcoming smile, though his deep-blue eyes carried a penetrating sadness. His manners were impeccable and his vast knowledge of all subjects astounding.

It was from his tutoring in Latin that I first learned about a place most appealing to my imagination. Père Charles owned a copy of the Itinerarium Kambriae by Geraldus Cambrensis. We used it in our lessons as a source of contemporary Latin to assist us in building the vocabulary of common words that describe places and their people. I was fascinated by Gerald's work as a priest and a pilgrim, for his rich descriptions brought the countryside of Wales alive for me. On numerous occasions I made mention of this enthusiasm to Père Charles. How could I have known that one day I would see and stay at the very places I had studied from the text? I, too, would venture on the exact same path as had Gerald, ending my pilgrimage as countless others had before me, at the cathedral of St Davids in Pembrokeshire.

At thirteen years old, my world turned upside down, for I experienced the death of my mother. One of her greatest wishes was to see that her three daughters were literate. I remember vividly that just before she died, she called me in to see her and to say farewell. As Maman lay on her deathbed with our chaplain in peaceful meditation, reciting from the psalter at her bedside, she gathered the strength to focus on me as she gripped my hand and whispered in a faraway voice: "Remember, Isabelle, your life is a prophecy from God upon mankind. Do not fear his instruction. Promise me, Isa, promise me to keep writing in your journal. Your journal, Isa. Capture your life in words and drawings before they slip from your memory forever." That is the last thing I remember her saying to me. And from that very day forward, I committed myself to recording in words and illustrations the experiences of my daily life, the people I met, and the places I visited, just as I had read in the work of Geraldus Cambrensis.

I
Showing of Love

My earliest vision from God came to me at age fourteen, not long after the death of my mother. From a deep sleep in the dark of the night, I shot straight up in bed, my whole body awash in a clammy sweat, unable to comprehend or control the steady stream of tears that fell from my eyes. Aroused from her slumber, my sister reached over and touched my hand.

"Isabelle, what has happened? What makes you cry?" she asked in alarm.

"Oh Margaret, I fear what I saw in a dream!"

"Can you recall what you saw?" my sister asked tenderly as she sat up in the bed next to me.

"I felt the presence of God as he held me close. His aura was ablaze in glory; it felt as though I was engulfed by flames, and yet I felt no pain in his touch. He told me my purpose in this life is to bestow his love upon a devoted son whom I shall come to know in time. He instructed me to not fear what terrors and sin my eyes will one day behold; Our Lord assured me that I will come to know the love of his blessed Son, Jesus Christ, as I share his love where there is emptiness and sin and unworthiness in this temporal world. I know not what he means by his instruction. I am so afraid, Margaret! What is meant by this? Why must the Lord speak to me of such things? With whom am I to share this love? And what is the love of which he even speaks? I fear I shall displease him, and what will become of me then?"

"Do not fear, dear sister," Margaret reassured me as she stroked my face tenderly. "Remember the divine prophecy made at your birth. This vision that awakened you is our Lord's confirmation of what he desires for you to do in this life. Recall the words from your psalter, found in psalm forty-two, 'Why art thou so full of heaviness, O my soul: and why art thou so disquieted within me? Put thy trust in God: for I will yet give him thanks for the help of his countenance.' Now, do close your eyes and go back to sleep. All shall be well, and all manner of things shall be well in the morning, I assure you."

II
Pestilence & Prophecy

"Have you heard the news from Paris?" Pey, our porter, exclaimed animatedly as he moved to sit near Jeanne, our cook, one afternoon. I had been in the cellar and had not noticed Pey's footsteps on the wooden floor above when he entered the kitchen. Drawing back, I was curious to learn more. In silence, I retreated into the shadows, craning forward to catch their exchange.

The two servants sat facing each other across the central worktable as they often did at that time of day, the ingredients of the evening meal spread between them.

"Well, come on then. Do tell me, Pey – do not leave me in suspense!" Jeanne's tone was excited.

"It is the plague: it is coming for us, even here so far away from the city. None of us will be spared." Pey made the threat seem frightening in its proximity to our home.

"How do you know all that? I have not heard anything about it. I think you are mad, that is what I think," Jeanne replied sceptically.

"My friends in Bazas tell me it has ravaged the city of Paris. Decaying bodies are piling up; there is no one to bury them. If you don't believe me, listen to the priests at the cathedral in Bazas. They are now saying prayers for the souls of those who have died from the disease."

"I see. Well, this is alarming news. How long do you think it will be before we are going to face the same fate around here?" Jeanne asked anxiously.

"I pray it does not come before Lady Margaret is wed to the Count of Foix," Pey replied, as I choked back my gasp of surprise.

"Our Lady Margaret is to marry the Count of Foix?" Jeanne asked in disbelief.

"Aye, that is what I hear from my friend who has a tavern in Cadillac visited by the count's retinue."

"But Our Lady is so fair a woman; the count may have ample wealth and lands but his wrath is vengeful. I cannot imagine Lord Philippe allowing Her Ladyship to enter into such a dangerous affair. I have heard the count does not even entertain strangers travelling through his lands at his castle. If Lady Margaret must marry him I pray she will survive his evil ways. Surely that will be a miracle of God!"

"The count's misdeeds have often been brought to the attention of the King's Council in Bordeaux. But the English who are in power there allow him to be pardoned from any wrongdoing. If you ask my opinion, I believe the count would be no match for the English if he were found to have violated Lady Margaret. Not with Lord Philippe's connections to the constable of Bordeaux and his army of English soldiers stationed in *les filleules*."

"All the same, I would not want to be in Her Ladyship's position," Jeanne concluded. "I certainly would not wish to be forced to marry such a wicked man. I have heard the stench of rotting corpses from his donjon fills the stagnant air of his castle at Benauges."

"And imagine how all those bodies, and the vermin who feed on them, must fill his castle with disease. It would seem to me if anyone was to be imprisoned there they would not come out alive." The disgust in Pey's tone was evident.

I could not stomach hearing any more foul details of his reports. I moved and cleared my throat, alerting the servants to my presence in the threshold of the cellar.

"Good afternoon, Your Ladyship." Pey jumped to his feet and bowed his head as I entered the kitchen.

"Your Ladyship." Jeanne did the same as I walked past them.

"I am grateful to have found these provisions," I declared, smiling as I tipped my basket to show them the apple and carrots I had collected for Peyriac.

"Indeed, Lady Isabelle, your horse does well by the treats you provide him," Pey acknowledged with a twinkle in his eye.

"I must be off to feed and groom him now." I nodded to both servants before stepping into the courtyard.

For a moment I closed my eyes, inhaling the fresh air deeply as I sought to digest all that I had overheard. Quickly I moved on, gathering my journal and writing instruments from my room before returning to the stable to care for my horse. I wished to note all the details of the alarming news Pey had divulged, fearful of his cruel prophecy that was about to unfold in our lives.

III
The Solemnization
of Matrimony

"Margaret, do you remember His Lordship, Bertram, the Count of Foix?" asked our father. "He joined us at the Great Hunt a fortnight ago and at the feast that same evening."

Over supper, our father had asked my sister to join him and our aunt to discuss a private matter in his bedchamber before Margaret went to sleep. Later that night, dressed in a long white nightshirt, I stood at the door. With my ear pressed firmly against the frame, in secret I listened to their dialogue.

"I do remember him, yes. He has come back to see you recently, has he not?" Margaret's voice remained cheerful, innocent of where the conversation was heading.

"Indeed, he has. We have met to discuss an alliance between the Albret Courteault family and the House of Foix. The count is determined to marry you, and in return has offered me a dozen members of his garrison should war with France reach our lands. When you bear him a child, our two families will be forever joined. He is prepared to give his heir an inheritance that will provide for us all after his death. The House of Albret Courteault will reap the benefits of ruling a portion of the lands he holds title to now."

My father fell silent and for several moments I could hear no sound. Presently, the faint sounds of Margaret crying drifted through the heavy door that separated me from my sister. It became clear that our father was trying to comfort her as best he could.

"There, there, Margaret. I have tried in vain to persuade him that this is not an appropriate time for you to consider the thought of marriage, so soon after the loss of your husband, Count Alfonse. However, as the eldest daughter you are to set an example for the others of what is expected of you all: to make good marriages that will benefit this family."

"Oh, Father!" cried Margaret out of desperation as she pleaded. "I do not even know this man at all. He is so much older than me and I am not ready to wed again. I have spoken recently to our chaplain, asking him for advice on pursuing a vocation as a nun. I much prefer to live my life with daily devotions and prayer."

"You put me in a difficult position, Margaret," our father conceded. "So be it. Let his hostile threats fall upon me. I will bear the responsibility of protecting our family and estate from any violence that might come as a result of your rejecting his marriage proposal."

"Now you listen to me, Margaret!" interrupted Aunt Christine's stern voice. "You shall do as your father instructs. You do not have a choice in the matter of whom you marry. This family must not dishonour the Albret name by rejecting the count's proposal of marriage. How dare Père Charles assert any authority over you and your future plans!"

She continued, unleashing her wrath upon my father.

"As for you, brother, you already bring shame upon the House of Albret with your insistence on remaining loyal to the English, even after your wife's death. Do not do us further injustice by allowing your daughter to reject this offer of marriage and title to the Foix inheritance. She must do as you ask of her, regardless of how she feels. Marriage is not a matter of love; marriage is for the contracting of property!"

There came another pause in their conversation. I could still hear the faint sound of Margaret crying.

With a sorrowful voice, she replied, "Do not worry for me, Father. I do not wish to see our family torn apart by a feud with the count. Perhaps I am wrong and I judge him too hastily. Though I do not feel it in my heart, I shall marry him."

"Very well, Margaret, I shall send word to him that you accept his proposal." My father's tone was cool and deferential.

I heard the rustle of my sister's skirt as she stood up, causing the floor to creak softly as she walked toward the door to leave the room. I hurried back to our bedchamber and sat on the bed, careful not to awaken Sarah, and took up my embroidery. When Margaret entered, her face bore the signs of distress at what had been asked of her. I acted as though I had heard nothing of her conversation, and she never spoke of the cause of her anguish. I had been shocked by my aunt's insistence that my sister marry the count. Her brazen criticism of our chaplain's role in advising Margaret made it clear that none of us would be spared from her domineering intolerance of our affairs.

My sister's marriage in late January 1452 was an intimate ceremony, with only immediate family and some members of the count's retinue in attendance. In the weeks following Margaret's departure, her absence from our home was palpable; we had become accustomed to her nurturing and motherly demeanour in our daily activities. Soon thereafter, Father was recalled to Bordeaux by the English council to work for the Gascon resistance effort at the *Palais de l'Ombrière*, the seat of the King's Council in the capital. My aunt remained with us, having assumed the role of governess to my younger siblings in my sister's absence. She was assisted by our chaplain, who gave us our daily lessons in Latin, logic, and rhetoric, in addition to celebrating daily Mass for us and our servants.

With Father and Margaret away from Rosete, as the spring wore on, Johan, too, began spending more time apart from us. He stayed with friends in and around Bazas, engaging in social activities with his companions. One evening in April he returned to Rosete full of good cheer, his spirits high. After supper, when Sarah and Christophe had gone to bed, we were seated together in a window seat of the great hall; my aunt and I sharing a stone bench on one side, its cold, firm seat covered in hand-stitched cushions; Père Charles and Johan sharing the bench directly across from us. The intimate space was illuminated by candles perched atop two massive standing candelabra. Our aunt worked on her embroidery, Père Charles silently read from a Latin text we were studying, I pored over the decorated pages of my psalter, testing myself on my memorization of the psalms as Johan looked on.

"Aunt Christine, Isabelle, Père Charles; I wish to share some important news." Johan's declaration broke the silence. We all looked up expectantly.

"Do not keep us waiting, then," Aunt Christine implored. "Do carry on."

"I have met a girl whom I wish to marry." Johan's face beamed as he spoke.

"How wonderful, Johan!" I exclaimed joyfully.

Hearing the news caused our aunt to sit up and put her sewing to one side.

"I see. And who is she? What is her family's name?" Aunt Christine cast a stern expression over Johan.

"I don't see how that is important, her family name," Johan retorted, fearless against our aunt.

"If I may," Père Charles interjected helpfully, "I believe what your aunt meant to ask was whether this girl is from a family known to your parents?"

"I would thank you *not* to put words in my mouth, Père Charles. Since this matter is none of your affair you may take your leave of us at once. I wish to discuss this further with my nephew and niece in private."

"I see. Very well." Père Charles nodded his head in deference to our aunt before collecting his books and retiring for the evening, softly closing the door to the great hall as he left.

"I am still waiting for your reply to my question, Johan," Aunt Christine insisted, her voice becoming more shrill.

With his face drawn up and showing no fear, only contempt, Johan took Père Charles's vacated seat directly across from our aunt.

"The girl I love is named Pharrah. Pharrah Said. Her family are spice traders from Tangier in Morocco."

A gasp of disgust escaped from our aunt.

"You cannot be serious. You are not permitted to entertain the idea that you love this girl. She is foreign: you are only allowed to marry within the Gascon nobility. You must stop seeing her at once! When I tell you father what you are doing he will certainly disown you." Our aunt's tone was determined.

"I do not have to remain here in your company and listen to you tell me whom I am permitted to love. How dare you! You are not my parent; I daresay my mother would have never spoken such unkind words. And you think that my father would disown me? How rich of you; it was your father and brothers, my very uncles, who turned their backs on our father when he told them he was in love with an orphan girl of foreign ancestry. Our beloved parents taught us what it is to love; it is not about one's family name. I care nothing for Pharrah's position in society. I love her; you will see. Take back what you have said to me or I will....."

"Yes, Johan? What is it that you will do?" Aunt Christine tested my brother.

Johan jumped up and away from the window seat alcove.

"I will leave Rosete! And I will never return!" he yelled.

"No, Johan, do not go!" I cried, standing up and reaching out to hold my brother's arm.

"I do not believe you – that you will run away to a life of no support," our aunt challenged.

"Then you refuse to apologise to me?" Johan pressed.

"I have no reason to apologise. I speak words that are the truth, which you simply do not like to hear. Marrying a girl from a trader's family, much less from north Africa, really, Johan? Is that the best you can do? Clearly the Albret family's behaviour to your own parents did nothing to teach you about why family ties matter. I suppose you really ought not to be a part of the limited inheritance the Albret Courteault family would offer you in seeking marriage to a proper bride. You see how your father's lands are so poor, the yield of crops barely provides for your own family, let alone those families of the peasants who work for you? No, it will be far better for your brothers and sisters if you go away and seek marriage to the girl you *love* and leave the inheritance to them. They will no doubt make good marriages. Certainly they will be better than yours."

As my aunt continued her cruel and demeaning rant against Johan and Pharrah I felt a sharp stab of ire build in my chest. I fought back the tears as Johan tore his arm away from my hand.

"Goodbye, Isabelle. Take care of Sarah and Christophe." He stormed across the floor of the great hall.

"Johan, no, wait!" I called out.

The door slammed behind him, and I felt numb; I had never imagined I would lose both Margaret and Johan in such swift succession. I turned back to the bench to gather my psalter and cloak. My aunt put out her leg to prevent me from walking past, the pointy toe of her poulaine catching briefly on the hem of my skirt.

"Do not dare to disappoint me, Isabelle. The house of Albret Courteault will not suffer the loss of your brother Johan."

I kept my eyes to the floor and did not respond. My aunt lowered her leg to let me pass. On the way to my room I stopped first in the stable, hoping to see Johan's horse still there. The stall was vacant, his horse nowhere to be found. Johan had indeed run away to be with his love.

I went upstairs to the room that I shared with Sarah. After changing my clothes for bed I knelt on the floor, my hands clasped in prayer. With my eyes closed I searched for comfortable words of healing after what I had witnessed that evening.

"Almighty Father, for the senseless berating that wisdom has endured on this night, keep your prudence, keep your justice, and let the true test be that which shall overcome all evil. For those who impart only hate and do not love, show your strength, that they may recoil for their wicked transgression against purity of heart and soundness of mind. Protect my brother Johan, and the girl Pharrah whom I have yet to meet. I ask that you guide and shield them along their course, that we might one day be united again as family. Amen."

IV
The Count of Foix

As the spring evolved into summer, I felt an increasing sense of anxiety for the safety of Johan and Margaret. Neither of them had written to tell us of their plans, and I feared for their health and well-being. I was eager to have my father return home to Rosete. He had written to us that he planned to leave Bordeaux before the Constable, Sir Edward Hull, locked the gates of the city against the French troops who were thought to be planning a siege on the city in the autumn.

To my surprise, late one night in August after I had checked on Peyriac before going to bed, I heard voices and laughter coming from the kitchen. As I crept closer I could distinguish that they belonged to our cook and porter who without doubt assumed that the household would be asleep. Undetected, I stood hunched over in the shadows that fell outside the doorway of the ground-floor kitchen.

"And have you any news from Benauges?" our cook asked our porter.

The two servants sat on wooden stools before the hearth, its glowing embers emitting a slow hiss signalling the end of the workday for both. Unaware that they were being watched, they took turns drinking from a ceramic jug normally used for carrying cider and wine to my family at our meals in the great hall above. The room was illuminated by the flame of a single fat tallow candle placed at the end of the work table closest to them. The outline of Jeanne's plump physique contrasted sharply with that of Pey's; his thin frame cast a haunting silhouette against the tiled fireplace surround.

"She is being kept a prisoner of the count, that is what my friends in the town of Cadillac tell me," Pey announced.

"Does the family know what has become of their sister?" Jeanne's tone revealed her alarm.

"I know Lady Isabelle has often sent written correspondence to Her Ladyship in the hope that she may receive some word. But no response has yet come back," Pey observed.

"That sounds about right. I have heard from those who serve the count and his retinue. She is locked in the top floor of the donjon; a grim place to be for a genteel woman such as Lady Margaret. The rumour I have heard is that she remains barren. The count believes she prays to God not to conceive by him and he punishes her for her piety and faith by keeping her imprisoned in the round tower."

"That would explain why she has not written back to Lady Isabelle," Pey stated confidently. "It appears he does not allow her to receive any messages from her family or to receive guests. What a pity that she was given in marriage to such an evil oxhouser!"

What I overheard of their conversation filled my heart with dread for my sister. I silently crept away to my bedroom, sick at the thought of Margaret's imprisonment.

———

"Lady Isabelle, are you still out here?" Pey called out for me across the inner ward late the next afternoon. I had taken Sarah and Christophe to read and play in our mother's garden. Looking up from my psalter, a canopy of delicate white roses framing the arbour over my head, I watched as his spindly legs carried him quickly in my direction.

"Yes, Pey, here I am," I announced, waving to him as I stood up.

"Very well, Your Ladyship. I could barely see you over the hedge. There is a visitor come to speak to you. She says she is a friend of your Lady Margaret's. I have taken her to the privy hall."

"My sister? She has word of my sister?" I exclaimed. "Sarah and Christophe, you must remain here until I return, do you understand?"

"Yes, Isabelle," my brother and sister answered in unison before returning to their game of chess.

I dashed away after Pey, quickly ascending the two flights of stairs before entering the privy hall behind him.

"Lady Bernadette, may I present Lady Isabelle," Pey announced.

"I am so very pleased you have come," I said, walking towards Lady Bernadette.

"As I am pleased to see you again. Look how you have grown so fair since I saw you last at the marriage of Lady Margaret and the count. Your dear sister has told me much about you; about all of you." Lady Bernadette's calm tone put me at ease at once.

Her Ladyship was truly exquisite, a widowed matron of about fifty years with fair white skin and ashen-blonde hair pulled up tightly under a conical sapphire hat covered by a gauze veil that draped down her back. Her long-sleeved, navy-silk dress was open from her neck to her chest, revealing a gold necklace, heavy with inset rubies, pearls and enamelled decoration. With her air of grace and refinement she instantly reminded me of my late mother whose presence in my life I missed dearly.

"Shall I send for your aunt as well, Lady Isabelle?" Pey enquired.

"No thank you, Pey, that will be all for now," I instructed the porter.

"Very well, then." Pey bowed to us both and closed the door gently as he left.

"Please, do have a seat," I said, gesturing to the cushioned stone window seat looking out over the inner ward.

"Have you any word from my sister?" I began in earnest. "I have sent her many letters, but I have never received a reply. I am greatly concerned for her health. I have heard horrible rumours about her situation, but I have no way to confirm their truth."

"Yes, my child, I can understand how difficult this must be for you, to be separated from your lovely sister Margaret while the affairs of the duchy continue to crumble about us. I fear this is not a safe time for the people of this place."

"What news have you, then? Is there anything you can tell me about how she is faring?"

Her Ladyship sighed heavily before continuing.

"I am afraid what I have to tell you will be very difficult to hear. I have visited your sister. She asked me to carry this letter to you. She said you can read and that you are a writer. Is this true?" Lady Bernadette took from her satchel a roll of parchment, secured only by a length of blue ribbon. I recognised it immediately as the ribbon I had given her to wear at her wedding.

"Yes; yes, I do write. I keep journals of the people I know and the stories I hear others tell. I wish to have a record of what my life was like so that one day I might share it with my children and grandchildren."

Lady Bernadette handed me the scroll.

"Then you should be able to understand this account. I have not read it myself. I can assure you, though, whatever your sister tells you, you must believe her. When I visited her this week she was in a terrible condition."

My eyes grew moist as Lady Bernadette recounted the state of my sister. Suddenly, with a violent push, the door to the privy hall swung open with great force, causing it to slam against the wooden wall that framed it.

"I see I am not too late to be introduced to our guest, if I am not mistaken, niece?" I could detect the lack of sincerity in my aunt's tone, of which our guest would be unaware, as she approached us in the window alcove.

"Why, is that Madame Christine d'Albret?" Lady Bernadette stood up and nodded her head towards my aunt.

"I am, indeed. And now that I have come closer I, too, recognise you. You are Madame de Tastes; Lady Bernadette." Once again, my aunt's pretence of enthusiasm was detected only by me.

"This is a most welcome reunion," my aunt continued, her silvery tone turning the pit of my stomach. I could tell immediately she had a great dislike for Lady Bernadette. Yet our guest made no acknowledgement of Aunt Christine's disdain.

"I have come to bring word of Lady Margaret's ill health; she suffers greatly in her marriage to the Count of Foix."

"Why, I thank you for showing such compassion and concern for my niece, Isabelle's sister," my aunt replied. "But these matters really must be judged by her father, my brother Philippe; he is away in Bordeaux but I shall be certain to pass along your report when he returns."

"I have enjoyed meeting Lady Isabelle, she has made me feel most welcome at Rosete." Lady Bernadette turned to me, her warm smile temporarily casting away my fears.

"That is good to hear. Though, Isabelle, the next time you are entertaining guests I expect to be invited to meet them," my aunt chastised me.

"Yes, Aunt Christine," I replied dutifully, not wishing to cause a scene. "Madame de Tastes, shall I walk you to your escort waiting downstairs?"

"Why, yes, I would welcome that," Lady Bernadette replied, standing up.

Leaving my aunt behind in the privy hall, we descended the steps and into the inner ward before Lady Bernadette stopped to face me at the gatehouse where her attendants stood to the side, waiting to help her into her carriage.

"You have the letter from your sister?" she asked, her tone low.

"Yes," I replied in the same hushed tone.

"Know that I will do whatever is necessary to help her, to help you, to be reunited. When the time is right, get her out. I pray you will not be too late." Lady Bernadette's solemn expression bore the pain of what she had witnessed.

I nodded my head, and she turned from me, stretching out her right hand to her attendant who helped her inside her cart. With a whisk of the driver's whip the horses came alive and the carriage pulled away; slowly at first, then picking up speed quickly by the time the thundering hooves passed through the gatehouse and away from Rosete. I knew I needed to read the letter from my sister. The only place where I could do so without fear of my aunt interrupting me was the chapel.

———

My dear Isa,

I trust you and the family are well. How I think of you all often, and our dear Maman, with memories of our beautiful Rosete. My marriage to the Count of Foix has been nothing like I expected. It is so bad that I find I wish for my life to end. I pray to our Lord that he takes me, that he frees me from the persecution I endure at the hands of these men; though it is not only their hands that do the torture.

It began on our wedding night. I could not lie with the count. I did not feel in my heart that I could bear to look at another man unclothed and in bed with me. I knew it would take some time to become comfortable in his presence as his wife, and I certainly did not feel amorous towards him. I hoped he would be compassionate and not force our love. But his anger overcame him and he tried to strike me that very night, while within the very walls of Rosete! I did my best not to cry, even as he threatened me. Thankfully, since he drank so much wine at our wedding banquet he became unsteady on his feet and he fell in a heap on top of the bed. I rolled off to one side and crept across the room, sleeping in the corner near the door in case he came for me again. Should he have been successful and raised a hand against me, I planned to run to Father and beg his forgiveness that very night, for I wished to never be alone with the count again.

He did not awaken until the morning, though. Kicking me awake he told me that once we arrived at Benauges I would suffer for not consummating our marriage on our wedding night. I am certain members of his retinue had been spying at the door of our bedchamber, waiting to hear the sounds of our lovemaking. Knowing that these men whom he prized for their brawn and fortitude would hear no noise of our copulation must have angered the count even more. I overheard his servants make fun of him out of earshot about his lack of manhood with his young wife on his wedding night. They would say these things in my presence, but not dare to say them in front of Bertram.

After our arrival at his castle, the count took me to his bedchamber immediately and locked the door. I begged him to leave me be, to give our love time to be nurtured and to grow, but my pleading seemed to only make him more determined to have control over me. He hit me hard across the face and I fell back onto his bed, crying. I attempted to scramble away from him but his strength was too great. He grabbed me from the back and pushed up my skirt, mounting me from behind, as a stallion to a mare.

I was devastated by what I had read so far. Anger seethed throughout my frame. I looked up from the letter, needing desperately to fix my eyes on something to help calm my mind, now filled with wicked thoughts and brutal images of the horrid treatment my sister had endured. As I glanced about, my vision caught on the cross placed in the centre of the altar. I was in our chapel. I was safe there. I closed my eyes and took some time before opening them once more to read the conclusion of Margaret's letter.

I have never felt so humiliated in my whole life. When he finished, I lay naked on his bed, my face and left eye bruised and swollen. He refused to even look at me and left the room, leaving the door wide open. Then one of his valets entered. The count had ordered his men to lock me in the donjon. Can you imagine how that felt to be left there in his room, a lady of my standing, disgraced, violated and exposed in such a way? His servant entered and said nothing to comfort me, he simply told me to pick myself up and follow him. I had no time to put on my clothes and no idea where I was being taken. As we walked through the courtyard towards the donjon, members of his guard peered at me, mocking me and my chastity. I felt so humiliated to be put in such a position. I soon learned the count's intention. I was to be locked in a cell at the top of the ancient tower, only to be released upon his command. I begged God every day that I would not bear his child, for I feared the future of the infant at the hands of such an evil man.

I close this letter to you with the hope that you will know how much I love and care for you all. I fear that by the time you are reading this it will be too late for me. All I ask is that you send for my body. Do not let Bertram do to my corpse as he has done to the others who have died here. I wish to be buried alongside our mother, in the garden at Rosete.

I pray you stay true to your divine calling, dear Isabelle. I love you, as I love all my family.

With great affection,
your sister Margaret

V

The Rescue

"Lady Isabelle?" Père Charles called my name softly from the bench behind me.

"Pardon me, I came to the chapel to pray; to find peace," I said, wiping my nose and the tears from my face while holding my gaze steady on the cross on the altar.

"I see. Well, I hope you have found it. I shall leave you then, I do not wish to disturb your meditation."

I heard my chaplain begin to step away and I glanced around.

"No, please. Do not leave me. I am so unhappy. I do not wish to be alone. May I confide something in you?" I asked, my eyes pleading.

"Why, of course you may. That is what I am here for. What troubles you?" Père Charles came to kneel by my side.

"Here; read this," I said, handing him the letter from Margaret.

I watched his expression as his eyes consumed the words. I had never witnessed him exhibit anything but a calm demeanour. Now I saw his face muscles move, his jaw grind; the visible outrage building in him was fearsome. For a moment my mind raced with the thought I had done something wrong to share my sister's private correspondence with our chaplain. Père Charles put down the letter, signalling he had finished reading it.

"I am so sorry," he said, handing it back to me. "Your sister is in grave danger for her life. I must go at once and help free her from the count; her marriage must be annulled."

"Then I shall go with you," I replied.

"No, Your Ladyship, you most certainly will not. I cannot risk having you taken prisoner by the count and abused by his men."

"Then I will get Peyriac and we will run away," I said defiantly.

"You shall do no such thing!" My chaplain's tone was fierce. "Your father and aunt will not allow you to ride unchaperoned across the duchy in lands that are held by feuding families. You are to remain here in the safety of Rosete."

"And what about you? How will you be safe from Count Bertram?" I challenged.

"You need not concern yourself with how I will free your sister; now enough of this, we are wasting precious time. I must explain to your aunt my reason for leaving."

We left the chapel together; I tagged along behind my chaplain as he dashed upstairs to the great hall where our supper was being set out.

"Lady Christine," Père Charles began, bowing to my aunt. "I am sorry, but I must take leave of you and the children at once. I have learned that Lady Margaret has taken seriously ill while in the care of her husband. It is critical that I recover her and return her to Rosete so she can heal at her familial home."

My aunt shot him a quizzical look.

"You are not in a position to take such measures on behalf of this family," she said, her tone commanding. "Margaret has made an important union between the House of Foix and House of Albret. I will not allow this contract to be broken."

"As the priest responsible for witnessing the marriage between Margaret and Bertram I bear the authority for protecting the wife

39

against abuse and neglect; both have been brought to my attention. I will write to Lord Philippe and seek his support for my actions."

"You are not to meddle in the affairs of this family!" Aunt Christine warned.

I stepped forward to stand next to Père Charles.

"I will be joining our chaplain to rescue my sister. If you try to block me, I will run away as Johan has. Then you will have lost two of father's children because of your cruelty. How will you explain that?" I challenged my aunt.

She glared at Père Charles and me.

"If you leave this home you do so at your own peril, Isabelle," Aunt Christine asserted, her tone sharp. "I take no responsibility for the behaviours of such impertinent children: you or your brother Johan."

Père Charles and I left Rosete that evening to ride to the town of Bazas and his friend Père Francis; our recovery of Margaret was underway.

———

Later that night we approached the town's arched stone gatehouse; Père Charles spoke briefly to the porter, explaining that we were there to visit Père Francis. The gate was unlocked and the portcullis raised, while a page was sent scurrying ahead of us to announce our arrival at the rectory. We passed through the entry and emerged into the quiet, open space of the central square. Only the steady clip-clop of hooves could be heard echoing through the warm, still night air that engulfed us. Under the heightened brilliance of the moonlit summer sky I took the time to survey my surroundings – in particular, the cathedral façade and the half-timbered townhouses and shops around the central market square. For the first time in my life I noticed the charm and character of our tranquil Gascon town. The serenity of the scene was interrupted by a familiar voice calling out to us from across the way.

"Charles, Lady Isabelle, welcome!" Père Francis's voice rang out cheerfully as he approached us on foot, accompanied by a fellow Franciscan.

"Do come along with me. Leave your horses for Frère Paul to put away and let us retire to the rectory kitchen. I can imagine you must be famished after your ride here," Père Francis said kindly as he led us towards the town's south-east ramparts where the rectory was located.

Once inside, a servant appeared holding a brass candlestick, its lively flame illuminating the hallway leading to the kitchen. As we entered the place where meals were prepared, our eyes quickly adjusted to the bright light of several tall tapers flickering along the walls and a group of seven bunched together in the centre of the workspace. We took our seats on wooden benches on either side of the rectangular table.

"Olivier, please provide our guests with some refreshments and then you may retire for the night," Père Francis instructed his servant.

Olivier bowed his head and silently set the kitchen table with bowls, plates and cups. We enjoyed an assortment of dried fruits, cheeses, freshly baked savoury pies and mulled cider, still warm from the kettle hung over the fire. After finishing his work, Olivier left us in private. While we ate, Père Charles explained to Père Francis about the letter I had received from Margaret and the need to rescue her immediately, before it was too late.

"I must first send word to Lord Philippe who is still in Bordeaux," Père Charles said, "and also to Sir Edward Hull. Intervention from the constable and his men will certainly aid in preventing Lady

Isabelle and me from falling victim to the count's wrath. Once Margaret is safely with us at Rosete I wish to begin formal proceedings in order for the marriage to be annulled. What do you know of such forms of appeal, Francis?"

"I have heard of such an instance, where a marriage was annulled under similar circumstances. I believe the year was 1296, in a town not far from Toulouse. A husband kept his wife locked away for several years before her family realised what had happened. The couple bore no heirs and eventually the wife was freed by an edict drafted under the direction of Pope Boniface VIII. He annulled the marriage and charged the husband with an unlawful act, which in the end resulted in his wife receiving more than half of his land and entitlements. I feel certain that something similar can be done for Margaret."

Père Francis was learned in canon law. Though of Moorish origin, from Cordoba in Spain, like our chaplain he had been orphaned at a young age when his family was killed during a clash between the Moors and Catholics. He was taken to live in a monastery where his curiosity about the Catholic faith grew, until one day he was sent by the abbot to study in Italy. It was there, Père Charles later told me, that he was awarded a degree in theology from the University of Bologna. On a trip to Rome he was introduced to another former student of the University of Bologna, Tommaso Parentucelli. In 1447, when Parentucelli was elevated to the papacy as Pope Nicholas V, Père Francis was invited to attend his consecration ceremony. Over the years, the two men had stayed in close contact and remained good friends.

"It is fortunate indeed that you arrived tonight; I am about to send a letter to His Holiness, Pope Nicholas. I must enquire whether he wishes us to prepare the papal residence at Villandraut for his forthcoming journey to Bordeaux in a month's time. I will include your concern about the annulment and seek his advice. I cannot promise that an answer will come back in short order, but I shall do my best for you."

"I am most appreciative of your help, Père Francis," I exclaimed gratefully. "Anything you can offer to help lessen my sister's suffering will be a blessing for her."

"I want very much to help Lady Margaret. The kindness your family shows to others in our parish has not gone unnoticed. Your late mother was most generous in how she cared for so many who were sick, regardless of their social standing or place of birth," Père Francis replied.

"I thank you, Francis," Père Charles added, reaching out to take his friend's hand in his own.

A lively discussion followed between the two priests; however, the events of the day suddenly caught up with me and my head began to droop.

"Why, Your Ladyship, forgive us. It is quite late. Shall I show you both to your rooms?" Père Francis asked with concern.

"Thank you, yes, please do so. I am suddenly very tired," I replied, my body slowly rocking back and forth from fatigue.

"Come, Lady Isabelle, allow me to help you." Père Charles came to my side and offered me his outstretched arm to help me to stand.

"Père Francis, there is one final question I have for you." I turned to face the priest who was extinguishing the candles affixed to the walls.

"Yes, do ask it of me; what is it?" he said, softly blowing out the flames.

"It is about Johan. He left Rosete in April. He said he was in love with a girl from Tangier named Pharrah Said. He told us he

43

wishes to marry her. I have had no word from him. Have you seen him?"

Père Francis was quiet for a moment. "I know of the Said family; they are traders here in Bazas. Pharrah is a beautiful and kind young woman. I can understand why Johan is in love with her. However, I do not believe her family will allow such a marriage to take place."

"But why ever not? Why should they not be allowed to marry?" I asked, confused.

"She is Muslim; she must marry someone who is Muslim."

"Ah, I see. Now I understand," I said, disappointed for my brother.

"I can tell that not having communication from Johan is upsetting you," Père Francis observed. "While you are away, I will check on him. When you return I will do my best to have some news to share."

We arrived at the corridor with our rooms. After showing me to my door, we agreed to meet at the break of day for matins in the cathedral. We said our goodnights and parted; I was ready to fall fast asleep.

———

I awakened as the first rays of light came streaming through the unshuttered windows, their long bands of brightness and warmth coaxing me from my rest. After quickly dressing I joined the others who had assembled for morning prayers in the cathedral apse. Following the service, we returned to the kitchen where we had met the night before.

"Charles, I have dispatched my messenger with your letter to Lord Philippe in Bordeaux. I have also given him instruction that he is to deliver by his hand a letter I have addressed to Constable Hull, asking for his intervention on behalf of the Albret Courteault family. I understand that Sir Edward is travelling with a small retinue along the Garonne. They are surveying the recent fortifications and repairs made to English-held towns that are the key defences against the French. Might I suggest a possible route across the river?"

"Why, yes, if you would be so kind," said Père Charles.

"Very well, here is what I suggest. Travel by barge from Barsac. Once on the opposite bank, take the river road west in the direction of Cadillac. Ask there for directions to Benauges. There can be little doubt that one of the count's rearguard stationed in the town will set out in advance to notify him of your arrival."

"And upon our return, might we seek your hospitality again, Francis?" enquired my chaplain.

"Why, of course, you must. I shall be eager to see that you have found Margaret alive, and to know that you are all safe."

As though reading my unspoken thoughts, Père Francis added, "You will have heard many tales of the count and his evil ways: stay committed to your faith in the Lord and your mission to rescue your sister. Remember, the Lord is with us always, so be of strong courage. Do not give up hope; your sister will benefit from your tenacious spirit."

"Thank you, Père Francis. It is all I can think of now; saving my sister and taking her away from her prison," I replied.

"Let us carry on, then; you must not tarry here, as you have still a full day's journey ahead of you. Here, Lady Isabelle, take this parcel I have had our cook prepare. It contains dried meats, fruit from our orchard and bread to sustain you as you travel today. I assure you, yours is an errand of mercy and God favours those who show such determination."

He then turned and led us through the corridor of the rectory and out into the stable yard where our horses were saddled and ready for us to mount. The peal of cathedral bells calling parishioners to mass rang out across the town square and signalled that it was time for us to depart.

"Thank you for your kind hospitality and fellowship," said Père Charles after mounting his horse.

"God bless you both and Godspeed," Père Francis replied.

Our horses trotted across the square and we left Bazas, taking up the route toward the riverside town of Langon. Later that day, from the vantage point of a hilltop above the town, we stopped and dismounted, gazing across the banks of the Garonne to the English-held town of Saint Macaire on the opposite side.

Père Charles pointed to the river. "Look, Lady Isabelle, there, on the river."

I turned toward the direction he was indicating.

"What is it?"

"On the river past the dock at Langon, do you see the barge approaching the town? That is how and where we will cross."

"But I thought Père Francis told us to look farther up toward Barsac," I reminded our chaplain.

"He did. But if we take the barge at Langon we shall arrive earlier in Cadillac. Come along now. We must head for the dock and enquire as to whether there is room for us on the next crossing."

We gathered our horses and quickly rode down into the town, entering through what looked to be a recently built wooden barbican, and on towards the river. We arrived at the dock just as the same barge we had seen making the crossing earlier was preparing to depart.

"Have you room for two horses and riders, sir?" Père Charles called out to the captain.

"All right, get on up there, though I have a full load and I want to pull out as soon as these here barrels are stored," came the captain's response.

We dismounted and hurried on board with our horses, calming them as we led them onto the barge. Once positioned, we hobbled them and took a moment to catch our breath. I produced the sack containing dried pork and boar sausage, pears, grapes, apples and bread baked fresh that morning. We stood as we ate, trying to keep our balance and soothe the horses, which were snorting and shaking their necks out of frustration at being hobbled on the moving vessel. Although a light rain shower overnight had provided us with cool, fresh morning air as we set out from Bazas, the weather had since turned balmy, and a blanket of warm, heavy air settled in around us as we crossed the middle of the river. The soft breeze we had felt along the water's edge at Langon had dissipated completely.

Père Charles stood watching the gentle wake left as the barge ploughed placidly across the river; I stopped to look at him, leaning against Peyriac. I closed my eyes and recalled all that had happened so quickly to bring me to where I was, floating along the Garonne to rescue my sister. For the first time I observed something striking in the character of my chaplain. His determination to save Margaret drew me to him in a way I had not felt before. Such thoughts conflicted me; in my heart he was more than a priest who looked after my spiritual health. That day as I watched him from afar, he seemed a mighty protector. In my mind I recalled the poetry Count Alfonse had written for Margaret. In his poems his description of the ascetic acts of the Knights Templar called to mind our chaplain and his chivalrous manner. He had shown himself to be fearless in the face of danger; in that quiet moment I imagined he was one of them. The divine prophecy I had received at birth echoed through my mind, that I was *to care for those whose lives were touched by devastating loss and feelings of unworthiness.* Though at that moment I could not imagine how this related to my chaplain, I felt a surge of compassion for him that I had not experienced before.

"Look, Lady Isabelle, there it is," Père Charles exclaimed, interrupting my thoughts and pointing upwards towards the outline of a castle perched atop a craggy hill.

With banners unfurled and lightly waving in the gentle afternoon breeze that reached the elevated promontory, the stout castle stood guard over all who entered the town below. As our barge floated closer to the town's riverside ramparts, I could see men-at-arms patrolling the rectangular castle from behind their protective crenelated barrier on top of the hill. I waved at one, and after checking to see that no one else was watching him, he smiled and waved back.

Our docking was bumpy; it took several attempts before we could be pulled alongside the pier and moored. Once the ramp was set out for us we disembarked. We set off, this time at a canter, eager to arrive in Cadillac without further delay.

As predicted, the town was well guarded with many of the count's retinue present and conducting business there on his behalf. Thick stone walls, one of which ran parallel to the Garonne, surrounded the town. We entered through a gate on the riverside called *Porte de la Mer* and followed the narrow street to where it intersected with another equally narrow road. As we rode toward the town centre, I glanced eastward where I noticed that a tall bell tower stood guard over an entrance at the far end of the street. Feeling dwarfed by the heavily fortified town with its labyrinth of narrow streets and alleys, I followed closely behind Père Charles as he rode up to the covered market in the arcaded central square. Shoppers and vendors alike stopped their activities to take us in, and the marketplace fell silent. The winded appearance of our horses only served to draw more attention to us.

"You two, what business have you here?" a stern voice called out from somewhere behind us.

We turned around to see a knight bearing Count Bertram's standard coming toward us. Almost immediately, the market came alive again, with the voices of vendors calling out to buyers as they passed by their market stalls.

"I say, what business have you here?" he demanded firmly again.

"Allow me to present myself. I am Father Charles Bonvinac and I wish to learn the direction of Benauges Castle. I seek an audience with His Lordship, Count Bertram of Foix."

"I see, and who are you travelling with, then?" He cast his eye over me with suspicion.

"May I present Lady Isabelle, sister of the count's wife, Lady Margaret," responded my chaplain on my behalf.

The knight glared at me, his piercing gaze causing me to shudder. After a brief pause he replied, "Very well, I shall escort you up to the castle myself. Wait here until I return on horseback."

It was not long before he returned and we followed him out of Cadillac on a road leading to the north in the direction of a town called Arbis. I noted that the scenery had changed dramatically since leaving Rosete and the south side of the river. Whereas the countryside of our estate was densely wooded and fairly flat, to the north of us from Bazas to the Garonne and beyond, the countryside was covered with rolling hills and vales. Such topography covered thousands of acres of farmland that favoured the growth of grape vines, from which was produced the duchy's most important trade item with England and the northern countries: a special red wine of Bordeaux called claret.

By late afternoon we had come within sight of Benauges Castle. As the mighty fortress grew ever closer, it would fall in and out of view as our path dipped and curved around little hills. I tried to imagine what it had been like for Margaret when she first saw her new home. For one who was not locked up within it, the castle might appear like a protective guardian rising above the undulating countryside. But given its present state as the prison that housed my older sister, I could not help but tremble at the thought of being held against my will within its massive, soaring walls. Its façade loomed directly ahead of us as we pressed on, and soon I could see soldiers walking about along the parapet. Suddenly the silhouette of its tall, cylindrical donjon rising above the height of the walls came clearly into view.

"Margaret, we are coming. Stay alive, dear sister. I pray you feel us near you," I whispered to myself.

As we drew closer, shouts and the sound of clinking metal could be heard from about the walls as the double portcullis was raised for our entry into the inner ward of the bleak and oppressive fortification.

VI
Château Benauges

Word sent via messenger from Cadillac ahead of our arrival had informed the guards at Benauges that our party was approaching. As we rode over the cobblestones of the inner ward, a groom appeared from the stable yard at the opposite end of the castle, ready to take our horses. I felt an impending sense of doom come over me that I could not shake.

"You are to follow me," ordered the knight who had escorted us.

After dismounting, he led us to the private range housing the refectory and privy hall. We entered through a heavy stone doorway and down a long hall on the ground floor, lined with various weapons and armour. In silence we made our way through the vast corridor to yet another doorway at the opposite end. This one opened to a turret with a flight of stairs. We climbed them and once we had reached the first floor, the knight muttered, "Wait here until I return," before striding off, hunching his shoulders as if displeased with the task he must carry out.

We looked about the room in his absence; it contained two long, roughly hewn rectangular tables and benches. On the side of the room facing over the inner ward were four wide windows with wooden shutters, each divided by a transom and mullion, the bottom halves of which were closed. A stale, musky odour emanated from the hay-covered floor; at the far end of the hall a fireplace had been lit in preparation for the cool of the ensuing nightfall. I can still recall the dank chill that penetrated the air that afternoon; the stench that filled my nostrils was a mixture of urine and sweat. I felt uncomfortable being there, for it felt unsafe, even with Père Charles as my companion.

Presently, our escort returned with the message that we had been granted an audience with the count.

We started forward. "Wait," he said, looking at me. "Only the priest. You must stay here."

"I pray, kind sir, that you will allow both of us to meet Count Bertram. I bring with me Lady Isabelle, who wishes to request that she might see her sister."

The knight looked at us with resentment before deciding to let us enter together.

"The Lord is with us, remember that," Père Charles whispered, and we entered the antechamber of the count's private reception hall.

The knight gave three quick knocks on the door separating us from Margaret's captor. As the door opened I felt a surge of weakness come over me. I clutched the back of Père Charles's garment and was steadied by his unshaken demeanour. He showed no signs of fear, only great intent.

Upon entering, my eyes beheld the rich furnishings that seemed to emerge from every corner. Directly across the room sat the count, his ornately carved chair covered in ruby-coloured silk and placed on a dais, resembling a throne. Behind it along the wall two tapestries hung, their narratives depicting scenes of the hunt. A small table and two carved benches were positioned to one side, providing some intimacy in the otherwise vacuous chamber. A servant quietly appeared from behind us, lighting the candles in the pair of candelabra towering over either side of the stately seat, before retreating from the room in silence.

We made our way toward the count. Père Charles bowed deeply, a gesture which I quickly copied; at once he spoke.

"Your Lordship, we have come to the castle of Benauges with a favour to ask of you."

The years had not been kind to Count Bertram. His portly body sat heavily in place, his pockmarked face revealed evidence of an earlier run of the disease. Though his beard was neatly trimmed, his hair thinly masked his misshapen head. I had spent so little time in his company when he had come to Rosete to marry my sister that I had not taken any notice of his appearance during that visit. Without hesitation he turned his face away and belched.

"And tell me, what would that be?"

"We have heard that Margaret is not well," Père Charles continued. "We request permission to see her immediately and ascertain whether she should be returned home to be with her family."

Count Bertram turned back and looked at us. "Do you think I would hand over my wife, who is my property, to you, a priest, and to you, her sister?" He began to laugh, his mouth forming a sneer. "What makes you think that you have the right to appear before me with such a request?"

"As you will recall, I am the priest who attended you both in your marriage, at the request of her father. I have a responsibility to ensure that the vows you both made do not impinge on Lady Margaret or cause her ill health."

"I can have you two taken to her donjon right now. That would do you well to observe how I treat her, and my other prisoners. Guard! Take these two away to the donjon at once. They want to see how well Lady Margaret has been treated. Let them learn for themselves!" Count Bertram let out a malicious chuckle.

"As you wish, sire."

After bowing to the count, the knight who had brought us in approached us, brandishing a halberd.

"You two, move ahead of me," he ordered, nudging Père Charles in the back first, then prodding me with the weapon.

We were pushed along by the guard in the direction of the donjon. Isolated, it stood across the inner ward, away from the other buildings. As we marched along we were joined by two other guards in the count's retinue. The distress of our situation sent a chill through my whole being. I could smell the stench of decaying flesh that wafted on the late summer breeze in the putrid air around us; it caused me to gag as acid bubbled up in my throat. I feared what was to become of us, especially if I became separated from my chaplain. Without the guards noticing, I reached out, grabbing Père Charles's arm. He shook his head at me discreetly and I released my grasp. When our gazes locked I felt at once steadied by his presence so near.

The guard bearing the halberd pushed us up the stairs to the first floor of the donjon, then hung his weapon with others mounted on the wall. My eyes adjusted slowly to the round, dimly lit room after we entered it; I stopped briefly to take in my surroundings. Two loopholes, at opposite sides, their splay large enough to suit small crossbows, pierced the castle's exterior wall. Along the courtyard side, a long, narrow ventilation shaft allowed for filtered light and fresh air to enter. Two pairs of iron hooks had been stuck into the walls, each bearing a trail of chains. A dilapidated wooden ladder stood straight ahead of us, leading up to the next level through a small, square opening in the floor above.

"And who have we here, then?" one of the guards asked of the other two, stepping so close to me that I could smell the foulness of his breath.

"The count has ordered the priest to be locked up. We can decide what we want to do with the girl; I don't think the count will mind," another guard replied.

"She is the sister of Lady Margaret," said the guard who had escorted us. "We will have our turns with her; look how young and fair she is. I wonder if she fights back like her sister."

The three guards laughed at the disgusting remark; my mind filled with terror.

"Well, there is one way to find out." One of the guards came towards me and I ducked to the side to avoid him.

"Leave her alone! Do not touch her!" Père Charles roared, springing to life and coming to my defence by putting himself between me and the three men.

"Well, well. A priest who thinks he can fight the likes of us? Join me, lads; this should be entertaining!"

The three guards pulled out their swords from the scabbards about their waists. As the men circled my chaplain I looked about in fear, desperate to help him. Suddenly I spied a row of lances hung along the wall. I pried one loose from the wall and threw it to him. To my great surprise he caught it and deftly deflected one of the guards' advances. *How could he be so skilled at bearing arms?* I thought to myself as I watched the guards continue to move around him. With each step they made to stab at him, he acted quickly with the lance. I felt powerless to do anything else to help save him. As my heart raced for fear of what they would do to me and Père Charles I silently prayed to the Lord. "*Kyrie eleison, Christe eleison, Kyrie eleison*", begging the Lord for mercy and to bring us an instant miracle of reconciliation.

VII
The Constable of Bordeaux

A t that instant, from across the inner ward there came a clattering of hooves under the barbican. Momentarily I cast my gaze away from the fight, peering out the ventilation shaft as the battle between the guards and Père Charles escalated around me. Panic and fear turned to hope and relief as I watched the swift arrival of a group of ten men in the attire of English officers. Their leader wore a cloak with two red crosses and his saddle blanket was different from those of his companions; it depicted three red leopards edged in white. He carried himself with great confidence. From the horses' exhaustion, it seemed as if the poor animals had just carried their riders at a gallop from a great distance. Their heads hung low and a sweaty lather covered their chests. The leader addressed a guard.

"I do not care. You will notify His Lordship, Count Bertram, *now* that Sir Edward Hull is here to see him!" Though he spoke in Gascon, the male voice that rose from the courtyard below was firm and his accent distinctly English.

The constable and five of his men strode purposefully toward the entrance of the private range housing the refectory and privy hall, while four others bounded towards the entrance of the donjon and quickly up the stairs.

"Are you Lady Margaret?" one of them asked me as the constable's men broke up the fight between Père Charles and the three guards.

"No, I am her sister, Isabelle," I replied.

"And who are you?" asked the guard who had carried the halberd earlier. "What business have you here, barging in on us like this when we are in the middle of locking up our prisoners?"

While the men were distracted I took a moment to retreat to my chaplain's side.

I noticed Père Charles's long black tunic was ripped along the hem. His face was red and he was hunched over slightly to his left, favouring his hip. I rushed to his aid.

"Are you all right? Did you get hurt?" I asked, my hushed voice full of concern.

"I am fine, I will be fine," he said, attempting to stand up straight. "I think I may have bruised my rib. But I am relieved we are now safe. It could have been a much worse outcome for both of us. It has been many years since I trained to fight."

"Listen to me," commanded one of the constable's guards. "You are ordered to release all prisoners being kept here from the Albret Courteault household at once. The priest and Her Ladyship will come with us to the privy hall. You three in the retinue of the count are to await further instruction from the constable."

He then turned to two of his fellow soldiers.

"Go upstairs now and fetch Lady Margaret. Prepare her for immediate travel."

His words elicited the first smile that had crossed my lips since I received news of how my sister had been abused by the count. I looked at Père Charles with disbelief.

"Do not be anxious, Your Ladyship." Père Charles's voice was barely audible. "These are the men Père Francis called upon to help us. You will see. Sir Edward Hull has spent many years as the constable of Bordeaux and his authority is far greater than that of any Gascon lord."

We followed the constable's men as they led us to the privy hall. This time, when we entered his room, Count Bertram sat hunched in his chair. He watched us with great disdain. His hair and face looked dishevelled, as if he had recently been in a physical altercation and lost the fight. Several men wearing the attire of the English retinue stood in a tight circle, listening to the words of another man with his back to us. As we approached their group, the central figure turned around and I instantly recognised his authoritative voice as that which I had heard in the courtyard earlier. It was Sir Edward Hull, the constable of Bordeaux.

Sir Edward stepped forward to take Père Charles's hand and embrace him. As he leaned forward he softly whispered the phrase "Who worketh wonders?" in a voice barely audible to anyone but my chaplain and me.

I was surprised to see Père Charles lean in to whisper back in the same low tone one word: "Immanuel."

The constable bowed to me.

"I have ordered the count to release Lady Margaret into your custody immediately. She is to remain in the care of her family until her health improves and a legal determination can be made as to the dissolution of the marriage contract."

As he heard the words spoken to us by Sir Edward, the count suddenly leaped from his seat.

"Leave my castle at once! All of you! I wish to have no further communication with any members of the Courteault family *or* the Seigneurs d'Albret. Now go! Leave my sight before I decide to go back on my word. I would love nothing more than to set my retinue on all of you – to fight to your deaths!"

We left the chamber at once, returning to the inner ward below. Our horses stood saddled and ready to ride along with the now rested horses of the constable and his men.

Coming close to us so none of the count's men could hear, Sir Edward calmly told us of his plans.

"Be assured, we are prepared to provide you safe conduct from Benauges. We must move on as quickly as possible. The count often reverses his word. I will not feel you three are safe until we are well away from here."

I was immediately taken with the constable's commanding presence.

"I feel as though this is a dream," I exclaimed, once the constable was out of earshot. "Margaret is to be released to us! She will be freed from her marriage and can return home!"

"Indeed, My Lady. We still have much work to do to make her well again. And to petition the Pope for his intercession in the annulling of her marriage. Even still, this is a most miraculous turn of events. Our prayers have been answered," Père Charles acknowledged joyfully.

"But until we are away from Benauges, let us curtail our enthusiasm," he continued. "It would not be wise to appear excited about the constable's intervention. We do not want to incite the count or his men in any way while we remain at his residence."

We did not have to wait long before we saw Margaret emerge from the donjon, supported on either side by two of the constable's guard. I fought hard to hold back my tears: I was shocked by her appearance. My sister had always taken great pride in keeping herself and her garments clean. As she walked toward us, her clothes stained in night soil and grime, her nails broken and dirty and deep, dark rings under her once bright eyes, I felt a wave of sickness wrench my insides. I feared my expression of shock might cause her further grief. Even her hair bore evidence of neglect, for it was off her face in a loosely matted braid. She appeared pale and gaunt after months being confined in isolation. Margaret let out a cry of disbelief as she recognised us and rushed to embrace us. We could not leave Benauges soon enough.

"Are you two ladies ready to ride?" Sir Edward called to Margaret and me after we mounted Peyriac.

"Yes, sir." I nodded my head in response to the powerful leader. I felt my strength returning. At last I felt secure knowing that Margaret would be safe in our family's care.

VIII
Madame de Tastes

Riding away from Benauges in the direction of the Garonne River, with the profile of the castle and her prison, perched high atop its craggy hilltop, diminishing at every bend we made along the road, I finally reclaimed my own peace of mind.

After covering some distance, we came to a fork in the road and drew up our horses to rest momentarily.

"How do you wish to proceed on the journey?" asked the constable. He had pulled up his mount to stand near us.

"I think it is best if we search for lodging in Cadillac," Père Charles replied. "I would like us to reach the English town of Saint Macaire by tomorrow midday."

"If I may interject, I am not comfortable with the thought of staying in Cadillac tonight," Margaret said. "I assure you, the count will have his guards on alert for us. I fear they will wait until we are asleep and take me away again. Rather, I think it is best if we stay with the count's cousin, Madame de Tastes."

My sister pulled a small parchment scroll from the pouch tied about her waist and unrolled it for Sir Edward and Père Charles to view.

"Her Ladyship secretly gave me this map on a visit before I was imprisoned; it contains directions to her home. She instructed me to seek refuge with her if ever I was to escape. It appears her castle is not much further along the route ahead, to the west."

"Let us be off at once to find her residence," Père Charles directed us after surveying its contents. "Sir Edward, on behalf of Lord Philippe, I personally thank you for intervening with your men to help us and Lady Margaret to escape from the count."

"I am glad we could be of assistance to you three. I will take leave of you, but two of my personal guard shall ride with you for the remainder of your journey. You will be safe at all times with them."

We bade the constable and his party farewell and kicked up our horses into a canter in the direction of Château Laroque, the residence of Madame de Tastes. The narrow road was no more than a dirt path in some places, and a great many weeds covered the trail, further obscuring our route. We soon rounded a bend and, to our surprise, Laroque Castle appeared ahead of us on the right. Upon arriving outside the fortified entrance gate, Margaret dismounted from Peyriac to announce our arrival. After some words were exchanged, the heavy wooden portal was pulled open from within. Our party dismounted, leading our horses and following my sister into the castle ward.

Just inside the entrance stood Lady Bernadette with two young guards at either side, long silver staffs in hand. They wore polished metal helmets and bright emerald-green vests over their hauberks.

A groom appeared and took our horses' reins from us while our two escorts joined him in search of their separate accommodation.

"*Adiu à Laroque*," Lady Bernadette welcomed us in Gascon. "How wonderful it is that you are here. Please, follow me. Let us retreat inside where I can hear you better, and Lady Margaret, you can tell me how you came to be released. I shall have my servant Monique prepare hot baths for you. You can wash and change before we share supper. And Lady Margaret, please accept the gift of one of my gowns which Monique will bring for you."

The thoughtfulness of our hostess touched us all. We followed her to the great hall where several candles and a fire at the end of the room were lit, their light and warmth comforting after the tense encounter which had nearly resulted in our assault and imprisonment at Benauges.

"Please, let us sit and converse while the water heats for your baths and my cook prepares something to eat," Her Ladyship instructed us. "Tell me what has happened. How did you gain Lady Margaret's release?"

Père Charles explained what had transpired with the Count of Foix, relating our efforts to seek her liberation.

"Allow me to caution you three," Madame de Tastes warned us. "The count will not easily forget that you and the English forced him to give up his wife and return her to her family. Those who cause him shame often end up becoming targets of his vengeance.

"However, at the moment, he needs the financial support of the English in Bordeaux for as long as he can maintain it. There are rumours that very soon the French King Charles VII, and his army led by General Dunois, will infiltrate our lands. If that is so, the count will be forced to forgo his loyalty to the English or give up his riches and face being sent to the Bastille Saint-Antoine in Paris. It is rumoured that members of the French royal courts who are disloyal and sent to prison there come out with their heads on pikes. Count Bertram certainly knows this; he will return to serve King Charles as soon as the English are forced out of Gascony. In doing so, the count could rescind his permission to have you released from your marriage contract, and send his men to abduct you. Only this time when they do so there will be no Englishmen to come to your aid. I am sure the count considered all of this as he agreed to the terms of your release with Sir Edward. I must insist that after your return to Rosete you do everything possible to leave this country at once for England. Your father must be forming some plan for your family to escape the French."

"I cannot believe what I am hearing!" exclaimed Margaret, alarmed. "I cannot imagine us leaving our homeland; I do not dare to think of such events!"

Her Ladyship stretched out her arm to take my sister's hand in hers. "I impart this information to you all so that you may prepare to face the possibility of evacuation. For your own safety, I do not believe you will have any other choice."

A heavy silence filled the room.

"Yet I do not wish for you three to despair. You are my guests tonight and you are safe here in my castle. Go take some refreshment and change your clothes, we shall meet here again for our meal."

Madame de Tastes rang a bell, calling her servant to her side.

"Monique, show my guests to their chambers and give Margaret a fresh gown to wear from my wardrobe."

"*Oui, madame*," Monique replied dutifully. "Please, follow me," she said to us, and we followed her out of the hall.

I was grateful to share the bath with my sister that evening. As our backs were scrubbed and our hair cleaned I was particularly pleased to see the colour returning to her cheeks.

Later, as we sat together in the great hall for our meal, our conversation turned to the other impactful change which had occurred since Margaret left: Johan's absence. I related to the others the events surrounding his departure. I felt safe in their company at Laroque that evening and openly shared my observations about Aunt Christine's growing hostility.

"I believe you are right to be concerned about your aunt's personality," Madame de Tastes acknowledged. "She and I have known each other for many decades. She has a reputation for being unwelcoming to strangers; whether they come from abroad or simply a neighbouring duchy, she shows little tolerance for others outside her social circle."

"What can you tell us of her resentment toward members of the clergy?" I asked.

"This is something new," Madame de Tastes said thoughtfully. "Are you suggesting that she has developed an intolerance of them as well?"

"Isa, I do not think it is right for you to judge our aunt's behaviour so harshly. I am not comfortable with discussing her in this manner," Margaret cautioned.

"But I am only expressing concern for what I have witnessed in her behaviour to Père Charles," I explained.

"I will tell you that I do know her husband was a Knight of the Holy Sepulchre," Lady Bernadette began. "When they lived in Paris they worshipped at the church of St-Leu-St-Gilles. After he became ill with the pestilence, Lady Christine spent several hours of every day there, praying with the priests and brothers of the order for the life of her husband to be spared. In spite of her deep devotion, he died: she lost her faith in God."

"I did not know that about her; she never talks about what her life was like in Paris," I said, saddened to hear of the loss our aunt had lived through.

"If I may," began Père Charles. "As a member of the clergy I feel we should judge people by their own words, rather than the words of others."

"Then I do apologise for questioning her treatment of the clergy," I said, suddenly feeling ashamed for my feelings about my aunt. "But there is still the way she behaved toward our brother."

I went on to explain to Margaret about Johan and Pharrah; my sister's eyes grew sad as I revealed our aunt's reaction to his announcement.

"It is upsetting to hear that Johan felt he had to leave," she said. "You are correct, Isa, our mother would not have been so easily upset by his admission of love for a lady of Pharrah's background and status. How has father reacted to the news?"

"Why, I do not know," I admitted. "Aunt Christine said she would write to him and tell him. But I do not know of his response."

"Nor do I," said Père Charles. "Since she instructed me not to be a part of the conversation I have not offered my counsel."

"Might I suggest that tonight we celebrate Lady Margaret's freedom," Madame de Tastes suggested. "Try not to concern yourselves with what lies ahead for your family and the future of the duchy."

"But what will happen to you, Your Ladyship?" demanded my sister. "You will also be forced to give up your castle and your lands when the French come, will you not? Where will you go?"

"I am far older than you, and I have seen the tide turn between the English and French in this region over many decades," Madame de Tastes replied. "From what I have heard, life in England is not much easier. There is the constant threat of an internal war between the rival families of York and Beaufort. I understand that Richard of York is displeased with King Henry's decision to cast him off to govern Ireland the past few years, while the king's advisor, Edmund Beaufort, the Duke of Somerset, was given Richard's previous position of Lieutenant of France.

"Yet I would still prefer the risks of a civil war in England than to stay here and face the French and what they would do to me for my family's loyalty to the English all these years. I, too, have considered moving to London, where I am welcome to stay at the residence of His Lordship, John Talbot, the Earl of Shrewsbury, who is a distant cousin. If it is a decision between life in a foreign country or death at the Bastille, I choose life and, therefore, I choose London."

There was a momentary silence as we waited for Margaret's response.

"Very well, then, London it will be for me also," she concluded aloud.

"I am glad to hear it. Now, let us prepare for bed," our hostess suggested. "Tomorrow, before you leave, I shall see you all once more."

With Margaret peacefully asleep at my side, my mind remained crowded by the concerns and anxieties raised over the course of our conversation. I could not imagine leaving Rosete for an uncertain life in England. My thoughts quickly turned to my beloved Peyriac, for what would become of him? I simply could not bear the thought of leaving him behind.

It seemed my eyes had been shut only for a moment before I heard the birds outside in the treetops, singing their morning songs to the breaking dawn. I slipped out of bed, careful not to awaken my sister, and walked over to peer out of the narrow lancet window near our bed. Through the iron grate I watched as the predawn sky slowly faded from sombre twilight into shades of pale pink, orange and yellow, their petal-soft hues extinguishing the last of the evening stars, revealing the glory of a new day. I took a moment to say a quick prayer of thanksgiving for the beauty of the Lord's creation that I heard and watched unfold before me.

With an air of felicity rising in my heart I quickly dressed and left the room, eager to record my observations while the household was still asleep. I made my way to the great hall where we had dined the previous night. Just as I completed my writing and was blotting the ink on the page before wrapping it closed with its leather strap, Madame de Tastes entered and sat down at my side.

"Lady Isabelle, what have you been doing in here by yourself so early in the morning? What is this book that you have here before you?"

"Pardon me, Your Ladyship, I thought everyone was still asleep; I hope I have not disturbed you. I simply wished to record our stay at your residence in my journal."

"I see," replied Her Ladyship, taking a seat next to me. "Then you enjoy a pursuit similar to a lady of Italian birth named Christine de Pisan who worked in the court of the French king. I have copies of her love poems, written in memory of her deceased husband, and found them greatly inspirational after I, like Christine, became widowed at an early age. I have a copy of her prose entitled *Le Livre de la Cité des Dames* that I would like you to have; it is a most notable tribute to the virtues of womanhood. I am certain you will be moved by what you read."

"Why thank you, Your Ladyship. You are most generous to think of me in such a way. I shall undoubtedly take great pleasure in reading and studying such a text. I will show it to my tutor, our chaplain, and ask that he incorporate it into our lessons."

"Ah, yes, your chaplain is indeed a most learned man. I have just come from my chapel where he kindly offered to recite the morning office with me, ending with our celebrating the Eucharist together. Reciting the words of the liturgy and psalms together with him has lifted my soul in a way I have not felt in many years. Your family is indeed fortunate that he shows such devotion to your pastoral care."

As we sat talking quietly together, Père Charles and Margaret appeared in the doorway.

"Good morning, Lady Margaret. I pray you had a peaceful sleep. Now that you are all gathered together, allow me to offer you some food for your journey. It will not take but a moment to have the cook pack it for you," insisted Madame de Tastes.

"You have been most gracious, Lady Bernadette, and we are indeed grateful for your generous hospitality," replied Margaret. "We should be most appreciative to you for anything you might provide."

After collecting our possessions from our bedchambers, and with our horses already saddled for our journey, we joined our two escorts and waited for Her Ladyship to return from the kitchen. After a few minutes she appeared, carrying Christine de Pisan's book of poems and followed by Monique, who carried a wrapped parcel for us. We exchanged our farewells and promised to remain in contact should our father decide to move our family to England. Our party took off at a canter down the narrow lane, with Laroque fading away into the far distance until it disappeared completely.

———

The rest of the journey that day passed uneventfully. We arrived in Saint Macaire by late afternoon, having stopped only briefly at noon to take our meal. After being presented to the English captain of the town, Robert Burnell, a scribe was called in to draft a short message to our father confirming the news that Margaret had been freed. Captain Burnell assured us that the missive would be sent out that night with other documents directed to the council in Bordeaux. While in his company, he shared additional news on the preparations underway in Bordeaux against the coming war.

"Madame de Tastes is correct about the possibility of the French army staging a final battle for the duchy," he confirmed. "Already preparation is under way in the capital with the production of small cannon and other ordnance to be dispatched throughout the region, as needed. They also await the arrival of English soldiers that King Henry has promised to send. However, you should keep your ears open for talk by traitors to His Majesty King Henry. Such discourse is considered an offence punishable by confiscation of lands and title, and even death. If you learn of any subversive plots, report them to an English officer at once."

After our visit, Captain Burnell accompanied us to the dock where we boarded the ferry crossing the Garonne River to the town of Langon, where we were made guests of the English captain in the town's castle. The next morning we set off for Bazas, arriving there by midday.

The town and the cathedral square were filled with merchants and buyers noisily going about their business. Carts carrying a variety of food items were lined up in three long rows across the town square. Children of farmers and butchers, fishmongers and bakers worked busily alongside their parents, who called out to those who passed to come and buy from their stall. Skirting the market activity in the centre of the square, we rode up to the front of the rectory and dismounted, waiting outside while Père Charles went in search of Père Francis. Soon the two men appeared together, approaching us from the rectory garden where we had met on our last visit.

"Lady Margaret, how wonderful it is to see you here," Père Francis exclaimed in greeting as he approached my sister.

"Thank you, Père Francis. I must tell you how grateful I am to be free from my marriage to Count Bertram," my sister replied. "I prayed every day for God to provide a miracle to release me, and then one day these two arrived, and now here I am with you again!"

"It was miraculous indeed," Père Francis began. "Come and join me in the garden for a cup of fresh cider and some *saucisson secs* and *foie gras*, won't you? I want to hear from you all how Margaret's release came about. As fortune would have it, there are two visitors with me now who also are eager to see you three."

We left our horses to be looked after by our two escorts and followed Père Francis, enjoying the break from riding as we entered the peaceful surroundings of the rectory.

"Why, Johan!" I exclaimed, rushing to embrace my brother. "What a welcome surprise to find you here! And this must be your Pharrah."

"It is wonderful to meet you, Lady Isabelle?" Pharrah said, her accent smooth and soft. "And you must be Lady Margaret? That means you are Père Charles. I feel I have known all of you already. Johan speaks of his family to me all the time."

Pharrah was a striking woman of about Johan's age. Her olive complexion complemented the thick, lustrous ebony locks that hung long and wavy down her back, partially visible from under the brightly coloured headwrap she wore. Her deep emerald eyes seemed to dance as she spoke. The fabrics of her costume, while different from our own, were as vibrant in colour as her headscarf. I felt immediately drawn to her.

"Do, everyone sit and be comfortable. We are reunited at last!" Johan said, a wide smile across his face. "Margaret, how good it is to see you. Père Francis has told me of your trouble. I am glad you are home again."

It was a heartfelt reunion that afternoon. We enjoyed being together and having time to spend with Pharrah. She appeared at ease with my brother, even playful, and he was the happiest I had seen him since our mother died. I was curious to know more about her, and would have liked to spend more time in their company. Eventually, though, it came time for us to leave.

"I am afraid it is time for us to depart for Rosete, Francis," Père Charles said, standing up. "Come along, we must get back to our horses."

"Very well. It has been a pleasure to have you all here," Père Francis said, smiling warmly.

"Johan, will you ride home with us?" Margaret asked. "Once we have Father back you can ask him to meet Pharrah and her family."

"I think it is time now for you to return with your sisters and chaplain, Johan," Pharrah admitted. "It will be different with your aunt, especially if your father is there."

"Only if you agree that you are promised to me," Johan replied, gazing at her.

"You know I cannot do that without my father's permission. But I can assure you of this: you have my heart. I will give it to no other. There; I have said it in front of your sisters and the priests as witnesses."

"Pharrah, we hope to welcome you soon into our family," Margaret said, embracing her.

"You are too kind," Pharrah answered.

"I hope to show you my books one day," I said with enthusiasm.

"I would love that, Isabelle," Pharrah said warmly. "I think you and I have many things in common. Let us hope that one day soon we will be free to make these discoveries as sisters."

Our visit over, we left the rectory garden and went in search of our mounts. Once we found them, and our two escorts, it was but a short time before Johan appeared on horseback. Our party rode back across the cathedral square in the direction of the town gate and the route home to Rosete. We were eager to arrive before nightfall.

After passing the town of Captieux we entered the safety of the lands of our estate. Père Charles thanked our two escorts and released them from their service. Upon our unexpected return that evening, Sarah and Christophe welcomed us all with elation and surprise, jumping around and circling us with glee, for no one in our household had yet been made aware of Margaret's release or the knowledge that Johan would return with us. However, our aunt remained cool and distant, her expression not one of joy but rather dismay that Margaret and Johan were home again. It was clear that she would rather my sister suffer in her marriage for the sake of upholding the reputation of the House of Albret than see her returned to us under the circumstances as she did; my sister's health and well-being meant nothing to her. It was clear having my brother home again did not comfort her either.

While I stood watching Aunt Christine's reaction of disdain, I felt my head become heavy. I urgently felt drawn to our chapel. Lifting a lantern affixed to the wall of the inner ward, I carried it with me to illuminate the chapel; once inside I knelt before the altar. In my unsettled state I experienced a shocking vision. I saw my aunt in what appeared to be a prison cell in a square white tower. She was dressed in an unadorned black sackcloth gown. An examiner stood at her side; she was being made to confess something, but I could not understand what was being said, for it was being communicated in a foreign tongue. She was then made to rise and leave her cell, walking down a set of stairs and outside to the gallows. A crowd had gathered to watch and they chanted in unison a word in English that I could recognise, for it was similar to the French word of the same meaning, "*Traitor, traitor, traitor!*"

Then a bright flash of light appeared before my eyes from nowhere and the vision ended.

Disturbed and fearful of what I had just witnessed, from the lantern flame I lit a candle on the altar, offering silent prayers of gratitude that we had Margaret and Johan with us again. I hoped that by doing so I might invoke a new vision, one that offered blessings of Christ's mercy and grace. But nothing appeared before my sight. Instead, my mind shifted to the memory of the traumatic events at Benauges. Piercing thoughts about marriage overwhelmed me and I began to weep out loud.

Unperceived, Père Charles had silently entered the chapel to pray. At the sound of my muffled crying he approached me.

"Your Ladyship, allow me to help you. What has upset you so? You rushed away from the others with such haste. Please trust in me – your confession shall go no further than this chapel."

I stopped my tears as I struggled to find the words to explain how I felt.

"What happened to Margaret fills me with such sadness," I admitted, my eyes downcast. "When we first saw her, I felt such anger towards the count and his men. How can someone exchange sacred vows of marriage and then treat their partner in such a manner? How does one know whether they can trust the marriage vows taken by their beloved to be honoured? Her first marriage to Count Alfonse was one filled with love and tenderness. Why did she have to experience such cruelty in her second marriage? Is what happened to my sister the way all wives are treated by their husbands? Does the Lord wish to see us suffer for our love?"

Stretching out his arm, Père Charles directed me to sit on a bench where he joined me, composing his thoughts before responding.

"I am afraid there is no one simple answer to your many questions, Your Ladyship. Our God is a God of love. He does not wish to see any of his children suffer – you must always remember that. Building trust with those whom you love requires years of courting and companionship. Love is fostered in our faith, as the Lord teaches us, by his love for his Son, Jesus Christ. We see this in the way Christ wishes for us to put our love for his Father above all else in our lives. Attentive love, Christlike love, shared and honoured by both husband and wife, builds a trust that grows and joins two hearts in a most holy union. Sharing a foundation in our Catholic faith provides both husband and wife with a means of seeking a most holy unity together. In that way, not only are they committing themselves to honouring one another in love as Christ honours his Father, but their own love for each other will also be blessed with the presence of the Holy Spirit that exists between and within them. Remember this: God is love. The only way there can be love in our lives is to love one another: there can be no love in the absence of fellowship."

He paused, allowing the divine truth of his words to settle into my soul.

"Know this, Your Ladyship: the Lord has called you to follow a special path in life. Lose yourself in your studies and continue to compose your observations in your journals. If you are indeed to marry one day, I am certain the Lord has a plan for how that will come to pass. You must give it time."

I leaned towards my chaplain, resting my head upon his shoulder for support.

"Thank you for sharing your wisdom, Père Charles," I said quietly, grateful for his words, which helped clear my head of its tortured thoughts of marriage and what lay in store for me. "Your words, like your actions, are always of such comfort."

IX
Farewell to Rosete

The very day after Margaret returned home to Rosete, Père Charles decided we must begin learning the English language in preparation for our likely move to England. All of us, including Margaret, took up our new studies in earnest. A few weeks later we received word that our father would return from Bordeaux with important news. We decided to prepare a feast in his honour to welcome him home. The event would be special for our family, since the last time we were together had been at Margaret's wedding to the Count of Foix in late January.

After finishing my lessons with the others one morning in early October, I decided to read in the privy hall. Sarah and Christophe had become increasingly bothersome, always wanting my attention to be a part of their play. The only quiet place I could study my texts by Geraldus Cambrensis and Christine de Pisan was in the formal chamber.

After entering I moved toward my favourite niche, the alcove overlooking the inner ward. As I crossed the room, I detected a scent I could not recognise while the glint of a fiery ember in the fireplace caught my attention; I walked closer to inspect it.

Stooping down, I realised someone else had been in the privy hall before me. A fire had been started and someone had attempted to burn a vellum scroll. But they must have walked away without waiting to ensure the document was completely destroyed. Curious to know what was inscribed on the letter that deemed such permanent destruction necessary, I picked it up. The outer cover was singed beyond recognition and fell away back into the fireplace. But the inside pages were still intact, the borders only slightly singed. My eyes grew wide as I read the contents.

30 September, year of our Lord Charles VII, 1452

To our most loyal sister Lady Christine d'Albret, from her brother, Charles d'Albret.

I write to you at this time while our French troops in the north are preparing to march south on Bordeaux. We believe we are still on course to lay siege on the duchy by surprise attack in the coming weeks. I wish for you to remain in the household of our brother Philippe and to forward to me any news you have from him regarding the production of guns and cannon which are rumoured to be underway in les filleules that line the Garonne River. Do not remove yourself from the family until you receive word from me that you are permitted to do so. Your information is critical to the success of the pending French campaign.

Should you abandon your post you will be considered a traitor and I will have no choice but to submit your name for imprisonment at the Bastille.

You do the Albret family well by your work for the French crown. Send me your news as soon as you are able.

With anticipation,
Your brother Charles

Alarmed, I recalled the words of the Captain Robert Burnell in Saint Macaire, "...*keep your ears open for talk by traitors to His Majesty King Henry.*" I carefully rolled up the sheepskin missive and tucked it into the inner pocket of my surcoat. At least now I had the evidence to show my aunt was guilty of espionage for the French; that her decision to live with our family was not born of good intentions. The only question was what to do with such knowledge.

———

A few days later, after returning home from an afternoon exploring the forest around Rosete with Peyriac, I noticed the familiar silhouette of a lone rider along the perimeter of the forest to the west of Rosete.

"Come, everyone, look, over there, near the woods!" I exclaimed as I ran breathlessly into the inner ward. "It is Father! He has returned!"

Our household and my siblings filed out of the gateway and joined me in regarding the horizon, while Aunt Christine gave instructions for his arrival: "Quickly, we must prepare the great hall. Pey, you are to position the d'Albret Courteault standard on the parapet atop the barbican. His Lordship will be in residence again!"

As my father approached, I ran out to greet him, ahead of the others. I wanted to speak to him privately before he rejoined the household.

"Dear Father, we have missed you so!" I cried as I rushed to his side.

He brought his horse down from a trot to a walk and then dismounted so we could walk back to Rosete together.

"I am pleased to be home. I received word that Margaret was no longer bound by marriage to the count; with what I must disclose to you all tonight about our future, I am much relieved that she is once again with us."

"So much has happened since you have been away," I admitted as we walked.

"Is there anything you wish to tell me?" my father asked, as ever, sensitive to my moods.

"I think it is best if the others explain for themselves," I replied, not wanting to speak on behalf of Margaret and Johan.

We continued walking towards the castle where we could see a small crowd already gathering. I decided to ask him about the changes that might lie ahead for our family in the immediate future.

"There are many rumours being circulated by our friends and servants. What will become of us? Will we have to move to England? And what about Peyriac? You know I cannot bear to leave without him."

"I shall disclose my plans for us and the future of Rosete tonight in the company of our family and members of our household. I have taken into consideration what is best for the safety of everyone. My work in Bordeaux will provide us with the means to escape the onset of war that is to come with France."

I knew that before we joined the others I must also address my fear about the vision I had had of my aunt.

"Since you asked, there is one thing that concerns me." I took hold of my father's arm and we stopped to look at each other. "It concerns Aunt Christine. I believe she is involved in activities that amount to treason against King Henry."

"Isabelle, be careful of the words you use and the charges you raise against my sister. I realise she is loyal to my brothers in the House of Albret who support the French king, but to suggest that she is involved in treasonous plots is unfathomable! She would not dare expose this family to such risk, especially as war with France is drawing ever nearer to our borders. I do not wish to hear you speak such words against your aunt again, do you understand me?"

We carried on in silence, and I tried to put the disappointment of his words from my mind. There was no time to discuss the letter, my vision or my aunt's loyalties further. By this time we had reached the path leading up to the castle gate. Everyone came spilling forth, encircling us and congratulating my father on his return. Soon we were standing amidst our tenants, who joined the servants and members of our family in calling out words of welcome in our native Gascon tongue: "*Adiu! Adiu, notre seigneur et maître!*"

"Thank you, all of you," Father acknowledged, looking around himself as he addressed everyone. "It is good to see you again and to be home at last. I have much news to share with you all. I am afraid there will be many changes in store for us. We must remain strong in our faith that the Lord will protect each and every one of us; we must be prepared to adapt to a new way of life. I wish what is best for us all, and I appreciate the dedication and loyalty you have shown my family. Tonight, let us prepare to feast together and celebrate that we are again reunited."

At that moment I grabbed Margaret's hand and pulled her out into the open, in front of the group, where our father could see her. His eyes filled with tears, and everyone fell silent, eagerly awaiting his reaction.

"Margaret, how pleased I am to see you again!" our father cried, embracing my sister. "You will have to share all the details of how you gained your release with me later."

He then turned to face our chaplain, and with great sincerity added, "I am so grateful to you, Charles, for ensuring the safety of all the members of my family and household while I was away for many months. How you managed I shall never know. I am truly indebted to you."

As our father imparted his gratitude to our chaplain I glanced at my aunt. The subtle expression of disgust she bore across her countenance was more telling than any words she could have spoken at that moment.

"To be reunited is a cause for great celebration!" Father exclaimed. "Let us not be anxious about what the future holds this evening; tonight is meant for family and friends. I wish to honour you all!"

With a cheery response, the group that had assembled to greet our father moved away, as there was still much to arrange before supper. Pey took Father's horse to be stabled and we children walked through the inner ward with our father amongst us, overjoyed to be in his company once again.

In the shadow of the barbican, and out of earshot of our aunt and chaplain, he stopped and turned to face us.

"Listen to me, everyone. What I have to tell you cannot wait. While our meal is being prepared, let us seek some privacy."

Together, we walked upstairs to the privy hall. From the open windows came the sounds of our servants as they merrily worked on the arrangements for the celebration.

"I do not wish to upset any of you with the message I must deliver tonight to our household and tenants," he began, once we were all seated comfortably in his presence. "You know that I have been away for many months in Bordeaux; during that time I have been made aware that war with the French is unavoidable.

At this point it is not a matter of *if* it will occur; it is a matter of *when* it will occur. I have heeded the advice of the members of the English administration and have begun to make preparations for our family to move to London where I shall seek a position as a peer in the upper house of Parliament. I have been told that my Gascon title should transfer to an appointment on the King's Privy Council at Westminster. My colleagues in Bordeaux are drafting the necessary documents now, and we shall leave at the end of October with the next shipment of wine headed for Portsmouth, on the south coast of England. We shall travel together as a family and with only as much as we can load into one cart, for we are unable to take the entire contents of our home; nor shall we take any members of our household staff, as there is too much risk in travelling with such a large retinue who do not understand the English language or customs. We will have a full household of English servants once I have determined where we shall live."

Upon hearing these words, Sarah and Christophe exchanged worried glances, their faces full of alarm and anxiety.

"I can tell by your solemn expressions that you are rightly concerned about moving from Rosete. But I wish to keep our family together. With the possibility of this land becoming a part of France, and my loyalty over the years to the English administration, it is likely that I would be imprisoned in the Bastille and we would lose everything we own. If we leave at once we can escape to England, where we shall have protection from persecution. I have made it possible for Père Charles to accompany our family and I shall ask my sister to remain with us; we shall take Peyriac too. I hope this pleases everyone."

As he mentioned Peyriac, he looked directly at me, and I could feel my expression soften.

"I do believe, though, that one day you children will have the opportunity to return to your cherished Gascony, and, by the grace of God, to your mother's home."

The room was filled with a heavy silence. We were all stunned by what had just transpired. Margaret was the first to respond to our father's announcement.

"You are correct, of course, Father. I can help prepare Christophe and Sarah for the journey and I am certain Isa can assist our servants in the selection of which household goods we shall take. We shall start on that tomorrow."

"Yes, of course," I agreed. "I shall help with the organisation of our belongings."

"Father," Johan began, "I must have time to speak to you; in private."

"Very well, son. We have some time before our feast. Stay and tell me your news."

We left them to their discussion; I knew it would involve Johan's new love Pharrah and how his desire to marry her would be affected by our move to England.

———

Later that evening the inner ward was filled with the aroma of roasting chickens and ducks. As we took our places in the great hall, surrounded by our servants and tenant farmers who had served us loyally for so many years, we were presented with a hearty feast. In addition to the roasted fowl from our farm, our cook prepared a gourd and parsnip soup and baked vegetables including large round cabbage, broccoli, cabbage sprouts and cauliflower. The produce was a generous contribution from the farms of our tenants who were attending the banquet.

After Père Charles said the grace, we took our seats and our father stood, with goblet raised, to offer a toast to all the members of his household.

"Let us raise our drink to each and every one of us – that we have survived the periods of war with France. I hereby toast King Henry, and may all of you continue to prosper in your everyday lives."

"Here, here!" everyone heartily chimed in, except my aunt, whom I noticed raised her cup but did not sip from it.

———

With the break of dawn the following day, I lay awake in bed, uncertain whether I should rise so early, not wishing to disturb either sister, who remained asleep near me. Margaret sensed my restlessness and spoke to me softly.

"Poor Isa, you must be quite worried. I could hear your heavy sighs all night as you slept. Let us not awaken Sarah. Come with me. Let us talk in peace."

After entering our parents' solar, Margaret closed the door behind us.

"Something is wrong, I can tell. Can I help at all?"

"I am sorry if I disturbed your sleep, sister. When we went to Benauges to rescue you barely one month ago, I could not have imagined we would have to move upon our return. I have never lived anywhere but here at Rosete. What will life be like in England? Where shall we settle?"

"You have so many concerns; remember, your journey is just beginning, dear Isa. Keep your trust in the Lord. Be strong and of a good courage; be not afraid, neither be dismayed, for the Lord is with you wherever you go."

She took up my hands in hers and we sat together on the bench in quiet reflection until we heard a soft knock at the door.

"Can I join you two?" Johan asked, poking his head into the room.

"Why of course, brother, do enter. What causes you to awaken at this early hour?"

"I spoke at length to Father last night," began Johan as he walked across the little room and took a seat on the floor in front of us. "I told him about Pharrah – about my desire to marry her."

"And what did he say?" I asked, hoping the response from our father was better than that of our aunt.

"He was quiet for a while. Then he told me it would not be possible for me to wed her."

"I am so sorry to hear that. What reasons did he give?" Margaret asked, placing her hand on our brother's back.

"There are many reasons. The greatest one is that there is not time for us to be married before we leave for England. But Father also said that as a Muslim woman she would not be allowed by her family to marry me."

"And you are not disappointed with what he said?" I asked, confused.

"I am grateful that he did not tell me I was forbidden to marry her. He just said that it would not be possible because of her family."

"And do you believe him? Have you asked Pharrah's father to marry her?" I insisted.

"Isa, our father knows of what he speaks. Do not try to convey that he might be preventing Johan from proposing this union," Margaret gently reprimanded me.

"I do believe him, Isa," Johan replied. "Pharrah has told me often that she did not think her family would allow the marriage between us. She has been promised in marriage already to someone from Tangier whom her family has chosen, but he has not yet arrived."

"I see," I said, saddened by this new information.

"Pharrah's ancestors are part of the Tuareg," Johan continued. "They are an ancient nomadic tribe who trace their roots back to before the time of Christ. Her people were traders across much of northern Africa until about two hundred years ago when her family set up a trade business in Tangier. Since then the family split and half still live in Tangier, the other half moved northward through Spain, settling in different places as they went. Her parents only moved to Bazas four years ago. But they have developed good relations with the townspeople and they feel safe here. Like Father, they have benefited from the English overseeing trade with the northern countries and London."

"How do you feel about leaving her?" Margaret asked, concerned.

"She is the first girl I have ever loved," our brother answered honestly. "I know our aunt says we are only to marry for the sake of preserving the wealth and power of the Albret family, but our father risked this to marry our mother. I do not feel our aunt should be allowed to dictate how we are to live."

Johan paused and I debated whether this was the right moment to tell them about the letter I had discovered. Before I could interject, my brother continued.

"I suppose now we must all look to what the future will be for us in a new country. For me there will be plenty of opportunities to join in with English lords who like to hunt, and there will be new friends to make in King Henry's court. But I shall be sad to leave Pharrah; I shall be sad to leave Rosete, and Maman."

"I believe we all share such sentiments, Johan," Margaret replied maternally. "But as I was just counselling Isa, we must now focus on the journey ahead. The move is coming and there are still many arrangements to be made. We shall return one day, as Father said; Rosete will always be our home. We must remain hopeful so that Sarah and Christophe do not perceive any doubts or fears on our part."

My brother and I agreed to do our best to keep in good spirits from that moment forward. I abandoned the idea of telling them about the letter. For on that day, as on those that were to come, there were countless tasks to be undertaken in preparation for our departure.

——

News of our impending move had spread quickly throughout the nearby villages, and even to Bazas. One day we had a visit from Père Francis, who came to speak to Father on business matters concerning the maintenance of Rosete and the keeping of the estate accounts. He also had news of Margaret's annulment from the Count of Foix. After coming down from the privy gallery, he silently crossed the inner ward to stand outside our mother's enclosed garden. Margaret, Sarah and I sat talking quietly on a bench under the garden's barren arbour, our backs to him, taking a break from the activities involved with our move; the last of the summer roses that had once covered the trellis with their fragrant perfume had long since fallen.

"Goodbye to you all. You will be missed," Père Francis said softly, not wishing to disturb us as he stood in our presence.

Upon hearing his voice we rose quickly to join him and say our farewells.

"Thank you, Père Francis. We shall always remain grateful to you for looking after Rosete and our mother's grave in our absence," said Margaret, her tone wistful.

"Yes, and thank you for your assistance in bringing Margaret back to us," I added.

"Ladies, I assure you, your father is a very wise man. His decision to move your family was not an easy one to make. Like you, he has his own concerns for the future and starting life in a new country. We shall do our best to protect your property and home. I look forward to the day when I shall see your family again, especially you, Lady Sarah." Père Francis smiled at our little sister.

Normally a shy child, upon hearing her name, Sarah came out from where she stood behind Margaret and me and embraced Père Francis with a hug.

"And Lady Margaret, I just shared the news with your father – I received the papal dispensation annulling your marriage on the grounds of the marriage being forced. Should you choose to marry again, you may do so knowing that your marriage to the count is void by the laws of the Church."

With one arm holding our sister Sarah, he bowed his head and asked us to join him in a moment of prayer.

"Dear Heavenly Father, this beloved family is about to leave their native home for lands unknown to them. Look after Their Ladyships Margaret, Isabelle and Sarah, and keep them from harm in their travels. Help them and all the family to settle into their new life in England and give them peace of mind, knowing their home is being cared for here in Gascony. In the name of the Father, and of the Son, and of the Holy Spirit. Amen."

Père Francis closed his prayer by offering each one of us his benediction.

"I wish your family a safe journey. One day we shall meet again, of that I am certain. The peace of the Lord be always with you."

"And with you also," my sisters and I replied in unison.

Père Francis bowed his head solemnly before turning to walk away.

———

At last the day came to bid farewell to Rosete. We would travel with one large cart full of our most valuable and essential possessions. In the late morning we gathered in our chapel, where Père Charles was preparing to lead Mass for the final time. With a heavy heart, I listened to the words he spoke, letting the sound of his deep, clear voice float over me and pass beyond the chapel walls.

The service moved me spiritually and I felt my soul lift. I closed my eyes as a vision came over me. I felt myself drifting through the air to one of the small hills beyond the forest neighbouring Rosete. I looked back at the castle, picturing our mother as she called for us to come in from playing so we could begin our lessons with Père Charles. Next, I watched my father and his fellow hunters at a feast, seated in the great hall, happily conversing and joking as they shared stories of hunting the wild boar that was their prize at dinner that night. The fire crackled as a piece of fat from the carcass melted, drizzling onto the flame. Then I saw Peyriac being led out of his stall for me by Père Charles. He helped me to mount and in my vision I watched his eyes follow us as first we trotted, then cantered off into the fields.

My thoughts then returned to Rosete, her silhouette against the evening sky; to the strength imparted by her impenetrable walls, the love that came from the sound of voices and laughter in the great hall, the solemn beauty of her chapel and Père Charles himself, always present in times of joy and sorrow about our home. Gradually, I drifted out of my dream, back into the present moment.

During the final prayer, I silently rose, wishing to make a last visit of my cherished home. Stepping outside into the fresh air, I had to catch my breath as I felt a wave of sadness wash over me. I climbed the central staircase to the wing that housed our rooms and entered my parents' solar. The room had taken on a vacant and empty feel, in spite of containing the furniture we would leave behind. With a heavy heart, I stopped and closed my eyes. When I opened them, Père Charles was there, patiently watching me.

"There, there, Lady Isabelle," he quietly whispered. I moved forward to embrace him, and he took me in his arms. I laid my head against his chest and silently wept.

"It will be all right. Allow me to comfort you, Your Ladyship," he continued as he stroked my hair.

I could not pull away from him. What I had needed so desperately since learning we were to move was someone to allow me to privately mourn the loss of my surroundings. I had never approached him in such an intimate way before, but I found that his presence brought me great relief.

"What do you say, shall we finish this visit together? Might that help?" he suggested, his voice full of concern.

"Please forgive me. I should have never let you see me cry. It is not proper. But I feel so upset at leaving Rosete, and you were here, and I, I…"

"There is no need to explain your sorrow," he said reassuringly. "I am always here to listen, and to counsel you. Do not ever forget that. And when we are in England, if you find you need to express your feelings in private, remember that as your chaplain I shall always be someone in whom you may confide."

I nodded my head in silent acknowledgement as he led me in the direction of the stairway. As I entered the castle's inner ward I took in the architectural details of the setting for a final time. The interior was set in paving stones, apart from a tiny area to the side nearest our lodgings where Maman had kept her hortus conclusus, protected by a low wooden fence. I recalled fondly how the only time we were allowed to enter the flower-and-herb garden was during the long summer evenings, when remaining inside our rooms was too warm for comfort and the serenity of the inner ward had a calming effect on us all. The medicinal herbs and plants growing there offered us and our household aid in times of sickness. An arbour strung with scented white roses hung above our heads, and under its sweet dreamy perfume we girls would read or work on our embroidered samplers, while the boys would complete their lessons quietly.

Our chapel and stable, placed on either side of the postern to the rear of the inner ward, had both been places of great joy in my childhood. Placed in the chapel wall that faced the inner ward were four narrow lancet windows, each pane filled with diamond shapes of crimson, azure, peridot and gold. A window in the east wall above the altar was capped with a roundel displaying our family crest in the centre. The thought of being separated from the sacred space that had been my daily refuge since I was a young girl heightened the disquieting fear that my family would be facing great danger in our move to England.

We crossed the courtyard, now empty and still, and walked together under the arched passageway of the barbican. Once outside the castle, Père Charles stopped and turned around, raising his arm in the sign of the cross, to give Rosete one last benediction. We found the rest of the family already assembled with the cart and our horses, ready for departure. Mounting my horse, I took a final glance back toward Rosete.

All the fond recollections of my mother and my innocent childhood came rushing through my mind in a flood. I was overcome with emotion, committing to my memory the way the late-morning sun cast a soft golden glow over her limestone walls, knowing in my heart that she would remain for all eternity: our safe haven, our stronghold, our Rosete.

Wiping the tears from my eyes, I turned Peyriac around and kicked him into a canter, eager to catch up with my family and Père Charles, who were already ahead of me on the road to Bazas.

X

Bordeaux and the *Salamanca*

O ver the course of the next few days we travelled to Bordeaux on the southern banks of the Garonne River, hoping to avoid confrontation with the Count of Foix and his retinue around Cadillac. Our father had arranged for our family to be escorted by three additional men-at-arms from our estate to ensure our safe arrival in Bordeaux. The autumn season had left its mark upon the fiery colours of the foliage growing along the verdant banks of the river's path. The grapevines that in spring and summer were clearly visible with their distinctive green leaves, even when set back at a distance from the road, had all disappeared, leaving behind only the spindly, skeletal remains of empty wooden vines hanging over arbours and running along posts planted like fences across the fields.

Our journey with the cart took longer than by horseback alone. Yet it was neither onerous nor tedious travelling so slowly. It allowed for quiet reflection as I took in the natural beauty of my beloved Gascony one final time. I enjoyed the long days of riding Peyriac upon Gascon soil, for I realised it would be some time before I would have the freedom to ride him in such a way again. And when I did, we would be in a new country, far from the duchy.

As we approached our point of entry into Bordeaux through the central gate called the *Porte Cailhau*, I noticed a marked change in my surroundings. In contrast to the quiet orderliness of the countryside around Rosete and Bazas, I found the capital to be lively and noisy, bustling with people and commotion.

From every direction came people rushing about their daily business, calling out greetings to one another, while carts and horses vied for space in the narrow roads that crisscrossed the city. Most of what I witnessed was new to me: the sight of men and women in an array of colourful and ornate costumes, the aroma of a variety of freshly baked breads from the corner *boulangerie*, the sounds of a local wine merchant busily constructing and filling wine barrels for export. Timber-framed houses lined the streets and were jettied in a cantilevered fashion, nearly blocking all views of the sky from the street below. I wondered with some trepidation whether this was what life would be like in England as well.

Our father led our group in the direction of our lodgings in the *Palais de l'Ombrière*, not far from the *Porte Cailhau* we had just entered. We were guests of the constable of Bordeaux, Sir Edward Hull, the same man responsible for Margaret's release. Father always stayed at the palace when he worked in Bordeaux. On this,

his final trip before our departure for England, the close quarters with other members of the King's Council provided him the access he needed to say his farewells and finalise his affairs in the capital. I learned that Peyriac was to be kept with Sir Edward's horses, and I was allowed to visit him as often as I pleased, a task that afforded me relief from the mounting anxiety I felt, witnessing all the changes around me.

The vessel on which we would sail to England, called the *Salamanca*, was berthed at a pier just outside the *Porte Cailhau*. Father met the captain to review what our requirements would be during the passage, and to arrange payment for the voyage in advance.

As the days wore on prior to our sailing date, we were confined to the palace. It was not practical or safe for me to take Peyriac out for a day of riding and adventure alone in the city. There was simply nothing I could do to relieve my feeling of being cooped up and restrained. We were only a week into our overseas odyssey, and already I was suffering from a combination of boredom and restlessness.

My siblings and I kept up our lessons and private Masses with Père Charles in the palace chapel. They were a welcome distraction from the worries about our pending sea travel that plagued my mind. While we had our tutorials, Margaret was away with Aunt Christine, calling on the wives of Father's associates on the council, for my sister hoped that the women in Bordeaux would provide her with introductions to other ladies at court in London. Once they returned they resumed their duties looking after the needs of Sarah and Christophe, leaving Johan and me free to take up our own interests. Johan had immediately become acquainted with members of the constable's retinue and I was free to care for Peyriac.

One morning, a week after we had arrived at the palace, we received word that we were to meet members of the King's

Council who were preparing our documents for travel to England. Our attendance was required in order for them to vouch for us in their letters of introduction and safeguard. All of us, Père Charles included, had separate interviews with five Englishmen who formed the committee. Their questions were straightforward enough: they simply wished to confirm that we were the family, sister and chaplain of Lord d'Albret Courteault, that we were members of the powerful *Seigneurie d'Albret*, that our mother was a descendant of Edward Plantagenet, the Black Prince of Bordeaux, and that despite other members of our noble family choosing to remain loyal to the King of France, we confirmed our allegiance to serve His Majesty King Henry. I was concerned that Aunt Christine would not swear an oath of allegiance to the king. But it was as my father had assured me the night he returned to Rosete. My aunt signed her letter confirming her loyalty to the English crown. In my heart I knew that she lied, but I dared not raise my concerns when my father had so adamantly admonished me earlier for questioning her motives. Once the scribe had finished blotting the ink on the parchment, each of our documents was secured with hot crimson wax and the seal of the constable of Bordeaux. Sir Edward Hull was present to hand the letters over to our father, who in turn was relieved to have our family's documents securely in his possession. At last we had everything we needed to start a new life in England.

The morning of our scheduled departure from Bordeaux, father left on an errand down the street from the palace; he visited a haberdasher to settle his account. After he had finished paying the merchant, as he left the premises, his attention was suddenly drawn to a cry heard from down the street.

"Hear ye! Hear ye! News of the French incursion! Hear ye! Hear ye!"

Stepping into the growing crowd of bystanders, he could hear the announcement more clearly being called.

"Hear ye, hear ye, the French have infiltrated the Guyenne! The English forces just beyond Fronsac have stopped them! All men of able body are instructed to take up arms and fight for His Majesty King Henry of England at once. There is to be no further transport to or from Bordeaux by land or water, and the gates of the city will be closed at midday. Hear ye, hear ye, the French have infiltrated..." The sound of the crier's voice drifted by as he continued his delivery of the startling news.

Our father rushed back to where we were waiting at the palace.

"We must leave immediately!" he exclaimed upon finding us. "It is as I feared would happen. We must not get caught inside Bordeaux after the city gates are locked. We must get to the *Salamanca* before it is too late. Let us gather our things as quickly as possible. Charles, you and Isabelle inform the grooms to prepare our horses and the cart. Christine, children, come with me. We must prepare to leave the palace at once!"

My family returned to our lodgings and quickly gathered our remaining items. The palace guards carried our parcels into the street where they were then hoisted up onto the cart and tied down securely. The grooms arrived from the stable with Peyriac and our other horses and we set off to find the ship, passing under the *Porte Cailhau* just as the guards prepared to secure and lock the gate. Carrying on, we rushed to the Bordeaux waterfront, hoping that we would still be able to board the *Salamanca* before the order came preventing any more ships from casting off and setting sail. As soon as we arrived at the wharf, Father went in search of the captain, while the rest of us watched as our personal belongings that we wished to have access to during the voyage were separated from the other crates. The remainder of the household goods were kept bundled together in the cart so that they could be easily wheeled onto the ship and stowed. The task had only just been completed when we saw Father and the captain walking down the pier toward us. Upon joining our group, the captain addressed his crew.

"All right, men, do not just stand there. Get the cart up onto the *Salamanca*. I want us ready to cast off as soon as the d'Albret Courteault family are safely on board." Captain Farley summoned several deckhands who assisted in stowing the heavily laden cart.

As I gazed upon the numerous sailing vessels tied up along the waterfront, it came to my mind that earlier in the year Père Charles had led us in a study of the text of Michael of Rhodes in our daily Latin lessons. The work and its illustrations familiarised us with sailing terminology and navigation techniques used by Venetian sailors. None of the boats moored along the waterfront resembled those depicted in the manuscript. However, I recognised that our sailing vessel was a type of merchant sailing ship that we had learned about called a caravel. It was designed to ferry passengers and cargo, including livestock and horses, between the ports of southern England and Bordeaux across the treacherous waters of the Bay of Biscay. Comparing the *Salamanca* to the other ships docked nearby, I felt confident in her abilities.

While the other cogs and galleys required a crew of up to a hundred and eighty rowers and had no enclosed cabins, our ship was fitted with two triangular lateen sails, positioned on masts at either end of the deck, designed to catch the wind and provide a fast sailing time between ports. In the middle stood a much heavier square-rigged mast. Glancing around, I noticed that none of the other ships in the port had two different types of sails. Once on board, I would discover another important distinction of our ship: enclosed cabins that provided shelter from the piercing winds that would suddenly whip up around us out of nowhere. It was clear that the *Salamanca* had been selected specifically for her speed and the level of comfort she afforded her passengers.

With my family watching as our cart was pushed onto the ship, out of the corner of my eye I noticed the captain discreetly embrace Père Charles. He said the words "Who worketh wonders?" to which our chaplain replied, "Immanuel" – just as I had heard him say to Sir Edward in Benauges! There was no time to think about the exchange I had witnessed, for the captain then turned back to us as he instructed my family to follow him up the ramp and onto the deck.

As the final preparations for our casting off were being made and orders called out to the sailors all around me, I followed behind my family as they boarded. I led Peyriac slowly, trying to keep his head low so he could focus on the sound of my voice as I attempted to calm him: his eyes and nostrils flared large at all the new sights and smells. His ears twitched to either side nervously as sailors scurried around us, throwing off the ties and setting the sails. Father remained briefly on the dock, making arrangements for the horses he and Père Charles had ridden during our travel to Bordeaux to be returned to Rosete and cared for under the direction of Père Francis. I approached him as he was talking to the captain.

"Excuse me, sir, where shall I stable my horse?" I enquired of Captain Farley.

"He must be stowed in the hold below deck. Tie him up in one of the cargo spaces. There are pens that have been used to store pigs and chickens on previous journeys; one of them should afford him the necessary space for the journey. Your father assures me that you will be responsible for feeding him and cleaning his stall every day; I do not have any extra men on board to take care of such duties. There are two large barrels of fresh water in the storage area that are used when we transport livestock. Use that for his water supply; do not give him seawater. And most importantly, keep him in cross ties until he is accustomed to travelling by sea."

"Yes, sir," I said, and I led Peyriac on a separate ramp that opened to the cargo hold. Upon entering the ship, my nostrils were overcome with the stench of the animals that had been carried there on previous trips. A damp and musty smell hung in the air and the wooden floors reeked of pig urine. I hated to leave my beloved friend in such conditions. Peyriac shied uneasily at every noise from above and pawed the floor impatiently, clearly nervous to be so closely confined on the unsteady vessel. Unexpectedly, the ramp to the cargo hold was slammed shut in preparation for casting off and, as I turned to leave, Peyriac softly whinnied at me. When I looked back, I could see the whites of his eyes as he strained his head in my direction, watching me. Though he was not usually a nervous horse, his rebellious stance and the movement of his ears flicking back and forth were evidence of his displeasure at being tied up below deck as the ship began tossing and swaying as she sailed out of port.

"Here, boy, here you are. Look what I brought for you."

Wishing to calm him, from my satchel I produced a small apple bought at the market in Bordeaux. I walked back toward him, trying to keep my balance on the moving vessel, holding it out to him in my palm. He stretched out his long graceful neck so that his silky brunette mane was caught up in the rush of air that came whistling through the hold from the deck above. He then moved towards me, still in his cross ties, and took a bite out of the apple from my hand, chewing slowly, cautiously at first, stopping to listen with his ears pointed forward as the ship groaned and heaved through the heavy current. I kept my hand near his muzzle to catch any apple that should fall from his mouth. As he nervously glanced around the space, I rubbed behind his ears to help calm him. At last his tension eased and he relaxed, taking a big bite of the apple and crunching through it without further hesitation. I could see that by the time he had finished his treat he had calmed; he had even stopped pawing at the floor. After watching him carefully for several moments, I was satisfied that he was at last subdued. By helping Peyriac to relax I had in turn helped ease my own initial panic and fear that had mounted in me as we raced to escape from Bordeaux. Satisfied that he was less anxious in his new surroundings, I felt I could leave him to join my family on deck.

"You have installed Peyriac securely below in the hold as you were instructed?" my father asked when I joined the group.

"Yes, but I do not think he is content to be there at the moment. The smell is so unpleasant and he is not accustomed to being on a ship at sea; I must check on him again later."

"Certainly; I would not like to see him go sick or lame as a result of the sea voyage," Father agreed.

My brothers and sisters fell quiet and we stood together, each of us lost in our own thoughts. Little Sarah in particular wore an expression of great concern as the ship it ploughed its way through the waves. She clung to Margaret, her arms wrapped tightly around our sister's waist. It had been quite a turn of events to pack up and get to the *Salamanca* so quickly, uncertain whether we would leave the city in time. Not surprisingly, we all showed signs of exhaustion as our bodies supported one another through the rise and fall of the waves. Shivering as we huddled together for warmth, we felt the bite of the wind whip around us from across the deck. Captain Farley approached us, offering us the use of his cabin for our meals and as a gathering place throughout the duration of the voyage. Grateful to have been given a space large enough to accommodate us all at one time, we moved inside at once to seek protection from the cold.

The comfortably appointed cabin was located directly below the quarterdeck at the stern of the ship. From the sheltered interior, we watched as the fortified towns of first Bourg, then Blaye came into and then passed from our view. Not long after we had sailed by the two towns, we came to the promontory of the Médoc peninsula, where the placid waters of the river Gironde meet the notoriously rough and expansive seas of the Bay of Biscay. I noticed that everyone had fallen silent. None of us were accustomed to travelling on the water for any distance, and the jarring motion of the ship as it fought its way through the surf gave us all a sense of overwhelming queasiness. Just as worries of falling ill at sea entered my head, our father interrupted my thoughts.

"Thankfully we were able to set sail quickly. I was worried that we might not make it out of port. As we boarded, the captain told me the voyage should take no more than five days, if we do not run into any trouble at sea."

"Father, what kind of trouble?" Margaret asked, startled by his suggestion.

"There have been reports of sea rovers operating along the route over the past few months. No ships have been taken or lives lost so far, but the captain asked me to help the crew keep guard and watch for them during certain hours of the day. The threat of aggression is very real and present; you are to keep together at all times during the voyage. We left port quickly and without the protection afforded by the two smaller, accompanying vessels that normally make the journey with the *Salamanca*. I must leave you now so that I can take my turn helping the crew keep watch over the sea. I shall return later to have supper with you."

He then donned his heavy woollen cloak that hung on a peg by the door and stepped out of the cabin. As he did so we were met with a rush of cool sea air.

"Children," our chaplain began, "I hope to make this trip comfortable for you. We will go over some lessons and then you may read from your psalter or entertain yourselves quietly. We need to stay out of the way of the sailors and captain as much as possible."

With Margaret listening to our lesson as she embroidered intricate floral patterns on a sampler she had started in Bordeaux, we took up our study of the English language. The fresh air and constant tossing of the ship in the rough sea soon affected the younger ones, who lay curled up asleep around Margaret's feet. Johan had been studying a text, but now he, too, was quietly dozing in his seat. My aunt sat slumped on a bench across the room, her eyes closed and one hand covering her mouth, the other clutching a basin at her side to catch her vomit. I recalled what I had said to my father earlier and left the cabin to check on Peyriac.

"May I join you, Your Ladyship?" Père Charles asked softly as he hastened to join me outside the cabin.

"Why, of course. I welcome your company," I gratefully acknowledged.

We made our way across the deck with our heads down, trying to keep out of the sharpness of the wind, and quickly descended into the depths of the hold below. Peyriac, upon smelling our approach from above, neighed softly. As we walked closer towards him, he nodded his head with anticipation and even let out a welcoming whinny. Père Charles approached him and rubbed his muzzle and ears affectionately.

"Why, I thought you had a fear of horses," I told him with a smile.

"Perhaps you are thinking of one horse at Rosete that I did not like to ride because it took a dislike to me." He looked over at me and chuckled. "But in fact I am quite fond of horses. When I was the age Christophe is now, my father had a warhorse named Pericles, whom I spent much time caring for while he was away in London. Pericles was rather more of a docile pet than a work animal, and I learned to trust his instincts when I rode him. As Peyriac protects you when you take your rides out into the countryside, my Pericles did the same for me across the fields of our estate in Cambridgeshire. That is why I am so pleased you were able to bring him with us. He is a noble and gentle animal. I hated the idea that you two might be separated from each other. I have watched you both for many years now and you have a very special bond: he watches over you and you are very safe with him."

These last words brought a smile to my face. "I never knew you had a horse when you were a boy. I am grateful to have both you and Peyriac in my life. I feel as if you both always keep me secure and free from harm."

I could see the colour rise in my chaplain's face: my confession had clearly taken him by surprise, yet he somehow seemed touched by my observation.

"Shall we feed him and check his water?" he asked.

I untied my horse, but kept a halter and lead on him. This allowed him to move about the open space of the hold while we gathered his food and fresh water, and cleaned out his stall. In spite of the rocking of the ship, Peyriac was able to maintain his balance and remained steady on his feet. Before leaving to return upstairs, I threw a rug over his back, but cold air enveloping the cargo hold felt tremendous as I reached over his haunches to lift the heavy blanket up to his withers. I shuddered as I pulled the thick cloth up around his neck. Père Charles reached from behind to help me, and in doing so covered my chilled fingers with his warm hands.

"Why, Lady Isabelle, I did not realise you had taken such cold! You should have said something; I would have given this to you sooner." He removed his long black cloak, unbuckling it from about his neck and draped it over my shoulders. "There, now, is that better?" he asked.

"Oh yes, that is very kind of you. But what about you? I do not wish for you to feel cold, either."

"Do not worry for me. I shall be warm enough. Let us return to your family and prepare for our vespers before taking our supper, shall we?"

Though the fierce winds from earlier in the day had calmed somewhat, there remained a distinct crispness in the air as we crossed back over the deck to join the members of my family in the captain's cabin. Soon after we had finished the service, the cook and his galley assistant brought supper to us. We took our seats at the table and heartily consumed the edible, though not particularly tasty, stew. The meat was over-salted and the vegetables were the consistency of mush, but it was precisely what we needed to nourish us after our first day at sea. When we finished our supper, my siblings and I returned to our cabins, leaving Père Charles and Father to finish talking in private with Captain Farley. They seemed to be in the middle of a serious conversation led by the captain. We would learn the nature of their discussion the following day.

——

The next morning, we gathered in the captain's cabin and I noticed that my family looked to be in better health and spirits than the day before. Through the night, I had struggled with the constant tossing and swaying of the ship. Several times I awoke in a sweat, certain that I heard Peyriac neighing for me, but it was just the wind as it whipped through the passage outside our cabin. Nonetheless, I was curious to know what had kept the men at the table so long after supper.

"I have some distressing news," Father declared once we were all seated around him. "A ship bearing a striking resemblance to one that crossed our path yesterday was spotted early this morning from the crow's nest. Captain Farley is not certain whether it is indeed a pirate ship, but he does not wish to take any chances. If the ship comes back around in our sight today, there may be trouble. This could become a dangerous situation for us and the *Salamanca*. Since last evening I have asked Père Charles to pray for our vessel and for us, which he is doing now in the privacy of his cabin. Today you all must stay here in the safety of this room. I am going to spend the day assisting the captain with preparations to secure the vessel. Johan, you are to assist us."

We were left in our aunt's care, and she attempted to answer our many questions and allay our fears. We spent the morning reading and playing games quietly. By the time we had finished our midday meal of hard bread and salted meats, boredom at being in the same room all morning with my siblings was starting to set in. I tried to write in my journal, but I found it hard to concentrate. Our chaplain eventually joined us in the afternoon, his face contemplative. He took a seat on a bench by the window, quietly reading from one of his classical texts and occasionally closing his eyes and dropping his head in slumber. I watched him, his head gently resting to one side on his broad shoulders, his hands folded over the book in his lap. He nodded his head forward with the rocking of the ship and slowly opened his eyes.

Looking across the cabin, our eyes met and neither of us turned away until Sarah's voice interrupted our steady gaze.

"Margaret, how do I make the leaf for my flower?"

My sister stopped her embroidery to help Sarah. I suppose I should have been doing the same, but I found that I could not concentrate on anything. I rose from the floor and put on my cape in preparation to go outside to the main deck. I needed fresh air, as I was overcome by a sudden rush of feelings I could not understand. I stood up and started to walk when I felt the walls of the room closing in on me, and I briefly shut my eyes to help steady myself. When I opened them again and stepped into the antechamber, the same feeling came over me, only it felt as if there was too little air. Stars darted past my eyes as I tried to take a few steps, but the ship was rolling and plunging. I reached out to grab on to something so that I would not lose my balance but it was too late. My body pitched forward, my head striking the wall of the corridor with great force. I collapsed on the floor in the antechamber of the captain's cabin.

Père Charles must have been close behind me, because when I awoke in the cot I shared with my sisters, I found him by my side, holding my hand, his head bowed in prayer.

"O Lord, I lift up Lady Isabelle to you and your safekeeping, that you might watch over her and help her body to heal. *Gaudent in caelis animae sanctorum, qui Christi vestigia sunt secuti; et quia pro eius amore sanguinem suum fuderunt, ideo cum Christo regnabunt in aeternum,*" he softly recited.

"Look, Isa is awakening now," interrupted Margaret. She held a cool damp cloth on my forehead. I glanced around the room, unsure how I had come to be there. My aunt stood to the side, her hands clasped in front of her. Her stern expression lacked any compassion as she looked upon me with dismay.

"What… happened?" I asked in confusion while trying to sit up.

"There is no need to speak, Your Ladyship," answered Père Charles. "This sea travel has made you weary, I am afraid. You fainted in the anteroom. I happened to step out behind you and witnessed you fall. You hit your head on the wall and floor quite hard. There is a large purple bruise and visible bump forming on your forehead. Just rest here and we shall look after you."

"But Peyriac! I must see him and ensure his stall is cleaned. I must get him fresh water and food!" I exclaimed in alarm.

"Lady Isabelle, you know that I am more than happy to look after him for you. You are in no condition to be moving about the ship. I must insist that you remain here in your bed and take rest. Allow your aunt and sister to care for you," my chaplain instructed as he rose and left the cabin.

"You are very fortunate, Isabelle, that your chaplain cares for you so," began Aunt Christine, her tone curt as she stepped forward to replace the damp compress over the bump on my head. "Now that I can see you have not suffered any lasting impact to your health from your fall, I must return to look after Sarah and Christophe. Margaret, I leave you to care for your sister."

"Do lie back and close your eyes," my sister instructed with a soft voice. "Give your body some rest. You have not slept soundly over the past week in Bordeaux. Try not to think of what the future holds for us. Father and Père Charles will not let us come to any harm. Your family is here with you and we shall take care of you, dear sister."

Margaret reached over and gathered the cloth off my forehead before wringing it out in a basin next to the bed. Kissing my face, she placed it again above my eyes and this at once had a calming effect. With her motherly care I felt transported back to my early childhood at Rosete.

After some time, I woke again. With Margaret and Sarah asleep on either side of me, I realised I must have slept through the remainder of the day; no one had disturbed me. But now I was wide awake. The combination of the swaying motion and stale air gave rise to a feeling of sickness in the pit of my stomach. I decided to go up on deck for some fresh air. Climbing off the straw mattress, trying to make as little noise as possible, I silently moved across the cabin. Donning my woollen cape, I slipped out into the pitch-black passage. Once my eyes had adjusted, I could make out a faint degree of light at the end where a narrow set of stairs with rope railing led to the main deck. The cool, fresh air helped relieve some of the nausea brought on by the deep throbbing pain in my head. Feeling my way along the wall to the stairs as the ship rocked and tossed, I carefully made my way up the ladder and outside.

The sky was a royal-blue tapestry of tiny twinkling lights. I drank in the cold sea breeze and felt immediately refreshed, the discomfort across my forehead fading with every deep breath. Then I felt a shiver as a hand appeared out of the dark, touching my shoulder.

"What is wrong, Your Ladyship? Why are you not with the others in bed, asleep?"

It was Père Charles. I had not seen him in the dark, for he was dressed in his long black cassock and cape. His bent figure had stood hunched over the ship's railing, blending in with the dark of the night.

He removed his cape and gently placed it around my trembling shoulders. I sank into the protection of its warmth, still bearing the heat from his own body.

"I apologise. You gave me such a fright. Allow me to catch my breath first."

He stood behind me, his broad frame protecting my small one from the cool night wind.

"I could not sleep any longer," I finally said, turning to face him. "Did I sleep all afternoon and evening?"

Stepping back and to the side, Père Charles replied, "Yes, Your Ladyship, you did. We did not want to wake you for supper, since it was clear that you needed the rest. But you should know better than to wander up here by yourself, especially in the dark. It is far too dangerous. Your father would be alarmed if he knew you had done this on your own."

"Since you are here, I shall be safe," I said with assurance. "I am not alone."

"I am afraid, Lady Isabelle, that I must escort you to your room before your sister finds that you are missing."

"Of course. I am grateful for your attentive care. What would my life be without you?" I queried, the tone of my voice an acknowledgement of how much I appreciated his concern.

"That is not a fair question for you to ask of me. Remember, I am a priest and your guardian. I shall remain a part of your life during this time of transition. Everything will change once we reach England and you are presented at court in London. I am afraid I shall not always have the fortune to watch over you, Lady Isabelle."

"You are my chaplain and tutor, Père Charles. In you, I have a connection to my life and childhood at Rosete. I cannot bear the thought of ever losing your wise counsel and guardianship."

"Of course I shall not abandon you, Your Ladyship. I would do anything you ask of me," he replied softly. "But now I must take responsibility for your safety and return you to your room."

He escorted me back downstairs to my cabin. After removing his cape from about my shoulders, he turned to leave my side as I reached out to put my arms around him, catching him off guard with my brazen move.

"Goodnight and thank you for your kindness," I whispered in his ear. As I kissed him gently on the cheek, my skin softly grazed the stubble of his unshaven face. I felt his body stiffen from the contact and I sensed his strong reaction to my bold move.

"Goodnight to you, my Lady Isabelle," he quietly whispered in my ear as we parted.

———

The next morning I awakened, finally feeling refreshed and clear-headed. Margaret, Sarah and I dressed and joined the rest of the family in the captain's cabin. I noticed that Père Charles was absent and felt an immeasurable sense of guilt about our intimacy in the passage as we parted the night before. I had determined to control my outward signs of affection better in his presence, no matter how difficult that might be, when Father interrupted my thoughts.

"Isa, you appear to be much better today. Does your head hurt where you bumped it?" he asked.

"I do feel rested and my head is only very slightly sore."

"Good, good," he replied with a kind expression. "My only news for you all is to continue to keep alert. We did not come across the mysterious ship yesterday, but it may well appear again today. Meanwhile, the winds have picked up considerably. I am afraid we may run into a fierce storm later."

The sea rovers! How could I have forgotten about them? Captain Farley came into the cabin and sat down to talk to our father. They were again deep in discussion at the end of the table when our aunt directed us to return to our lessons. I excused myself to go below and check on my horse.

Later that morning when I returned back upstairs to the warmth and shelter of the captain's cabin with the rest of my family, I noticed that our chaplain had not joined us. Finally, I could not bear wondering about his absence any longer and asked whether anyone had seen him.

"Oh yes, he was up quite early," answered Christophe. "I passed him outside my cabin as he was entering his own this morning. He asked that we not disturb him; he said he was in need of solitude and quiet meditation."

"Why do you concern yourself with his presence, Isabelle?" my aunt asked pointedly. "You need not worry yourself with his well-being. Your father and I will see to that ourselves."

I did not appreciate my aunt's dismissive tone and turned to my sister instead.

"Margaret, my head has begun to ache. I feel I must take some rest in our cabin."

"Of course, Isa. Please go and lie down," she said, looking up from her book. "Would you like me to walk with you?"

"Oh no, thank you. That is not necessary." I stood and took leave of my family.

Upon returning to the privacy of the cabin, I felt an overwhelming sense of sadness come over me. I feared that I had ruined the very special friendship that was developing between Père Charles and me. I lay down on the cot, drifting off to sleep. Images floated through my dreams – Father arriving at Rosete after being away; Maman talking and laughing with Margaret; Johan and I running around the castle playing hide-and-seek. And then I saw myself lying in a field outside Rosete with Peyriac nearby, looking up as milky-white clouds drifted across the backdrop of a brilliant blue sky.

And then I experienced a new vision from the Lord. In it I saw a foreign place where I had never been, in a land where I could not understand the language. Père Charles was with me. He was introducing me to someone I had not met before, a bishop wearing a brilliant white alb with a stole around his neck embroidered in gold thread. We stood by a windswept barren cliff overlooking the sea; a ship was anchored nearby. He carried with him a weathered brown leather pouch; inside was a worn cloth stained with what appeared to be dried blood. We knelt before the bishop and looked up to the heavens. A flash of light and a dove appeared above us. In my dream I saw the presence of the Lord as he stood between us, in the human form of his Son, Jesus Christ, wearing the crown of thorns, his body wounded and bleeding where he had been tortured upon taking up the cross. Smiling at both of us in turn, the Lord reached out and took our hands in his own and I heard him reveal himself in glory to us, saying, "You are the blessed children of my creation; in you I place my love and devotion. If I could suffer more for your sins, I would gladly do so, to lessen your own pain and suffering. Your deep friendship with each other is a blessing upon you from heaven; may the Holy Spirit remain within you and join you together always."

XI
The Tempest

I fell in and out of slumber that afternoon, bundled up to keep warm against the damp chill as the pitch of the *Salamanca* rolling back and forth grew stronger at more regular intervals. With my eyes still closed, my mouth filled with the astringent taste of bile as a wave of sickness came over me. Suddenly came the sounds of creaking and groaning, and the ship shuddered strongly. A terrible clap of thunder followed by loud shouts of the sailors on the main deck directly above my cabin prevented me from hearing the persistent sound of my name being called. Without any warning, before I could make sense of what was happening around me, Père Charles rushed in to be at my side.

"What is happening?" I demanded of him as I sat up, startled by his sudden appearance.

"You must come with me at once, Lady Isabelle! We have sailed into a mighty storm; you must get upstairs to take shelter in the captain's cabin with the others! I have been given the task of collecting you. The ship has been struck by lightning already, though at present the damage is not great enough to cause us to sink."

"Oh no!" I cried, my thoughts turning to my horse. "I must see to Peyriac then, too!"

"We must first think of our own safety," he instructed forcibly. "Come along! We must return upstairs at once!"

There was a flurry of activity on deck, with Captain Farley shouting orders and his men completing them. A torrent of rain poured down over the deck as we crossed, flooding its already slippery surface, making the deck treacherous to navigate. It seemed a change in wind direction increased the velocity of the ship, taking her into the heart of the brutal storm. We dashed into the captain's cabin, our clothes and bodies thoroughly soaked, where we found my father instructing the others.

"Collect yourselves, children! Prepare to do as I say. Good, Charles and Isabelle, you are here now. Charles, you are in charge while I assist the crew and Captain Farley."

"Certainly, Your Lordship."

We felt the full force of the storm as the fierce winds caused the waters around us to rise and swell. In turn, the *Salamanca* was tossed about through the waves that pounded her relentlessly. From inside the cabin we felt pitched and thrown; we had to cling to whatever we could to keep our balance. Several times I caught sight of my siblings becoming ill, their faces and clothing strewn with the contents of their stomachs. The stench of vomit in the cabin was almost worse than the continual rising and crashing of the ship as we crested a wave only to be dashed down hard on the other side. Father left us and the yelling outside continued at irregular intervals; what made it worse was that we could not understand what was being shouted. Sarah threw her arms around Margaret, whose expression did little to mask her panic over the brutality and force of the storm. Crying aloud and with tears streaming down her face, my little sister was visibly frightened; yet through it all our aunt sat stoically, in spite of the fear and utter dread displayed on my face and on my brothers'.

As our ship was rocked by a succession of great waves that caused us to list heavily to one side and then the other, our aunt directed her attention upon our chaplain. With a mocking tone, she gave him instruction.

"Well, Père Charles, I believe it is time for you to invoke the mercy of the Lord, is it not? Let us see if he will indeed save us from the perils of this mighty tempest that seeks to destroy our vessel and us along with it."

Doing as he was told, our chaplain bowed his head and began to pray out loud.

"O Father in Heaven, we ask that you watch over us and our vessel as we are carried forth into this destructive storm. Protect our family and the sailors as we are led away from our intended course. Watch over us and keep us from harm; save us from all perils and from drowning at sea. We pray now together the Lord's Prayer. *Pater noster, qui es in caelis, sanctificetur nomen tuum. Adveniat regnum tuum. Fiat voluntas tua, sicut in caelo et in terra. Panem nostrum quotidianum da nobis hodie, et dimitte nobis debita nostra sicut et nos dimittimus debitoribus nostris. Et ne nos inducas in tentationem, sed libera nos a malo. Amen.*"

While we were praying aloud, another terrifying clap of thunder erupted directly above us; its impact was felt throughout the ship as the vessel shuddered and groaned in response. Both Margaret and Sarah shrieked in alarm as we heard a mast crack and come crashing down across the deck. Johan and Christophe sat holding each other in anticipation of the next lightning strike, their faces ashen with fear. We could feel the pressure in the air changing around us as we sailed deeper into the storm.

"It would appear that your God does not approve of your prayer, Père Charles," Aunt Christine sneered, her dislike of our chaplain and his piety evident in her tone.

Suddenly I heard a piercing whinny over the cries of men and rolling claps of thunder all about us. Without even thinking, impulsively I rushed from the cabin, desperate to get to my horse.

"Isabelle! No! Come back!" I heard Margaret cry, but I paid no attention.

"Stay here, children. Stay here and follow your aunt's instructions!" shouted Père Charles as he ran out of the door after me.

Remarkably, I was able to get down into the hull and Peyriac's makeshift stall without injury. Out of fear, the poor frightened animal had worked his blanket from his back and had managed to hobble himself with it. When I reached him, he was overcome with aggression. He even bared his teeth at me, something I had never seen him do before. As the ship pitched and tossed I lost my balance, clinging to his neck, my fingers clutching his mane to steady myself. I reached out and was about to untie one of his cross ties when I heard a voice shriek from behind me.

"Lady Isabelle! What are you doing? You will be killed!" yelled Père Charles as he approached me from across the hull. Doing so, he lost his balance as the ship made a sudden deep dip and I could hear the anger in his voice mounting as he raised himself from the floor unsteadily.

"Let go of him! Let go of him at once and come here to me, I say!"

His harsh words and the shock of the situation were too much for me. I turned back to Peyriac and closed my eyes, my legs frozen in place. The ship pitched heavily to one side and then rocked back, the impact casting my body against that of my chaplain as Peyriac attempted to rear up in fear. Grabbing hold of the stall's railing for balance, Père Charles caught me and held me tightly, securing me against his body, his arms wrapped low around my waist, shielding me from Peyriac's hooves as he repeatedly thrashed about. The ship continued to rise and fall with every colossal wave that washed over her, causing us to sway haphazardly as we stood together. Grabbing my face, Père Charles looked into my terror-filled eyes, wide with alarm. I could immediately sense his pain at having to be so stern with me.

"I am doing this for you, Lady Isabelle, to try to save your precious life. Leave Peyriac, I command you! We must seek shelter upstairs. *Now*!"

"No, I refuse to leave my horse!" I insisted stubbornly.

There was more yelling heard above us on the main deck, followed by another series of deep rolls and pitches. I felt a mounting sickness rise in my throat as the *Salamanca* struggled to remain upright on the turbulent seas. Peyriac whinnied loudly and we both turned to look at him.

"Oh, very well, I do not have time to argue with you. Come quickly and help me! We must get the blanket away from his feet!" Père Charles commanded. "Move all the other equipment out of his way! Give him room to step about more freely!"

I did as I was told, for I anticipated we would be tossed to the side at any moment. We had just moved the blanket away when within seconds our ship listed heavily again. The impact was so strong that it threw us both across the floor; this time I landed on top of my chaplain. I slid off him and we picked ourselves up, hurriedly making our way back up to the deck, dodging the crew who scurried past us, doing their best to keep the ship afloat in the treacherous seas, knowing we had only moments before the next wave came crashing down over us, potentially washing us overboard as we rushed back to the security of the captain's cabin. Peyriac could still be heard, his whinnies loud and shrill; he continued thrashing around below deck, the hammering of his hooves as they came into contact with the sides of his stall audible in spite of the thunder that cracked and pounded overhead. As we entered the cabin, soaked through to the skin from crossing the deck in the incessant pounding of wave upon wave and sheet upon sheet of drenching torrential rain, I could see Sarah sobbing in Margaret's arms. We braced ourselves in anticipation of further dipping and rolling, but instead the winds appeared to have changed again and we were now sailing beyond the outer barrier of the violent storm.

Though the cold blasts and sheeting rain would continue for the remainder of the afternoon, we were no longer sailing directly into the eye of the storm as we had previously been. At that moment, our father and Captain Farley ran into the room to check on us.

"We are so pleased to see that you are all safe!" Margaret exclaimed to them as they greeted us, their expressions full of relief.

"Miraculously we have all survived, by the grace of God," our father exclaimed joyfully. "Charles, your prayers were answered. I believe we have been spared a much worse fate. We must give thanks to the Lord, for he has watched over this mighty vessel and kept us safe from harm."

As our father bestowed his praise upon our chaplain and the Lord, I glanced at my aunt's expression. She rolled her eyes and looked askance, clearly dismayed that her brother felt the need to bestow gratitude upon Père Charles and God.

"I agree, Your Lordship," replied Captain Farley. "Our crew put up a brave fight against the elements and we have indeed survived. We did sustain some damage, but nothing that will prevent us from continuing our voyage up the coast. Tonight we shall share in a special celebration. Father Charles, might you permit the crew to join the family at vespers before we dine?"

"Yes, you may attend our worship this evening," he answered with reverence. "It is indeed right and just to give thanks and praise to the Lord for his safeguarding of the crew and family."

"I shall inform the sailors. Let us meet in the cabin on the quarterdeck; there is room enough there for all to attend the service. Now please excuse me. I must direct the crew in the repairs that require urgent attention – but I look forward to celebrating with you all tonight."

Captain Farley left us to help the sailors recover and untangle the broken mainmast of the square-rigged sail that lay strewn treacherously across the deck. The two other masts remained undamaged; we would rely on their triangular lateen sails to help us navigate our way up the coast to Portsmouth without further delay.

After going down to the hold to feed and care for Peyriac together, Père Charles and I returned to our cabins to change out of our wet clothes. When I returned alone to the main deck, I found that the crew and my family had assembled in the cabin on the quarterdeck for the brief service of thanksgiving. I joined the group as the prayers began. The time spent in worship was good for us all, for we arrived at supper refreshed and in high spirits.

The conversation over dinner that night dwelt upon the subject of the afternoon's storm – of what we had witnessed and survived. Presently, it came time for Sarah and Christophe to retire; I told my aunt I would return with them, and Margaret joined me. We left to put the young ones to bed and to steal some precious quiet time for ourselves.

Once we were installed in our cabin, I came to realise that it had been a long time since I had felt so comfortable being alone with my sister. Initially, after her return from Benauges, I had carefully avoided any topics of discussion relating to her marriage. But over the past few weeks, since learning of our departure for London, I had noticed her smile and laughter returning. Sitting together on the floor of our cabin that evening, after Sarah fell asleep, her little snores barely audible as she rested soundly, at last I mustered the courage and asked Margaret about her ordeal of being married to the count.

"Margaret?" I began, keeping my voice low to avoid disturbing Sarah's sleep.

"Yes, Isabelle, what is it?" she replied in a whisper.

"What you experienced with the Count of Foix has made me fearful of men and of marriage. I know Father expects me to marry into a noble family after we settle in England. But how shall I know when I have met someone in whom I can trust to bestow my love? I am so uncertain about courting; I regret that I must burden you with my concerns."

"Do not be anxious about such things, dear sister," Margaret said, her voice distant and reserved. "You must remember, I wed the count out of a sense of duty to our family. I did not marry him for love. I thought my marriage would benefit our family and prevent any feuding between the Houses of Albret and Foix, for nothing would have pleased the count more than to engage in war had I refused his proposal."

Margaret's expression became contemplative.

"Just know that you are far stronger a woman in here," she said, pointing to her heart, "than any man will ever think you are. What happened to me I pray will not happen to you. I am the eldest daughter and as such I was bound by my obligation to serve the family's best interests. It was critical that through my marriage I maintained peace for the Albret family. I must caution you: do not judge all men by the cruel actions of one, dear Isa."

After a few moments of reflection, Margaret continued, "I believe that the Lord has provided me with this opportunity to find a new life in England. We have so much to be thankful for, Isabelle. Do not worry about marriage for the time being."

Margaret's tone had lightened and she turned to me, smiling.

"You came to rescue me. You are very brave, dear sister. If you ever need my help, I want you to ask it of me. Our mother was always so proud of you for keeping up with your writing. I see you with your journals, and I assume you are still noting down all you see around you."

"Why, yes. Father brought me additional journals from Bordeaux when he returned home from his trips to the capital. I have used them to record our family history. I describe the events in our lives that we have lived through and the people who have been a part of them."

"Someday, Isabelle, you will make a man very proud to love you," Margaret continued, her voice soft and maternal. "You offer so much to a fortunate suitor. You love with all your heart and care for those whom you treasure deeply. Though you are sometimes impulsive, your desire to do good unto others by putting their needs before your own is one of your greatest gifts."

My sister knew how to make me feel important, loved, needed. We stopped talking and prepared for sleep.

"Before I join you, I must see that Peyriac is installed safely in case the waters become rough tonight."

"Should you be inspecting him by yourself?" Margaret asked with concern. "It is dreadfully dark out there."

"Do not worry. I shall be cautious as I make my way to him," I assured her. "Go to sleep and you will see me again in the morning."

"Very well, then. Goodnight. Do not remain out in the cold for long," said Margaret as I stood and moved quietly to the door.

When at last I reached Peyriac in his stall, he neighed softly and pawed the floor calmly in a greeting. It was only when I was close to him that I discovered he was already in his cross ties and that the rug had been placed securely over his back.

"Peyriac, who took care of you tonight?" I asked him out loud. I gave him a kiss on his muzzle, holding his head steady in my hands. He waited patiently for me to finish hugging him and then, after bobbing his head, he gave a heavy snort of content. Seeing him so calm after his frantic behaviour earlier that day in the midst of the storm brought me great relief.

Returning upstairs, I saw the familiar shape of Père Charles leaning against the guardrail, his head lifted upwards to the star-filled sky. Not wishing to interrupt his moment of peaceful reflection, I stood patiently to one side, waiting for him to sense my presence and address me.

"Why, Lady Isabelle, is that you?" he asked, his voice full of concern as he moved toward me. "What are you doing up here again after dark?"

"I went to check on Peyriac, but it appears you have already done so for me," I said, inching closer to stand at his side.

For a few moments we remained together in a comfortable silence, the cool sea air feeling crisp and light around us.

"Père Charles…"

"Yes, Your Ladyship, what concerns you?"

"I have come to wonder about you," I stated, hoping he would not be put off by my inquisitive nature.

"Oh?" he said, raising his eyebrows and tilting his head to the side. "And what do you dare wonder?"

"I am curious about where you came from, before you joined our family. I hope that you might tell me about your childhood and where you were brought up. Is life in England so very different from Gascony?"

He regarded me for several moments, and then took a deep breath, gazing out across the sea before responding.

"Let us move away from the railing where we might be more comfortable."

Together we walked over to the steps leading up to the quarterdeck. In the rush of sea air that continued to blow over us intermittently, we sat down, side by side. I continued with my questions.

"Margaret has told me you spent time in England. Please tell me the truth. You are more than a simple country priest, is that not so? You left England to come and live in Gascony – are you able to tell me why?"

After a few moments of silence, he draped his clerical cloak across my shoulders protectively to help shield me in warmth as we huddled together against the chill of the night.

XII
Père Charles

"I was born in England, the eldest son of four children, two boys and two girls. My father, Sir Robert Goodwyn, was a fellow of the Hall of Valence Marie in Cambridge, where many of his college pupils were of French noble birth. When I was four years old, the Earl of Warwick invited my father to take leave from his work in Cambridge and join him in providing instruction for King Henry, who was only eight years old at the time. My father was responsible for teaching the future king a variety of subjects, most notably the French language and the importance of obtaining peace through diplomacy. For his years of loyal service, the king rewarded my father with the title of Earl of Huntingdon, which included a deed to the lands and associated annual rents.

"At the same time, Cardinal Henry Beaufort, the Bishop of Winchester, who sat on the Regency Council with the Duke of Bedford and Duke of Gloucester, sought my father's advice. While he was in London instructing Henry, my father would privately meet Cardinal Beaufort to discuss the language of various treaties the cardinal wished to propose between England and members of the royal court of France.

"Although my father remained highly regarded by many scholars at the colleges of Oxford and Cambridge universities for his knowledge of the French language and customs, certain noblemen in the King's Court did not favour him or his style of rapprochement. In particular, his views on how to attain *détente* with the French, with whom we had been at war for nearly one hundred years, were considered controversial amongst several of his peers.

"One year, in anticipation of a congress between the courts of England and France to be held at Arras, my father advocated that Henry VI should marry one of the daughters of the French king as an attempt to further legitimise his claim to French throne. But the negotiations turned out poorly. The French refused to acknowledge the English regent as King of France; they had their own legitimate heir to the throne in King Charles VII.

"Instead, a separate treaty was reached between the King of France and Philip, the Duke of Burgundy, who had previously been a long-time ally of the English. It came as a great shock to the English noblemen serving in the King's Court that the duke switched his allegiance and joined forces with the King of France in the language drawn up in a document called the Treaty of Arras. My father and Cardinal Beaufort were blamed for the failed marriage negotiations at the congress."

"But surely they must have understood that your father and Cardinal Beaufort desired the best for England and wished to see a peaceful end to the war with France," I said in disbelief.

"I am afraid unfortunately not, Lady Isabelle. At that time a group of English noblemen, all members of the king's inner circle, began to assert that the King of England should no longer answer to the Pope in Rome. They secretly wished that a new Church be formed, a Church of England, independent from the Holy See. They felt that the representatives of Pope Eugene IV and the Council of Basel, in attendance at the congress in France, had facilitated the Treaty of Arras by providing correspondence absolving Duke Philip of Burgundy from his obligations to serve the English crown. This act, carried out by those with ties to the Pope in Rome, angered those English noblemen who felt that the French king was able to control the members of the papacy. Since the start of this century the popes have styled the French monarch as *Rex Christianissimus*, the most Christian king. Members of the English nobility have long taken offence that such a significant designation should be granted to their adversary by the Holy See, whose members are meant to remain impartial in such matters. To this day, there remains a secret movement underway to separate England from the powers of the Church in Rome."

"Does that mean the congress at Arras provided no benefit for England?" I asked, with some alarm.

"That is correct. Following the Treaty of Arras, nephews of the peace-seeking Cardinal Beaufort – John Beaufort, the Duke of Somerset, and his brother Edmund, with their associates in Parliament – repeatedly circulated rumours and lies about my father at court. The group of noblemen claimed that my father was in possession of a most sacred artefact. They said it had been stolen and brought back centuries earlier with the Knights Templar returning from the third crusade to Acre. They believed it to be a holy relic relating to the Passion of Christ, one that should have remained in the custody of the Pope in Rome, yet was of such importance that it could provide them with the foundation of a new Church, to be headed by the King of England and separate from the Roman Catholic faith. They believed my father to be a member of the Order of the Passion, a chivalric order started during the reign of Richard II and of which Richard's half-brother, the previous Earl of Huntingdon, had been a member. In the end, their thirst for power culminated in a terrible act carried out against my family."

Père Charles paused, casting his gaze downwards before continuing, "In the late autumn of 1435, my father returned home from teaching the king in London one week earlier than expected. Over dinner that night he revealed that he felt as though his life was under threat by a hostile group at court headed by the Beaufort brothers. My father told us how on the previous evening, as he was returning to his inn from the Palace of Westminster, he had been forcibly detained in a dark corner of the lane. A masked man held a knife to his throat and asked whether his family was 'safe' at home. He told my father to leave London at once to check on them or else he would return home to Cambridgeshire and find his family missing."

"That news must have been frightening to hear as a young boy!" I interjected, full of concern.

"Indeed, it was. My father explained to us that after his encounter with the mysterious figure, he ended his affairs immediately and returned home, grateful to see that we were indeed safe and no harm had been done to us. Before my siblings and I went to bed that night, he kissed us all and begged us to be careful, especially whenever he was away. The household went to sleep with his warning in mind. But it turned out that his presence in our home was not enough to save us."

Here he stopped speaking and looked away. I could see it was difficult for him to continue, so I too looked away until he was ready to proceed with his story.

"You see, Your Ladyship, during the night intruders stole into Huntingdon Castle and murdered my entire family as they slept."

I let out an audible gasp, horrified by his revelation.

"That is terrible! What about you? How did you escape them?"

"When they came to the room where my brother and I lay sleeping in separate beds, I was awakened by the sound of the floor creaking. Alerted, I sat up straight, alarmed and wondering who was there, but fear overwhelmed me and I dared not utter a sound. They carried no torch, so I could only see a vague silhouette of three men in the dark of our shuttered room. At the next instance my brother, who slept nearby, was savagely stabbed repeatedly in the chest, his cries muffled by a pillow held firmly over his head by one of the assassins. I could hear him shrieking my name, but instead of running to help him, I crept silently away into the shadows."

"I am so sorry for what you witnessed as a boy!" I exclaimed. "I cannot imagine how horrifying it must have been to hear and watch your brother being murdered in the same room as you!"

At this point, looking at Père Charles, I could see how excruciatingly painful it was for him to recount the vision from that terrible night. I longed to reach over and hold him, to offer some consolation and to comfort him for his terrible loss. But I feared his reaction to such behaviour, so instead I sat patiently, awaiting him to continue.

"With the assailants' attention focused on my younger brother and his valiant struggle to overcome their attack, I escaped down the stairs and outside where I hid in a ditch until I heard them ride away. That night I cried and cried. I asked God why he had allowed me to be a witness to the murder of my younger brother. Why had I not been killed too? It was only in the predawn light of morning, as I went about the castle, searching for my parents and sisters, that I discovered my whole family and three of our servants had been murdered as they slept, in the same manner as my brother. Moving from room to room, all I could smell was the rancid scent of death. In every bedchamber I came upon the members of my family and our household, their faces frozen in a state of agony, their eyes open and staring, yet unable to see, their blood splattered across their nightshirts and the sheets on their beds. Each had been hacked to death in a most violent way; the assassins had spared no mercy on them, not even upon my sisters, who slept together in the same bed. At first I thought they might have survived and were just lying still, but when I reached out to awaken them, their heads rolled back; their necks had been snapped and broken like the branches of a tree! What kind of human being could afflict such torture on innocent children?"

He paused, sighing deeply and looking away from me across the open expanse of sea, the deep and steady rocking a comfort against the narrative he had just described.

"I have never shared the story of my family's murder and what I witnessed with anyone, except God. The guilt of surviving that night has stayed with me for many years now. To this day I feel a sense of isolation and heartache from the absence in my life of my mother and siblings. I loved my father dearly. To me, there was no greater man than he."

"Please, continue only if you are comfortable doing so. It grieves me to learn of your suffering. I can see that relating the story of your childhood is distressing to you," I said, my voice full of concern for his well-being.

"On the contrary, Lady Isabelle," he replied, looking up and locking his eyes with mine. "Feelings of my great unworthiness have plagued me since childhood. I have never had anyone in my life with whom I felt I could confide the memory of that night."

I reached out my hand to cover his. He acknowledged my intimate gesture by gently squeezing it. At last he continued.

"I ran away from Cambridgeshire and the love of my family that it represented. The only other place where I thought I might be safe was in Oxford. I recalled that my father had often spoken of his colleagues who were fellows of the New College of St Mary.

It was while at Oxford, begging in the street, that I encountered one of them, Master James Redding, a priest and former fellow from the Hall of Valence Marie in Cambridge. James later told me that when he saw me, he barely recognised me. I bore no resemblance to the boy he'd known in Cambridge, for I was dressed in rags, my face and eyes dark and hollow from malnourishment. On that day, James directed me to follow him and we walked along the city walls until we came to the hall where he was a fellow; it was the very college of which my father had often spoken. Making no issue of my identity with the porter as we entered, he had me bathe and presented me with clean clothes to wear. They were far too big, but his generosity and paternal kindness touched me deeply. On that very day James enrolled me as his pupil. I did not have the wealth of worldly goods that I had been entitled to before, but I had the advantages afforded by an Oxford college education."

"How fortunate you were to be recognised by Father James!" I exclaimed.

"That is indeed true. Over time, he felt he could share with me the aftermath of my family's murder. According to James, my father's friends and colleagues had assumed I was dead, for my body was never found on the Huntingdon estate. Certainly, they reasoned, a boy of my age and nobility could never survive on his own without the aid of his retinue of household servants. James explained that whoever ordered the killing of my family would want to silence me as well, if they were to discover I was still alive."

Père Charles began to collect himself at this point in his story; his demeanour became more assertive and less anguished.

"When I was sixteen, James took me with him to Wales, where we followed the path of Geraldus Cambrensis as described in his *Itinerarium Kambriae*. It is the very same text that I have used to instruct you in your Latin lessons. While on our trip, James convinced me that becoming a member of the clergy could provide me with a safe living. Carrying letters of introduction to other clergymen in France, I made my way to Paris. I took my sea passage from St Davids, which lies directly along the Pembrokeshire coast in Wales.

"Within days of arriving in the capital city, I was introduced to Archbishop Pey Berland following a service he had led in the cathedral of Notre Dame. He was from Bordeaux, and he and his delegation had stopped in Paris on their way to England to address Parliament on the plight of the impoverished Gascons. Archbishop Berland, like my father, was something of a diplomat. He was well known for his tireless efforts to help the English administration in Bordeaux, who were at the time struggling against constant threats of invasion from the French. Archbishop Berland sent me to Bordeaux with his letters of introduction, confident that I would find life in the south-west agreeable."

Père Charles paused, and with his characteristic humility, enquired, "Lady Isabelle, perhaps you are tiring of my story. Have I shared enough for one night?"

"No, I wish to hear more. Please do continue, if you will," I replied in earnest.

"Very well then. Not long after my arrival at the Cathedral of Bordeaux, the Bishop of Bazas visited the clergy, seeking a few priests who would benefit from working in a rural setting with a smaller congregation outside the city. He chose me, determining that I could best serve the Church by working at the parish of Bazas. Upon meeting your parents at Christophe's baptism, I found that they reminded me of my own in many ways. I thank the Lord every day for sending me to Gascony, and for your parents and siblings, for all of you have helped me to feel again the love of family I knew only as a young boy."

He became silent and turned his gaze out beyond me, across the rolling waters that surrounded us. I looked at him, quietly thinking of all he had divulged, how he had lived through such a tormented childhood.

"That, my dear Lady Isabelle, is the story of who I am and how I came to know your family," he said, concluding his tale. Pausing, he gently added, "And how I came to know you."

"I am overwhelmed by all you have shared with me. I am astounded that you have been witness to such loss and sadness in your life, for in your outward appearance you mask your sorrow completely. With all that happened to you as a child, are you comfortable returning to England with us?" I asked with concern.

"Certainly. I am pleased to accompany your family to the country of my birth. My knowledge of English customs and language should prove advantageous to your father as he enters the upper house of Parliament. I have heard that there is an ongoing feud between the Duke of Somerset and Duke of York. Richard Plantagenet, the Duke of York, whom the king sent away from court to govern Ireland, has recently planned a return to London to call upon His Majesty and seek acknowledgement as heir apparent. What is alarming is that two years ago Richard of York's supporters in Kent and Sussex staged a rebellion. It ended in London where the king's Lord Treasurer James Fiennes, Baron Saye & Sele, was murdered at the hands of the rebels. There is a strong possibility of similar violence and rioting during the time we are in London."

His voice suddenly became very serious, and he fastened his eyes on mine.

"Lady Isabelle, what I have told you this evening must not be shared with anyone. Not your sisters, nor your brothers, not even your father can know about my past. I implore you, never share my background with anyone else. If word were to circulate in England that I am alive and have returned, it could impede your father's work at court and put my own life in peril."

"Of course, I understand," I said, nodding my head in affirmation. "I only wish I could provide solace for you in some way."

"Oh, but you have and you do," he acknowledged sincerely. "I should have you know that what I have shared with you tonight about my identity is the most I have shared with anyone, ever."

"I promise to guard your secrets close to my heart. I cannot imagine what it must be like for you to have experienced such devastating loss in your life. Here I sit beside you, full of anxiety about moving to a new country with the support of my family and chaplain, but you, you lost everything and everyone whom you loved, and at such a young age! You had no choice but to run away to save your own life. You had to escape on your own, to an uncertain future in a new place. You are so much more than the modest priest that most people see."

We continued to sit together on the steps of the quarterdeck, the long silence between us satisfying after hearing the many truths disclosed by Père Charles.

"It is time for us to take our rest. Allow me to escort you downstairs," my chaplain offered, taking my arm and leading me safely to the passage with our separate quarters.

Once again we found ourselves alone in the dark of the corridor. He carefully removed his clerical cape from about my shoulders as he had done the previous evening. Alone with a man of such remarkable character in the dark of the hallway, I felt timid;

I sensed an intense passion for him developing in my heart. It confused me, for I had never before experienced such feelings for anyone.

"Are you not going to say goodnight to me?" he asked softly, and my attention returned to the present. "Tell me your thoughts, for your mind seems troubled."

"I am afraid I cannot tell you just yet," I answered hesitantly. "But know that one day you will understand."

"Then goodnight, Lady Isabelle. I am touched by your kindness and friendship."

We stepped closer to each other and he placed his arms around me. Feeling secure in his embrace, I held on to him. We silently stood together, lost in the power of the revelations that had come forth that evening, neither one of us wishing to be the first to withdraw.

"Goodnight, my honourable lord," I said, looking at him directly.

"Lady Isabelle, you enchant me," he whispered lovingly.

He lowered his head, his hands gently raising my face as his lips touched mine. For several moments we stood together in the hallway, locked in an intimate exchange of our deep desire for one another. I did not wish the moment to end. I did not wish him to leave me. I vowed secretly to myself that I would stand by him and with him from that moment onward. With his tender kiss, I knew in my heart that I was his. From the very lips that imparted God's love and mercy, the lessons in Latin and subjects so varied and lively, came a new instruction, slowly, and devotedly, with no trepidation laid. As he gently pulled away from me, I already longed to feel the intimacy of his kiss again. He put his fingers to my lips to ensure our secret, brushing his mouth against my cheek in a lingering gesture of his affection. I knew I would never wish for anyone as much as I did for him at that parting moment.

———

Upon awakening the next morning, I could sense the presence of someone watching over me before I opened my eyes. My sisters had already left our cabin; it was my aunt who stood glaring at me, a stern scowl drawn across her face.

"I woke in the night when I heard voices in the corridor. I witnessed what you and our chaplain did. How dare you ruin your reputation in such a sinful and lustful manner! You continue to disappoint me, Isabelle. You refuse to consider marriage, you spend far too much time with your horse and engrossed in worthless scholarship. A woman of your age and station must learn her place in this world! I will tell your father what I witnessed. This family will be rid of that loathsome priest once and for all. And as for you, I shall personally make sure that you are made to do as is expected of all ladies your age!"

My aunt's cruel words and accusatory tone sickened me; she was evil, an enemy with a malicious and vindictive desire not only to control her brother's affairs, but also to direct the paths my siblings and I would take. I knew then that I must risk her wrath even further by sharing the knowledge I had kept hidden of her ties to those in the service of the French king.

"Before you tell my father anything, Aunt Christine, you should be aware that I hold in my possession correspondence that you thought you had destroyed by fire. Do you remember its contents?" I exclaimed with confidence, knowing that my aunt would be alarmed by my revelation.

"Allow me to give you a hint," I continued with courage. "It is a directive from your brother, my uncle, who is in the French king's army, that you are to remain with our family and report to him all developments concerning the English and their plans to protect Bordeaux from battle with the French. You are a spy and if you dare tell Father what you witnessed then I will produce the evidence that will see you imprisoned for treason!"

"Surely you would not trade the life of your chaplain for the life of a blood relative?" my aunt asked incredulously.

"That is a thought you will have to consider as you make your way to England with us. I know you think little of me, little of my love of God and the visions I have from him, and even less of the man who has committed himself to providing us with instruction in our faith. But his is a most noble vocation and he a most compassionate representative of our Lord. I suggest you keep your judgements about others and their behaviour to yourself, lest you yourself be judged by your own, dear Aunt."

"My, but you *are* a wicked thing, are you not?" she replied, a sinister grin forming across her lips. "So be it. You have managed to get away with your illicit affair for now, but surely one day you two will not be so fortunate. You will be caught outright in your deception and I, for one, will do nothing to protect you from the corporal punishment you both will deservedly receive. May you both burn in hell for your indiscretions!"

Aunt Christine then turned and stormed out of the cabin. Left to my own thoughts, my composure fell. What if she was right? What if the feelings we shared were nothing more than the work of the Devil? I knew I must turn to prayer and seek God's forgiveness for my sin the night before. Yet somehow in my heart I could not bring myself to acknowledge the deepening friendship between us as something improper or worthy of concern. For in my chaplain I felt a direct connection to the love in my soul that burned for God the Father. In my prayers later that morning, I asked the Lord for his protection from my enemy, who sought to cast me in the teeth.

The final days of our sea voyage passed without incident. I looked after Peyriac and read quietly from my psalter, committing several of my favourite psalms to memory. After saying the morning office with us, Père Charles would retire for the remainder of the day and take his meals alone in his cabin. I wished to find him for confession, yet I was afraid to approach him, knowing in my heart the reason he sought solitude and distance from everyone was because of the guilt he felt for his attraction to me.

XIII
The London Road

The day of our arrival in England was one of great elation for our family and the ship's crew. At the first shout of "Land!" from the scout in the crow's nest, everyone came out on deck, cheering and rushing to get a glimpse of the coast. After a week at sea, it felt wonderful to at last be within sight of our future home. A feeling of restlessness had set in amongst my siblings and me during the final days of our journey. We were all experiencing bouts of boredom, and even Sarah and Christophe, who were normally quiet and well behaved, had taken to squabbling over their games. During that time, I captured the precise details of my conversation with Père Charles – from our night on the quarterdeck – in my journal before they faded from my memory forever. I wanted to have a record of the names of people, places and descriptions he had given me. Somehow, reading and rereading the story of his tragic childhood and how he had come to join our family in Gascony consoled me in the absence of his physical presence.

As the *Salamanca* sailed into Portsmouth Harbour in the early afternoon, the activity of the deckhands and sailors increased all around us. Once the ship was anchored and securely bound, the crew transferred our cart and belongings onto the dock. I followed them off the ship, leading a very anxious Peyriac down the ramp and onto solid footing. He appeared confused, twitching his ears and tail nervously and taking short breaths, his head darting about, nostrils flaring as he looked around at his surroundings, unsure of the strange new sounds and smells. After thanking the captain for the use of his cabin during our voyage, our father posed a question to him.

"Tell me, William, where might I find some horses for sale nearby?"

"I can help you with that, Your Lordship. Come along; I shall take you," Captain Farley replied.

They eventually returned with the horses and driver who carried provisions for the journey. I helped my sisters and aunt prepare for the journey in the cart by covering them with several dense layers of woollen blankets, tucking in the corners tightly to keep them warm. My father gave me an ermine-lined hooded cape to wear over my surcoat and the others donned heavy woollen hats with rabbit-fur lined flaps to cover their ears. Our hands were covered with heavy leather gloves that provided an additional layer of protection against the frosty air. The autumn weather in England was much colder than in Gascony. Even with the light of day still about, a distinct chill had settled in around us.

Once we were prepared to set off, Father asked our chaplain for his advice.

"What do you suggest we do, Charles? Should we stay nearby for the night or press on?"

"Your Lordship, I am afraid I am at a loss. I am not familiar with the south of England. I shall have to enquire in the public house up ahead as to how far we are from Oxford or London."

He returned after a short time, joined by two men-at-arms who would accompany us on horseback.

140

"I have some unfortunate news," he said, his tone serious as he rejoined our group. "We are about five days out from London. For that reason, I feel we must begin our travel north this afternoon. I have arranged for us to be escorted by these two men, who will accompany us to London and ensure the safety of our travel along unfamiliar roads. They will also guard our cart and possessions at the inns where we will stay on our way north. We shall journey now in the direction of the next town along the London Road. We should try to make it as far as Petersfield tonight."

"Then let us be off without further delay," commanded my father.

The low grey sky that blanketed the horizon enhanced the feeling of cold dampness that hung stiffly in the air. Père Charles and I took the lead as our horses set off at a slow trot that allowed the cart horse to keep pace without overturning the wagon. It became a struggle to keep our bodies, heads and hands from feeling the bone-chilling cold brought on by our rapid movement. I glanced back occasionally to see how Margaret and Sarah were faring, being bumped and jostled in the cart. They were still huddled together under the blankets with our aunt, their heads just barely visible. We eventually came to our first stop, a village called Clanfield. Père Charles suggested that we take a brief rest in the village inn to eat a meal and warm ourselves. We all heartily agreed, and eagerly stopped for a break.

"There you are, Sarah," Father said, helping my little sister down from the cart. "And you two next, Margaret and Christine. Let us move inside and have something to eat and drink."

Johan and Christophe joined us after dismounting and our family filed into the establishment while our two escorts and the driver stood guard over the cart and horses. The heat from a giant fire in the corner welcomed us the moment we entered and closed the cumbersome wooden door. At first I was nervous in the dimly lit interior but soon the warmth of the blazing fire proved inviting and helped me overcome my initial apprehension. Two long tables and benches ran the length of the room and a low ceiling with solid timber beams imparted a feeling of intimacy with the other patrons already seated there.

As we walked through the centre of the room to our table, I could feel the eyes of the other guests watching our every move. We were dressed differently from them, and with Père Charles in his clerical attire speaking to us in Gascon, our little group must have puzzled them even further.

Our meal was similar to what we ate in Gascony – roasted venison and a vegetable bean stew served with thick, crusty bread that we used for mopping up the remnants left in our bowls. As we finished, Père Charles and the man who had served our meal exchanged some words in English. It soon became apparent that their dialogue concerned the ordering of several hot drinks.

"Now, try this, everyone, and see if it does not help to settle you," Père Charles suggested after the steaming cups were delivered to our table.

Our chaplain entertained Christophe and Sarah with his drink that arrived in a puzzle jug. As its name suggested, it was designed with many spouts along its cylindrical core. Père Charles managed to find the one which held the drink without pouring the contents down his front. My brother and sister giggled with glee as he demonstrated what could happen should he have chosen the wrong spout. The dark green enamelled earthenware had a glossy finish, giving the many faces that adorned it a realistic look.

I did not recognise the drink he had handed me at first. I put my nose to my mug; my face was immediately met with the heat of rising steam. The sweet aroma of fruit and spices pleased my senses. Taking my first sip, I found that the delicious drink warmed me even to my toes, but surprisingly did not burn my tongue.

"This is wonderful. What is it?" asked Margaret.

"It is a special drink called mulled wine. It is a traditional English winter drink. It should help comfort us on the next leg of the journey as we head to the town where we shall sleep tonight. The owner of this hostelry said we need travel only another few miles before we shall see the sign for Petersfield. It is just off the London Road."

"Excellent!" replied Father, smiling. "You are a blessing for us, Charles. I could not have managed on this trip without your guidance."

"I am pleased to be of assistance to you and the family, Your Lordship," he replied humbly.

Sarah and Christophe, having hurriedly finished their drink and meal, were already in front of the fire, laughing and playing while Margaret and my aunt looked after them. I sat back and watched Père Charles as he drank his last sips of the mulled wine. In my mind I imagined him wearing a cloak and mantle, leggings and a feathered hat, attributes of his social standing as a powerful and wealthy young lord. He could have very easily been seated in a public house like this one, sipping from a toasty mug of mulled wine while travelling to his manor house in Cambridgeshire. Instead, he was returning to his beloved homeland an impoverished priest with an adopted alias and an adopted family.

When we prepared to return outside, Sarah became obstinate about leaving the comfort of the inn. Margaret had to tempt her with a piece of dried apple to make her get onto the cart. With the sun having set, the wind had lessened quite considerably, but the air was still bitterly cold. The lanterns attached to the cart provided a limited source of light for us as we continued on the last leg of our journey. In silence we progressed, carefully navigating the path in the dark to prevent any of our party from riding into one of the ditches running parallel on either side of the road. I was so cold that I almost fell asleep, numb in the saddle, when Peyriac bolted to the left, following the other horses; we had at last come to the final stretch of road leading into Petersfield. The village was dark and silent, with only a few cottages dotting the roadside. For a moment my heart sank. What if there was no inn here and we had to keep riding? Despite being covered by gloves, my hands felt stiff from the cold. My nose and ears felt no better. We had ridden only a few more paces when Père Charles called out, "There it is, over there on the right; there is our lodging for the night."

"What is it, Charles?" called Father, bringing his horse up to the front of the cart. "That looks like a cottage."

"Oh no, Your Lordship, that is a hostelry. See the sign there in the front, hanging to the side of the door? It says it is an inn. Now let us pray that we may be accommodated for the night."

The two men slid off their horses and entered the establishment. I turned and looked back at the cart. My aunt, Margaret and Sarah were still huddled together for warmth under their blankets. Covering my face with my hands to warm it with my breath, my nose slowly began to thaw, my sense of smell returned and I noticed the scent of earthy bitterness from a fire in the air. Glancing up at the roofline, I could faintly see puffs of smoke drifting into the night sky. Thankfully, at that moment the door to the inn opened and my father and Père Charles emerged. Approaching us, they each bore an expression of relief.

Coming around to my horse, Père Charles looked up at me as he made his announcement.

"Good news, everyone, there is room for us to stay here tonight. First, we must get the horses stabled and the cart stored away."

"Yes, children, let us not waste another moment in the cold," instructed Father. "Christine, take Margaret and Sarah in and prepare for bed. We will put up our horses and store the cart, and then join you all shortly. I have made arrangements for our driver and escorts to sleep in the barn tonight. In the morning let us meet as the cock crows so that we might travel farther along the London Road before the cold of the night sets in. Sleep well, everyone."

"Thank you and goodnight, Father," Margaret said, as she was helped down from the cart.

Sarah slid down wearily behind my aunt and Margaret. Everyone was exhausted and eager to get inside to the warmth of the inn. I, too, was ready to get the horses put away and go to bed.

Once inside the barn our group soon finished caring for their mounts and the cart and they returned to the warmth of the inn, leaving Père Charles and me alone with our horses in the quiet of the stable. We worked quickly and in silence, each of us lost in our own thoughts. Then without warning, as I finished brushing Peyriac in his stall, a familiar hand came from behind to take hold of my own.

"Why, Your Ladyship, you are still so cold. Come to me and I shall warm you." My chaplain's tone was of concern for my comfort.

I did as he suggested. I put down the brush and stepped forward. He opened his long woollen cape and wrapped us both inside it. Standing there, united against the cold, I could feel immediate relief as the heat from his body penetrated my garments.

"If it were not for you, Lady Isabelle, my return to England would be far more difficult," he confided in a low voice. "It is as if I am experiencing everything for the first time, since I can share the journey with you. You have said that I give you a great sense of security; well, I must confess, you do the same for me."

"I am so glad to hear you say that; I do care for you so." I embraced him from under his cloak, wrapping my arms tightly around his back in a show of affection. As I did so, I felt the tension mount in his frame, and he pulled away from me, removing my arms from his body and leaving me without the protective barrier of warmth offered by his cape.

"I beg your forgiveness, Your Ladyship; my feelings for you have been sorely misinterpreted. For some reason I feel compelled to protect you and guard you from potential harm. But I am wrong to do so; that duty must be saved for the man who is to become your husband. Once you are presented at court in London you will soon forget about this moment and the feelings you have for me. You must remember, my vocation is to serve the Lord through the teachings of the Church. The longing you feel is better directed towards a nobleman of rank and means who can provide for you. But I am not that man. I cannot be that man. I am afraid I simply cannot assume the responsibility of loving you."

"Then you do *not* feel love for me?" I said, my voice low, my eyes moist with tears. His rejection left me surprised and confused after the intimacy we had shared on the sea voyage.

"Your Ladyship, how can you ask of me such a thing? Please understand, since arriving in Paris at the age of eighteen I have followed my calling: to remain celibate and serve the Church. I have taken the rule of St Benedict as my guide. I am meant to provide you with instruction, to be your chaplain and a guardian to you and your family; yet with you I feel such a yearning. On the ship I sought isolation from you only because the feelings I have for you are forbidden to a clerk in holy orders. I am sorry, but what you desire from me I can never fulfil on my part. Please try to understand, Your Ladyship – it is not that I do not love you; it is that I cannot allow myself to love you in the way that you wish."

I backed away from him, shaking my head slowly, bumping into Peyriac along the way.

"I do not believe you! I do not understand how you can say such things! Does not the Lord wish his children, who are of this temporal world, to experience the very love that he bestowed upon his own Son, Jesus Christ? And can that love not be expressed in the joining of two souls through the bond of the Holy Spirit? I do not understand how what we feel for each other can be denied; certainly the Lord wants us to be joined in our love for each other as it comes directly from him. We have been granted the fortune to be together in each other's lives; you told me once at Rosete that love fostered in the trust and faith of Christian friendship can lead to a most loving union. Why does that not apply to us? I cannot imagine there will ever be another man towards whom I shall feel such devotion. No, I refuse to believe that you do not love me; there will never be another whom I care for as much as I do for you!"

My tears fell freely as I determined to keep away from him. I continued to step backwards until I felt the wall behind me. As I did so, he remained close. Then, when I could go no further, he took up my wrists in his hands, placing them to his chest, nestling them under the soft textured cloth of his muslin shirt. He held my hands against his skin and I felt the beating of his heart. Looking straight at me, through the soft flickering glow of the lanterns positioned along the walls of the stable, I could see there were tears in his eyes. He never let them fall; he held them back and then abruptly he released his grip. With one hand, he caressed my cheek, his penetrating gaze never leaving my own. Moments passed and neither of us moved. Then, he broke the silence at last.

"No, I cannot do it, Lady Isabelle. It is not right." He shook his head slowly. "For many reasons, I cannot. Do you not see? I wish to hold you close to me; I wish to kiss you deeply; I wish to lose myself in you. Can you imagine I could feel such a longing? But I am a priest – a priest, Your Ladyship, a man of God. I have vowed my life to serve the Lord, and I simply cannot break that commitment. You must believe me when I say to you that I wish to love no other being than you. Were my life different and were I the nobleman I was born to be, with my land and my position at court, then our situation would be different. But the irony is that even under such circumstances, with the riches of the world to bestow upon you, I would have never had the fortune of meeting you."

He stopped and collected himself before proceeding.

"Instead, my path has been directed by the Lord to care for you and your family to the best of my ability. Was I to allow myself to give into temptation, I would do nothing but destroy that relationship and trust. You must believe me that I do care for you, I do love you, more than you will ever know or I shall ever be able to share with you again. Please always keep that thought in your heart. I need your friendship, Lady Isabelle, and I rely on it, for it sustains me in my darkest hours. Yet, given my vocation, I cannot give you anything further of myself."

He turned his head from me as he tried to hide the tears that fell down the side of his cheek.

"I am so sorry to hurt you. That is the very last thing I should ever wish to do – to cause you any pain or hurt whatsoever."

I did not know how to respond to his honesty. I knew his confession was so very difficult for him to admit. But in revealing his feelings to me in such a way he had planted the seed of love between us. Like all the Lord's creation, it would need time and attentive love to cultivate and grow, if one day it was to survive and bloom. He took my hand and kissed it, the way I imagined he would if he were able to openly show his affection. At that moment we had to accept that neither of us would ever be able to act upon the love we secretly shared.

One of the horses softly nickered, reminding us of the work still to be completed. With his hand gently guiding mine, we walked back to Peyriac and finished brushing him together. After extinguishing all the lanterns illuminating the interior stable walls, we stopped before the stable door in the dark. He made a step forward to unlatch the handle, but I stepped in front of him to prevent him from opening it.

"Wait, please, there is something I must tell you before we go back inside," I began, putting my hand out to hold his back from the door latch.

"It saddens me to hear you say that we are destined to only remain simply companions, and nothing more. But if that is what must be, then you have my promise that I shall do all in my power not to distract you from your work. I do not regret what has happened between us. Know that I shall need your friendship, now and always. I cannot imagine not having your wise counsel and guardianship in my life. I shall never crave the attention of another man. I would rather die than be the object of a lesser man's affection."

I took his hands into my own, and, raising them to my lips, I kissed each one. Without thinking of the consequences, I leaned up and placed my lips upon his in one last, lingering kiss. We pulled away from one another, and he silently lifted the latch on the door. In the faint shaft of light that spilled forth from the moonlit sky above, I could see he was staring directly at me. In a hushed voice he gave his response.

"The feelings you have confessed tonight will stay with me for all eternity. I am not worthy of the attention and affection that a lady of your standing places upon me. I must refrain from allowing myself to reciprocate your love, though I shall guard your affection in my heart as I continue to care for you as both your friend and your chaplain. All I ask is this; do not ever doubt me, for the love I have for you shall never be replicated or replaced by that of another maiden."

Upon hearing him utter his statement of devotion, I stepped forward to take up his embrace one final time. After several moments had passed, with great reluctance we separated from each other and made our way across the yard to the inn. As we entered, we passed our two escorts and driver, who were returning to the stable to guard our horses and belongings. Parting from each other that night, we knew in our hearts that we shared a secret, sacred union – one that no man could tear asunder.

———

Over the next several days as we made our way to London, the road carried us along hilltop ridges under the canopy of densely forested lands, their barren, exposed branches forming a skeletal archway over our heads. The long days of riding gave me time to put my feelings for Père Charles in perspective. Though I wished we could be open in our love for one another, I accepted the danger of doing so – especially given that he must maintain his secret identity. I found that I was content just being in his presence as he directed our movement, along with the two men-at-arms who were our escort.

Throughout the remainder of our journey my prayers turned to our safety, for I could sense the roads were a dangerous place for our foreign family should we be stopped by mercenaries who had fought in the war with France. From Petersfield we made stops overnight in Haslemere, Leatherhead and finally Mitcham, only eleven miles to the south of the capital. With every day we travelled closer to London, I could sense a mounting eagerness in our father's demeanour as he anticipated his arrival at court in Westminster. As we rode toward London on the final day of our journey from Portsmouth, I wondered where we would stay once we arrived. We had been without any lessons for several days, and I looked forward to the time when we would stop travelling and return to our daily routine of study and prayer. I was also about to turn sixteen and acutely aware that at such an age other ladies were already married and producing heirs.

XIV
The Collegiate Church
of St Peter

12 November 1452, Westminster, London

It became clear after departing from Mitcham that we were close to the capital. As we approached London, the road became more congested with horses, carts and travellers on foot all sharing the same route towards the river crossing on the banks of the River Thames. In many places we were forced to stop along the side of the road so that rapidly moving carriages could pass us at their faster pace.

Arriving on the south bank of the river in the outskirts of the bustling city, my first impression of Greater London was that it was an inhospitable and unpleasant place. The streets were brimming with a variety of unpleasant activities; the fetid stench that settled in around us seemed to blanket my sense of smell with its putrid odour. As we journeyed along the cramped alleys and passageways to the dock where we would make our crossing to Westminster by ferry, we had to dodge the contents of chamber pots that were constantly being discharged over the streets above our heads. The malodorous mixture of urine and bodily waste wafted through the air about us; we feared being caught unaware by the falling human refuse and becoming covered in its noxious slime.

Navigating through the capital with any speed proved a near impossibility as throngs of pedestrians, horses and carts vied for space along the narrow, filthy streets. Cantilevered houses and buildings that lined the streets nearly blocked any light piercing the low grey range of clouds hovering motionless overhead. It made for a tedious journey and it was mid-afternoon when we finally arrived outside the walls surrounding the Palace of Westminster.

As with the previous nights, finding safe accommodation was of utmost importance. Père Charles made a suggestion.

"From Portsmouth I sent word to the abbot at the Collegiate Church of St Peter, asking if we might seek lodgings with the Benedictines. The entrance to the abbey is up ahead, just on the other side of the palace walls."

"Such an arrangement sounds quite suitable for our family, Charles," Father agreed. "Please carry on and we shall follow you. I would feel more secure staying in monastic surroundings, particularly in the event that I must be absent during the day. Since the palace is adjoining the church grounds, I would not have to travel far to appear at court."

"That is correct, Your Lordship. I shall call upon Abbot Gervase Stockard and enquire whether he can accommodate us," Père Charles replied.

Riding along the outer wall of the palace we soon came to the back of the massive abbey church. Continuing on a short distance, we rounded a corner and arrived at the abbey gate, to the side of the church's façade under construction. Père Charles dismounted and entered the quiet sanctity of the abbey grounds. While we waited outside the gate for him to return, we, too, dismounted and took in our new surroundings. I watched the faces of labourers employed in constructing the extensive church building that stood towering over us as they passed us on the street, noticing their hard-set and stern demeanour. I felt overshadowed by the façade with its sheer height and use of lofty wooden scaffolding. From the street level, I could hear and see the sounds and sights of construction: men calling out to each other; endless hammering; pulleys screeching as they hoisted large pieces of wood and stone for placement in the abbey church's walls.

As I stood facing the exterior, I pondered the scale of the unfinished nave. Upon completion, it was certain to be taller and more imposing than our cathedral back in Bazas. On that frigid autumn day, filtered light falling from the leaden skies cast a dark, dull reflection on the abbey's sombre stone walls. As I contemplated the design of the church's interior, Père Charles returned to us, wearing a pleased expression.

"We shall remain here. The Benedictines have kindly offered us hospitality for as long as we must remain in London," he told us. "We shall use the private guest apartments in the back of the property. Our horses may be stabled with their livestock. Come along now and let us get inside."

After releasing our two escorts from their service, our chaplain instructed us to follow him. We split up, he taking my sisters and aunt to the abbey to wait for us while my father, brothers and I rode to the stables with the cart and driver close behind. Johan and Christophe quickly dismounted and rushed back to join the others in the shelter of the abbey church.

"Are we meant to stay in London for long?" I asked my father, loosening the girth of Peyriac's saddle once I had dismounted.

"I anticipate we shall be here for a while, until I receive confirmation of my position at court. Why do you ask, Isa?" enquired my father after handing the reins of his horse to the groom.

"I do not wish to seem ungrateful, but we have not had time for our lessons since our first few days on the *Salamanca*. I do hope we shall not have to reside in London; is there any possibility that we might live in the countryside, as we did at Rosete?"

"Isabelle, you have so many concerns," he replied, giving me a quick embrace and stroking my hair. "I thought you should wish to live in London. It is soon to be your time to seek a husband and to make a good marriage; you cannot remain unmarried forever. Living in the capital and joining the queen's household will afford you many opportunities to meet the right group of suitors."

"Oh, come now, surely you jest!" I implored, stepping away from him. "I am not interested in marriage, now or ever! Being some distance from the city would truly benefit us all."

"I can see you are not like Margaret, who wishes to stay in London and make new acquaintances amongst members of the queen's court at once. I shall do my best to accommodate you and your siblings outside the city; although while we are guests of the abbey I expect everyone to show gratitude for the generous hospitality we receive from Charles's associates. And, yes, if I am presented with an opportunity for us to acquire an estate outside London I shall consider it. Tomorrow I shall learn whether my Gascon title will be transferred to a position on the King's Privy Council."

My father's tone became grave and he looked me straight in the eyes as he spoke.

"But, Isabelle, there will come a time when I shall expect you to come to court and be presented to Their Majesties. It is imperative that you do so: my future in Parliament depends upon making good marriages for all my children. You, Johan and Margaret must do your part for the integration of our family with members of the English nobility. Do we have an understanding?"

Before I could reply, Père Charles returned and together the three of us walked to the abbey church. From across the courtyard floated the rich tones of the church bells pealing, calling us to vespers. We quickly joined the rest of the family, who were already seated in the sanctuary, and watched as a group of friars, followed by a group of monks, processed in silently past us. Prior to vespers that evening, I had never experienced the beauty of a choral liturgical offering. I found that over the course of the service the repetitive harmonies in the chants somehow caused my mind to feel at one with the Lord.

With my eyes closed, I concentrated on the words of scripture being expressed through the range of voices unfolding one over the other, simultaneously deep and yet soft. For the first time in my life, I felt the presence of the Holy Spirit shepherd me into the comforting love of the Trinity where all was as one. As I went deeper into meditation, the simple message that was conveyed through chant reminded me of God's desire for us *that whatsoever is true, whatsoever is just, whatsoever is pure, whatsoever is lovely, whatsoever is of good report; rest in your heart knowing by faith in Jesus Christ, virtue and praise by him will be learned, received, heard, and seen done by his work. The God of peace remains always.* As vespers came to a close, all the concerns that had weighed upon my soul when the service begun had disappeared, leaving me in a state of lasting peace.

At the conclusion of the evening's service, the abbot kindly invited us to take our supper in his private residence. We followed closely behind our chaplain, who was joyfully talking with friends whom he had left behind when he had moved to France twelve years earlier. We travelled as a group, our family and the monks and clergy, walking through the main abbey cloister. A carpet of fresh hay and straw covered the stone floor, pieces of which caught in the long robes of the monks and my aunt and sisters' hems as we traversed the central corridor connecting the abbey church with the refectory and the abbot's residence. A bitterly cold air hung about the cloister corridor, for only the top halves of the windows facing out into the garden were glazed; the bottom halves were covered in wooden shutters.

Outside in the cloister garden, a long wooden pergola stood to one side. Withered, brittle rose branches were draped across the top, their telltale pinnated leaves and pendulant fragrant flowers long since lost in the late-autumn season. I later learned that pink peony shrubs were planted at the base of the arbour, their vines clutching the posts as they grew up the pillars so that in spring and summer a heavenly scent floated in the air to the pleasure of those who passed through the cloister.

I immediately felt my spirit lift in the quiet solemnity of the abbey's arcade. Over our heads a series of ribbed vaults seemed to unfold above us as we carried on through the hallway. It was a stark counterpoint to the noise and filth of the street just beyond us on the other side of the abbey wall.

When we arrived at the dining hall, we took our leave of the members of the monastic community, following the abbot instead to his lodgings in an adjacent building.

After saying grace, Abbot Geravase told us of the recent political developments affecting the abbey. He spoke to us in French so that we could understand him more easily. As we listened to him, I watched our chaplain respond animatedly to his friend in a way I had never seen before. Père Charles must have felt my eyes upon him, for he turned to smile at me as he asked his friend to explain to all of us the significance of the abbey church.

After pausing to take a sip of wine from his cup, Abbot Geravase continued, "As you can imagine from seeing the state of the buildings as they are today, there is more work to be completed than can be carried out in one lifetime. It may well take another fifty years to see the church nave completed. The work is slow to progress, as our financial resources have never been as plentiful as they were under the patronage of King Henry III.

"We remain grateful for what we can afford to do to honour our kings and queens and the noblemen who lie entombed within the walls of our church. Unfortunately, there is one royal painting – once housed in the abbey church – that has been missing for over fifty years. It was a depiction of the Madonna and Christ Child, surrounded by eleven angelic maidens, each wearing a badge with a white hart, the emblem of the king for whom the diptych was created, Richard II. On the opposite side of the wooden panel was a portrait of the kneeling king with Saints John the Baptist, Edward the Confessor and Edmund the Martyr. With the panels closed, the cover depicted the king's emblem – a most elegant and regal white hart, gorged with a crown around its neck, and chained while lying on a carpet of grass and flowers. The niche remains vacant in the chapel where the king once prayed. It is our hope to learn who possesses it and have it returned to us, for it was one of the most important devotional works we had and it attracted many pilgrims. As many came to view it as come to see the shrine of St Edward.

"I hope that you will enjoy your time here," Abbot Geravase continued. "It is my pleasure to welcome you and offer you accommodation for as long as you require it. Unfortunately, I am afraid I must excuse myself now to prepare for the service of compline. Please stay and finish your meal in my absence."

Later that night we were shown to our guest apartments. They suited us well, for they sat in a separate private building away from the principal abbey ranges and off the Little Cloister Garden path at the back of the abbey. My siblings, aunt and I shared one large room, leaving the other two smaller rooms for Father and Père Charles. In the room shared by the six of us there was a small corner fireplace, but no window. The spartan furnishings included two large hay-filled cots, and a simple table and two chairs, likely the handiwork of the monks themselves. In spite of our austere accommodation, we soon settled into our beds and fell soundly to sleep.

The same graceful tolling of bells that had called us to vespers the previous evening awakened us the next morning. We dressed, and assembled downstairs, walking into the church together to join the community for lauds. Again the service was simple and serene. Afterwards we were invited to break our fast in the refectory, though we were alone as the monks did not take a morning meal. We sat at the high table and as we ate, our father told us of his plans and instructed us how to spend the day in his absence.

"I am leaving you in the care of Père Charles, who assures me you shall again take up your studies in English and Latin. While we have the opportunity to stay in London, you will also benefit from hearing the monks practise the music they will perform for vespers."

Our father soon bade us farewell and excused himself, eager to meet Lord Dunstall, his contact from the Privy Council. With our aunt escorting her, Margaret left to join Madame de Tastes, who, they had learned, was a guest of Sir William Talbot, son of the Earl of Shrewsbury. It was William's father, Lord John Talbot, who had arrived in Bordeaux with his men as we fled the city. He had been tasked with strengthening the armies ready to fight the French incursion. That left my brothers and Sarah and me under the vigilant supervision of our chaplain once again.

XV
Like As The Hart

"Sicut cervus desiderat ad fontes aquarum, ita desiderat anima mea ad te, Deus."

Psalm 42

15 November 1452

"The lesson plan for today is as follows," our chaplain began. "We shall spend the morning going over our English vocabulary, our Latin declensions, and continuing our analysis of the *Itinerarium Kambriae*. We will resume our study of the text from where we left off back at Rosete. In the afternoon we shall have a tutorial in music theory before we hear the choir rehearse their Gregorian chants. One of the monks from the abbey will instruct you on the fundamentals of musical composition. You will attend two services today, one just for us at midday and one with the monks at vespers before supper. Please excuse me for a moment."

Père Charles left to ask the abbot what room we could use for our lessons. While the others chatted quietly, my mind began to wander. I wondered how much longer we would have to remain in London, for I had become increasingly unsettled with every day we were without a permanent home.

Soon our chaplain returned and we followed him in silence, respectful of our surroundings in the quiet abbey environment. Abbot Geravase had offered us the use of the chapter house. While it was comforting to return to our daily lessons with Père Charles, my anxiety about our future in a foreign land made it difficult to focus on his English and Latin instruction.

Far too soon, the morning soon came to a close and it was time for our midday prayers. Père Charles conducted us through the doors leading into the transept of the abbey church in a silent procession. We followed him to the apse where, after climbing some stairs to a raised memorial behind the high altar, we found ourselves encircled by the many tombs and effigies of English kings, their queens and famous knights. Standing before us was the beloved shrine of St Edward the Confessor. I had never seen such a finely decorated tomb; the monumental stone sepulchre was covered in brightly coloured Italian mosaic tiles. Their Byzantine colours of gold and crimson glittered warmly, reflecting the ambient candlelight of two massive candelabra that stood lighted on either end. We approached the great memorial and knelt before it as our chaplain quietly led us in our prayers of thanksgiving and peace. I prayed silently that day for our family to have word of our new home, that Margaret would find Madame de Tastes, and for my mother's soul in Heaven and that she might know how much she was missed by us.

Later that afternoon, Père Charles arranged for special instruction to be given by an Italian monk called Brother Giovanni Cortelli. Amongst his many talents was musical notation, a skill he had learned as a young orphan left in the care of the Benedictine monks in Florence. In our lesson, we learned of another Benedictine monk of the reformed Camaldolese order named Brother Guido d'Arezzo. Brother Guido's lasting contribution to music was his treatise on neumatic notation, a work largely responsible for helping singers to remember the keynotes in Gregorian chants.

Brother Giovanni proved to be a lively instructor, full of kindness and good cheer, a sharp contrast in personality to the austere English monks with whom we shared the abbey. From him we learned the basic notes found in the chants we had heard sung at vespers the previous night. In our lesson he explained how he came to possess the piece we would hear that day, written by a composer named Johannes Ockeghem. The two men had met briefly in Paris when Brother Giovanni was travelling to London from Italy. At the time, Johannes was writing a special requiem Mass that would eventually be sung at the death of the King of France. The only part of the *Missa pro defunctis* he had completed upon meeting our instructor was the fourth movement, a *Tractus* entitled *Sicut cervus desiderat*: the words were taken directly from Psalm 42. Brother Giovanni found the piece so moving and so unlike any Gregorian chant he had previously heard in Italy that he asked his colleague whether he might copy it and bring it with him to England. Fortunately for us, Johannes had graciously obliged and allowed him to make a reproduction. In our lesson that afternoon, we learned that the piece was written for four voices using the paraphrase technique of plainchant. We listened for the melody that was heard in the top voice. After he had instructed my siblings and me, we sat quietly as our instructor then turned his attention to directing four monks in their rehearsal of the song. It would be sung during vespers a few hours later. I found that the sweet melody of the high notes echoed perfectly the expression of love and longing found in the words of the psalm. I committed the heavenly piece to memory, and in my prayers expressed gratitude to the Lord for Ockeghem's gift of choral composition.

Following our lesson, Père Charles announced that we would be dismissed from our studies for the remainder of the afternoon.

We were to listen for the pealing of the church bells calling us back in to worship with the members of the monastic community. I eagerly went in search of the stable to seek privacy where I could write in my journal while visiting Peyriac. Johan set off on his own towards the palace where he was to be introduced to other young male courtiers. Aunt Christine had already returned from her outing and she agreed to mind my siblings back in the chapter house until we met for vespers only a few hours later.

Stepping into the cloister from the abbey church, I heard footsteps behind me. Turning around, I was surprised to find Père Charles there.

"I thought you wanted some time to yourself," I said, my voice full of confusion.

"I thought I did too, but what I really wish is to be with you. Do I impose on you? Do you prefer to be alone?"

My eyes scanned the corridor, confirming that no one was present who might overhear my response.

"You know that I long to be in your company. Of course; please, join me. I miss your companionship."

We walked together through the corridor of the cloister and across the courtyard to the stable. A steady drizzle fell through the low, misty clouds that blanketed the abbey grounds. When we reached the stable, I could not keep my disappointment to myself any longer.

"Why must the weather be so cold and grey? If only we were free from the confinement our travel has brought upon us!" I exclaimed. I closed the stable door against the chill of the afternoon breeze, my face and hair moist from the heavy, damp air.

"I am afraid it will take time for you to become settled here, Your Ladyship. I speak from experience, as you know. Come, allow me to find you something to keep you warm while your cape dries out."

We moved farther into the stable, where Peyriac, upon smelling us and hearing our voices, nickered a gentle greeting.

"All right, boy, I shall be with you in a moment," I assured him.

Père Charles managed to find a cloak for me to borrow.

"This should be better. I would worry too much if you were to fall ill because of wet clothes." As he draped the material about my shoulders he cast his eyes over me and slowly tilted his head. His expression softened and I could feel the warmth of passion and desire in the depth of his stare. I sensed what he was thinking, and had to contain my own yearning to be comforted by him.

"I must tell you, Your Ladyship, you seem to grow more striking by the day. It will be only a matter of time until you are introduced to your betrothed."

I turned away. How could he say something so cruel? He knew I loved only him. How the import of his words felt like the sting from a wasp, so painful and so lasting! Yet he remained innocently unaware of how his compliment affected me. Impulsively I wished to say something to hurt him as he had done to me with his words. Instead, with petulance I ignored him and, without responding, I turned and walked toward Peyriac.

"Isabelle," Père Charles said, following after me. "Do look at me. What is it that I have said to upset you? I speak only of what is so clearly obvious; do not resent me for it."

I refused to turn and look at him. With my back to him, I began busily tending to Peyriac.

"I can see you wish to be alone with your horse, after all. I shall depart from your company, then."

With heaviness weighing on my heart I groomed Peyriac, taking as much time as possible, for I did not wish to leave the stable and return to my siblings in the chapter house before the evening service. When I had finished caring for my horse, I swept the floor of the stable at the entrance to his stall and covered it with clean hay to sit on, all the while thinking of my chaplain and how I wished our lives were different, that I would know his love and he mine. Peyriac could sense something was wrong and from time to time he came over to check on me, bending his neck in a graceful arc over the stall door. I gathered my journal and writing instruments and began to record my observations and impressions of the abbey since arriving in London the day before.

XVI
Albus cervus

Why your gaze so sweet,
it makes the heart take leap?
With longing, with knowing deep,
your ears cocked up, our eyes first meet.

You take me in, into your garden fair;
the grass strewn with flowers,
to pick them, I should not dare –
for no desire have I to break your stare.

No, I wish not to disturb the scene
of you, lying there, your face so keen;
you have me locked in your space,
at once so regal; so full of grace.

Later that afternoon I decided to pause from my writing and return to the interior of the abbey church. Curious about what Abbot Geravase had mentioned the night before over supper about a missing devotional painting used by King Richard, I walked along the apse, stepping into each side chapel in the hope of finding a clue that might indicate where the king had once prayed before his painting. Coming to the last chapel, upon entering I looked up and saw the image of a white hart painted on the wall. Certain that this was the correct place, I knelt before the tiny altar and offered a prayer of blessing upon the departed soul of my ancestor. As I opened my eyes a tall, thin figure emerged from the shadows behind me.

"You have found the chapel of St Mary de la Pew, Your Ladyship. It is fitting that you should come pray here, since this was where your forbearer once held his private devotions."

"I apologise, Abbot Geravase. Am I allowed to enter the chapel?"

"Yes, of course you may. You are welcome to visit any part of our church; that is, those that are not currently under construction."

I stood and joined the company of the abbot.

"I am intrigued by what you told us about the missing painting last evening. Is this where it was once placed?"

"It is indeed. The painting was portable, so King Richard was able to take it with him when he travelled to different palaces and castles. It was kept in a leather pouch, bound with a thick leather strap and buckle. It is a shame we do not know where it is. It could provide the people with a reminder of the legacy of a pious king whose reign was marked by a return to the chivalric ideals espoused by his predecessors in the Plantagenet family. This country is in desperate need of a unifying icon that can restore a sense of peace and stability to the realm."

"I have heard from my chaplain that there have been plots against King Henry to see him removed from the throne, and there is a desire to sever ties with the Pope. Is this true?"

Abbot Geravase stepped closer to me and pointed to a bench. We both sat. He continued, his voice hushed.

"The future of the Church in this country is uncertain, Your Ladyship, though the desire for a change in Church doctrine is not new. John Wycliffe, a prominent Oxford philosopher and theologian, led a group of followers called the Lollards to pursue similar ideals late in the last century, during King Richard's reign. Wycliffe wrote of supporting controversial changes in the Church's doctrine. He believed it was individuals, not those offering the sacraments, who were ultimately responsible for their actions and the way in which they lived a moral life. His followers felt that the Church had grown too extravagant in its religious ceremonies and its lavishly appointed churches. The Lollards sought to establish a new Church where the clergy would no longer have power over the king. In fact, to the contrary, they believed that the Pope, as the appointed head, must answer to the monarchy. Wycliffe was protected for many years by Sir John of Gaunt, regent of England during his nephew King Richard's minority."

"But certainly the Catholic faith cannot be abolished here – would the people of England not defend their Church and Pope against such actions on the part of few noblemen?"

"I am afraid it is not so simple, Lady Isabelle. The population of the country would be forced either to follow the new church doctrine or to face certain demise. It has been suggested that there exists a holy relic, hidden somewhere in the realm, which could provide the new Church with legitimacy in the eyes of the greater population."

"What is the artefact of which you speak?" I asked, recalling the relic mentioned by Père Charles in relating the story of his family's murder, while trying not to sound alarmed by what the abbot had divulged. Placing his fingers to his lips to indicate silence, we listened for the sounds of footsteps in the apse outside the chapel. Hearing nothing, he continued, his voice just louder than a whisper. I leaned in to catch every word.

"Your Ladyship, the *Mandylion*, the shroud that covered our Lord and Saviour after he was taken down from the cross, it is here in our country, secretly cared for and kept hidden by the Brotherhood of the Knights Templar, although not in the place where they regularly meet and worship in London, Temple Church. It is kept in another location, and though for centuries it has been searched for by many, it has never been discovered."

"My only knowledge of the Knights Templar is from poetry describing their chivalrous actions. I did not know that the Brotherhood still exists!" I exclaimed in amazement.

"Oh yes, exist it does. Over the past one hundred years, since the order was officially disbanded in France and outlawed in England, the members have continued to meet throughout the realm from the north in Scotland to the west in Wales and even here in London. The brothers and their lay associates come from all ranks of society. Some are scholars, some are monks or priests, others are theologians, lawyers, members of Parliament, and others still are builders and master craftsmen. Though they do not possess as much wealth and property as our ancestors once did, their primary tenet remains the same, to guard and protect the one true sacred *Mandylion*. Their mission is to prevent it from falling into the hands of those who do not observe a life of charity and service to all mankind as the Christian Brotherhood of the Knights Templar do. It is believed that one day the shroud must be returned to Rome when the Pope calls for it to be brought to the Holy See."

Abbot Geravase stopped and cleared his throat, resuming his speech in a normal voice.

"I realise I have spoken about many different topics, but what you were most interested in was where your ancestor prayed and his devotional icon. Tell me, would you like to see his tomb?"

"Oh yes, please!" I said, thrilled that I would see the very tomb where the king lay buried with his queen.

We made our way up the short flight of wooden stairs to the shrine of Edward the Confessor. Turning around, we stood facing a grand tomb in cast bronze, the top draped with a heavy azure-coloured cloth, in the centre of which was sewn the image of a white hart. The king and Queen Anne lay together, side by side, holding hands in a sign of love and devotion. Seeing the regal final resting place of the pious couple, I felt my heart swell with a sense of pride for them both.

"Here they are, My Lady." The Abbot gestured with his left arm. "Your ancestor and his queen. Do you see the seated hart in the garment he wears? All that is missing is his broom-cod collar. This creature and the broom-cod are two of the lasting symbols of his marriage to his French Queen, a young girl named Isabelle, like you. Both details were depicted in his portable diptych. The white hart on the outer cover was especially graceful. The artist left a detailed record of their time working with the king and his icon, though that tome has long since vanished from our library. No one can recall the name of the painter, either. We do believe that they were a member of Queen Isabelle's court, sent to London by her uncle, the Duke of Burgundy. Losing both the king's treasure and the account of its origins has created quite a mystery for us."

As he finished speaking we heard the sound of footsteps rushing up the stairs leading to the raised platform where we stood.

"Abbot Geravase, are you here?" came a voice, calling softly; it was followed by a tonsured head of one of the monks of the abbey, peering around the corner at us.

"Ah, I have found you at last! Can you please join me? Two of the monks from the chapter have been discovered gambling at one of the markets they visit. Here we thought they were simply spending too much on provisions for the order when it appears they were in fact spending the abbey's funds on games of dice!

Your advice and counsel are needed in the matter of how to punish them for their vice and sin."

"Yes, of course, Brother Martin. Do carry on. I shall join you directly."

The monk bowed his head in the direction of the abbot and took his leave, silently this time, retreating back down the stairs.

"You must see to your affairs in the running of the abbey, Abbot Geravase," I began. "I appreciate the time you have spent with me this afternoon and all you have told me."

"Your Ladyship is most welcome." His voice then lowered back to a whisper. "Though please be cautious with what I have told you and do not reveal what I have said about the Knights Templar."

I recalled Père Charles asking me to do the same regarding his past.

"You may be assured I shall keep your secret. I have only one last question for you, though. How do you know my chaplain so intimately?"

"Why, I thought he had explained our relationship to you. But perhaps you do not know about his childhood? We attended the New College of St Mary in Oxford at the same time and sang together in the choir there. He has a deep fondness for song, fostered in the years he spent at the college, first as a chorister, then as an academical clerk. Though from what he tells me, he has not performed plainchant in a choir over the past decade while he served as your family's chaplain in Gascony. He is indeed pleased to be back in England and to hear our sung Masses and services once again."

"I thank you for telling me all that you have, Abbot Geravase. We shall see each other again at vespers."

"Indeed. Until then, enjoy the remainder of the afternoon in our abbey. I leave you to continue your visit."

XVII
Vespers

After returning to the stable to feed Peyriac before the evening service, I heard the church bells calling worshippers to vespers. The sun had long since set and a damp chill hung about, settling into my lungs as I breathed in the heavy air on my walk back to the abbey church. In the distance, the path leading to the cloister was lit by torchlight. The afternoon drizzle had let up, leaving the courtyard, its walls affixed with many torches, aglow with tiny beads of watery mist that stuck to the surfaces and hung in the air, reflecting the flickering flames of the ample sources of light. Walking past the abbey gate on my way to the cloister, I heard a familiar voice from just beyond the entrance. Glancing through the gate's passageway, I noticed my father descending from an elegant carriage.

"Thank you again, Lord Dunstall. I know my family will be very grateful to you."

He closed the carriage door and entered the abbey compound. Looking up and straight ahead, he was surprised to see me standing there, waiting for him.

"Isa, is that you?" he asked in astonishment.

"Yes, Father, welcome back. We did not expect you to join us for vespers tonight."

"I am glad to have returned so early. Tell me, how were your lessons today?"

"This afternoon we had instruction from an Italian monk, Brother Giovanni. He taught us the music we will hear tonight; it is a sung setting of the psalm *Sicut cervus desiderat*. I have never heard such beautiful sound! You are just in time to attend the service where you can hear it for yourself," I explained over the pealing of church bells, still ringing their call to worship.

Together we walked through the cloister toward the sanctuary. We had not gone very far when I reached out my hand to touch his arm and he stopped, turning to face me.

"Father, I must tell you something in private before we join the others in church. It is something I have wanted to tell you for a long time; I must tell you before you meet with any other members of the Privy Council," I warned him in a hushed voice.

"Yes, Isabelle, what concerns you?"

With courage I tried to maintain a steady voice as I continued.

"It is about Aunt Christine, Father. I have a document that proves she is working as a spy for those in the court of the King of France."

My father glanced around us nervously.

"Keep your voice down! How dare you raise this subject again – especially in this place, where we are so close to the palace and the walls have ears that tell all they hear! If you do possess such a document, you are to destroy it at once! I do not wish to hear you ever mention this topic with me again, am I understood? I am aware that you two have your differences of opinion relating to your visions and how you conduct yourself in your devotions and faith, but I insist that you do not tell anyone your thoughts about her loyalties."

Taken aback by his harsh response, I let go of his arm.

"Very well, Father. As you wish," I replied dejectedly, and we resumed our walk in silence.

We found our seats with the others just as vespers was about to commence. I noticed my older sister's absence and silently prayed for her safety. Only when the choral offering came to Ockeghem's lovely piece did my mind finally settle. I closed my eyes as I listened to the male voices unfolding, one over the other, like the gentle ripple of water in a stream. Layer upon layer, then wave upon wave of peace came over me. The music caused my vision to be set on things above, where I remained in the company of Christ, whom I envisioned seated at the right hand of God. My focus turned to that which lay in heaven, not the earthly world I occupied with all its troubles and doubts. I felt in my heart that when Christ showed himself to me, then I, too, would be released and revealed with him in glory.

After the service and with a quieted soul, I followed the others as we again joined Abbot Geravase for supper in his residence. With our full attention, we listened closely as Father told us what had happened on his first day at court.

"I return here tonight with wonderful news that should please you all. I met my advocate in London, a man named Lord Dunstall, who has facilitated my appointment to the Privy Council. Fortunately, I have been made aware that the council meets in the Pyx Chamber, located in the abbey environs. It comes as a great relief to know that I shall be working in the vicinity of the church. I learned today that Richard of York has left his castle in the north and rides for London with a small retinue of men. I know I can seek shelter in the church if indeed there is to be rioting in the streets around the palace upon his arrival."

He paused briefly, allowing his news to sink in before continuing.

"As for our accommodation, Lord Dunstall has seen to that as well. I shall reside, while in London, in one of his properties near the palace until I can find one to my liking. Meanwhile, he has suggested that I send you all out of London, to the safety of the countryside, so that you might become better adjusted to life in England. There have been many incidents of pestilence striking London in recent years; residing in the fresh country air will do you all well.

"The royal castle of Boarstall has been made available to us through the heirs of the Rede estate, whose tenure of the property has recently ended. They have already moved out to their new manor, and the castle stands currently vacant. Should we find it suitable, I may petition King Henry to seek its title. It is located in Buckinghamshire, close to the hilltop village of Brill, which is home to one of the king's royal hunting lodges, and there is even a neighbouring royal wood called Bernwood Forest where we may continue our annual tradition of the Great Hunt."

"When are we to move?" Johan questioned our father.

"And if you are to stay in London, must we stay with you here until you are free to leave court?" I asked.

"You may leave London tomorrow for Boarstall. I am uncertain how much time I must spend with the council at the moment. I learned today that the final battle for Gascony is drawing ever closer. There is concern that over the winter the French plan to mass their troops along the northern border of the duchy. They may well begin making war with our former neighbours and allies as far south as the town of Saint-Émilion by the middle of December. There is no talk of them waiting until the winter is past to continue their assault. I can be of assistance in helping the English devise a strategy for saving Bordeaux and the lands to the southern foothills of the Pyrenees, if indeed the English lose the lands to the

175

north in the Médoc peninsula and east to Fronsac. The thought of war ravaging our homeland gives me no pleasure. But if I can help maintain some degree of peace for our friends and former neighbours around Bazas then I shall do so."

As he discussed the plans concerning how the English were securing Bordeaux, I turned my focus upon my aunt. She sat, staring at her brother, listening intently to every detail he gave. With sadness in my heart, I could tell from her keen expression that she would likely pass along all she had learned over dinner that night to her network of spies in London. I wished my father had not spoken so openly of his first day at court in her presence. He took no notice of his sister's countenance as the conversation turned to our departure for our new home.

"You will make the journey to Boarstall with Aunt Christine as your governess and Père Charles as your guardian in my place. The castle stands unlocked and unguarded now; its location near the royal forest and village of Brill is considered to be safe but I trust you will be vigilant while there until the household arrives. You will have plenty of new lands and woods to explore."

"I am sure that we shall be very happy with what you have arranged, Father," I interrupted excitedly.

"Can Christophe and I go hunting after we arrive?" chimed in Johan excitedly.

My brothers exchanged pleased glances.

"Of course. Perhaps I can leave that for you to organise, Charles?" Father directed his attention to our chaplain.

"It would give me great pleasure to do so. I shall take Their Lordships out to survey the beasts that roam the neighbouring forest," Père Charles replied with an air of responsibility.

As Father finished speaking, a monk approached our table with a message for him.

"Allow me to share some good news," Father informed us after the messenger had departed. "Margaret will be staying with Madame de Tastes at the London residence of Sir William Talbot, son of the Earl of Shrewsbury, for the foreseeable future. She has accepted his invitation of hospitality."

Our father paused briefly, surveying our sad expressions at his news.

"I shall miss the company of sister Margaret, Father." Sarah's soft voice and sad eyes did little to mask her heartache.

"We count on her to check on us as we play our games of chess," Christophe added.

"I realise her absence will mark another transition for all of you to bear but you are all aware that your sister must find the right companions here. We shall send word to her tomorrow of your move to Boarstall. In due course I expect that Johan and Isa will both seek appointments in service to Their Majesties."

"Your Lordship, you may entrust your family and residence to my care and supervision," Père Charles acknowledged. For a change, our aunt said nothing and kept her thoughts to herself, though I was certain she would have preferred to remain in Westminster and take up a position as a lady-in-waiting to Her Majesty, rather than acting as our governess far away from the news and activities of the royal court.

"This is a wonderful development for your family, especially so soon after your arrival," Abbot Geravase interjected. "You will be well placed in Buckinghamshire. Boarstall lies close to Oxford, a prominent town with a university. If you require any assistance from us as you are settling, please do not hesitate to ask."

"You have already done so much for us, especially in providing us with a safe place to stay upon our arrival in the capital. It shall be my honour to reciprocate your courtesy. I should like to offer you and your fellow members of the abbey hospitality at our home in the future. Please do stay at Boarstall if you are in need of lodging when travelling to Oxford."

"You are most generous, Your Lordship," acknowledged the abbot. "We shall do so at your invitation."

"Charles, you and the family should leave at daybreak. I was told that the journey will take you several days. Return now, all of you, to your rooms and take your rest, for tomorrow morning will be soon upon us," instructed our father.

"Since you plan to depart at dawn, do come to the kitchen before leaving, Charles. I shall have the cook set aside some food for you tomorrow. I bid you all goodnight, and peace be with you," Abbot Geravase stated warmly. We returned to our lodgings for sleep.

XVIII
The Earl of Hillesden

We awoke before sunrise the next morning, a feat not unusual in late autumn as the length of daylight grew increasingly shorter. After we assembled at the abbey gate with Abbot Geravase and Father in the early-morning hour, I noticed that Père Charles had already collected the generous assortment of breads, dried meats and dried fruit packed for us by the abbey cook. The two mounted men-at-arms who had escorted us from Portsmouth had been pressed back into service. Father had arranged for them to accompany us to Boarstall and remain with us until our permanent household arrived.

"Good morning, everyone," the abbot's cheerful voice called out to us. "I see you are all well prepared for your trip to Boarstall, a journey of about four days. Let us bow our heads for a moment of prayer before you depart.

"Dear Father in Heaven, you have guided this loving family safely to our shores in England. I ask that you grant them further safeguard as they embark on these final days of their journey to their new home. Provide them happiness and joy in their new surroundings, care for them and protect them from harm, bestow the glories of your love and peace upon them. In your name we pray. Amen."

"Amen," we whispered softly in unison.

We each approached our father in turn to bid him farewell. He assured us he would come to Boarstall to see us at the earliest opportunity. Père Charles and I mounted and walked our horses through the courtyard, followed by Johan and Christophe on their horses, and then the cart and driver carrying my aunt and Sarah. Entering into the street and the serene quiet that pervaded the city prior to sunrise, I looked back and waved farewell to my father and Abbot Geravase, who stood watching us depart from the abbey gate.

Over the course of the next three days we followed the London Road towards Oxford, stopping overnight first in Uxbridge, then High Wycombe. On the third day we arrived in Thame just after sunset. Stout timber-framed homes lined the high street leading into the centre of town. After locating a hostelry where we would spend the night, we had dinner while Père Charles asked the proprietor for information pertaining to Boarstall. They enjoyed a lively conversation, very little of which I understood with my limited knowledge of the English language. When he had finished talking to the owner of the establishment, Père Charles came and sat down at the table with us, explaining that we were only eight miles from Boarstall.

"We are very close now," he told us, his tone reassuring. "There is no need to rise before the break of dawn tomorrow, as we have previously on this journey. I have been assured that we can arrive at Boarstall by nightfall, even if we leave here by mid-morning. I want you all to have a peaceful rest tonight with the assurance that tomorrow you will be in your new home."

The next morning, we bought simple provisions, including meat pies, apples and pears, and freshly baked bread. The townspeople of Thame were soft-spoken and kind, advising Père Charles where to find the various goods we required. After our chaplain finished placing an order for meats and produce with a village merchant at his market stall, he asked the man for directions to Brill. As he did so, they were approached by a well-dressed young nobleman on horseback. He appeared to be a little older than Margaret. Overhearing the conversation between Père Charles and the merchant, the stranger interrupted them and insisted that he show us the way himself.

"Oh no, My Lord," Père Charles interjected. "I simply cannot permit you to do such a thing for us. You are clearly here in Thame on personal business. I cannot ask to take up your time with such a matter."

"In fact," the stranger replied, "I have finished my affairs here in town. I am about to return to my home. It is just past Brill, near a place called Steeple Claydon in Buckinghamshire. Whom are you planning to visit there, if I might enquire?"

"No one in Brill, My Lord. We are headed to Boarstall Castle, where we are to take up residence. Might you know the route?" Père Charles answered, lowering his voice.

"Why yes, I do. My family is closely associated with the Rede family, the ones to whom the castle was formerly entitled. Perhaps you consider acquiring the castle and its title?" said the stranger, attempting to coax more information from our chaplain.

"Oh no, not I, Your Lordship." Père Charles made it clear he had nothing more to impart to the stranger.

"I see," the young nobleman replied, slowly eyeing each of us in turn. "And who is the fair young maiden riding on the silver stallion? Does she find herself already promised in marriage?"

"Come, shall we continue on our way?" Père Charles interrupted the nobleman's scrutiny of me without answering his question.

"Of course," the young lord replied, wheeling his horse around in the direction of the road to Brill. "Follow me. I shall lead you to Boarstall."

With our two mounted escorts accompanying us, we followed the stranger out of Thame. Although he was dressed with an impeccable quality of refinement, something about the stranger unsettled me. I especially did not like the leering look he gave me, nor his inquisitive nature. I felt certain this was the type of man Margaret had cautioned me against. I stayed back on Peyriac, choosing instead to ride in between the two men-at-arms where I felt secure. Père Charles and the young lord were lost in conversation; I did not care to know of what they spoke.

It came as a great relief to discover that Brill was only six miles from Thame. Arriving that afternoon in the tiny hamlet perched along a hilltop ridge called Brae Hill, I felt a sense of joy pervade my thoughts. I turned my attention away from the man who escorted us and instead focused on taking in the details of what was to become our new home. Whereas the character of Thame was that of a quaint and orderly small market town, Brill was a place of royal patronage. The hamlet was home to a manor house used by the kings of England when they, with their hunting parties, came up from London to pursue wild boar in the neighbouring Bernwood Forest.

I immediately felt an attachment to the place as we rode past the royal residence with its little parish church. Pulling his horse back so that he was within earshot of us, Père Charles explained that the church's foundation had been laid in the twelfth century and that it belonged to the Priory of St Frideswide in Oxford.

Continuing along the scenic road to Boarstall, we crossed over several little rounded hills as we made our way out of town. Passing by many fallow fields, at last we saw the castle barbican rising up ahead of us through a copse. I wondered why our guide had not yet turned off the road to depart for his own home. He finally decided to leave our company only after much insistence from Père Charles that we could carry on without his aid. But not before he asked our chaplain a most disquieting question.

"I am curious, Father," the young lord began. "You brought up an interesting fact as we rode through Brill. You mentioned the church's twelfth-century foundation and association with the Priory of St Frideswide in Oxford. How is it that a man of your background would know such a thing? Did you reside in Oxford at some point in your life?"

The nobleman looked upon him with pointed suspicion, as if he knew something about our chaplain that might compromise his position and trust with our family. Knowing Père Charles's secret past as I did, a sudden wave of fear came over me, for I sensed this man could imperil the safety of our chaplain.

"Why, Your Lordship, I am simply repeating what was told to me when I sought directions in Thame. As I teach His Lordship's children, I felt I should impart that information to them so that they might become familiar with the history and significance of their new surroundings."

"Very well, then," the young lord replied, his tone turning sinister. "You seem somehow familiar to me, Father Charles. Perhaps I shall recall where and when we have met. Maybe it was while in the company of the Duke of Somerset? The Beaufort family is closely aligned with my own. I must check with them; perhaps they will remember you. When I do find out who you are, you can be certain that I will call upon you again."

Spinning his horse around to face me, he bowed from the saddle and addressed me directly, his words easy enough to understand, in spite of my still limited knowledge of the English language.

"I shall be returning to visit you one day, Your Ladyship – in private. I pray you settle in well," he said as he turned and rode off.

After he was well out of earshot, Johan asked the very question that had been on my mind.

"Père Charles, who was that person?"

"He introduced himself as a second cousin to Lord Dunstall. His name is Sir Henry Lormont, Earl of Hillesden. I am not sure though whether he can be trusted. He asked many questions, which, as your chaplain and guardian, I felt were far too personal in nature for me to provide a response. As he is our neighbour, I am certain he will return to visit us at some point."

"Since we are newly arrived in this country, I believe we should remain open and hospitable to our neighbours, Père Charles," my aunt interjected, her tone condescending. "We are in no position to judge whether fellow members of the nobility who show us a good turn are worthy of our trust; how arrogant of you to suggest such a thing! And you, being a priest, not even of noble birth, how dare you impose your concerns in such a way! He will be welcome back, whenever he might return. I daresay he took quite an interest in you, Isabelle. It is time for you to become better acquainted with potential suitors. Should he ask after you, I shall be more than happy to chaperon you two."

"Certainly, Your Ladyship," Père Charles conceded. "For now, let us not concern ourselves with him. We should rejoice, for at last we are here at our new home."

With our escorts riding ahead first and ensuring it was safe to enter Boarstall, we followed them into the inner ward and began unloading the cart. My aunt and I searched for some means of lighting the courtyard, for by the time we arrived it was already dark. I found a few lanterns in a ground-floor room that I would later discover was the kitchen below the great hall. We lit and carried them, one by one, back outside and hung them on some pegs fastened to the walls. The lanterns illuminated the area considerably and aided my family as they unloaded the parcels from the cart.

From what I could tell in the semi-dark, with only a torch to provide light, the castle was of a regular plan, similar to Rosete. The moated main entry gate had two polygonal towers on either end, a design I had never seen before in other barbicans. There was a stable yard with a postern at the far end of the inner ward, opposite the barbican. With one of the soldiers joining me for safety, we entered a large building on the north side of the courtyard and climbed a wide stone staircase. The first level housed an incredibly ornate great hall, with substantial fireplaces at either end, both crafted in herringbone-work. Stone benches had been built in the large window openings overlooking the inner ward below, but there were no windows placed in the exterior wall of the room.

We proceeded upstairs to the privy hall; its layout was similar to the great hall, although the windows on this level faced out over the inner courtyard as well as to the exterior. Each window had a carved stone window seat, and, similar to its counterpart below, it also had two massive fireplaces, one at either end of the room. In the dark of the night I could just discern that a colourful scene of the hunt with fanciful beasts and foliage was painted on both fireplace hoods.

Briefly peering out from one of the windows, in the distance I could faintly see the outline of trees inhabiting Bernwood Forest set against a large expanse of rolling countryside. I felt elated at the thought of what lay just beyond our castle walls. That landscape was exactly what I had longed for since leaving Gascony and enduring many weeks of travel.

After returning downstairs to the castle ward, my aunt, Sarah and I carried the remaining small parcels to the kitchen for sorting in the light of day, while the two soldiers, Johan and Père Charles put away the cart and our horses. I was so tired that I asked them to groom Peyriac for me.

Once the group had returned from the stable, Père Charles suggested that we have a moment of prayer and make a meal from the provisions we had acquired in Thame. I knew which parcel contained our cups and pitcher and quickly opened the wooden trunk, instructing Sarah to collect water from a well I had noticed in the inner ward. As she did so I unpacked and handed Christophe and Johan the cups we would use with our meal.

Upon Sarah's return, and after unhooking one of the lanterns from a peg in the wall of the inner ward to light the way, my family followed me up the stairs to the great hall. Using the flame from my lantern to help him, Christophe ignited a fire in one of the fireplaces while I lit several tapers that I found stacked on one end of the table, left by the royal hunting party. The warmth from the blaze could be felt immediately as it permeated the cold, damp air. As the room filled with illumination, we took our seats in the centre of the long wooden table that ran the length of the hall. I opened our food parcels and Père Charles gathered us together to pray.

"Our most gracious and loving Father, we call upon you in this late hour to thank you for all that you have granted us. You have made us strong in spirit and have provided a roof over our heads to shelter and protect us. Bless this home and keep us all safe and in your sight. In the name of the Father, and of the Son, and of the Holy Spirit. Amen."

The silence that ensued gave little hint of our true exhaustion. We ate without conversation; the only sound in the room came from the cracking and popping of the fire, as embers from the logs burst through the air, dropping onto the stone hearth surrounding the fireplace. From the nourishment provided by our small supper, we at last managed to find the strength to retire across the inner ward to the building housing our new bedchambers. We quickly said our goodnights and parted, tired and thankful to be in our new home at last.

XIX

Boarstall Castle

20 November 1452, Buckinghamshire

For centuries, the ownership of Boarstall Castle had been a mark of distinction amongst noble families fortunate enough to have acquired title of the royal property. Many amongst the peerage sought to attain the right as a reward for their years of loyal service to the crown; to be granted the title Lord of Boarstall indicated a close relationship with the court at Westminster. The fact that our family had been permitted to reside in such a prestigious royal property signified the king's recognition of our father's service to his administration in Bordeaux.

We later learned that Boarstall Castle and the lands that made up its demesne were closely linked to the royal manor in the neighbouring village of Brill, whose foundation had been laid by the Anglo-Saxon kings. In the eleventh century, Edward the Confessor had used the ancient palace there as his hunting lodge when he and members of his court explored Bernwood Forest in search of a particular wild boar. The beast was rumoured to have killed several peasants whose farms lay upon the boundary of the forest. When at last the terrifying beast was slain by a member of the king's guard named Nigel Crossman during a royal hunt, the king granted him neighbouring lands to be held in cornage, which in ancient times required the landowner to blow a horn to announce an invasion of the territory. On his newly acquired lands outside Brill, Nigel built a manor house and named it *Bore-stall*, an ongoing reminder of how the property had come to be in his possession.

Over the centuries, custodianship of the estate passed from one powerful noble family to the next, the term of tenure stipulating that it could not remain in any one family for more than fifty years. The once tiny eleventh-century manor house had become the formidable Boarstall Castle by the time we moved into it, the most recent addition being that of the barbican, which had been built prior to the tenure of the Rede family. The history of the castle was about to enter an altogether new period, with Gascon descendants of the *Seigneurie d'Albret* becoming the owners once the horn of ownership was passed to our father.

———

When I opened my eyes that first morning after so many days of travel, I was initially uncertain as to my surroundings. Then I heard Sarah stirring in her sleep in the bed next to mine. Her presence in the room we shared reminded me that we were indeed installed in our new home. No longer were we on the move, wondering where we would lay our heads that night.

Not wishing to awaken my sister, I silently slipped out of my bed and got dressed. I left the room and made my way down the stairs to the inner ward. Once outside in the freshness of the morning air, I felt my spirits lift. A fine mist hugged the ground, the low clouds certain to be burned away with the break of dawn that cast its first rays of filtered daylight across the distant sky.

Glancing in the direction of the barbican tower, a movement in the distance along the crenelated parapet caught my eye. A figure sat there, and in the dimness of the early-morning light, at first I could not distinguish who it was. As I stepped further out into the centre of the yard, the silhouette of a man came into sharper focus. To my shock I recognised it was Père Charles; he sat with his legs dangling off the ledge of a crenel! He leaned forward, as if preparing to fall, and then back, his body moving in a rocking motion. I could not believe what I saw, for it looked as though he were about to cast himself from the roof to the ground below – a fall that would end in his death! I raced to the barbican, my heart pounding, unsure whether I would arrive at the top of the tower in time to save him. Continuing up the two flights of newel stairs until I reached the rooftop, I called out when I came upon him, as he was rocking forward, about to fall over the wall of the parapet.

"Père Charles! No, stop! What are you doing up here?" I had to catch my breath as I ran up to him, throwing my arms around him from behind. "Why are you doing this? Come down from here. Allow me to help you!"

I held on to him with all my strength and felt the tension in his frame dissolve in my grasp as he took notice of me.

"Lady Isabelle, you must not stop me! They are coming! Do you not see them?" My chaplain's normally calm voice was erratic; his breathing came in short gasps. "Over there, in the woods; I hear them, and their horses. They wish to find me and kill me. I will not let them – I would rather take my own life than allow them the satisfaction!"

"You are talking nonsense. There is no one there. The dawn has just broken – do you not hear the birds as they call their song to the new day? We are the only ones here," I said with a strained voice, trying to convince him.

A slight breeze came up and caught in my long blonde hair, causing it to drape delicately across my face and onto Père Charles's shoulder. Grabbing his upper arms and turning his torso towards me, I slowly moved his body and lifted his legs from over the parapet to the rooftop safety of where I stood before him.

"Come here, come to me," I said, gently coaxing him off the ledge and into my embrace. "What happened just now? Why did you come up here?"

"I— I do not know, Lady Isabelle." My chaplain's voice had calmed and he allowed me to pull him forward, away from the crenel. "From somewhere outside my room I heard a stranger call out my name, beckoning me to follow him. I pursued the sound of the voice up here and then I heard another voice whisper in my ear, instructing me to leap. I caught a glimpse of fiery torchlights in the distance. I assumed the voice was one of the assassins who wish to kill me. I know they are out there in the forest somewhere, waiting for me."

"But there is no one else about. There is no one here at Boarstall, only our family and the two escorts. I do not understand what you think you see and who you think you hear. Come along, let us recite our morning office in the chapel together. I shall stay with you and you will see that there is no one here but us. Take my hand – follow me."

I took him by the hand and led him back downstairs, where we crossed the inner ward still hand in hand. The chapel was at the opposite end of the castle, next to the postern, not far from the stable. An ornate ocular window pierced the wall above the door and four rounded stone steps led up to the entrance. As we entered I felt my spirits uplift after what I had just witnessed on the roof of the barbican. Père Charles moved directly to the altar, where he dropped to his knees in prayer.

I quietly took in my surroundings. The interior of the chapel was plastered in alabaster white with a slightly protruding apse pierced by five narrow lancet windows, each set with panes in diamond-shaped jewel tones of ruby, sapphire, emerald and citrine. The first rays of dawn continued to break free across the sky outside, increasing the intensity of the light piercing the ocular window and casting the chapel in a splendid palette of deep hues. A small carved stone gallery raised upon six decorative stone pilasters stood to the left of the altar. Presumably this private space had provided the king and queen with an elevated place from which they could pray in private when they visited the castle. Underneath was a confessional, made of the same quarried stone, its chambers enclosed by carved wooden doors.

Without a sound, I moved to a bench behind Père Charles and knelt to join him in silent prayer. I closed my eyes and searched within my soul to find the words of concern that I might offer to the Lord after the tragedy I had just prevented. I knew it was a mortal sin to take one's life, so the fact that my chaplain would seek to end his own life left me perplexed and searching for a possible explanation for his abnormal behaviour. I prayed for his soul, that the loving embrace of Jesus Christ would calm him and shower him with mercy. Before I opened my eyes, I could feel Père Charles's presence as he stood over me, watching me in silence.

"Thank you, Lady Isabelle. You saved me this morning. I do not know what came over me. I pray you forgive my foolishness. Please do not speak again of what you witnessed."

"Why, of course. I shall not tell anyone what I saw." My voice was full of concern. "Though I must have you know, your behaviour shocked me. It is not right that you should hear voices telling you to take your own life. Please, always remember, you are safe here with us. There is no one nearby who will harm you. I never saw you behave in such a manner when we lived at Rosete."

"While living in Gascony, I never feared my family's assassins discovering my identity and coming for me as I do now that I have returned to England. I can only profess my profound unworthiness, Your Ladyship. I am afraid the episode you observed this morning may not be the last of its kind."

"Do you think Sir Henry's observation yesterday that he might know you, or that his associates in the Beaufort family might remember you, caused you to hear the voices? Yet you never mentioned that you knew any of these men when you described the time you lived in Oxford with your tutor Father James. Are you concerned that someone from your childhood might recognise you?"

"Sir Henry's words to me last night were startling. I had rather hoped it would be some time before I was identified. Thankfully he did not place me outright. But now you can see that I have put great trust in you, Lady Isabelle. You understand why you must never divulge to anyone the secrets I have disclosed to you. After supper I asked the two men-at-arms to remain with us. Once the servants and porter arrive today and our household is again full, it shall be much safer for all of us."

"I hope for your sake you are correct, for I did not like the way Sir Henry spoke to me as if I were someone he wished to possess. His behaviour reminded me of the Count of Foix on the day Sir Edward Hull forced him to release Margaret. Sir Henry is not someone I wish to encounter again."

"If only that were the case; but as he is a distant relative of the very family who are helping us acquire this property, I believe that was not the last either of us shall see of him or his associates," admitted Père Charles. Changing the subject, he sat down on the bench next to me. "Tell me, how do you find your new home? Are you pleased with what you have seen so far?"

"Oh yes," I said in earnest. "Yes, I am truly much happier here than in London. I think I shall be content to live here for the rest of our time in England."

"I am glad to hear of it. It pleases me greatly to know that you are satisfied with your new home in my country," Père Charles said, his tender expression a silent acknowledgement of the secret we shared.

XX
Rebellion

It was only one week after our move to Boarstall when a messenger arrived early in the evening with an important letter
from our father. After reading it, Père Charles asked our aunt to
prepare Sarah and Christophe for bed and then to join us in the
privy gallery. While she did so, he gathered three candlesticks from
the great hall and Johan and I followed him upstairs, each of us
carrying a light to illuminate the room, eager to hear the news
from London. Once my aunt had joined our group, our chaplain
bolted the door to prevent any servants from disturbing us. We sat
together near the unlit fireplace.

"I have received word from His Lordship concerning affairs at
court that may affect your family directly," Père Charles began, his
tone grave. "He has drafted a detailed description of the events
involving the recent rebellion outside London staged by the Duke
of York. It would appear that we were fortunate to have left the
city when we did, for that very day word came that York and his
small army had advanced up to the capital's walls from the north.
Upon learning that the group intended to enter the city and proceed to Westminster, the king's chief advisor, Edmund Beaufort,

Duke of Somerset, ordered that the city gates be locked at midday. Such action forced York and his men to the east of the city, where they set up camp at Dartford, in Kent."

"Are our father and sister safe?" I asked, as Johan and I exchanged concerned glances.

"It would appear that they are both in secure surroundings. Your father is still at the residence of Lord Dunstall. Margaret is with Madame de Tastes and remains a guest of Sir William Talbot. I shall read to you from His Lordship's correspondence, for I believe you should be made aware of what is happening at court. Though we have only recently arrived here seeking safety after decades of war in Gascony, it seems the peace and stability that we had hoped to find in England is not to be."

Père Charles picked up the document from his lap and began to read from it.

"*The king's army was dispatched to Kent where Richard of York has made his camp. The Lancastrian contingent heavily outnumbered Richard's small group of soldiers and Edmund of Somerset pushed for a battle to be staged that would see Richard of York finally defeated. King Henry did not permit this to happen, for he preferred to attempt reconciliation with York.*

"*At the insistence of Edmund of Somerset, both Richard Neville, Earl of Salisbury, and Richard Neville, Earl of Warwick, who were normally allied with York, were dispatched as emissaries on behalf of His Majesty King Henry. Though both men openly oppose the Lancastrian king's rule at court, Somerset directed them to appeal to their confederate – failing which, the two men would face charges of treason. To save themselves, they agreed to meet with York on behalf of the king. York told his two allies of the series of charges he had compiled against Somerset, which he intended to use as a means of turning the king from his trusted advisor. When they learned of this, the two Nevilles returned* to the king and informed him that York simply wished to present his accusations before His Majesty. The two men convinced the king that York should be pardoned from any treasonable charges he faced. King Henry agreed and the men were dispatched back to York's camp, where they told Richard to bring his plea before His Majesty in the royal tent."

As Père Charles continued, I could sense that the letter's contents had alarmed my brother as much as they had me. Yet my aunt's expression remained blank and unfeeling.

"The Nevilles met with and convinced York that he should seek an audience with the king, assuring York that King Henry sought a diplomatic means to ending the dispute. York agreed to meet the king and make his petition in person, but when he entered the king's tent he was startled to see that it was not Henry who sat in wait, but his nemesis, the Duke of Somerset. Queen Margaret had convinced her husband to put Somerset in his place, allowing for York to be captured and arrested. Three days later, York appeared in London, where he was made to process through St Paul's Cathedral before myself and other members of the peerage and swear an oath to never raise an army against the king. His Majesty then released York to return to his home in the north. The king hoped that by showing York mercy, the duke would stand by his promise and not return to London under such circumstances again.

"But York has secret allies amongst his peers at Westminster. They recognise that one day they shall be called upon to support the reforms he has proposed against Somerset. This group of men wishes to see York usurp the throne, though Somerset has made it clear that he intends to place himself there as the king continues to show a lack of leadership. Those at court say that Somerset's role as the king's chief advisor has been riddled with acts of embezzlement and poor management of the war with France. They blame Somerset as much as they blame the king for the loss of Normandy and the territories in Northern France, as well as the trouble we have faced in Gascony in recent years. What I am witnessing here as a member of the King's Privy Council is a breakdown in trust and signs of betrayal amongst the king's staunchest supporters. As such, I am uncertain what the future will hold for England, and what will become of us if the country goes to war with itself. Our family will remain loyal to the Lancastrian king whatever the outcome, for it is his favour that has provided us with an estate and my rank amongst the peerage of Westminster.

"There is one more development I wish to share. I have heard secret talk amongst my peers on the Privy Council that a schism of the Church is being planned amongst certain members of the nobility. I am not yet aware of the details, but it would appear that there is a growing desire to move away from the direct influence of the Roman Pope. I have overheard members of the council conversing in hushed voices about a sacred relic they wish to possess. They believe that the artefact proving Christ's existence is hidden somewhere in England, brought back from the Crusades with members of the Knights Templar who reside at the Temple Church in London. They seek to acquire it by any means possible, for with it they will have the means of founding a new Church. I have been witness to their claims that they no longer wish for England to answer to the Pope, who, they believe, is increasingly controlled by the French monarchy. As such there may come a time when we shall be persecuted for our faith. We must remain steadfast and show great resolve through all these new trials presented before us.

"I hereby conclude this letter to you. Once you have read my words you must destroy what I have written by fire. I pray the Lord keeps us all safe from harm, and in good favour with those in power who hold our destiny in their hands."

After he finished reading the lengthy missive, Père Charles moved from where he was seated to stand by the fireplace. Using the candle he had brought with him to ignite a piece of kindling lying near the hearth, he then tossed the letter onto the pile of logs stacked in the centre. Slowly the flame moved from one side of the pile to the other until, at last, the fire roared to life.

We watched ends of the parchment curling under the heat of fire that eventually consumed the entire document. The evidence destroyed, Johan voiced his concern.

"How will this affect us, Père Charles? I plan to join in the king's summer progress next year; I am keen to join others at court. Will it be safe for me to do so if the country is on the brink of a civil and holy war?"

"I am afraid we must wait and see what develops in the course of the ongoing rivalry between the houses of Somerset and York. Until we learn more about the creation of a new Church, we must remain silent on the news your father has imparted. He would not put his life or the lives of his family in peril for the sake of loyalty to the king – let us take comfort in knowing that. It is important for us to remain aware of the situation unfolding around us. Do not despair, any of you. In our daily prayers we shall continue to seek God's protection from those around us who may wish to harm us."

"I do not agree with you whatsoever," Aunt Christine inter-jected, her tone hostile. "This news is most alarming for our family. Surely we are in great peril if the king, whose favour my brother seeks, is removed from the throne. Philippe should have listened to me back at Rosete and aligned himself and his children with the French king! We should be in the safety of the House of Albret this winter in Gascony, not living as strangers in a foreign land where everyone looks upon us with suspicion!"

"Will our father have to remain in London for long?" I asked, deliberately ignoring my aunt's malice.

"It would appear that he will stay there until Parliament breaks for the advent season next month. He is fortunate to have been accepted into the peerage so quickly. It is imperative that he becomes familiar with the customs and requirements of such a significant standing at court. To become a member of the Privy Council signifies that the king and his advisors felt he could be trusted with guarding the nation's secrets. He will undoubtedly be working directly with the Duke of Somerset on affairs concerning the war in Gascony."

"I pray this move to England will not become a liability for our family, for the country here is by no means stable." Wearing a deep frown, Aunt Christine rose and crossed the room, then left the privy gallery. Johan stood up, preparing to leave as well.

"I do hope we are safe in England. I hate to think that I left behind Pharrah and my friends in Gascony only to be caught in the middle of this turmoil at court in London," Johan said, before striding away toward the door. "Are you joining me, sister? It is time to check on Christophe and Sarah."

"Do go ahead, brother. I will return in a moment. There is something I wish to ask our chaplain in private."

"Until tomorrow, then," Johan said, closing the door behind him, leaving Père Charles and me alone in the gallery.

"Yes, Your Ladyship? Tell me, what is on your mind?" he gently queried me.

Now that we were alone, I moved closer to my chaplain, taking a seat in the chair at his side.

"There is something I wish to confess," I began, slowly. "Father mentioned in his letter that there is a hidden relic guarded by the Knights Templar. I know of what he speaks – it is the *Mandylion*, the shroud that covered Christ at his death."

"And how do you come to know such a thing?" my chaplain asked, alarmed.

"It was Abbot Geravase who divulged the truth about the holy artefact to me," I admitted. "What I was told by him has now been confirmed by Father. Our lives may be in peril if there is a separation from the Catholic Church, is that not so? How will the creation of a new Church affect us?" I asked, my voice mirroring the concern I wore on my face.

"I am afraid that the time is nearing for a break from Rome, Lady Isabelle. Do you remember what I explained that evening on the deck of the *Salamanca*? That my father and Cardinal Beaufort were blamed for the failure of the congress at Arras? And that in the wake of the Treaty of Arras certain noblemen serving in his court began to plan a breakaway Church? I fear we are now facing a time of great change in my homeland. The day is fast approaching when it may no longer be safe for us to remain followers of the Church in Rome."

"That saddens me greatly. I cannot imagine living my life without the familiar comforts of the Catholic religion," I admitted.

"There is no call for alarm at the moment." Père Charles's tone was reassuring. "If the country does break from Rome, we shall find another place to live where we are safe to practise our faith – do not despair."

"I am also concerned with what you said earlier: that Edmund of Somerset will be working closely with Father on the King's Council. Do you not think this could imperil us if we are favoured by someone whom the Duke of York and his men wish to see charged with crimes against the realm?"

"I wish I had an answer to your question. It is too soon to know what the outcome will be of the recent events in London. Clearly the king favours his advisor Somerset over York, though he does not wish to see either party arrested and imprisoned. I believe I know your father well enough to reassure you that he will take every precaution necessary to avoid being placed in either camp. His neutrality in the matters of state will be what defines him amongst his peers."

"I am thankful that we are well away from London and all the intrigue at court, though I shall feel much relieved when Father and Margaret join us at Boarstall to celebrate the Christmas holiday next month," I acknowledged.

"It will indeed be a joyous reunion for us all. Is there anything else you wish to discuss tonight, Your Ladyship?"

I paused momentarily, casting my gaze upon the floor, wondering if I should dare to tell him how much I wished I could be held in his arms and comforted. Then I thought about his divine calling; his vocation. I did not wish to make our deepening friendship fall under any scrutiny that would blemish my reputation or his. I decided against opening my heart to him.

"No, I should retire now and ensure that Sarah is sleeping soundly. I shall see you in the morning."

"May you be at peace and enjoy all the blessings that deep slumber brings," Père Charles said with tenderness.

Picking up my candlestick, its taper flickering gently in the rush of air about it, I rose from my seat and walked to the door, silently departing and closing it behind me.

XXI
Winter

January 1453, Boarstall Castle

We had been accustomed to feeling the change of seasons in Gascony. Winter would melt delicately into the fresh spring season. The abundant new life that sprang up in the temperate period was indolently followed by summer, when the warmest days of the year extended over several months before the heat of the season gradually abated into a mild autumn. Cooler air would follow, indicating that the time was right to gather the grapes before autumn turned to winter. Soon the landscape would take on the appearance of another world, the terrain devoid of any signs of the life that lay dormant. And yet, with all the subtle changes from one season to the next throughout the year, overall our Gascon climate had certainly been tolerable, enjoyable in most seasons. And even during the coldest moments of our winters we were never as cold as we were that first winter we spent in England.

After our arrival at Boarstall, any plans for hunting were delayed as we turned our attention to caring for Sarah and Christophe. Their health was the weakest it had ever been in their young lives. In the bitter cold of our initial winter, they almost perished from repeated illnesses affecting their lungs.

My brother and sister remained sick with fevers for much of December and January. Before Christmas Aunt Christine and Johan had moved to London with Father to avoid catching the illness. I had insisted that I stay at Boarstall with our servants and Père Charles to help care for my brother and sister. They were so weak and frightened that I could not bear the thought of leaving them and possibly never seeing them again if they succumbed to their fevers.

Late one night towards the middle of January, I awoke to hear Sarah's breath coming in raspy, intermittent intervals, the silence broken only by a deep, rattling cough. She otherwise lay limp and unresponsive as I tried desperately to awaken her. Her face was flushed with the sign of a high fever. I rushed upstairs to Père Charles's room, knocking loudly to raise him.

"Père Charles, you must come at once! Père Charles, please wake up!" I continued my banging on his door. "It is Sarah, she is burning up and she cannot breathe!" I yelled frantically outside his door, my breath visible in the freezing air of the corridor.

Our chaplain emerged, his hair tousled, still tying his long black woollen cape about his shoulders. One of our servants, who slept in the room with Christophe while caring for him, had heard my frenzied yelling and run upstairs to see what he could do to help.

"You two go at once to the kitchen," commanded our chaplain. "You must act quickly. Make me a hot compress of valerian, thyme and oregano to lay upon Lady Sarah's chest. Then prepare a decoction adding comfrey, elecampane and hyssop. Bring me horehound, honey, the root of fennel, radish, wild celery and anise with the mortar and pestle. I will mix them into a syrup to help calm her cough. Hurry now – do not waste a moment!"

The male servant and I rushed out into the cold of the night and across the inner ward to our kitchen and storeroom, searching for the ingredients as instructed by Père Charles. Thankfully the embers from the fire laid to cook our meal that evening were still glowing and it took only a little additional fuel to bring them roaring back to life. I filled a pot with water from a pitcher kept on the sideboard and hung it from the iron hook that swung out from an arm over the fire, taking care not to burn myself in the process. When the water came to the boil I prepared a large mug of ptisan as directed. I set everything on a tray so that I could carry the basin with the compress and the mug at the same time. With my companion not far behind carrying the other ingredients to make the syrup, I quickly climbed the stairs to my room. When I entered the bedchamber, the chill almost took my breath away.

"I had to open the windows to allow fresh cool air to enter; doing so should aid in bringing her fever down more quickly," Père Charles explained as he worked with determination to help my little sister. "Apart from applying these remedies and making her drink the ptisan, there is not much more we can do for poor little Lady Sarah, I am afraid."

I bowed my head, leaning against the wall for support. Suddenly my brother appeared in the doorway, wearing only his nightshirt to guard him against the cold.

"Why is everyone up?" he asked tiredly, rubbing his eyes and yawning. "Why do you congregate around Sarah's bed?"

"She is gravely ill, Christophe. And since you have not fully recovered, you must return to the warmth of your bed at once," I insisted.

"Come along, Lord Christophe. I will carry you back." The male servant lifted him into his arms, where the poor boy collapsed – the sheer exertion caused by walking to my room had been too much for him.

"Lady Isabelle, please come here and rub this compress along your sister's chest while I prepare the syrup," Père Charles said, directing my attention back to my sister.

I knelt by the bed and when I reached into the basin our hands touched as we both simultaneously sought to wring the excess water from the cloth. We stopped and looked up, our eyes locked in a fleeting moment of acknowledgement before we continued seeing to our respective tasks, desperately fighting to save Sarah from the illness that seemed to steal her every breath.

After Père Charles had readied the syrup, I raised Sarah's head, her eyes still closed. Our chaplain opened her lips to place the syrup in her mouth. In spite of its bitter smell and taste, she did not resist him, and in her weakened state swallowed as best she could. The concoction left a lingering stench in the room long after it had been prepared.

We sat by her side for the rest of the night, taking our sleep in turns, as first one then the other reapplied the compress, heated more water and prepared more ptisan, which could be administered only one spoonful at a time. Fatigue took over and I fell asleep, awakening when I heard the cock in the outer yard begin to crow, announcing the coming dawn. I opened my eyes to find Père Charles deep in prayer, bent over Sarah, his eyes closed and his lips reciting the words of scripture that brought healing to her frail body, ravaged by illness.

Sarah opened her eyes wide, and looked about the room, frightened, as if awaking from a nightmare.

"Isa," she cried upon seeing me, her voice small and weak. "I am so frightened," she whispered as I rushed to sit by her side, stroking her hair.

"I could not breathe. I saw Maman and she held me." Her body began to shake as she softly sobbed, recalling the phantom sight of our mother in her vision.

"There, there, Sarah. You were experiencing a dream, that is all. You had a very bad fever in the night, but Père Charles was here to help you," I said, soothingly.

"It feels as if her fever has subsided," I added hopefully, glancing in his direction.

"Lady Sarah, it appears the worst of what you felt in the night has passed you now," he said, gently stroking her arm to help soothe her after her nightmare.

"Lady Isabelle, continue to treat her using the same herbs as you did in her compress. I shall summon the physician to come out from Oxford. Until then, if we continue to give her the syrup and decoction every few hours she should show continued signs of improvement. I shall also send word to your father in London to come at once."

"I will watch over Sarah," I replied, looking at my sister tenderly before gazing at Père Charles. "Thank you for coming to aid us. I would not have known what to do to help her."

"I will leave her to your care, then," he said with an encouraging smile as he rose and stepped to the door. As he was about to open it, I stopped him with a question.

"Wait, please tell me, where does your knowledge of plants and medicine come from?"

"While I was a student at New College, my tutor James assigned me to work in the college's infirmary. I studied with a learned physician who taught me how to use different plants and compounds to heal. We used the text written by Hildegard of Bingen as our primary reference."

With the door closing quietly behind him, my sister closed her eyes and settled her head back into her pillow. I moved to the window seat in time to watch the man I secretly loved cross over the inner ward in the direction of the porter's lodging. He climbed the stairs two at a time and then disappeared into the first floor of the barbican tower to wake the porter and have his messages dispatched. His gallant effort to save Sarah had touched me deeply, and I could feel my heart ache for the love I wished to share with him.

"Do try to rest now, Sarah. I pray your body will show signs of healing," I said calmly, returning to my sister's side and kissing her forehead.

Sarah did as I told her, laying her head to one side and closing her eyes. Her fever had broken in the night and her cheeks bore only a slight rosy glow. The breathing that had awakened me in a panic the night before was now passive and regular, with only a thin raspy sound emitted as she exhaled. I thanked God at that moment for Père Charles and his wisdom, for he had indeed saved little Sarah's life.

XXII
Broughton Castle

F ather came to Boarstall at once after receiving the message
urging him to visit our sister, while Johan and Aunt Christine
remained in London. Since arriving there in the Christmas season,
Johan had joined the other young noblemen in the King's Court
and quickly settled into a life as a courtier. The business that kept
my aunt in London was never disclosed to me by our father. I had
my suspicions but dared not raise them given my father's prior
reprimand.

Upon arrival, Father went immediately to Sarah's bedside, where
he remained for several days as her fever continued to subside.

We all continued taking turns to care for my little sister. Thankfully none of us was taken by the illness that had infected her lungs
and nearly caused her to die.

During Father's second week of visiting Boarstall, Sarah joined
us one morning with her usual appetite. She was playful and full of
energy. We were thrilled to see her looking so well and back to her
usual sweet demeanour, with no evidence of the almost fatal ordeal
she had been through only weeks earlier. Over our meal, my father
gave instruction for a short journey he wished to take.

"Seeing that Sarah and Christophe are now well and truly healed from their illnesses, I would like to pay a visit to the son of the late James Fiennes. James was King Henry's Lord High Treasurer when he was killed in the London riots a few years ago. His son is Sir William Fiennes, Baron Saye & Sele. Through his marriage to Lady Margaret Wykeham, a descendant of Bishop William of Wykeham, he resides at Broughton Castle, not far out of Oxford, to the north near the town of Banbury. Before I left London to call upon Sarah and visit Boarstall, Sir William invited me to attend a special banquet at his castle if the family was well enough that I could leave them. Charles and Isabelle, you shall accompany me on my visit. I wish to leave shortly so that we might arrive there in time for the feast tonight," Father instructed, rising from the table to leave.

"How long do you plan to stay at Broughton, Your Lordship? Shall I send word by messenger this morning that we intend to seek the baron's hospitality?" Père Charles enquired.

"Yes, Charles, you may make the arrangements for our visit," my father instructed. "Tell them that we plan to stay for two nights. I shall meet you both in the stable. I want to leave as soon as you are ready."

Sarah and Christophe finished their meal and left the hall soon after our father. Père Charles then joined me on the bench where I sat.

"Why do you think Father wants us to attend the banquet with Baron Saye & Sele? I am surprised that he has asked me to join you two."

"Yes, I was thinking the same thing. There must be a reason for it; I am certain your father's invitation to the banquet at Broughton is related to his joining the peerage and his position on the King's Privy Council. We must do as he asks, yet I do not wish to be presented at court to the king, nor do I wish to risk being identified by the king's courtiers. It is safer for me to stay away from people who might question my past. I know how these men and women gossip around the halls of Westminster; I wish to play no role as a subject of their rumours."

"Have you heard something about them that gives you cause for alarm?" I asked, concerned for his safety.

"At this point it is not the Fienneses whom I am particularly anxious about; it is the company they keep that may prove troublesome for me. I have a strong suspicion that amongst those invited to the banquet are men who could identify me if I were to be questioned about my family and where they came from. I will not know until we arrive and I learn who is in attendance; but I shall plan to keep silent and listen to what those around me say. The Fienneses have enjoyed close ties with all the Lancastrian kings, and their steadfast support of King Henry comes as no surprise. Given your father's work on the King's Privy Council, the young Sir William, who resides at Broughton Castle, is someone with whom your father should be on good terms."

"If you would rather that he had one of our male servants accompany us, ask him whether you might stay back and watch Sarah and Christophe instead," I suggested.

"I wish to ride with you and accompany you during your visit. I feel I should be there in case I am needed to translate something for either of you," he explained, rising from the bench and extending his hand to assist me. "Shall we prepare for our journey now?"

"Whatever the reason for your accompanying my father on his visit, it will be all the better for your joining us," I said in a hushed tone as we departed from the great hall.

"As your presence will be for me, I assure you," Père Charles replied, before taking leave of me to send word by messenger to our hosts of our anticipated arrival that evening.

———

We rode for Broughton later that morning.

It was dark upon our arrival and the castle's exterior was not clearly visible. As we entered the inner ward, a servant approached us and instructed us to dismount and follow him. A groom appeared and led our mounts to the stable yard while we were escorted to the range housing the great hall.

Once we entered the building we were led along a narrow stone hallway pierced on one side with recessed windows formed from pointed arches. Tapestries depicting an assortment of subjects lined the opposite wall – unicorns danced with fair maidens dressed in diaphanous gowns and wearing crowns of flowers; a group of hunters entered a darkened wood in search of a wild boar barely visible in the depths of the forest; a battle scene depicted Crusader knights with a tall crenellated castle on a mountainside. Twelve brass candelabra, dripping with wax and each holding seven tall, slow-burning tapers, illuminated the long passageway brilliantly; a roof comprising delicately ribbed vaults hung suspended over our heads.

Reaching the end of the corridor, the servant opened the door to the great hall where dinner was about to be served. As we entered, my eyes beheld a room far grander than even that which I had seen at Benauges. A large fireplace in the centre of the room roared with life, the energy from the flames sending embers cracking and popping into the air. An elaborate chevron pattern was set into its stonework, and the hood was decoratively painted with foliage and birds. Guests were seated on two richly carved wooden benches on either side of a long wooden table laid with a variety of highly polished silver plates and goblets that reflected the light of dozens of candles placed on candelabra similar to the ones in the corridor we had just walked through.

Upon entering the room, the servant announced our names to Sir William and Lady Margaret, while those around the table, in particular the ladies, giggled to each other as they nodded their heads in our direction.

As I stepped forward to bow to our host and hostess, I became aware that in our haste to join the other guests, who had already assembled, we remained yet in our riding clothes. While this was not a serious concern for Père Charles and Father, whose costumes were suitable enough for a banquet, I wore boots and breeches, and a long woollen shirt, belted around my waist, peeked out from under a heavy surcoat. I had packed a gown and small headdress for the occasion but there had been no time to change. Now, only my long blonde hair, pulled to the side in a simple plait tied with a red silk ribbon, gave any clue of my feminine identity. In spite of this, our host and hostess were polite enough not to make any mention of it.

"Welcome to Broughton," exclaimed Sir William heartily, rising from his carved chair at the head of the table to come and greet us. "We are about to dine – please do join us. Lord Philippe, my guests have shared with me how the Privy Council has benefited from your wisdom and experience of living in Gascony, and your influence over the king in the decisions affecting the war with France. I wish to hear of what changes might be in store for us and how they may affect our family's finances. We are often called upon by His Majesty to pledge monies in aid of the ongoing campaigns abroad."

Turning to me, he bowed his head as he took up my hand and kissed it.

"Ah, the fair Lady Isabelle d'Albret Courteault, it is my great pleasure to make your acquaintance at last. You remain a person of great mystery at court by your absence there. Why do you not reside in London as do other ladies of your same age? Living out here in the shire, you are far away from any suitors. Unless you have intentionally chosen to live here?" he asked in French, his tone mischievous, yet harmless.

I did not know how to respond to such an overture, so I simply curtsied and smiled, keeping my eyes low to avoid his penetrating gaze.

"Come with me. I should like to introduce my brother, Sir Rupert Fiennes. He has come to stay with us from Kent where he resides with our mother at Hever Castle. You will dine with him this evening. He speaks some Gascon and French, so you two already have something in common."

Sir William led me to a vacant seat on the bench at the opposite end of the table from where my father and Père Charles were to sit. When I arrived at my place, Sir Rupert stood up and bowed, to which I curtsied in return.

Over a lively dinner, our conversation covered many topics. Amongst them were our family home at Rosete, the journey to England, and how I had found the transition to living in the English countryside from that of Gascony. As we spoke, I took in the details of Sir Rupert's face, for he was a ruggedly handsome man, with dark-brown hair and the shadow of a neatly trimmed beard covering the chiselled features of his cheeks and chin. His smile was gracious and sincere and he laughed easily as we spoke. To my surprise I found I enjoyed being in his presence.

Towards the end of our meal, Sir Rupert excused himself from our conversation. He turned to a male guest seated next to him and they began to converse. I could not understand what they said so I finished my meal in silence. As I glanced down the table to Père Charles, looking past the animated faces of Sir William and Lady Margaret's family and guests, it was evident from my chaplain's sombre expression that he was not comfortable in the company in which he was placed. After what he had told me that morning, I could understand why he looked so quiet.

As my attention was drawn back to my own dinner companion, the nature of our discussion took an entirely different tone.

"So tell me, Lady Isabelle, why is it that you prefer the countryside to the city? Do you fear the company of men?" Sir Rupert asked offhandedly, leaning back from the bench and slurring some of his words, for at this point in the evening he had drunk almost the entire pitcher of wine placed at our end of the table.

Shocked by his questions, I was at first unable to utter a response. He continued to demean me.

"Your Ladyship, while it may be customary for ladies of your standing to wear men's clothing and ride their beasts astride in the duchy, you are *now* in England. No lady of noble birth would dare do such a thing in our country, let alone appear at a formal banquet attired in her brother's clothes. Is it true what they say about you? That you are the virgin maiden from Gascony who seeks neither husband nor lover, and prefers to spend time with her horse rather than her suitors? I am afraid I am unable to compete for your affection if it is indeed a beast whose heart you seek. Or is there a man whom you take to your bed in secret, away from the prying eyes of your family and attendants?"

His shift in demeanour and derogatory questions disgusted me. I had been enjoying myself at the banquet in spite of my initial awkward feelings about the way I was dressed. But now I sensed a change that made me ill at ease in his presence, even with members of my household seated in the same room.

"I find your questions inappropriate and rude, Sir Rupert," I began. "I was pleased to make your acquaintance earlier but I am offended that you should talk to me in such a manner. You will please excuse me."

My abrupt reprisal shocked him and he sat speechless as I stood up from the table and quickly left the room, eager to find a servant who could show me to my lodging. Sir Rupert's words had sickened me. So this is how I was to find life in England, I thought to myself. A court of lords and ladies who had nothing better to do than spread wicked lies and untruths about those whom they did not even know! Apart from the one encounter with Sir Henry Lormont in November, I had never met any of these people, yet nonetheless they felt compelled to spread awful rumours about me. Tired and unsure of where to go next in the long hall, I heard footsteps fast approaching.

"Lady Isabelle, please wait for me. What happened? What has caused you to retire so quickly from the banquet?" Père Charles enquired, his voice full of concern as he joined me in the corridor leading away from the great hall.

"I did not mean for you to abandon your place at the feast, Père Charles. Please do not concern yourself with my affairs. I need to take some rest after such a full day," I replied, unable to look him in the eyes as I spoke.

He gently inclined my head towards him with his hand, fastening his eyes on mine.

"Tell me what happened at dinner. I can see something is not right. Shall we take a walk to the stable and visit Peyriac?"

"Yes, let us do that," I replied as I took up his arm.

We found our way to the stable and came upon our horses, groomed and fed for the night, dozing in the corner of their stalls. Upon sensing us nearby, Peyriac woke up and wheeled around, coming to the door and letting out a low nicker of greeting.

After glancing about to ensure that we were alone, I explained what had transpired during my conversation with Sir Rupert. "How cruel must someone be to imply such things when they do not know anything about me and I know nothing about them?"

I turned away from Père Charles and reached out my hand to stroke Peyriac's head.

"What you have shared with me now is most distressing. It is right that I approach your father privately and relate to him Sir Rupert's inappropriate conduct. Will you allow me to speak on your behalf?"

"Yes, I would be grateful if you would describe the course of events at supper to him. Let him decide for himself whether he wishes me to be treated in such a boorish manner by a suitor."

"I shall speak to your father of this matter tonight confidentially, My Lady."

Pausing momentarily, his tone became even more serious. "There is something else of which you should be made aware: I believe I know why I was invited to attend the banquet with your father."

"Oh? Why is that? What else did you learn over dinner?"

"I was sitting near a nobleman named John Paston, an attorney from Norfolk who I believe may be a spy in the commission of Richard of York, seeking to uncover those who are most loyal to Somerset and the Lancastrian dynasty. He said very little over supper and drank no wine, whereas everyone else around me drank heartily and spoke freely.

"As you know, York has been attempting to see his rival Edmund Beaufort of Somerset stripped of his position as the king's chief advisor for many months now. Even after swearing his oath of fealty last November, it is rumoured that York still aspires to take over the running of the country. I believe he has in his employ a network of spies who are collecting the names of those fiercely loyal to the king and Somerset. It appears the Fiennes family may be unaware that by aligning with members of the Beaufort clan they shall ultimately become ensnared in the battle for control of the throne that threatens to bring down the House of Lancaster.

"With their wealth and privileges at King Henry's court, the Fienneses may feel that they are shielded from the consequences of civil war. But I fear we are heading towards a time when Englishmen, former brothers-in-arms in the wars against France, will rise up and fight one another, here in the open fields and towns of our very own country."

Père Charles paused, allowing time for me to digest his observations before continuing, "But even more shocking for me was that tonight I learned that two of the men who murdered my family were the brothers John and Edmund Beaufort, the Dukes of Somerset – indeed, the very same Edmund of Somerset who is now the king's most trusted advisor and someone with whom your father is working closely on His Majesty's Privy Council!"

Upon hearing him mention the names of the two men, I gasped as a cold wave of fear washed over me.

"How did you come to learn so much over supper?" I asked, my tone one of incredulity.

"As the dinner wore on and those around me continued to grow merry from the wine they consumed, John Paston suggested that Edmund of Somerset had blood on his hands from a heinous act, committed with his brother John when he was in his adolescence. From where I sat, those around me fell silent at the utterance of such an accusation, for words spoken against a minister of such high rank as Somerset are tantamount to treason. Sir John de Vere, the Earl of Oxford, who is a keen supporter of both King Henry and Somerset, asked Paston to explain himself and the rumour he had mentioned.

"Paston described the night my family and our household servants were murdered, even naming my father as the person on whom the attack was directed. He claimed that the attack was mounted because of my father's support of peace treaties with France, and because the Beaufort brothers believed that my father possessed a sacred relic so esteemed that its ownership could provide the foundation for a new Church, separate from Rome. Paston referred to the denomination as the Church of England, and whoever is monarch will have complete control of the person appointed to be its head. The artefact of which he speaks is, as you now know, the *Mandylion*. From what he described, it is believed that as the only surviving member of my family I would know where the relic is located. If captured, I could be forced to disclose its whereabouts."

"That is terrible!" I cried. "But surely they were not aware of who you really are. They did not know your true identity."

"I believe the disclosure of such sensitive intelligence tonight was made intentionally. Paston hoped to provoke a reaction from me so that I might be shown to be the Earl of Huntingdon's surviving son. But I carried on eating my meal and showed no visible change in my demeanour upon hearing who had murdered my family."

"What else did he say?" I asked, fearing for the life of my chaplain.

"He continued, describing how, upon his return from serving in France, John Beaufort was overheard by a servant in his household making confession to his uncle, Cardinal Henry Beaufort, about the murders he and his brother had committed. The Duke of Somerset was found dead two days later. Speculation at court has always been that he killed himself over the losses he incurred during his lieutenancy of France, but it would appear that he was also plagued by the demons of the crime he had committed against my family.

"As for the reaction of the other noblemen seated around me, they accused Paston of deceit, claiming that if he continued planting such seeds of sedition they would bring his treasonous claims to Somerset himself. Paston then sat back and finished his meal in silence, having been put in his place by the loyal members of the King's Court, and yet appearing content with the uproar he had caused. I fear that if Paston begins to suspect me, my identity may eventually be called into question by Somerset. And by his very association with me, and the letters of safeguard he arranged for me as we left Bordeaux for England, your father's own life may be at risk."

"Will you tell Father what you have learned?" I asked anxiously.

"Indeed, I shall share what I overheard with him. There is great concern amongst the nobility for the future of England. The king is still without an heir and certain noble families wish to make the crown their own. Eliminating those of us who support the Lancastrian line of succession would make it much easier for one of them to usurp the throne."

"I worry for Father. I fear he may not be aware of the plots that are being devised around him by other members of court."

"Lady Isabelle, be comforted that I shall share with His Lordship all that I know and all that I hear. The last thing I wish is to see any harm come to him, or to any of you, his family," Père Charles said, placing his arm around my back reassuringly.

We sat together in silence, as the consequences of what had been learned at the banquet settled into our minds.

"Come along, Your Ladyship," my chaplain instructed, interrupting my thoughts as he stood and assisted me in doing the same. "We have spent too much time away from the feast; doing so may give those at supper reason to suspect something untoward about us. We should return now and thank our host and hostess for their hospitality."

Arriving back in the great hall, I remained by the door while Père Charles walked to where my father was seated and bent over to whisper a message in his ear.

"I am afraid it has been a long day for us and we wish to retire for the night. We shall see you again in the morning," my father said, directing his comment to our host as he rose to leave the table, his countenance bearing no indication of the message Père Charles had privately imparted.

"We are pleased you could join us this evening, Lord Philippe. Sleep well, Father Charles. Until tomorrow, then." Sir William waved his hand in the direction of one of the servants standing to his side, who approached us and asked us to follow him to our rooms.

———

Upon joining the others in the great hall to break our fast the following morning, I found Sir William and my father deep in discussion by themselves at one end of the table, while Père Charles, Sir Rupert and Lady Margaret, the wife of Baron Saye & Sele, sat quietly talking amongst the guests and family members at the other end. After I had finished my meal, Père Charles approached me, asking me to join him in the chapel for our morning office.

We left the group still eating and conversing, and entered the corridor we had walked through the previous evening upon our arrival, this time turning left at the far end, climbing a vaulted stone stairway to reach the chapel. As we did so, a design in the vaults overhead caught my eye and I stopped momentarily to take a closer view. Four stone bosses were carved with rather arbitrary items: a sheaf of wheat, a crenellated castle tower, a square and compass, and a sheep bearing a rod and standard. I thought nothing more of it at the time and continued to make my way up the long flight of stairs to the privacy afforded by the chapel.

After reciting the liturgy and responses together, we took a few moments for silent meditation. The morning office said, Père Charles turned his attention to his discussion concerning Sir Rupert's inappropriate comments at dinner.

"Your father was most concerned when he heard of your treatment last night, Your Ladyship. He feels responsible for putting you in a position where your reputation might be called into question. We shall leave Broughton this morning as you requested; at the moment, he is simply making apologies to Sir William in the most diplomatic way possible, for he does not wish to compromise his position at court over this incident."

"Thank you for your wise guardianship and counsel. I am grateful to you for explaining what happened last night," I placed my hand on his arm and gave it a gentle squeeze.

"I must admit, what you told me you learned over the course of the meal gives me cause for great worry," I added in a hushed voice.

"We should not speak of it here, Lady Isabelle. I fear not even in the chapel are we free from those who might overhear us."

He directed my attention up the wall behind us, where two wooden shutters opened from a gallery where those who wished to pray in private could do so.

———

A short time later, we stood in the entrance court of the castle, awaiting my father's appearance so we could depart. In the light of day, I took in the architectural details missed in the early-evening shadows as we had entered the night before. Running along the perimeter of the castle ward was a low, crenellated wall with a wall walk. Though it encircled the main building housing the private rooms, kitchen and chapel, its low height indicated that its purpose was more decorative than functional. A moat surrounded the castle, giving the place an air of pastoral serenity, even in the late winter season when the adjacent fields and trees were barren and empty. Presently Father and Sir William emerged from the door of one of the private ranges and came to join us where we stood waiting with our horses.

"It has been a pleasure to welcome you at Broughton. I trust you will have a safe journey back to Boarstall."

"We thank you for your most generous hospitality, Sir William. I shall see you again in London next – we have many more matters to discuss concerning France and Gascony," replied my father. Turning to address us he continued, "Charles and Isabelle, let us be off."

We returned that evening to Boarstall and the quiet life of seclusion from courtiers that suited me best.

XXIII
Spring

O ne week later, the night before he returned to London, my father summoned me to meet him privately after supper. I entered the privy gallery that evening and sat down next to him, where he was already installed comfortably in front of the blazing fire. I took comfort in knowing that my aunt was still in London; I would have my father's attention without her scrutiny or her interfering ways.

"Isabelle, I have asked you to join me because I wish to apologise for the treatment you received while a guest at the residence of Baron Saye & Sele. When I was asked by Sir William to bring you to the banquet to meet his brother, Sir Rupert, I felt it was an appropriate invitation for you to meet a potential suitor. Over dinner that night it became clear to me that Sir William intended for you to become offered in marriage to his brother, and from where I sat it appeared that you were enjoying his company. When Sir William brought up the subject, I heartily agreed that you two should marry. After Charles told me in private of Sir Rupert's disgraceful behaviour towards you I realised the mistake I had made."

"I know you intended me no harm, Father," I replied, reaching across to him and laying my hand upon his. "You wish for me to make a good union for our family with an Englishman of noble birth, as Margaret will no doubt do, and Sarah, too, when she is of age. But I must assure you, I am most content being here at Boarstall. At this time, the thought of marrying someone and bearing his children gives me no pleasure. I apologise, I know this is not the news you wish to hear. I am grateful for the liberty you have provided; I do not wish to disappoint you."

"Isabelle, you will never disappoint me. You are your mother's little scholar, and with each day that passes I come to understand why she called you that. Your love of learning and writing are your two greatest strengths; they are gifts that our Lord has bestowed upon you. Indeed, it was our Lord who at your birth foretold that your life would be devoted to imparting his love to others. Who am I to stand in judgement of you otherwise?"

"Thank you for understanding, Father. I do not yet know how, but someday, somehow, I shall make you proud of your decision to allow me to continue with my scholarship."

"I have no doubt about that, Isabelle. You already honour me with your strong faith and firm courage in times of adversity. You must believe me when I tell you how appreciative I am that you are so like your mother in this regard."

Candelabra stood either side of where we sat; the flickering light from their candles illuminated the space around us. Gazing upon the steady swaying of flames ablaze in the fireplace, we became lost to the calming effect of its soft glow. Only the sounds of the fire as it crackled and hissed broke the comfortable silence that hung in the air between us. After several minutes had passed, I excused myself and kissed my father goodnight, bidding him farewell, for I would not see him again before he left Boarstall at the break of dawn the following day.

———

As the cold winter months faded into those of spring and the days lengthened and warmed, on occasion Père Charles and I would take excursions into the neighbouring village of Thame.

Upon returning home from one such journey in mid-March, we learned that Father had come from London on business matters concerning the running of the estate. Later that evening, after Sarah and Christophe had retired from the dinner table, he sought our advice on the arrangements for a celebration.

"I have decided it is time to host a special feast at Boarstall. King Henry and Queen Margaret will be in attendance, as well as members of their court. I wish to have the royal banquet in a month's time. In my sister's absence I ask that you, Charles, help the head of the household to prepare for the royal visit. Isabelle, I expect you to assist him if necessary since your sister Margaret is unable to do so."

"It will be my pleasure to do as you ask, Your Lordship. Lady Isabelle and I have been waiting for your instruction to host such an event since our arrival here in November."

"Then it is settled. Isabelle, I understand there are many lords who wish to make your acquaintance at the banquet. One in particular, Sir Henry Lormont, Earl of Hillesden, has made himself personally known to me at court. He revealed that he met you in Thame and served as your guide from there to Boarstall. He and the Rede family are to be invited, as are Lord Dunstall and other members of the King's Privy Council and peerage whom you met during the banquet at Broughton Castle. I imagine Margaret will also have many young lords and ladies to invite."

Upon hearing the name Sir Henry Lormont, my voice froze in my throat. Over the course of our first winter and the perils we had faced, I had forgotten the unsettled feeling I had experienced when we first encountered him. Père Charles immediately noticed the shocked expression on my face and quickly changed the subject, while I regained my composure.

"I think some roasted spring lamb, beef marrow fritters, whole sturgeon and baked eel will make a fine menu. Her Ladyship and I have discovered a wine merchant in Thame; we were just there at his stall today, in fact. We shall order three casks of his finest claret. I shall also make arrangements so that we may have proper entertainment for the event – a troop of talented minstrels will make everyone wish to join in the dance."

"I leave it all to your capable oversight, Charles. You have been a part of our family long enough and attended numerous banquets at Rosete. I am certain you know what I expect to have done."

My father's acknowledgement of Père Charles and his contribution to our family made my heart fill with pride; I could see from the smile in his eyes that my chaplain was also pleased by the recognition.

———

A week later, I was up early to pray my morning office before the household awakened. I entered the darkness of the chapel interior and lit a candle on the table by the entrance.

Walking down the centre aisle, I was surprised to find I was not alone. Someone else was already at the altar, and as I drew closer I could hear a muffled whimper coming from him. At first I thought it might be one of our servants or the porter, but as I stepped up to his side I was shocked to find Père Charles there, a blade in his right hand, the skin of his left wrist exposed and bleeding in several places where he had cut himself! Blood trickled down his arm, dripping onto his black robe.

"Père Charles, look at your wrist!" I cried, grabbing the bloodied knife from his hand. "What are you doing? Why are you cutting yourself?"

My chaplain appeared dazed and disoriented, a thin layer of stubble covering his normally clean-shaven face adding to his dishevelled appearance. I reached my arm around him, helping him to stand. With a faint voice he gave me a set of instructions, his body still too weak to move.

"Find me hot water, a clean cloth, some bee balm and fresh spirits from the kitchen. Prepare them and bring them to my room at once. You must hurry. And Isabelle, please forgive me for this."

"Of course I forgive you. Do not trouble yourself with such thoughts. I shall go now and collect those things straight away. But I still cannot comprehend why you would want to hurt yourself. Are you sure you can return to your room on your own?" My mind remained in shock at what I had witnessed.

"Yes, I will need to move slowly, but I can go there unassisted. Your Ladyship, please tell no one what you have witnessed. You will remain my confidante, will you not?" he asked, his voice weak from the painful wounds he had inflicted upon himself.

"Fear not, I shall not reveal your secret." I replied, walking with him to a bench with a back where he could place his hand for balance. Stepping away from him I turned towards the door and rushed to the kitchen, his blade still in my hand.

Thankfully none of the servants had yet appeared and I was alone to collect the items. Returning quickly up the stairs leading to his chamber, I knocked first and then entered, finding him seated on the edge of his bed, gazing vacantly across the room. I placed my tray on the table along with the blade, and he rose to join me. Taking a seat on the bench near the window, he cleaned and dressed his wounds himself. In time, I broke the silence.

"What happened to you in the chapel this morning? Can you tell me why you were cutting your wrist?"

"I wish I had an answer – the events are still unclear to me, even now. I awoke early this morning hearing voices shrieking in my head. They told me they were coming for me; I had to do something to escape the noise that filled my thoughts. I grabbed the only weapon I had, my blade, and ran down the stairs. But the voices only increased, becoming louder and louder as I stepped into the yard. Soon they were all around me, encircling me, taunting me, and then I saw faces appear before me, the faces of death that my family and our servants bore the morning I found them slaughtered. I ran into the chapel to seek the Lord's mercy in evading the phantoms."

"You poor soul! I cannot imagine how frightening that must have been to be awakened in such a way!" I exclaimed, my voice tender.

"Then, as I kneeled to pray in the dark, I heard the voice of a man whisper in my ear. He instructed me to take the blade and slit my wrist so that I might kill myself before they found me and did it themselves. So I obeyed, fearing the assassins who had come for me. I felt my body grow weak and my head became light as the edge of the knife pierced my skin. I found that once I had started I could not stop. By attempting to end my life I felt empowered over those who sought to harm me. I had almost sliced through my vein when you discovered me."

Père Charles hung his head in shame. His tears fell freely as his shoulders slumped forward. He could not look me in the face.

"Please accept my apology, Lady Isabelle. Please forgive me for my repeated sins; for placing myself in such a dishonourable position. I do not understand what is happening to me – I cannot control these demons who are plaguing my soul."

"What can I do to comfort you? What can I do to help?" I asked, reaching out and touching his arm gently.

He raised his head and looked at me as he replied. "I fear there is nothing you or anyone else can do. I am unable to control these thoughts of great unworthiness that race through my mind. I am constantly burdened by the knowledge that my life was spared when all my family was killed around me. Why, oh why, did I not stay and help my brother? Why was I able to escape the assassins as a boy?"

His voice trembled as he spoke these last words, and in that moment I witnessed him recede into the depths of his traumatic memories of murder and death. We sat together in silence; his vacant stare made it clear that he could not see me there in the room with him.

Believing he was still lost in his thoughts, I stood up and gathered the items he had asked me to bring from the kitchen, placing them back onto the tray. As I walked towards the door, Père Charles sprang up and rushed to me, blocking me with his body before I could leave the room. His voice was at once strong and firm.

"Your Ladyship, I must ask you again to keep this episode between us. Please do not share what I have done with anyone."

"Not even with my father, Père Charles?" I asked in a small voice.

"No, Lady Isabelle! No! I am afraid I cannot allow you to do that!" Père Charles growled aggressively, grabbing my wrist and twisting it sharply until I squealed in pain, upsetting the items on the tray and nearly scattering them across the floor.

"I will tell him myself if and when I believe the time is right. I insist that you must keep this between us. Do you understand me?"

My chaplain's eyes bore a look of rage that I had never seen before. I nodded my head in reply, swallowing hard, afraid to say anything else in response.

"Good, we comprehend each other. Carry on, then. I shall see you in the chapel with the rest of your family for morning Eucharist shortly."

He released me from his grasp and stood to the side, opening his door, casting his eyes away as I passed by him.

Walking slowly down the stairs, I took several deep breaths to regain my composure, still in a state of shock over what I had just observed and the sudden shift in my chaplain's demeanour. My mind was fraught with fear – he had never spoken or behaved in such a physically threatening manner to me. I looked down at my throbbing wrist. It was red and sore from where he had wrenched it tightly.

I felt conflicted – I could not decide whether it was better to tell someone what I had observed or do as I had been asked and believe that he would confess his behaviour to my father himself.

Indeed, who could I tell at Boarstall? Certainly none of our household. Knowing how my aunt despised Père Charles, I could not entrust her with knowing that he was demonstrating the onset of some form of madness.

For the first time since learning of his tragic past I felt burdened by the confidence he had placed in me. At that moment, I knew I must call upon my faith in the Lord. I closed my eyes and reflected upon the simple beauty captured in the opening line of chant, "*Quemadmodum desiderat cervus ad fontes aquarum, ita desiderat anima mea ad te, Deus*; As the hart desireth the water-brooks: so longeth my soul after thee, O God." Repeating the line of the chant several times in my mind I felt calmed and returned to a state of peace.

Later, during our service in the chapel, I noticed that Père Charles had covered his left wrist with a piece of black fabric so that it blended in with his clerical robe. I found it odd that after nearly taking his own life earlier that morning he gave no indication of a man whose troubled soul was possessed. His recitation of the liturgy that morning was flawless, something that did not seem possible for someone who had tried to kill himself only hours earlier.

After my family and our servants had left the chapel following the service, he approached and sat down on the bench next to me. With a quiet voice, he sought my forgiveness.

"Please, Lady Isabelle, allow me to humbly apologise for my behaviour in my room earlier. You were very good to help me. I am so grateful that you intervened this morning. You have saved me again. I should not have treated you the way I did as you left. I assure you, I shall tell your father when the time is right to do so. I shall leave it to him to decide whether he wishes for me to continue to serve in his household."

With my eyes locked steadily upon his, I took my chaplain's hands in my own as I felt the Lord's presence in my heart.

"Know that I am increasingly frightened by the changes I am seeing in you, in the way you act and the voices you hear that tell you to commit such atrocious sins. Remember that in you is life eternal, for the love of Christ is a flame that enlightens your soul far stronger than the evil voices of the demons who taunt you. As you keep your love fixed upon the Beloved, so will he return his blessings and mercy upon you, and he will shield you from the feelings of unworthiness that cause your mind to weaken. Through Christ's love you will be saved, and through my devotion to the Lord I shall always remain your friend. Let us never forget, the fire of the Holy Spirit engulfs us both with its flame; together we are drawn deeper into Christ and the mercy bestowed upon us by his Father."

Père Charles gently squeezed my hands, a silent acknowledgement of the divine love and wisdom I had imparted.

XXIV
A Royal Banquet

15 April 1453, Boarstall Castle

The morning of our banquet I initially occupied myself with Sarah and Christophe, staying clear of our servants, who were hurriedly making the final preparations around our home – all the fireplaces fully stocked with enough wood to keep the fires burning throughout the evening; extra tables and benches carried upstairs to be set for the supper; construction of a temporary raised dais from which the king and queen would preside over the meal. That day, new banners displaying the d'Albret Courteault coat of arms under the royal seal and arms of King Henry VI and the red rose of the House of Lancaster were hung from the barbican parapet to demonstrate our family's loyalty to the English king.

A few hours later, with our servants and cook assisting us, Père Charles and I oversaw delivery of the food that we had ordered at the market in Thame, including the spring lamb, barrels of Bordeaux wine, fish and cheese. As we worked, the aroma of baking bread and roasting lamb escaped through the door and windows of our ground-floor kitchen, the savoury smells making my appetite swell as I anticipated the delicious feast to be consumed that evening.

Close to midday, the minstrels, grooms and extra servants we had hired to help serve our guests began to arrive and assemble, ready to be given their instructions. Amidst all the commotion, the familiar faces of Margaret and Johan suddenly appeared in the doorway of the kitchen, silently smiling, waiting for someone to look up and notice them. I was the first to do so.

"Why, sister Margaret, brother Johan, you both have come! Welcome!" I exclaimed, rushing forward to embrace them.

"Greetings to you, fair sister," Margaret replied, addressing me warmly in return. "Boarstall Castle is as our father described it; I am so happy we may call it our home. It reminds me of Rosete. I am sure you must love living here."

"I do love it here. The longer we remain, the more I hope we never have to move again… unless of course we return to Rosete!" I said, and we both giggled.

"I shall leave you two," Johan began, looking out across the courtyard filled with the noise and activities of preparation for the arrival of the royal party later that day. "I wish to see whether any of my friends from court have arrived."

"Until later then, brother Johan. What a joy that our family is together again!" I called out as he stepped from the kitchen.

"Come, let me look at you," Margaret insisted as she twirled me around in front of her. "You are so grown up! I believe you have matured since I saw you last in London! You are now sixteen and look what a beautiful young lady you have become," she observed, her eyes shining.

"Oh, I do not know about that," I replied, casting my glance aside, embarrassed. "But do tell me about you, and about Sir William, too. Is it true what our father says? Is he courting you?"

I took up my sister's arm and led her through the groups of minstrels and servants who stood milling about in the inner ward.

Once we were installed in the privacy of my bedchamber with the door closed, we sat together on the end of my bed and she began to tell me all about London.

"Isa, I must tell you what has happened. I have wanted to tell you for so long, but there never seemed enough time to come and visit Boarstall. With my work at court and serving Her Majesty, Queen Margaret, I have found my new life. And that life includes Sir William. He is a kind man who has never married, though there have been many families who have wished to be aligned with his through marriage. Her Ladyship cautioned me that I should take his affection seriously, since I would find no more honourable a man in all of England. I heeded her advice and he has been my suitor ever since."

Margaret paused and took my hands in hers as she shared her special news with me.

"Isabelle, we plan to marry. William will join us here this afternoon and before the banquet he intends to ask Father for my hand."

I squealed with joy at her news.

"Oh, Margaret, how excited I am for you," I said, embracing her. "I look forward to meeting him. He must be a most gracious man if you are so in love."

Margaret nodded in agreement, too overcome with emotion to speak. We sat for several moments in the peace and relative quiet of the room, before she described in detail what it was like to serve as a lady-in-waiting. I found my sister's stories of the lords and ladies who served at court intriguing, though admittedly I remained grateful for my life away from the scandals and games played by courtiers against each other.

When we returned to the inner ward a short time later, Margaret was joyfully reunited with Sarah and Christophe. She answered their many questions about her newfound life serving at court in London. In the meantime, I assisted Père Charles in directing the servants, who were busy arranging the inner ward and great hall, now filled with much noise and activity as the final preparations were underway. By mid-afternoon we were ready for our guests to arrive.

Returning to my room, I quickly changed into a new emerald-green silk and velvet gown that had been made especially for our royal banquet. I let down my long blonde hair out of its plait and donned a jewelled headband. Looking out of the window in my bedchamber, I saw my family standing together, talking. Hurrying to pin a pearl-encrusted hair net around my loosely wavy locks as I left my room, I rushed downstairs to join them. Everyone was in a jovial mood as guests began to arrive on horseback and in carriages.

A few moments later, Père Charles emerged from the chapel. He had chosen to wear formal clerical attire for the royal banquet and was dressed in a royal-blue velvet tunic with gold cord trim and a matching velvet belt. The high collar of his surcoat framed his face and blond hair perfectly, and as I cast my eyes down his legs I saw he wore dark-purple-coloured silk leggings and long boots. Normally dressed in the plain black robes of his clerical vocation, I had never seen him look so elegant. I was instantly drawn to my handsome chaplain, and yet I found I could not even find the words to tell him so.

"Good afternoon, everyone," his deep voice greeted us. "I trust we are all in good spirits?" he asked, wearing a broad smile and embracing my sister. "Lady Margaret, how blessed we are to have you with us on this special occasion."

As he spoke we were joined by Madame de Tastes and Aunt Christine, who had journeyed together from London by separate coach from Margaret and Johan.

"What a pleasure it is to see you again, Your Ladyship, and welcome to Boarstall." I directed my greeting to Madame de Tastes.

"Thank you. I am so glad to be here with all of you, too," Madame de Tastes replied, seeing my sister's face aglow and knowing the joyous news that would soon be announced.

Then I turned to politely address my aunt, but she looked away and barely acknowledged me.

After our exchange of greetings, conversation amongst members of the group resumed, and Père Charles turned his attention to me. Once we were standing slightly apart, he cupped his hand under my elbow and put his lips close to my neck.

"I must tell you, Lady Isabelle, you look exquisite this afternoon," he softly whispered to me. "You will attract much attention tonight, but know that I shall admire you from afar."

As he finished speaking to me, our first guests arrived. The strikingly handsome Sir William Talbot rode in under the barbican with his retinue of six men-at-arms, dismounting when he came upon our group. Our grooms led their horses away as he approached Margaret, bowing to her and then taking up her hand and kissing it. He then did the same to Madame de Tastes and Aunt Christine. Margaret introduced him to each of us, after which he asked to speak to our father in private. They excused themselves and retired to the chapel, the only secluded place left in the castle with all the activities under way for the banquet.

Father and Sir William returned from their private discussion to join us in the inner ward just as a loud clattering of hooves and the sound of cries were heard in the distance. Shortly afterwards, a party of twelve carriages and riders entered Boarstall. The king and queen had arrived followed by the Duke of Somerset, the Earl of Oxford, Baron and Lady Saye & Sele and members of the Percy and Neville families, in addition to other lords and ladies from the court in London. Suddenly Boarstall was alive with joyous activity and boisterous shouts as friends greeted each other.

Père Charles took command of the moment and summoned the musicians and minstrels to perform for our royal guests. Our servants began pouring wine and very soon my siblings and I were caught up in the excitement of the festive atmosphere, enhanced by the presence of the king and his courtiers. I looked over to see our father greeting the king and queen in turn. Standing next to His and Her Majesties, I watched as my father signalled for us and Père Charles to join him.

"King Henry and Queen Margaret, may I have the honour of presenting my sister, Lady Christine d'Albret, and my children, Lord Johan, Lady Isabelle, Lord Christophe and Lady Sarah? You have already made the acquaintance of my daughter Lady Margaret at your court in London."

As each one of us was introduced in turn, we bowed or curtsied accordingly. Meeting the king and queen for the first time at Boarstall was an event I would never forget. They were both so young; the king was only a few years older than Père Charles and his queen appeared to be only a little older than my sister Margaret.

"And may I present Father Charles Bonvinac, a most trusted member of our household. I entrust to him the running of my estate and the tutelage of my children."

"Why, Lord Philippe, you never mentioned you had such a fine member of the clergy in your employ," began Queen Margaret, her voice sultry as she cast her gaze in the direction of our chaplain. Père Charles bowed his head solemnly in acknowledgement.

"Father Charles, perhaps you might consider joining our household as a member of the Chapel Royal?" she enquired. "Do give serious consideration to my proposition, for I am in need of a young priest in whom I may confess my most private matters."

"Your Majesty, I am humbled and honoured by your invitation," Père Charles replied, bowing again, this time deeply. "I shall give your proposal of service much thought and reply in due course."

"Pray do," Queen Margaret replied with a seductive smile.

"We are most pleased to meet you here at Boarstall this evening. I cannot think of a more deserving family to occupy this royal property," King Henry stated, oblivious to his wife's flirtatious nature. He turned to address my siblings and me.

"As you are aware, your father has proven his loyalty to our country while in Gascony. He served under my lieutenants and the constable of Bordeaux for many years. Now that he is in England I rely on his advice and wisdom regarding matters concerning the war with France. I trust you all will be happy in your new home and country." King Henry's sincerity was evident in his warm demeanour.

As the king spoke to us, I glanced over his shoulder and saw his queen and the Duke of Somerset whispering to each other behind his back. Her Majesty let out a coquettish giggle that went unnoticed by all except me. Somerset then kissed her on the ear and she gave a slight squeal as she playfully slapped his face away from hers. The mark of her deception was apparent, for although I could not tell for certain, the queen appeared quite full in her chest and a little round hump lay about her waist, as if she were early with child. I privately gave a quick prayer of thanksgiving, for what England needed most at that time was news of an heir to the throne, whether it was a bastard child or not.

"If it pleases Your Majesties, we shall begin the celebration." Father turned to the musicians and requested they stop playing while he made an announcement. Addressing the guests and his family, he conveyed a quiet sense of composure and assurance.

"I wish to share some joyful news with all of you in attendance this evening," he began, a smile beaming across his face. "I have just given my approval that my eldest daughter Lady Margaret and Sir William Talbot are to be wed. They wish to share their happiness with all of you this evening, and at the ceremony of their marriage this summer. So, please, everyone, raise your cups and join with me in toasting their blessed union."

A raucous cheer rose up from the party around us, led by His Majesty the King. It gave me great joy to see members of the King's Court and English nobility honouring Margaret and her betrothed. As the crowd parted, the couple approached each other and Sir William gently laid a kiss upon Margaret's lips. Such an open sign of affection on his part brought even more cheers from our many guests. The musicians suddenly took up their instruments and began to play again. I felt a hand graze my back and, surprised, I turned around. To my horror, I found myself face to face with Sir Henry Lormont.

"You must be happy for your older sister, Lady Isabelle," he said with an air of confidence and a sinister smile. "Tell me, what would it require for someone to seek your hand in marriage?"

"Why, Sir Henry, I thought you would know the answer," I replied smugly, remembering the rumours spread about me through the court in London. "According to what has been said of me, unlike my sister, Lady Margaret, I do not intend to marry anyone, apart from my horse." I searched the crowd, looking for Père Charles.

Before Sir Henry could offer a response, we were joined by a group of young lords, including Sir Rupert Fiennes, whom I had met previously at Broughton Castle. The men wore broad grins as they approached us, as if in on a secret together.

"What lies are you telling the fair Lady Isabelle d'Albret Courteault, Sir Henry?" began Sir Rupert haughtily, as he advanced and stood between us, blocking Sir Henry from me with his body. Turning then to face me, he presented the other members of his party.

"Allow me to introduce some associates, My Lady. This is Lord Crispin of Dunstall, Lord Malcolm of Stroud and Lord Edward of Restormel. As you know, my brother has worked closely with your father to ensure that you and your family are well cared for in this country. You may trust in me to continue his work. Whatever you desire, Lady Isabelle, it shall be yours."

I was momentarily overcome by his attention. I smiled graciously and continued scanning the crowd of courtiers for my chaplain, but he was nowhere to be found.

"That is most considerate of you, Sir Rupert. Should I seek your assistance, I trust that you or your companions would help me," I replied as I took a step back from the group.

"You know, Sir Rupert, *dear* friend," Sir Henry began with arrogance, "I met Lady Isabelle many months ago. We travelled up from Thame together and I made certain that she found Boarstall without any incident. Where were you at the time? In London fraternising with the ladies at court, no doubt. She is quite taken with me; I am afraid you are too late."

Upon hearing this, Lord Edward interjected. "I do believe the choice is up to the lady as to with whom she wishes to associate, Sir Henry."

"You will have to excuse him, Your Ladyship," Lord Malcolm warned. "You see, Sir Henry will often say things that are untrue and in the end he simply reveals himself to be nothing more than a complete imbecile. Please do heed our advice and stay well clear of him in the future."

"I thank you all for showing me such concern," I replied. "However, as I imagine Sir Rupert has shared with you, I am quite content with my life here at Boarstall. Please do not take offence

242

or misinterpret my lack of interest in being courted by you. I am certain you are all gracious gentlemen who will find suitable brides amongst the ladies at court in London."

I had no sooner finished speaking to my group of suitors when we were called to supper in the great hall. I excused myself and went in search of Père Charles. I found him, standing quite apart from the crowd, looking rather dejected.

"Why, whatever is the matter?" I said, extending my arm and placing my hand upon his in a show of concern. "Why do you stand over here by yourself? I looked for you earlier when Sir Henry and his associates surrounded me after the toast to my sister and Lord William."

"Pray, forgive me, Lady Isabelle," Père Charles began, casting his glance over the guests making their way to the great hall staircase. "I feel rather uncomfortable in the presence of those who are of much greater youth and rank than me. I am only your chaplain and guardian. What business have I interrupting the attention of so many fine suitors? I no longer have my title to give me courage in the presence of such an entourage."

He looked away, his face bearing the full import of his deep sadness. I ached to put my arms around him, to comfort him and tell him he was the only lord whose company I desired. But with so many witnesses standing nearby, I dared not step any closer.

"You must be my partner at supper; you must sit next to me. Must I beg? Do come with me and be my companion this evening."

Père Charles's expression softened.

"Lady Isabelle, it will be an honour to accompany you at supper, you may rely on that," he replied, offering me his arm.

"Let us move upstairs, then, and enjoy the rest of the evening together," I said, smiling, and I took up his arm as he escorted me across the now deserted inner ward.

The ceremonial banquet began by passing the ancient and ceremonial horn of ownership between Lord Thomas Rede and King Henry, and then from King Henry to Father. As of that night he accepted the horn and the rights and entitlements thereof, which included an English title: he became Philippe d'Albret Courteault, Lord of Rosete & Boarstall. Meanwhile our guests enjoyed themselves with the rich selection of foods, hearty wine and festive music we provided. Père Charles sat at the high table with my family, Sir William, the king and queen, and Madame de Tastes. Our honoured guests, including the Duke of Somerset, the Earl of Oxford, Baron and Lady Saye & Sele, Lord and Lady Dunstall, and members of the Rede family, sat amongst other members of the peerage and royal household.

Following supper, the musicians took up their instruments and the servants moved the tables and benches to the side walls of the hall, leaving the centre of the room open for dancing. The king and queen were asked to preside over the festivities. I stayed to watch as the first dancers made two large circles of eight participants each, their left arms outstretched to the centre like the spokes of a wheel, their bodies moving rhythmically in unison to the cadence of the music. I had never witnessed an English dance before and I found the intricacy of the steps fascinating. All our guests knew where to place their feet and when, for they were by no means novices to this form of entertainment. They clapped their hands and swung around as if on cue, with one of the musicians singing the words that brought a smile to our guests' faces.

After the first dance had ended I excused myself, intending to say my evening office in the chapel and then visit Peyriac in the stable, thereby avoiding being asked to join in the dance by my group of suitors. As I rose to leave, Père Charles looked up at me and I nodded my head subtly in his direction.

Moments after entering the inner ward, I heard men's footsteps quickly coming up behind me.

"Would you care to join me in the chapel for our devotions?" I asked without turning around, expecting to hear the deep voice of my chaplain in reply.

"Finally, we are alone, Lady Isabelle," came the response that froze me in the place where I stood.

"Why are you not dancing with the other guests?" I demanded as I turned to face Sir Henry, wondering what had prevented my dinner companion from joining me.

He slowly inched closer to me, a menacing expression appearing across his face.

"When I saw you leave, I took it as my cue to come and follow you. I will make you submit to me, and you will say nothing."

I felt trapped, as a rabbit becomes caught in a snare. I could not move. I was too frightened even to look at him. His face and mouth were so close to mine that I could smell the stench of alcohol on his breath. Overpowering me, he forcibly grabbed both of my wrists with one hand, binding my arms above my head as he pinned my body against the wall. I let out a cry of pain. My thoughts turned to how Margaret had described her treatment by Count Bertram during her marriage. Terrorised with panic, I felt his fingers move across my bodice then grope my breast as they continued upward. His hand found my neck and he was about to press his lips to mine when Père Charles came rushing up to us.

"Lady Isabelle, there you are." He reached my side just in time to make Sir Henry recoil, dropping his hands and taking a step back from me. "I am terribly sorry for my delay. You do still wish for me to lead you in compline this evening?"

"Why, yes, please," I sighed, stepping behind my chaplain, weakened from the assault by Sir Henry, yet relieved that my companion had appeared in time.

Sir Henry looked at him and then at me, seemingly trying to decide whether I was meant to have private worship with my chaplain at that particular moment. Once he realised I intended to remain in the company of Père Charles, he slowly began to back away.

Pointing his finger first at Père Charles and then me he continued, "I know about you two now. Neither of you will escape me. I will be back for you." He looked at me directly as he imparted his final words, his voice low and threatening.

He then turned and stormed away.

Père Charles could see I was in a state of shock at what had just occurred. He wrapped his arm around me as I buried my face in the soft velvet pile of his outer garment. Kissing my forehead, he whispered, "Forgive me, I am so sorry for what just happened."

Taking up my hand in his, he guided me to the chapel. We entered in silence and lit several candles before both kneeling at the altar, where he began to recite the comforting and familiar liturgy which included reciting the *Magnificat* and *Nunc Dimittis*.

Hearing his voice in the sanctity and safety of our chapel, after such an ordeal with Sir Henry, I closed my eyes, my mind deep in meditation. I did not notice that he had stopped praying aloud until I felt him wipe away the tears that fell from my eyes.

"There now, Lady Isabelle. Here, come close to me; you are safe now."

Securing me in his embrace, I felt his lips softly brush against my hair.

"I wish I had been able to follow you out of the hall immediately. His Majesty and your father delayed me as I attempted to leave the dance. If I were not bound by the rules of my vocation, I would have taken on Sir Henry and flogged him for how he treated you. The man is wicked; you are right to be fearful of him. I am so sorry for what you endured. It should have never happened."

I leaned against his shoulder, still shaken from my earlier encounter.

"Lady Isabelle, you realise I must tell your father about your assault. Since he serves with Sir Henry at court it would not be right to keep this from him."

"No, I cannot allow you to do that." I sat up, pulling away from him and collecting myself. "I believe that Sir Henry knows who you are. It is in the way he regards you – I can sense that he met you sometime, maybe in Oxford. Or Paris. Sir Henry can ruin my father's reputation at court. Please, I beg you, what happened tonight must remain between us."

"Very well. I shall consider your feelings again in the morning, and make my decision then. As for now, shall we check on Peyriac together?"

I nodded in silent agreement, and he carefully helped me to stand. As we stepped through the chapel doorway into the castle ward we were stopped by my aunt, who stood blocking our path.

"I knew I would find you two here. Prayer? At this hour, while your father is hosting a royal banquet upstairs?" she began, her tone incriminating. "Why do you two secret yourselves away? In particular, you, niece, you should be with your family, entertaining our royal guests and the members of their court. Leave your chaplain this instant and return to the celebration at once!"

"If I may interject, Your Ladyship," said Père Charles with conviction, "Lady Isabelle sought the peace of the chapel for solitude and prayer, as she often does in these circumstances. I have cared for her since her childhood and she does not express an interest in participating in song and dance. Her father permits her to remain in my guardianship during such events, as she will do again tonight."

With an expression of disbelief, my aunt replied with disgust, "I see. So be it, then; I cannot force you to return with me, Isabelle. But know that I am watching you both. Your friendship is most unconventional and rumours are certain to circulate amongst members of the court as a result of your absence tonight. There will come a day when you will no longer be free to live by the customs of your Gascon heritage, Isabelle. You must accept that we are in a new country, with traditions to which all young ladies of noble birth must conform. Margaret adopted these immediately and I expect you to do the same. Do not dare to do anything that might bring shame upon your family," my aunt warned me before turning and making her way back to the great hall.

After the alarming confrontation with Aunt Christine, my heart was divided. I knew what she said was true. My absence at the banquet was certain to give rise to speculation about my activities with our chaplain, feeding my group of suitors with even more about which to gossip. Yet joining the group of courtiers assembled at the banquet that evening would serve me no purpose. I could not imagine how any of them could relate to what it was like to carry the love of the Lord, as I did, in one's heart. I wished to be set apart from those around me who participated in activities that went against the teachings of God's grace and mercy. From what my sister had described to me earlier that day in private, the young lords and ladies at court were full of debauchery and lust. I wanted no part of that life.

The remainder of the evening was spent in the stable, away from the festivities, while the sounds of our guests and musicians could be heard floating across the castle's inner ward. I remembered my curiosity about the lyrics of the first dance and asked Père Charles to translate them for me.

"Well, to begin with, it is a traditional song that musicians will perform at the start of most dances. The verses relate the words of a famous poem. A fair maiden from the grange falls in love with a handsome young man dressed as a pauper whom she sees at market one day. He invites her to join him at a special banquet that night and she gladly accepts, taking no care that he is penniless and without any finery to wear. It is only later, when she appears at the dance, that she learns he is actually a prince. He is so taken by her striking beauty and kind heart that he seeks her hand in marriage. The song ends with a stanza dedicated to true love, finding a prince and fair maid through the steps of the dance."

"Oh my, that is rather complicated! Perhaps I shall enjoy these English dances much more when I can understand the meaning of the words being sung."

Sitting together on a rug opened across the floor of the stable, my head resting comfortably on his shoulder as we leaned our backs against Peyriac's stall for support, he began to relate from memory full passages from *The Canterbury Tales*. I felt my love for my chaplain intensify as I closed my eyes, listening in comfort to his eloquent and expressive voice narrate the first three tales.

Later that night, as the celebration drew to a close, our guests could be heard moving downstairs into the inner ward. We cautiously departed from the stable, careful to remain unnoticed amongst the crowd. Together we made our way across the inner ward to the stairway leading to our separate bedchambers.

Père Charles walked me to my door, where he stopped and bowed. Then he took up my hand and kissed it. "You are an elegant lady, full of grace. It was a privilege to be your escort this evening."

"The honour was mine. I am indebted to you for your protection and friendship this night. I pray I do not need your guardianship in such a way again."

"Should you find yourself in danger, you need only beckon, Lady Isabelle," he replied, before retreating quietly away to walk up the stairs to his room.

XXV
Innocence Lost

Père Charles honoured my request and said nothing to my father about Sir Henry's assault the night of the feast. With the royal party now behind us, in the days following the banquet, Margaret, Aunt Christine and Madame de Tastes began at once to make plans for the summer wedding. My sister sought my opinion on certain details, and I felt privileged to be included in the discussion of her forthcoming celebration. The month of April wore on and eventually the time came for the group to return to London. Word had now spread amongst the members of King Henry's court that Sir William and Lady Margaret were to be wed, and their many companions wished to offer their congratulations and share in the engagement festivities.

Johan returned to court immediately after the royal celebration, eager to make new acquaintances with other noblemen and prepare for the coming summer progress. That left Margaret, Lady Bernadette and Father to return to London; Aunt Christine decided to remain with us in the country. Once the party of three had departed, a tranquil atmosphere returned to Boarstall. I resumed writing in my journal and taking long rides exploring the nearby countryside and forest. Père Charles once more took to instructing us in our daily lessons in Latin, English, rhetoric and logic. I made a point of staying out of my aunt's surveillance and with the days increasingly longer as the spring season wore on, I gradually spent more time away from Boarstall in the afternoon. Sometimes Père Charles would accompany me and we would explore the country-side around Brill or the wooded depths of Bernwood Forest. But lately the bookkeeping necessary for managing our estate kept him occupied, and I was often unaccompanied on my frequent rides.

On one fine, clear afternoon in late April, I set out on Peyriac, planning to look for a convenient place to sit and write in my journal. I rode him for a few miles before dismounting in the shade of some saplings by a stream. As I watched him drinking deeply from the shallow creek that flowed leisurely by, I recalled the weeks leading up to Margaret's engagement, intending to record my observations in my journal. There were many particulars I wished to remember and I added more details to earlier entries as they came to mind. The combination of warm weather and fresh country air soon enveloped me and my thoughts began to wander. I lay on my back, my face lifted to watch the sea of little white clouds that drifted indolently above my head. I closed my eyes for a moment, enjoying the peacefulness of my pastoral refuge.

The next thing I heard was the sound of Peyriac as he grazed nearby on the tender grass upon which I lay. Standing up, I noticed that considerable time had passed during my nap. The sun had moved further down in the sky and it was time for me to return home. I collected my journal and writing instruments, placed them in my saddlebag and then mounted Peyriac.

A short time later, as the sun hovered along the horizon and dusk approached with its telltale shades of pink and golden-orange light spreading across the evening sky, I arrived in the dimly lit stable, still sleepy from my nap, and proceeded to put Peyriac away in his stall. At that hour of the day our servants were busily preparing the meal in the kitchen that would follow our evening prayer service in the chapel. I dropped my saddlebag behind a great barrel of oats. As I was about to reach down and scoop out a serving, Sir Henry Lormont leaped out from behind the barrel, surprising me.

"Ah!" I shrieked, catching my breath and dropping the scoop, scattering a sea of grain across the stable floor. "What are you doing here?" I demanded.

"You know what I am here for. Do not dare play innocent with me, Lady Isabelle," he sneered maliciously. "At your banquet you pretended not to show interest in me. You attempted to shame me in the presence of my associates and later before your chaplain."

As he spoke, he stepped closer until he was standing directly in front of me, his hands covered in thick leather gloves. He reeked of ale, and the sour stench of his breath reminded me of our previous encounter. My thoughts turned to my chaplain, whom I expected to appear in the doorway of the stable at any moment.

"My family awaits my company in the chapel. Go now and leave me in peace!" My voice grew louder and more high-pitched with every word. "Why do you continue to pursue me when you have your choice of many ladies at court? You must believe me when I say I do not seek your attention or that of anyone else!"

"That is a lie. You are no different from the other ladies-in-waiting I know. You taunt me with your prudish ways, but you shall learn to do as you are told when you are forced to succumb to a man's will. I know you have a lover – no maiden as fair as you would still be a virgin at your age. Who is he? A local boy from Thame? One of the servants whom you take to your bed when the rest of your household is asleep? Or is it that priest with whom you are always seen? I, too, would join the brothers in the Church if it meant I was able to fornicate with the likes of you!"

"You wicked man! How dare you talk to me in such a way!"

I attempted to scream for help but before I could make a sound he pressed one hand around my head while the other covered my nose and mouth to prevent me from uttering any noise. Glaring at me, he continued his derisive commentary.

"I have watched you two for many months, as you visited the market in Thame together and took your long rides to Brill through your countryside estate and Bernwood Forest; you innocently assumed that you travelled undetected and unobserved. Your laughter and gaiety when together reveal a far more intimate relationship than you suspect others can detect. But I was right all along – you two share a secret liaison. It was I who spread those rumours about your chastity at court so that no other nobleman would take you as their wife," he added with a wicked smile.

Snarling at me, he forced my arms behind my back. I spat in his face, yet that only caused his fury to increase. I felt the sting of pain as he hit me hard across the side of my head with the back of his hand. Dazed, I slumped to the floor. In my momentary weakness he bent down and grasped both my arms. Holding them behind my back with one hand, he stepped forward and used his other to put his blade to my throat.

"Do not dare to defy me. Do not utter a sound or I shall slit your throat immediately, as I have done to others who have disobeyed," he said with a grimace, before placing the knife between his teeth and forcing a shred of cloth into my mouth.

Turning me around, Sir Henry pushed me face down into the hay piled outside Peyriac's stall. Reaching into a leather pouch tied about his waist, he pulled out a coarse braided rope made of rough twine and metal wire with barbed spikes that ripped open the skin. He tightly bound my wrists with it. I could feel the sharpness of the cord as it cut deep under my flesh with every twist I made to try to free myself. Blood coursed from the wounds opening in my wrists. I lay there, in such agony from the pain of the wounds that I was unable to look, unable to cry out, unable to even move.

But he had no intention of stopping what he had started.

"It is not marriage I seek from you, for I know your little secret. The man whom you call your chaplain, your tutor, your friend – he is none of these, he is a traitor to our kingdom. I knew I would one day place him. The Duke of Somerset has confirmed his identity. His spies intercepted correspondence from the constable of Bordeaux to others in London, confirming it was him. He sent me to intercept you when you arrived in Thame. The more we spoke during our initial encounter on the ride to Boarstall, the more I was reminded of a story my deceased father once told me when I was a young boy. Your priest is the son of an apostate and escaped the murder of his family in Cambridgeshire. We have searched for him throughout the realm for nearly two decades, and here he returns, right under my nose.

"My father was there the night members of your chaplain's household were murdered. I bear his legacy upon my shoulders – that should I ever encounter Lord Richard Goodwyn I am to complete the task and assassinate him myself. Since he has evaded my attempts these past few months I shall take your life in his place. He will no doubt suffer from the loss of your soul and will seek to confront me. At last! He will be forced to disclose the secret he guards!"

Sir Henry then pushed me roughly onto my back as I felt the blade of his knife slash the inside of my legs, near my groin. Laughing as I writhed in agony beneath him, he continued to taunt me.

"Where is your chaplain now? Where is your God to save you? You see? There is no one to answer your cries for mercy! May you bleed to death!"

In response to the actions of my assailant, at that very instant the Lord sent me a new vision, of Christ at the moment of his greatest suffering upon the cross. I felt the acute pain of what the Son of God suffered in the Passion when the crown of thorns was pressed down upon his head by his executioners with such force that the sharpened tips pierced his skull, filling his eyes with blood. In despair and with my mind focused on the torment Christ had endured for the sins of mankind, I lost consciousness, with no memory of the horrors that were to follow.

XXVI
Silence

Gentle Reader,

The following two chapters are based on the observations shared later with me by my chaplain. Owing to the violent force and shock of the rape and torture I had experienced, I lost my ability to speak for several weeks and had an overwhelming desire for my life to end. I felt as though the brutal nature of the attack had extinguished the light of the Holy Spirit in me. Over time, Père Charles would reveal his recollection of the moment he found me. It is from his later confession that I submit to you the following events in the wake of the assault against me.

———

The smell of my blood brought Peyriac to attention. Whinnying loudly to arouse me and seeing no response from my lifeless body, he began thrashing about in fury. He became increasingly frenzied, his hooves lashing out as he attempted to break down the railing of the gate to his stall. He was on the point of succeeding when Père Charles appeared in the doorway to the stable.

"All right, boy, all right," he called out, trying to calm the enraged horse. "What causes you to be upset?"

Approaching the stall, Père Charles came upon the sickening familiar sight and smell of blood. He could not help but recall his own family's murder.

Peyriac continued to bob his head in the direction of the hay pile, while furiously kicking the door of his stall. Père Charles came closer and was alarmed at what he saw before him. I lay across the bloodstained hay, my entire body exposed, my ashen face drained of all colour, my fair hair entangled with crimson-coloured straw.

He dropped to his knees and began to weep as his eyes travelled further down my body, for they came upon my legs, spread wide open, a trail of blood indicating the brutal nature of the penetration that had occurred. My thighs were deeply cut in several places, and blood continued to trickle slowly in tiny rivulets from the wounds.

Peyriac's shrill whinnying brought my aunt to the stable in haste. She, too, wished to know what was agitating my horse. Upon seeing Père Charles bent over my bloodied, naked body, she gasped audibly in alarm.

"What is this? Who has attacked Isabelle? Quickly! We must remove her and clean up this mess! Quiet her horse at once! We cannot draw any more attention to the stable. You are witness to the shame my niece has brought on the House of Albret! If only she had done as she was told! If she survives, her reputation will be destroyed. What nobleman will ever marry her now? She will have no choice but to enter a convent!"

Gathering a rough woollen horse rug in her arms, she draped it over my body and directed my chaplain to carry me to my bedchamber.

"Tell no one what has happened to her. I will join you shortly. Do not permit her siblings to see her in her present state. You will await further instruction from me, am I understood?" My aunt's tone was dictatorial.

"Yes, of course. As you desire, Your Ladyship," Père Charles submissively agreed as he tenderly lifted my limp frame from the bloodied pile of hay on which it lay.

Once in the privacy of my room, he gently placed me on my bed. Stepping away from me, at last, overcome with grief, he felt his knees buckle beneath him as he stood in the centre of the room. Bowing his head and crossing himself, he then offered a prayer to the Lord.

"O Heavenly Father, were I not your servant, were I instead the nobleman I was born to be, I would search for Lady Isabelle's attacker until I found him; I would seek to destroy him limb from limb for the torture and rape he has inflicted upon my dear friend.

"Instead, I ask you, Lord, help me to save her precious life. Guide me in the direction of her salvation. Lead me on this path I have never journeyed before. I pray for you to help me show her my deepest compassion. Lord, I seek your strength in this dark hour."

Having borne witness to my suffering, he found solace in whispering the words of the psalm *Quemadmodum* to himself as he continued to pray over me.

"*As the hart longs for the flowing streams, so my soul longs for you, O God. My soul thirsts for God, for the living God. When shall I come and behold the face of God? My tears have been my food, day and night, while people say to me continually, 'where is now your God?' … Deep calls to deep at the thunder of your cataracts; all your waves and your billows have gone over me … Why are you cast down, O my soul, and why are you so disquieted within me? Hope in God; for I shall again praise him, my help and my God.*"

Père Charles was uncertain whether he should make some attempt to reach out to me. He feared he might startle me, but he ached to hold me, to offer comfort and assurance of his devotion. After watching me for several moments, he finally decided to risk my rejection. Rising, he came over and sat by my side on the bed.

"Your Ladyship, I know you can hear me. Please, oh please, forgive me for not being there when you needed me most. I feel this never would have happened if I had gone riding with you today. I shall live with that guilt for the rest of my life. I beg of you that when you are able, you find it in your heart to pardon me, for I have done you a great injustice. I promise you this, Lady Isabelle: never, never will I trust myself that you are safe in the company of another man. I shall remain by your side to look after you now and help you to heal."

He could see the corners of my closed eyes moisten at his confession, and he reached over to gently stroke my face.

"When you are ready to talk, know that I am prepared to listen. We shall heal together," he said tenderly as he pulled the blanket up around me and leaned toward me, kissing my cheek.

——

When I awakened the following morning after an excruciatingly painful and restless night, I looked about my room, at first uncertain how I had come to be there. Glancing to the window, I saw my chaplain seated on a bench, his head bent over in prayer, his lips silently reciting the words of scripture from the open pages of the psalter he held in his palms over his lap. So deep in his own meditation was he that he took no notice of my stare. With a puzzled expression, I tried to remember whether, the night before, I had seen his head covered with the bloodied bandage that was now wrapped across his left cheek, masking one side of his face. Still unable to speak and ask him what had caused his injury, I silently prayed for the healing of the Lord to be upon his wound.

I learned that immediately after the attack, Aunt Christine had sent Sarah and Christophe to stay in London with our father. She wrote to him, telling him of the rape, assuring him that he need not leave court to visit me; it was better for me to remain in her care.

At the initial meeting with the physician who rode from Oxford to treat me later that morning, it was decided that my chaplain would tend directly to my wounds since he had a general knowledge of medicine and plants. With my aunt watching over him as he worked, Père Charles treated my lacerations, regularly cleaning and dressing them, as if willing them to be healed by his compassionate and attentive touch. Over the ensuing month, I remained on my own to rest and recover in my bedchamber.

During that time, feeling defiled and unworthy, my mind returned repeatedly to the question, why had the Lord spared me? I lost the will to live and became increasingly weak as I refused to eat. My aunt took no notice of my depressed condition; it was as though she secretly wished for my life to end. But my chaplain refused to give up hope that I could be healed. In moments of complete despair and emptiness, it was recalling the calming repetitive lines of chant in *Quemadmodum desiderat cervus* that helped fill my mind with the healing presence of the Lord. From my meditation, I turned my thoughts to memories of happier times spent with my mother, brothers and sisters at Rosete, away from the brutality of the violent attack in the stable at Boarstall. Over time, and with my chaplain's encouragement to do so, I eventually accepted food and drink.

As much as he was able, Père Charles remained at my side, praying for me each day, determined to see me recover through his faithful vigilance. As a result of his repeated visits and attentive care, my body came to be healed, though the scars on my wrists and down my legs would remain forever as a permanent reminder of the heinous assault that had nearly taken my life.

XXVII
Father James Redding

17 May 1453, the New College of St Mary, Oxford

In addition to caring for me, Père Charles continued overseeing the many administrative tasks required in the running of the Boarstall estate. In spite of such a full schedule of work, he managed to find a day to visit his old friend in Oxford, Father James Redding. He wished to bring the man who had attacked me to justice and sought the advice of his former mentor on how to proceed.

His visit to the New College of St Mary was his first to Oxford since leaving the college twelve years earlier. As he rode into the town, he felt a sense of nostalgia for the place that had been his home and refuge during the darkest years of his young life. Riding down the familiar narrow lanes on horseback, he was reminded of the beauty of the collegiate setting that had become his second home.

Père Charles arrived at the college gate. The porter recognised him from his youth, even though he now bore a deep scar across his left cheek.

After first stepping into the great quadrangle, my chaplain then entered the cloister for a moment of quiet reflection. There he stopped and listened, for in the hushed sanctity of the arcaded garden the only thing audible was the distant ethereal sound of sacred music being rehearsed by the boys and men in the adjacent antechapel. Their beautiful high-pitched melodies seemed to float in the air, surrounding him with the welcoming breath of love. It had been in that very location, the central garden of the cloister, that he had felt the Holy Spirit awaken in him, nearly a year after being taken into Father James's care. The feelings of guilt and unworthiness he had suffered in the aftermath of seeing his family and household brutally murdered had stayed present in his mind. Yet the Lord's love proved to be unrelenting. While he sat in the garden listening to Father James deliver his lesson beneath the fragrant canopy of several blooming linden trees, he recalled gazing upon the simple beauty of the delicate flowers planted in the raised beds surrounding him. The heady scent of lime, mixed with heliotrope, violet and lilies, created an aromatic essence that was intoxicating to his senses. It was while in these surroundings that the warmth of a holy presence enlightened his soul.

Confused by the mystical experience, he seemed to hear the voices of angels. He gazed through the cloister arcade, transfixed in his place, his thoughts uplifted by the innocence and passion echoing through the musical phrasing and layering heard in the choirboys' treble voices. That incident changed his life forever. So taken with the singing was he that Father James asked the choirmaster to allow my chaplain to join the choristers; from there grew his love of sacred music. While he had been away in France he had not forgotten the beauty and serenity of his life at New College, the lasting impact of the music he had sung in the choir as a boy, and the fraternity the monastic setting had offered him.

Père Charles recalled that the last time he had stood in that very spot was the day he left for his trip to Wales and St Davids. As he visited the college that morning, he was once again overcome with a sense of being home at last, amidst familiar faces and surroundings.

Images of his youth came flooding back through his mind. He felt compelled to kneel in the cloister, offering a silent prayer of thanksgiving for his fortunate return and affirming the friendships he had made with his fellow singers that would remain a grounding force in his life.

As he knelt, his head bowed in meditation, he sensed a figure quietly approaching from behind. Continuing in his prayer, with his eyes still closed, he heard a slight gasp from someone near to him. He turned to see who was standing there.

"Why, Richard, Richard, is that you? How did I know I might find you here?" his mentor cried, holding out both arms to greet his former pupil.

"Yes, James, it is me," Père Charles replied, a broad smile crossing his face as he stood and embraced his friend.

"Richard Goodwyn. Or shall I address you as Father Richard?" his tutor asked with a slight chuckle. "Either way, come along. You must join me in my chambers and tell me the news of your life since leaving your homeland."

The two men walked together to the stairwell leading to James's rooms in the great quad. They climbed the familiar steps and James opened the door to his former pupil. Even as an adult, my chaplain could vividly recall the safety he had felt living within the protective walls of the college, certain that the men who had killed his family would never find him. Then his thoughts returned to the primary reason for his trip to Oxford.

"Do come in and sit down. Let us share some wine and you can detail your experiences abroad for me, Richard."

"That would please me very much, my friend, but I first must tell you that I am now known by my priestly name, Charles. I have returned to England with the identity of Father Charles Bonvinac. It has been safer for me to travel in such a manner."

"Yes, of course, it would be so," James agreed. "But come now, tell me. You have returned to Oxfordshire. You must explain what brought about your journey here; it has been many years since we last had communication. Surely the adjustment to life in England has been arduous for you. Have you heard the news of the ongoing rivalry between Richard of York and Edmund of Somerset? I fear it is as your father and I predicted many decades ago. Our country stands on the brink of a war that will bring down the House of Lancaster and all those associated with it. You have not returned to England at the safest moment."

"I believe you are correct. I am concerned for the future of the monarchy and the stability of the country."

"There is a rumour circulating through Westminster that Her Majesty is pregnant. Perhaps only that can save us from the talk of civil war that appears to be dividing members of the nobility. I have also heard it said that the child may not even be King Henry's, for the queen is often seen with the Duke of Somerset escorting her to her bedchamber at night. Bastard or not, I pray we remain free and clear of the feuding and do not get caught up in the persecution of loyalists that is certain to follow. But I say too much; here you have come from such a great distance. You must apprise me of all that has come about in your life, for something must have drawn you away from the safety of France and back to England."

Handing Père Charles a cup of wine and then taking a seat across the table from him, James listened closely while his former pupil confessed the events of the past twelve years of his life. He kept nothing from the kind man who was in many respects a father to him. My chaplain felt it was important to share the deeply rooted affection he felt for me. Suppressing his anger as he tried to retain his priestly composure, he described the events surrounding his discovery of me and the aftermath of my rape. He also expressed his desire to take me to Wales to visit the towns and places described in the *Itinerarium Kambriae* of Geraldus Cambrensis.

When his former pupil had finished relating the recent events affecting his life, James merely sat, quiet and visibly moved. It was several long moments before he could reply.

"Richard, you are certainly fortunate to have been installed in the d'Albret Courteault family, for they are indeed one of the most noble families in all of Gascony. They have provided you a living most suited to your interests and abilities. I never imagined that you were intended to lead a large congregation or minister to those with whom you had no personal affinity. Their family has welcomed you as one of their own, and for that I am immensely grateful," James began.

"As for this young maiden whom you care for, Lady Isabelle, I am doubtful that you should dare risk your own life in pursuit of a love that you know you can never fulfil."

James's words struck Père Charles at the very core of his being.

"Why do you suggest my love for her can never be fulfilled?" he asked, his expression one of confusion and hurt.

"Have you forgotten that you are a priest *and* a member of the Knights Templar, my son? You have taken your vows to serve in the ministry of the Church and the Brotherhood. Are you to tell me now that you wish to end your commitment to the priesthood in order to pursue a carnal lust rooted in the secular world, one that provides you with so little in return? I am certain that you may offer this young woman security as her guardian and priest. After all, who better to honour and protect her than her family chaplain, one who in different circumstances would be a powerful and wealthy nobleman? But as a priest and Templar Knight you have abstained from such corporal desires to follow in the path of the Lord. Am I correct to believe that you consider leaving the Church and Brotherhood an option, to permit you to love this woman openly? Do you not see the harm that will bring to you?"

Père Charles was not pleased with his friend's reaction.

"I think we interpret the situation in two very different ways. You see, I do take my relationship with the Lord very seriously. I do not wish to make a drastic or hasty departure from the Church or the Knights Templar that so kindly have offered me much in the way of fraternity and protection – it is the teachings of scripture that have enabled me to renew my faith in the good deeds of my fellow men.

"Yet I am confounded by the longing I feel when I contemplate a future with Lady Isabelle. Do not forget, I made my decision to join the Church at a young age and in large part because it provided me with a safe means of escaping from England and seeking a new life, free from my family's assassins. Try to understand that, before their murder, I had wanted nothing more than to one day wed a beautiful lady who might care for me as my mother had done for my father. As the firstborn son, I wished to live out my life in Cambridgeshire, inheriting the lands and title to Huntingdon Castle from my father. Over the years I have prayed to the Lord, seeking his direction in the path he wishes me to follow. I have come to accept that for some reason I have developed a particular friendship with Her Ladyship, one that is founded on the principles of our shared Catholic faith and her eagerness to pursue her knowledge of many subjects; no finer pupil could I ever wish to teach.

"For all that I provide in the way of scholarship and prayer she returns in her acceptance of who I am and my limitations. Yet I feel conflicted in my soul. I have felt a developing attraction to Her Ladyship. I have come to trust her, and I believe that she truly wishes to care for me, as I wish to honour her through the love we share in our faith. She has never asked that I cease administering the teachings of our Church to others."

"Then you have told her the details of your secret past and how you came to reside in Gascony?" James asked.

"She knows about my past and the night my family was murdered, how you came into my life and when I was called to the priesthood. I now wish to provide a safe future for her. I desire to take back my English family name, and I intend to come out of hiding."

James paused, looking across the room as he reflected on all that his former pupil had shared before giving his thoughtful response.

"So permit me to clarify the points you have presented, Richard. You are in love with Lady Isabelle d'Albret Courteault, whose attacker is still at large. You wish to avenge the violation against her by finding the man responsible and ensure that he is slain for the brutal acts of rape and torture that he committed. I must interject that, for a priest, such thoughts of violence are not in keeping with the vows you have taken to serve the Church. Yet with the argument you have put forward about the intentions you had as a young boy, I can well understand how you might believe your feelings would be justified in the eyes of the Lord. You were raised with the trappings and entitlement of a wealthy and powerful family and, from what you describe, it sounds as though you now seek a return to that life." James then shook his head slowly.

"Now listen to me, James," Père Charles responded adamantly. "Do not judge my character to be one of little merit. From what you describe, it would appear that since moving away from England and finding placement with the d'Albret Courteault family I have lived without values or morals, in pursuit of greed and lust," he added, his expression full of disappointment.

"I realise it has been many years since we last met. In that intervening time I have matured; my perspective on life has broadened. Yet what I treasure most in my memory are the years I spent here with you and the opportunity I had, right below us there in the cloister, to find the love of God in my soul again. All I ask is that you bear an open mind to the struggle I find raging in my heart. You are the only man whom I would permit to stand in judgement of me. And yet I ask you, I beg you, do not judge me. Instead, be my friend and father, for I seek your advice. I do not wish to disappoint you in my actions. You must counsel me, for my mind is in turmoil over what my heart tells me to do and the limitations placed upon me by my chosen vocation."

"Yes, yes," James said, moving closer to Père Charles and looking him directly in the eyes. "I can understand how the situation has encumbered you. I advise you to allow your heart to guide you, for you have endured a life of pain and yet shown great resilience in spite of all you have lost. Only you know the right course of action. You know Lady Isabelle far more intimately than I; if you implicitly trust her with knowing your secret past and she shows only patience and compassion in return, then she must be a most remarkable friend."

James paused as the full import of his sage words of experience sank into Père Charles's conscience.

"Tell me, how did you receive the wound that caused the scar on your cheek? Does this have anything to do with Lady Isabelle's assault?"

Père Charles once again found solace with his mentor as the conversation turned to the chief reason for his visit that day. They discussed at length the manner in which justice could be brought against Sir Henry Lormont.

"Now that you have disclosed your concerns to me, I feel I must apologise for what I said earlier," James admitted. "I am not the one to judge your life. You must do that for yourself. I admit I was startled by your honest revelation that you might truly love and cherish this young noblewoman, Lady Isabelle, of whom you speak so passionately. Richard, you must decide what is appropriate for you. Nothing is impossible in this world. And if you should choose to leave the Church and the Brotherhood to pursue her love, know that I shall support you."

"I very much appreciate your guidance, James," Père Charles replied, taking his tutor's hands into his own. "I must tell you, the comfort it brings to hear you speak such words is immeasurable. I feared that you might be disappointed in me for what I have confessed to you. I wish to honour our friendship in every way possible."

"You have already, my son. You have returned to me after many years away and you have followed a well-intentioned path in life, serving others with piety before yourself. What more could I ask for in a pupil? Your own father would be proud of you and the choices you have made. I assure you of that."

James, whom Père Charles remembered as having been full of energy and vigour in his youth, had begun to show signs of age. With the serious nature of the confession now behind them, they spent the remainder of their time together revisiting the landmarks of the college where my chaplain had felt so comfortable in his youth. The hall, the chapel, the garden: all brought back fond recollections of the time he spent within the peaceful Oxford college walls. Presently, it came time to leave. Père Charles gathered his horse and mounted, with James walking alongside to see him off.

"Thank you for visiting me," James began, his voice nostalgic. "It has meant so much to have seen you now as a grown man. Do come and visit me again, and bring Lady Isabelle with you. I shall make special arrangements for her to have access to the college and chapel."

"It is I who wish to thank you for your kindness and charity towards me," Père Charles replied. "I would not be the man I am today had it not been for your careful instruction. I shall keep you in my thoughts as I return to Boarstall and prepare for my journey to Wales with Lady Isabelle. When you took me on that journey, it forced me to look at my past and the pain I had suffered from afar.

In Wales I found my strength and my will to go on, and I hope the trip can do the same for my lady."

Their farewells completed, Père Charles rode off. When he glanced back, he could still see his friend standing at the gate, watching him as he disappeared down the narrow lane and into the distance.

XXVIII
Revelation

Towards the end of May, I was once again riding Peyriac, though at first only in the proximity of the castle with my chaplain leading him by the rein. With every ride I took, my confidence and strength returned until one day, in the first week of June, Père Charles decided we should revisit a place we had both enjoyed before my attack: the market in Thame. He believed that if I was strong enough to make the excursion to the neighbouring town, we could then set off on our trip to follow in the path of Geraldus Cambrensis through Wales soon thereafter.

We had just finished our daily circuit with Peyriac around the exterior perimeter of Boarstall when a courier arrived from London on horseback with a written message for my aunt. Our porter escorted him to the privy hall, where she sat working on her embroidery. We soon learned the contents of the missive. As we finished unsaddling Peyriac, she appeared in the doorway of the stable, wearing a broad grin.

"I have been summoned back to London and shall leave you both immediately. I am glad for the break from this wretched country life. I have been invited to attend the queen at court. I shall again be amongst members of the English nobility where I belong. Of course, this means I must leave Lady Isabelle in your care, Père Charles, something I am loath to do knowing how you two relate to one another in such an intimate way. But I have no choice; I must see to my own affairs."

"You have no reason to be concerned, Your Ladyship. I shall take care of your niece and ensure her safety and well-being while you are away. With whom will you be staying, may I ask?"

With a look of incredulity, she looked upon my chaplain and responded sharply with a mocking tone.

"You most certainly may *not* ask such a thing. My activities are of no consequence to someone in *your* vocation."

"I see. We shall await your return, then," Père Charles replied with grace as he humbled himself before my aunt. I wondered who in the queen's court had sent the invitation; I assumed it was Margaret who had asked her to join in the company of the other ladies-in-waiting. I put my aunt's departure from my mind. Her overbearing presence at Boarstall would not be missed.

Two days after my aunt had left, we took our first ride to Thame since early April. The seemingly endless days of sunlight leading up to the summer solstice were typically filled with warmth. This particular day was no exception. I felt as if I were back in Gascony, visiting Bazas on a summer day, feeling only the whisper of a breeze in the air against my cheeks as we rode.

After procuring some items for our journey to Wales, Père Charles suggested we follow a different route home than the one we had taken earlier that day. We decided to stop outside the village of Shabbington. Lying along the banks of the River Thames, the village consisted of a few thatched cottages and the tiny church of St Mary Magdalene, where we first stopped to offer a silent midday prayer of thanksgiving.

After finishing, not far from the village centre we found the crest of a knoll affording a view of the route we had just ridden. From the hilltop vantage point we could see the far edge of Bernwood Forest in the distance, some four miles away. We stopped there and let the horses out to graze. I spread a small rug on the ground while Père Charles proceeded to unwrap our savoury treats. In the absence of any cups, we shared wine from his wooden canteen while we ate.

As the afternoon wore on, I felt the desire to say something rise in my throat. But just as I was about to speak, fear overwhelmed me and I remained quiet. Père Charles, too, seemed lost in his own thoughts. After some time, I began to feel drowsy from the combination of fresh air, rich food and red wine. I moved my belongings to one side and lay down in the shade of a Tilia tree; its sweet linden perfume filled the air while its towering branches offered a broad canopy of protection from the sun.

Soon Père Charles did the same and I could hear his breathing turn heavy as he began to fall asleep. I was so comfortable in his presence. I trusted him implicitly. Then why, I wondered, could I not find the strength to confess what had happened? He had never asked me to tell him the details of the attack. He knew it would take time and he was prepared to wait.

As he dropped off in slumber, I watched him, my eyes following the steady rise and fall of his chest. He was at peace, and I was more determined than ever to join him in his tranquillity.

"It… it began that afternoon when we stopped in Thame to ask directions to Boarstall," I began, my voice hoarse as I felt a tickle rise in my throat after so many weeks of silence.

Père Charles stirred in his sleep. I turned my gaze in the direction of the fields nearby. I could not bear to look at him. I continued, cautiously and with hesitation, unaware that Pere Charles was now fully awake and gazing at me.

"He was so self-assured; he seemed to relish my discomfort at being in his presence. From the moment I made his acquaintance I sensed that he wished to hurt me physically in some way, though what gave rise to such antipathy toward me I do not know, for what could I have done to warrant such malice on his part?"

I brought my knees up to my chin and sat there for several moments. With my arms wrapped around my legs, hugging them to my chest, I wished to make myself as small as possible. I wished I could disappear. And then suddenly recollections came spilling out, my silence finally broken. Yet I suddenly found I could go no further with them.

"I have said enough. I am not comfortable continuing; please forgive me. Might we depart for Boarstall now?" I suggested.

"No, Lady Isabelle. Leaving for home at this moment would be a detriment to you. We have not far to go now. Please do continue. What happened after you put Peyriac away in his stall?"

Swallowing hard and taking a deep breath, I shifted my focus back to the narration of my ordeal. As I thought about what I was to describe, I felt a stab of anger and indignation build in my chest. Père Charles moved forward to comfort me, and I lashed out at him in anger.

"Where were you that afternoon?" I cried, my face feeling warm as the colour rose in my cheeks. "If you had been with me, I would not have been assaulted and my innocence stolen by that wicked man! I trusted you as my closest friend and companion, and you stayed away! You never came; you did not protect me!"

In my anger and pain, I threw myself against Père Charles, the sudden motion catching him off guard and knocking him backwards. Raising my fists as if to strike his face, I stopped myself; I could not bring myself to lay a hand against the man whom I loved.

I could not even look him in the face. I fell over him and wept until I could no longer catch my breath. He patiently waited, permitting me to express my anguish and disappointment without his interruption. Eventually, I grew tired and closed my eyes. He reached around me and slowly raised himself up, embracing me while I remained collapsed against him, listening to the steady rhythm of his heartbeat and feeling reassured of his protection and nearness.

"Oh, look what I have done; I have hurt you now with what I have acknowledged. I am so sorry," I whispered regretfully.

"Do not apologise. You have every reason to be angry with me," he assured me, stroking my hair and gently kissing my forehead. "I should have been there with you that afternoon. You are far too precious to me. I should have known better. I pray you forgive me; I failed you at the time when you needed me most." Père Charles's sombre tone was a clear indication of the torment he bore.

I collected my thoughts before slowly pulling away from him to finish my story.

"And then, prior to losing consciousness, I remember Sir Henry told me what I feared most. He knows who you are. It was his father who was the third man you watched enter your room and take the life of your brother. Sir Henry admitted that he must fulfil an obligation shared with his associates, to see you brought out of hiding and made to confess your secret."

"Oh, Isabelle, can you ever truly forgive me for allowing this to happen?" he asked, his voice barely louder than a murmur.

"Of course I forgive you. Please do not burden yourself. I cannot hold you responsible for my attack. I had buried Sir Henry's final statement so deep in the recess of my mind that I failed to recall his words until now. What does this mean for us? Neither one of us is safe at Boarstall, are we?"

Reaching my hand up to stroke his left cheek, my fingers lingered along the jagged scar that now permanently disfigured his noble features. With concern I asked him to tell me how and when he had obtained the mark.

Père Charles bowed his head. "It was the same evening as your assault. I returned to the stable after dinner, carrying a lantern in my hand to illuminate the space. I noticed the metallic glint of something protruding from behind the feed barrel. As I bent over to pick it up, I was attacked from behind. Sir Henry had come back, searching for his blade, which I held in my possession. He caught me off guard and the knife fell to the ground where he picked it up. Wielding it at my face, he attempted to slash my neck with it but, thankfully, as you can see, he missed and instead sliced my left cheek. I became enraged and tackled him, throwing him to the floor and taking back the blade. I sat on him and raised it over his heart, about to strike him with a fatal stab. But then I heard the voice of the Lord speak to me, commanding me not to take the life of another by my own hand. He assured me justice would be done and that I must release my prisoner. I jumped off Sir Henry, dropping his knife in the process. He grabbed it and taunted me, saying what a fool I had been that I did not kill him when I had the chance.

"Ever since that encounter I have been fearful that he might return to Boarstall and attack you when I was absent. I now realise that my first instincts about him were correct. With what you have just divulged about Sir Henry and his acknowledgement of my identity, it is imperative that we depart for Wales tomorrow, as much for your education as to leave the premises for our own safety. I shall send word to your father immediately upon our return today. He has already given me permission to take you on our pilgrimage to St Davids. I will tell him we must leave at once. I hope you will find the trip as healing as I did when I was your age."

"I am shocked to hear you describe what Sir Henry did to you. How painful it must have been to receive such an injury on your face! As difficult as it is for me to admit, you were right not to kill him by your hand. God will administer his justice to serve us both. I am grateful that we can ride to St Davids. I have eagerly anticipated following the path of Geraldus Cambrensis since our first reading of the text so long ago back at Rosete."

"Very well, Lady Isabelle. Then let us return now to Boarstall and prepare to leave tomorrow at dawn."

———

Over our dinner later that evening in the great hall, Père Charles told me about his recent trip into Oxford to visit his friend Father James Redding.

"Your mentor sounds like a lovely man. I do hope to be presented to him one day."

"He would also like to make your acquaintance. I have told him about you and your family. He asked that we might visit him on our journey." My chaplain's tone then turned serious. "There is something else you must know. When I met him, I told him about the attack, and I asked for his assistance in seeing Sir Henry brought to justice."

I stopped and stared at him, unable to believe what I was hearing.

"What... what exactly did you tell Father James?" I began slowly, trying to keep my voice steady. "Is that why he wants to meet me? So that I can discuss with him at length the ordeal I went through? How could you tell someone I do not even know something so private about me?"

"I assure you, I wish you no discomfort, Lady Isabelle. You will have to provide written testimony that James and a notary will witness, along with the constable of Oxford. Since it will be notarised, the document can stand as your evidence at Sir Henry's trial."

His deliberate and wise counsel was born of a desire to protect me as I returned to the life I had known before. With my innocence since lost, I thought about our friendship, about the trust we placed in one another, and concluded that his assessment could only be correct. Reluctantly, I nodded my head slowly in consent.

"I feel responsible for what happened to you, Your Ladyship. I believe you can and must do this, and I maintain that you will ultimately be grateful that you did. You know that I shall always provide you with all of my support. We shall face this together."

I looked down and stared at the food on the table before me, unable to eat. I could not look him in the face, but he did not turn his gaze away from me. So many images coursed through my mind. The thought of recalling the terrifying scene in the stable before several men elicited a feeling of nausea and weakness. I closed my eyes to steady myself, wishing to extinguish the images of the rape from my memory.

"Open your eyes, Lady Isabelle," he insisted, speaking tenderly. He had come to sit by my side. "Perhaps it is too soon to think about pursuing this matter. If you should one day decide to have Sir Henry tried for his actions, you know that you need only mention it to me and the deed will be done. Does that allay your concerns?"

I sighed long and heavily, clearing my head. "I wish to put my thoughts on our trip to Wales. It has been my focus for the past month while I have been recovering. I do not wish to disappoint you or Father James, though. Perhaps we can stop in Oxford tomorrow to visit him."

"Certainly. I shall ask the porter to send word straight away that we shall stop in the morning on our way to Gloucester. You should take rest this evening. Tomorrow's ride will be the longest you have made in several weeks. I expect it will tire you. Making a stop in Oxford will help break up the distance we travel on our first day. Sleep well, My Lady, for tomorrow you will begin a journey that will change your life forever."

Glancing upwards as I crossed the inner ward later that night after dinner, I noticed that the midsummer twilight sky was filled with a particularly fiery glow – the first stars of night dazzled with their infinite brilliance. I took a moment to linger under the radiant canopy, marvelling at the Lord's creation. Closing my eyes, I offered a prayer of gratitude to the Lord, for sparing my life, for my recovery, and most importantly for the presence of my friend and chaplain. It was his attentive love, bestowed so willingly, that had given rise to my desire to speak again. I prayed that one day I might provide him with similar comfort in his time of need.

XXIX
Facio Depositionem

8 June 1453, the New College of St Mary, Oxford

Père Charles knocked on my door to awaken me well before dawn on Wednesday morning. With our household servants still asleep, he prepared food parcels in the kitchen for us to carry on our journey, while I set off to the stable to saddle our horses for the trip. Just after sunrise we left Boarstall, riding towards the west, feeling the radiant first rays of the rising sun against our backs.

When we reached the crest of Headington Hill, just above the town of Oxford, we stopped to view several stone towers that rose above the treetops in the still of the valley below. Père Charles pointed out to me where we were in relation to the principal colleges of the university. I was moved by the quiet beauty of the place and immediately felt drawn to what I saw. The golden limestone of the buildings reflected the early-morning sun; the glow generated by the light as it spread across the vista filled me with a sense of calm. My companion patiently waited while I recorded some notes in my journal before suggesting that we continue down the hill and inside the town walls.

After crossing the high-street bridge spanning the River Cherwell, we soon entered the city walls. Continuing up the high street until we reached the church of St Mary, we turned right onto Catte Street, passing construction work being carried out on the College of All Souls. Riding along to New College Lane, we turned right again and entered the narrow passage, arriving at what looked like a fortified gatehouse at a bend in the road. It was not what I had expected to encounter as an entry into the college. High walls capped with machicolation and devoid of any fenestration or decoration rose up along either side of the lane; it was not immediately apparent that we were about to enter an academic hall. For a brief moment, I contemplated how Père Charles must have felt as a young boy entering through such a bleak and inhospitable passage, for it resembled nothing of the grandeur and openness of the short ride we had taken along the high street. Without warning, the college porter opened the gate before us and we entered on horseback.

"I beg your pardon, Father Richard; I did not see you coming down the lane. Father James has already been by to notify us of your anticipated arrival. He has made arrangements for you and Lady Isabelle to attend the morning service in chapel."

"Has it already started?"

"You are not too late, if that is what you are after. It started a few minutes ago, but you may join them at any time."

The porter whistled to a scout who was busy sweeping the corridor of the cloister to our left.

"Peter, come over here!" he called. "Take these horses for me, will you? Stable them up inside the warden's barn with the other horses."

We dismounted and handed over our reins to the scout, and the porter motioned for us to follow him to the chapel's entrance.

"Here you are, Father, Your Ladyship," he said, bowing slightly in deference to me outside the chapel door. "Father James indicated that there will be two empty seats in the stalls at the end of the nave, near the high altar. You may sit there for the service. Please send word when you wish to depart and I will ensure your horses are brought to the gate for you."

We entered the twin-bay antechapel and then turned to the right, walking under a carved wooden screen and passing the choir, who were standing near the entrance just inside the nave. Two rows of wooden misericords placed against the north and south walls ran down the length of the interior. There were not enough places for all members of college to be seated during the service; several junior members stood in the centre of the chapel, some with their heads bent together, their eyes watching us, murmuring to each other as we walked past.

First bowing our heads in the direction of the altar, we then stepped into our separate stalls, joining the others around us in silent prayer. Kneeling, we wished not to divert attention from the service being sung by a choir composed of both adult men and young boys, who appeared to be about the same age as my brother Christophe. While in meditation, I recognised the words of the chant were the very same as those I had first heard at the Collegiate Church of St Peter in London, only in this version of the psalm, the beauty lay in the high-pitched range of the young boys' voices. This new sound was unlike anything I had previously heard. As their choral offering continued, a lightness entered my soul. The Lord had sent me the grace of the Holy Spirit, felt as a whisper, through the breath of the choristers' song. I wept silently, oblivious to the stares of the men seated around me who were both shocked at my presence in their chapel, and my visible sign of emotion.

At the close of the chant I turned my attention to the fine architectural details of the chapel, recalling what Père Charles had told me before we attended the banquet at Broughton Castle. The college and castle were both works of the same master mason, William Wynford and his master carpenter Hugh Herland. The plain wooden timbers of the roof were set off by a series of tie-beams painted in bright colours of azure and vermilion, with white and gilded accents. Set in the reredos that ran the full height of the chapel wall behind the altar were rows of statues, some displaying scenes from the life of the Virgin Mary, in whose name the college had been founded.

In the centre of the wall toward the top was a statue of Christ on the cross. The niches in which the statues were placed were painted in the same bright colours and gilding as the tie-beams overhead. That morning the chapel was filled with a kaleidoscope of colours and radiant warmth as bright sunshine streamed through the immense stained-glass windows in both the nave and antechapel. Once the choral service had ended, the members of college walked past us, some of them laughing, pushing into one another and talking loudly amongst themselves. It was not long before we encountered Father James Redding in the crowd.

"Good morning to you both. I am glad to see you here. It is indeed a pleasure to welcome you to New College, Your Ladyship," he said in English, smiling warmly as he walked towards us.

"Before we convene in the privacy of my chambers, you must take a moment to visit our cloister. It was there that your chaplain felt the presence of the Holy Spirit awaken in him when he was my pupil."

Accompanying Father James through the arcaded corridor, we entered the tranquil setting of the central garden. While standing to the side of my companions, marvelling at the space, suddenly a pair of doves appeared overhead. They circled our group before landing on the roofline of the cloister. Watching their movement, my mind began to drift as I witnessed a new vision. In it was the seed of love, planted many months earlier. A single stem emerged from the ground, its bloom, a pure white lily. Once opened, the star-shaped flowers released their delicately sweet scent in the air around us, uniting the souls of my chaplain and me. I closed my eyes as I offered a prayer of thanksgiving to the Lord for what he had revealed to me in that showing.

Father James interrupted my contemplation. "May I ask whether you found the morning service to your liking, Your Ladyship?"

"Oh yes, I certainly did. I have never heard a choir composed of boys and men. There is a lightness and texturing of the chants that is not heard in the adult male voice alone."

"You are correct in your observation," Father James replied. "In fact, it was our founder, William of Wykeham, who decreed in the college statutes that the choir must include ten priests, three lay clerks and sixteen choristers to sing the chapel services. The sound you heard is indeed the innocent voice of youth before it changes into one of manhood."

We returned to the great quadrangle and up a narrow stairway leading to the floor housing his chambers. It suddenly struck me that now I was granted access to the private room of a senior fellow. Normally, women were admitted to the college only for the purposes of cleaning and food preparation, or for delivery of goods; and if the latter were the case, then no farther than the porter's lodge housed in the postern gate.

"It is fortunate that we could meet on such short notice," Père Charles announced as we entered the room. "This is Her Ladyship's first trip into Oxford. I thank you for making it possible for her to visit New College."

"Know that I would do whatever necessary to accommodate you both. Please, do take a seat. I will return in a moment."

Father James's paternal tone made me feel at ease in his presence immediately, and I felt secure in the quiet surroundings of his rooms. They overlooked the quadrangle and chapel and were comfortably furnished with carved benches and chairs. A circular wooden table for his pupils stood in the centre of the room. Along one wall was a fireplace. Tall shelves filled with manuscripts were set in the space between the room's two windows. In the far corner of the room near the fireplace was a desk where Father James was at work, its surface covered with several documents lying open, ready for his examination. He was clearly a very learned man, yet for all his wisdom he revealed a charming twinkle in his eye as he spoke. It was immediately apparent to me that he looked upon my chaplain as though he were his own son. I reached over to hold Père Charles's hand. It was so exciting for me to be there, in the very room where he had been as a young man.

Father James had once again joined us. A scout had followed him, carrying a tray that he placed on the table in the centre of the room before leaving.

"Well here we are. Do help yourselves." He directed us to take a cup of cider. "I am grateful to you both for taking the time to stop and visit me."

The faces on the green earthenware vessels immediately reminded me of those I had seen on the puzzle jug at the tavern in Clanfield where our family stopped on our way to London the previous year.

"We would not have missed the opportunity to see you. I have told Her Ladyship so much about you that I felt a meeting was in order."

"Yes, that is right," I agreed. "And in fact, I have been told that you have been made aware of my attack."

"Lady Isabelle, you need not bring that up now," Père Charles quickly interjected, surprised at what I had stated.

"But, yes, I believe I do," I said defiantly. "I have given it more thought since you and I spoke of it in private. I have decided I must give my account of the events, as you recommended. Perhaps, Father James, you could call upon the constable and bring in a notary. I would ask that you also be a witness to my testimony."

"Why certainly, Lady Isabelle, as you wish," Father James replied, his tone serious and deferential. "I shall call upon our college notary and the procurator at once, and send for the constable as well. But I must caution you – making a witness statement will not be a pleasurable experience, especially given the nature of the subject matter to be recounted. Perhaps you might consider waiting until you are a little stronger."

"I thank you for your candour, but I have given it much thought. Last night I decided that if I am to go through with this trip to Wales, I must first make my legal testimony."

"You have my full support, Lady Isabelle, be assured," Père Charles confirmed.

"Yes, My Lady, and mine as well. Now, if you will please excuse me, I shall summon the different parties we need present in order to document your account."

Father James stood and headed for the door. Once he was outside and we were again alone, Père Charles directed his attention to me.

"Lady Isabelle, you never fail to astonish and impress me. I shall remain by your side throughout the entire process, that I promise you," he vowed.

He moved closer to me, placing his arm around my back and I closed my eyes as I leaned towards him for support. After several long moments of quiet, all at once we felt the presence of someone near and we both looked up to see Father James smiling at us. I quickly straightened my posture, trying to appear as if I had not been sitting in such an intimate position with my chaplain.

"Do not let me disturb you, Lady Isabelle," his gentle voice assured me. "Do not alarm yourself. I am not one to stand in judgement of your behaviour."

"I… we did not hear you enter, Father James."

"Seeing you both together in such a manner bears me no discomfort. It is only fitting that you should find solace in the company of each other. The world is such a lonely place in the absence of feeling the love of another. I well know, for I have chosen to live as a priest in a cloistered academic hall since I was a young man."

"Father James, thank you. You are a man of great understanding and wisdom. I can see why Père Charles reveres you so."

"Richard is a remarkable man and he is like a son to me. Since he cares so deeply for you, I wish to accord my friendship to you also."

After taking a seat across from us, he continued, "Now, to keep you informed about the events taking place. I have sent for Constable Matthew Parish to come at once. I have instructed the porter to also send for the college notary and procurator, both of whom live here in town. They are all expected to arrive within a short period of time. However, once we begin I am afraid recording the witness statement may take up the remainder of the morning."

"Thank you for making the arrangements on my behalf," I stated with appreciation.

"Know that I shall do whatever I can to help you, Your Ladyship."

"James, since we have a few moments before they arrive, perhaps you might discuss the journey we are about to embark upon to Wales," Père Charles suggested.

"Why, of course. When Richard and I journeyed there together, we stayed with my associates in several monasteries and castles. I assume you have planned to do the same on your trip. I understand that under Richard's instruction you have studied the Latin text of Geraldus Cambrensis. I wonder whether he has shared with you some background on Gerald's manuscripts and why they are so significant. He was unknown to me until I came across copies of his *Itinerarium Kambriae* and *Descriptio Kambriae* in the university library housed in the university church of Saint Mary the Virgin. I later learned that he was a scholar and clergyman who had aspired to become the Bishop of St Davids in Wales, but his ambition was never realised. However, the manner in which the countryside and people were described in the *Descriptio Kambriae* fascinated me. Throughout our travels we found that the country had not changed much in the course of the past two hundred and fifty years.

"I understand from Richard that you, Lady Isabelle, have a particular interest in architecture, is that correct? If so, would you like me to recommend some places Gerald stopped during his journey? I believe I have his manuscript here somewhere amongst my collection of sacred and secular texts."

"Oh, yes, please, Father James," I said eagerly. "If you feel there is time, that is."

The tutor rose up from his seat and began sorting through the pile of manuscripts on his desk. Having located the text he was looking for, he carried it over to the bench my chaplain and I shared, and opened it across the table before us.

"There is always time to share a little history with such a keen young pupil," Father James replied, his eyes smiling. He began to describe what we might see as we followed Gerald's path through Wales to St Davids.

"From what I gather, your trip will cover the route through the southern region of the country. Departing from the Benedictine Abbey of St Peter in Gloucester will afford you a point of comparison with the Welsh buildings you will stay in along the route. Incidentally, it was while he was a student of a monk named Haimo at St Peter's Abbey in Gloucester that Gerald became a scholar of classical and medieval Latin texts, which would later influence his own writing style."

The lesson continued with further details relating to the building campaign of King Edward I in north Wales.

Father James took several moments to check something noted in the margin of the manuscript. Before he could continue, a sudden knock at the door abruptly ended his scrutiny of the document. Our host crossed the room to open the door and I glanced at Père Charles expectantly.

"I am afraid here ends the brief lesson. Do not worry, Your Ladyship. We shall take care of you," Father James reassured me before he greeted the guests.

He returned in the company of three men, dressed in the robes of their office.

"Lady Isabelle, may I present to you Constable Matthew Parish of Oxford, our college notary Edmund Writte and our college procurator John Law. Gentlemen, please be seated."

While the two other men greeted me, I noticed Constable Parish lean toward Père Charles, whom he embraced and in a low voice asked, "Who worketh wonders?" Père Charles gave his answer – "Immanuel" – in the same low tone. I did not wish to appear as if I was eavesdropping, so I took my seat with the other men.

"I have not yet told the constable of the reason we have summoned him here today. If it pleases Her Ladyship, would she have me speak on her behalf?"

"Yes, you may proceed, Father James," I answered quietly.

"Very well, then. Lady Isabelle d'Albret Courteault wishes to bring charges against Sir Henry Lormont, Earl of Hillesden, for the violent crime he enacted against her in late April of this year."

"Let us begin." Constable Parish sat across the table from me. His face showed no emotion as he gave instructions to the others. "John, you and Edmund prepare the proper documentation for the case. As you do this, I would ask that Her Ladyship recount to us her personal details and how she came to be acquainted with the man she claims to have violated her."

I proceeded to describe my life since arriving in London with my family for the officials, answering their questions. After some time, I began to feel tired. With my head feeling light, I knew I needed to stop and take in some fresh air.

"Gentlemen, may we break for a moment so that Her Lady-ship may step outside with me?" asked Père Charles, reading my expression.

"You may. But please remember, we still have much to cover and the morning is quickly drawing to an end," Constable Parish cautioned.

Père Charles carefully guided me to the door and down the stairs. Once outside I felt relieved. The morning air revived me; I was glad to be outdoors in the presence of my friend and confessor.

"Take your time. If it is difficult for you to talk about this in front of the others, please just look at me and I shall help you."

I nodded my head in silent agreement and felt comforted by my chaplain's hand in the small of my back, gently guiding me towards the stairs. Upon entering James's room we sat apart from one another.

"Now, Lady Isabelle," began Constable Parish, regarding the written document the scribe presented before him, "where were we? Ah yes, I see. You have described your past and how you have come to reside at Boarstall Castle. Perhaps we can skip ahead to the details regarding your attacker and the identity of the aggressor."

With that I opened up and began to recount the moments leading up to and including the night of the banquet and Margaret's betrothal, the assault in the courtyard during the dance, and the day I was raped in the stable. None of the men showed any signs of surprise at my attacker's malicious comment that I was not the first woman to be killed by his hand. I chose not to mention Sir Henry's statement that my attack was meant to bring my chaplain out of hiding, for I did not know whom I could trust amongst the men seated before me. Upon finishing my statement, I was relieved to see the notary and procurator finish their final markings on the document and hand it over for me to sign in the presence of my witnesses, James Redding, Matthew Parish and John Law.

"I believe we have all the information we shall need from you at this time, Lady Isabelle. Your testimony will be filed with the court in Oxford this afternoon. Though I must alert you that in the absence of any witnesses to your attack it is likely that Sir Henry will be acquitted of the crime, since there is no precedent in our court of rape cases resulting in punishment for the attacker. If you had someone to vouch for your assault, that would strengthen your witness statement."

"Then might I add a few lines of testimony to Her Ladyship's account?" my chaplain quickly interjected. "You see, I was later assaulted by Sir Henry that same day as I held in my hand the weapon he had used to savagely attack her. He attempted to grab it from me and stab me with it, and in our altercation, he instead drew the blade across my face, resulting in the scar I now bear on my left cheek." Père Charles then described his encounter with my assailant in the stable. When he had completed his own witness statement and signed it, Constable Parish rose up from his seat, gathering the parchment and preparing to leave.

"Father Richard, your additional testament will certainly strengthen the case Her Ladyship has brought against Sir Henry. We shall bring him in immediately," the constable disclosed.

"And you will not need me to remain in Oxford any longer? I may now take my leave for Wales?"

"You may, Your Ladyship. Though I urge you to be cautious on your journey. Sir Henry is a powerful lord with a large retinue in his service."

"We thank you for your wise counsel, Constable. We shall heed your advice," Père Charles soberly replied.

"Yes, thank you, gentlemen, for joining us so promptly this morning," Father James added. "I shall show you out of college."

I watched as the men filed past me, following Father James through the door to the stairway. He escorted them downstairs to the quadrangle, affording Père Charles and me a moment of privacy.

"You took an incredible risk in adding your own witness statement to mine. If you are made to answer questions about your identity, how will you respond?"

"Do not concern yourself with such matters, Your Ladyship. That is unlikely to occur; if it does I will seek James's counsel on how to proceed. What is more important is that Sir Henry is arrested and imprisoned. The longer he remains free to carry out his violent acts the more likely we, or someone else, may fall victim to his crimes. I imagine this morning's confession has made you weary. What would it please you to do now?"

The bells in the tower overlooking the cloister began to toll the noontime hour, reminding us that the morning had come to an end.

"I would like to say farewell to your tutor and then leave Oxford at once before they bring in Sir Henry."

"Very well. We shall wait for James."

XXX
Judgement Day

We had not long to wait before we were joined by Father James once more. After entering he motioned for us to sit together at the table in the centre of the room.

"You have performed a courageous act, Your Ladyship, and you too, Richard. Constable Parish mentioned to me in private just now that he is certain Sir Henry is a man wanted for a number of crimes. Because of his association with the Beaufort family, led by the Duke of Somerset, he has evaded any past charges. You can be assured that the constable will do whatever possible to bring him to justice at once. Have you two heard of the recent assault accusations made against Sir Henry that resulted in the death of an Oxfordshire judge?"

"No," I replied slowly, glancing at my tutor nervously. "Were they similar charges to mine?"

"Quite similar. It was about two months ago that the attack took place," Father James began, his tone solemn, "around the time of the royal feast at Boarstall."

"What attack was this?" Père Charles queried. "I do not recall hearing about the incident either."

"Oh, I see. Well then, allow me to briefly describe the events. One night in April this year Lady Ann Whitmore of Binsey, a village less than one mile from Oxford, was attacked in her home. Lady Ann is known in Oxford for her generosity and kindness and as one who cares for the sick and those in need. She is a young crippled widow. Though her body is quite weak and she feels constant pain in her shoulders and legs, Lady Ann works with the nuns of Godstow Priory in feeding the hungry and visiting those who are infirm and close to death. She lives off the proceeds of the rents left to her by her late husband. In fact, such is her generous nature that on the night of her assault she was home alone, having given her servants the day and evening off to attend a spring fete. He attacked her, leaving her for dead and stealing her most precious deeds and jewellery."

"Are you talking about Sir Henry? That he committed these heinous acts?" I exclaimed in anger.

"Yes, indeed, from Lady Ann's account made before the judge and tribunal, it seems the act was committed by him. She identified Sir Henry by name even though he was not present. She described how, as he attacked her, thinking he was killing her, Sir Henry admitted what he did was an act of revenge for a business dealing he had with her late husband that went badly. A rumour surfaced that the judge had accepted money in return for sheltering Sir Henry."

"What wretched judge could hear this evidence and not condemn him to death, if not at least jail him? Had Sir Henry been jailed and sentenced to death then Lady Isabelle would not have suffered through the vicious attack he made on her at Boarstall!" My chaplain's tone was fierce.

"That is true, Richard. What happened next is likely to astound you both. It certainly caused me great alarm when I heard it."

"Do continue, Father James. We are listening," I said gravely.

"Upon hearing that the judge ignored Lady Ann's pleading and her evidence, and knowing they were provided by the lady who helped so many in the community, a large mob made up of local residents decided to take justice into their own hands. Under the cover of darkness, their identities masked by the black capes and hoods they wore, the terrorising mass descended upon the judge's residence, to the shock and horror of his own family. With blazing torches in hand they broke through the front door and entered, a dozen or so of them racing up the stairs to the judge's bedroom, his wife and children shrieking in fright as he was dragged outside to the forecourt of their manor house. The family's servants were outnumbered by the angry horde, some of whom chanted, 'Give him a taste, give him a taste!' The judge pleaded for mercy but the mob would have none of it after he had ignored Lady Ann's testimony in his tribunal. Holding him down, members of the group stripped the judge naked and one drew a long blade, castrating him right there and then. They stuffed his mouth with his own bloody genitals, leaving him to writhe in agony, dying in a pool of blood at their feet."

"Oh, that is awful!" I cried, wincing and turning away, sickened by the description of events.

"But they did not stop there. According to one of the servants who managed to escape and watched the events unfold from the safety of the stable, that is not all they did. They forced the judge's wife, children and servants back inside the home, tying them up and setting the house on fire. No one has claimed to know anything about who the leaders were, but I assure you, there is now fear among the judges here in Oxford that they must abide by the complaints issued by women against Sir Henry, or face a similar fate. I believe your testimony will go far to helping re-establish the credibility of the previous case against him."

"All this murder and mayhem could have been avoided with one simple act, had the judge accepted Lady Ann's testimony. He should never have dismissed her claims, allowing Sir Henry to remain free. He has paid for such an abuse of power with his life and the lives of his family and household. May God save his soul," Père Charles stated, bowing his head and crossing himself.

"Precisely. And that is why I am confident that with the depositions you both have made today, Sir Henry's life will not be spared again, no matter what he does to pay those in power to protect him," Father James concluded.

In silence Père Charles and I exchanged glances, our sombre expressions bearing the shock of what had been disclosed. Sensing our disgust, Father James turned the discussion to a more palatable subject.

"I realise that your next meal may not be weighing heavily on your minds at this particular moment, but I certainly could do with a change of setting and some food. Though it is well past noon, would you two like to stay and dine with me in the hall or do you prefer to leave Oxford to get moving onward in your journey?"

"You make a generous offer, James. However, Her Ladyship would prefer that we take our leave. If we would be permitted, might we visit you on our return from Wales?"

"You may indeed, Richard, that is understood. As you are so late now leaving Oxford for Gloucester, perhaps tonight you might stay with an associate who lives along the Burford Road in the direction of Gloucester. Lord Lovell is a most generous host and he will offer hospitality to you both. Here, take this letter of introduction from me. I drafted it before you arrived this morning, thinking our visit might take longer than anticipated. Lady Isabelle, I am certain you will find Lovell Hall and its location to your liking."

"Then I suppose this is farewell. We shall set forth. Will you accompany us to the gate?"

"Why of course. Nothing would please me more," Father James replied, bowing his head slightly.

As we proceeded down the stairway and into the quadrangle, Père Charles and Father James held back. They stood in the centre of the yard, talking in hushed tones. When Père Charles saw that I had stopped to wait for him, he motioned for me to continue. The porter then took notice of me and called out to the scout to fetch our horses from the warden's barn beyond the main gate. I could not imagine what Père Charles and his former tutor were discussing, but I did notice out of the corner of my eye that Father James passed a document to him under cover of his gown.

Our horses were brought to us and we mounted them, preparing to ride out of the college, while Father James walked forward to stand at the gate, bidding us a final farewell. As we passed him out of the gateway, he grabbed hold of Peyriac's rein to halt him. Beckoning me to bend down, I stooped over to the side to hear the message he wished to impart.

"Lady Isabelle, you are a remarkable and accomplished scholar, and a good friend to my former pupil. God speed you well on your journey. I pray that you bear with an open mind and heart what you will learn from Richard on this trip."

There was no time for me to respond, for as soon as he finished his statement he released the rein and Peyriac took off at a trot, quickly catching up to Père Charles's horse. Once we had brought our horses under control after rounding the corner at the intersection of New College Lane and Catte Street, it struck me that we were at last on our way to Wales, with no turning back.

XXXI
Minster Lovell Hall and the Abbey of St Peter in Gloucester

9 June 1453

We rode to the west out of Oxford in the direction of the manor house of Lord William Lovell. Tucked along the banks of the sleepy River Windrush, Minster Lovell Hall sat at the bottom of a vale off the well-travelled Burford Road. Surrounded by copses of elms whose full branches provided seclusion and privacy from the outside world, no lovelier setting for a manor had I ever visited.

After being presented to His Lordship, I was led away and shown to my guest chamber. Glancing back before leaving the entry hall, I noticed Père Charles handing our host the letter from Father James as Lord William and he exchanged whispered greetings. Father James's mysterious parting message, asking me to be accepting of what I was to learn about my chaplain on the trip, weighed heavily on my mind as we settled into our accommodation that evening. Having borne witness to the moments of madness that had nearly caused him to take his own life, I feared the worst: that what Father James referred to were the demons plaguing my chaplain's mind.

Lord and Lady Lovell provided us with generous hospitality, and over dinner His Lordship described the measures he had taken to build a residence befitting his family's noble lineage. When he learned of my interest in architecture, he proudly showed us the manor, pointing out that the recently completed courtyard-plan house had been built with three separate wings. One included a great hall, a chapel and a solar, another accommodated the bakehouse and kitchen, and the third held the apartments for family.

No expense was spared in the design and detail of his home. The carved stone bosses and delicate quadripartite vaulting found in the chapel, great hall and even on the entry porch were fitting additions to a manor built for a nobleman of Lord Lovell's standing. Windows were placed in most rooms of the hall, some quatrefoil, others cinquefoil, all of them a further attestation to the wealth of the owner.

"At last, we come to my favourite room in the manor: it is my chapel. Do step inside and follow me, I have something very beautiful to show you two."

We followed our host into the sacred space, located on the ground floor.

"It brings me great joy to share this with you." Lord Lovell placed in my hand his most prized possession; a *cloisonné* astel.

"Why, what is it?" I remarked, holding the delicate object up to the light of a candle for better inspection.

"It appears to be an instrument used in the reading of Biblical text, Lady Isabelle," Père Charles replied.

"That is indeed correct," Lord Lovell confirmed. "This artefact was given to my ancestors by King Alfred. It has survived many centuries of use and travel. I keep it here, in the chapel, where it is safe from the prying eyes of visitors."

I was fascinated by the shape and design of the pointer. The craftsmanship of the Lovell astel showed a remarkable level of detail. Delicately shaped gold *cloisonné* and contrasting blue, green and white enamel covered the jewel. As I gazed upon the object I held in my hand, the shape of a cross appeared before my eyes. I felt the Lord confirming his blessing on England as he had done for the king who had ruled over five hundred years earlier.

As we parted company from Lord Lovell the following morning, he invited us back to stay with him again when we returned from Wales, an offer we gratefully accepted.

Our trip to Gloucester continued through an affluent pastoral region called the Cod's Wold, and proved to be a most agreeable journey. We passed through many tiny villages including Burford, Little Barrington and Northleach. As we rode through them, Père Charles pointed out the many wool churches, so called because of the area's wool trade that had led to their foundation. The pretty churches were all built of the same golden limestone as the colleges and town wall of Oxford I had seen the previous morning from the vantage point of Headington Hill at daybreak.

We covered a great distance, stopping only to give the horses rest at a public house in Northleach. That afternoon we enjoyed fine weather as we rode along towards the River Severn and the city of Gloucester. As we approached the town's centre, I noticed a number of barges tied up along the banks of the river, indicating Gloucester's prominence as a trading outpost for the west country.

Our accommodation for the evening was at the Abbey of St Peter, where Father James had suggested we seek hospitality.

The abbey complex was massive, on a scale similar to that of the Collegiate Church of St Peter in London, and upon our arrival the monks welcomed me to stay in their guest quarters. Such lodging was normally only accorded to members of the nobility. It was through their benefactions that the monastery had survived through periods of the Black Death, while neighbouring towns and villages were decimated in the wake of the plague.

After dismounting, I was taken to my guest room adjacent to the porter's lodge, while Père Charles was directed to the monk's dormitory. With my personal possessions securely stored, I patiently waited in my room until I heard his footsteps coming up the stairs. He first knocked and then peered around the door that I had left slightly ajar.

"Shall we join the other members of the abbey for vespers?"

Joining him, we were halfway down the stairs when Père Charles pulled me aside. In a low voice, so that no one else would hear our exchange, he asked about our ride to Gloucester that afternoon.

"Lady Isabelle, what has kept you quiet all day? It is not customary for us to ride in complete silence for so long. Even when we took our rest at the hostelry in Northleach, you kept your thoughts to yourself. Please, confide in me. Are you concerned about our trip to Wales?"

"Father James said something to me as we left New College that has left me wondering about the true purpose of our journey. We are not merely following the path of Geraldus Cambrensis, are we? This is not simply another academic exercise as part of my lessons, is it?"

"No, you are quite right. We must speak, but this is neither the moment nor the place to do so. I assure you, Your Ladyship, do not fear. What I have to tell you will clarify everything you have come to know about me."

As we reached the bottom stair, still speaking in hushed voices, we were greeted by two monks who asked us to follow them into the abbey church. I hoped that the tranquillity of the sung service might help me think through the events that had occurred since meeting with Father James in Oxford the previous day. As we joined the community of monks for vespers that evening, I prayed that our time in Wales would not result in any harm falling upon us. The parting message and the passing of a secret document between the men had left me with a feeling of apprehension that I could not abandon.

Over the course of the service, from the deepening shadows grew the sound of male voices, their highs and their lows, unaccompanied in full plainchant. Against the flicker of soft candlelight came a holy sound, full of God's might, first from one side of the nave, then repeated on the other. With my eyes closed I listened and something stirred from deep inside. Suddenly my heart was aflutter. For in every note, sung with precision, came the response of scripture achieved with such vision, leaving my soul enraptured.

The chanting had worked; in quiet meditation I shut out the sounds of the world around me and remained deep in silent prayer, seeking comfort in unburdening my concerns.

"*O Lord in Heaven, all-powerful and merciful Father, please grant that I might be guarded in your safekeeping on this journey. Many troubling matters fill my mind and I pray for the soul of my chaplain, that he continues to do what is right in following the teachings of your Son, Jesus Christ. Absolve him, Father, of any sin that he has committed, whether in thought or by deed. In the name of Jesus Christ I pray. Amen.*"

I opened my eyes to the dimness of the candlelit interior of the church. Père Charles stood waiting at the end of our row.

"I apologise for my tardiness, I did not realise the service had ended," I said in a hushed voice as I joined him. My eyes searched the nave for the members of the abbey, who had long since walked silently past.

"You were consumed in prayer and I did not wish to disturb you. Join me now, I see the abbot in the doorway there, waiting for us to join him at supper."

Over the course of our meal that evening, I remained so preoccupied with my own thoughts that I heard not a single word of the conversation around me until I was drawn into the exchange.

"Abbot Seabroke, have I told you that our journey to Wales will follow the path of one of your noted scholars, Geraldus Cambrensis?" enquired my chaplain.

"Why no, I had not been made aware of that. He was indeed a man of great repute here in our abbey. Our monks still copy his Latin texts chronicling the history of Wales and the Welsh people."

"We are embarking on a trip to provide Her Ladyship with some context for his writings. Like Gerald, she keeps journals of her experiences and the places she has travelled."

"The church has many interesting styles of building. Might you have time to tell me about its history?" I asked, delighted that the conversation was turning to topics of interest to me.

Though lively and filled with rich historical detail, as our conversation carried on, my eyelids felt increasingly heavy with fatigue. I caught my companion's gaze. He nodded in my direction, and I looked back wearily, for it had been a full day of riding.

"I am afraid I must interrupt you here, Abbot Seabroke. We are quite tired from our journey today. Might we excuse ourselves and take some rest?"

"Why, of course, you may. Lady Isabelle, I hope you find our guest quarters comfortable and to your liking. Agatha, our laundress, will see that you are well looked after here. Father Richard, we have made up a cot for you in one of the cells of the dormitory where you left your satchel earlier. If you two are ready, you may be excused."

"Thank you, Abbot Seabroke," Père Charles replied. "Your hospitality to weary pilgrims is greatly appreciated. We have much distance to cover tomorrow if we are to arrive at Tintern Abbey in time for vespers there."

We took our leave from our host and stepped out of the refectory into the hushed cloister of the monastery. When we reached my lodgings, my chaplain turned his back to me, as if to walk away without a word of farewell. Then he turned again and stopped. Looking me straight in the eyes and leaning in, he gently cupped his hand around my neck, pulling me towards him, bringing my ear to his lips. In a whisper, barely audible even to me, he simply said, "You shall soon know."

As he slowly drew back, I had to resist the temptation to hold on to him. I longed to take his face in my hands, to force him to look at me and recount the hidden details of his past that I sensed he had omitted from his earlier confession on board the *Salamanca*. Instead, we stood there, unable to speak another word to each other. Several moments passed, until finally a door at the top of the stairway opened and a shaft of light poured down from above.

"Lady Isabelle, is that you out there?" The voice could only be that of Agatha. "Do come upstairs; I have your chamber ready."

"Yes, Agatha, thank you. I shall be up presently," I responded, trying to temper my annoyance at the thought that she had been watching us.

I stepped away from Père Charles and climbed the stairs to Agatha and the source of light. I wondered whether he read the disappointment in my face at having to part from him when I really wished to stay and hear what truths he might have to impart.

XXXII
Itinerarium Kambriae

11 June 1453

After attending morning prayer and Mass with the monks of St Peter's at dawn, we left Gloucester for Tintern Abbey. When we stopped to rest at midday, I found I could not contain my doubts about our journey any longer.

"I cannot blame you for having such thoughts," Père Charles affirmed tenderly. "Yet there is no reason to fear, I assure you. I have told you about my life, who I am and why I am here. Please have faith in me that I do care deeply for you. We have spoken of this before."

I turned away, looking out across the rows of thin saplings in the distance before responding.

"Then tell me; what is the burden that Father James told me I shall discover and why do you not confide in me as I have so often in you?"

"I do apologise, but there is nothing more I can share with you. I bear a great responsibility in caring for you. Yet it is one that I accept with great pleasure."

"How can you refuse to tell me the truth? What am I asking of you that is so great you fear you must hide information from me?

Have I not proven to you that I can be trusted?" I demanded with frustration.

"If only it were so simple," replied my chaplain. "Please know how grateful I am for your friendship; that I have been able to confide in you about the voices I hear and the fears that do not abate from my childhood memories. Listen; do you notice the birds in the trees?"

I nodded my head in silence.

"Even here, so far from the court in London and the courtiers who still hunt for me; even amidst such natural beauty and the peace that surrounds us, where we have seen not another soul on our journey; even now do I worry for who or what might appear around every bend in the road, in the shadowy depths of the forests, from behind the boulders along the route. I cannot even begin to feel calm until we are in the safety of those who offer us hospitality."

"Then why, oh why, did you agree to make this journey with me? If you knew it might be difficult, we should never have endeavoured to come!"

"I have wanted to escort you to St Davids since you first took an interest in the work of Geraldus Cambrensis; please do not ask me to forsake such pleasure. I asked James to send letters to various constables and abbots who will host us on our journey. This will ensure us of our safety overnight. These men know me by my English name, Richard Goodwyn, and James will certainly have provided our hosts with information about you."

"Your episodes of madness are of great concern to me," I pressed him. "I want for your mind to be healed and the demon voices silenced. I fear this trip will only serve to make them louder and stronger. I have seen you attempt to take your own life – a mortal sin – several times; you frighten me in those moments. This is what Father James cautioned me about, your state of mind, is it not?" I asked, determined to uncover the truth. "And what is it that you promised me I should know soon?"

"Lady Isabelle, you must stop. Do not take this conversation any further."

With mounting trepidation I could see the rising vexation in Père Charles's demeanour.

"For the last time, do not mention this subject again!" he jumped up from the boulder on which he sat and glared at me. "Do not concern yourself with what James said in Oxford!"

———

We arrived at Tintern Abbey in time to attend the vesper service. Although it was not included amongst the places visited and described by Gerald, it proved, as predicted by Father James, to be a notable example of the simplicity and light that characterised Cistercian architecture. The abbey's idyllic location, situated along the wooded banks of the tranquil River Wye, suited the venerable building.

We sat in the church's sanctuary, where I was given special permission to remain alongside my chaplain during vespers. With candlelight illuminating the fine architectural details throughout the interior, I gazed about in wonder. Deep pointed arches were repeated throughout the building, drawing my eyes ever upwards to the soaring clerestory windows towering overhead. At the ends of the transept and nave were monumental lancet windows capped with traceried roundels. After the difficult discussion with my chaplain and his heated outburst earlier in the day, the contemplative worship brought spiritual relief. My shoulders and back, having borne the tension of the ride and our conversation, relaxed as I inhaled and exhaled deeply during the course of our peaceful mediation.

In the midst of the service, after staring intently upon the altar and crucifix for some time, I suddenly felt the world around me disappear. With my eyes closed in silent reflection I experienced a fleeting vision. An ephemeral figure clutched at me, pulling me close. For several brief moments I felt the rapture of transcendence; my wearied spirit became safely nestled in the Lord's presence in my heart: He reminded me that I was not alone on my journey.

Hearing the choral melody chanted by the monks helped to soothe my mind, offering it a respite from the thoughts of what possible dangers lay in wait for us along our pilgrimage through Wales. That evening I sought an affirmation of my calling; that I might be made to know how best to love and serve the Lord, with all my heart.

———

The next morning a monk knocked on my door to collect me for the predawn service of prime. As the service wore on, sunlight poured through the numerous massive windows, filling the entire space with bright illumination. We departed from Tintern Abbey not long after daybreak, travelling towards Cardiff, at last on the path taken by Gerald and mentioned in his *Descriptio Kambriae*.

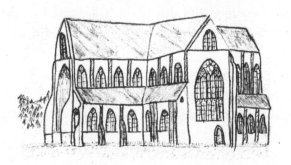

The evening stars had appeared when we finally arrived at Cardiff Castle. After presenting the captain with our letters of introduction, we were shown to the constable's privy hall. As we prepared to take our seats at the dinner table, the constable entered the room and approached my companion. The two men exchanged pleasantries. They embraced each other as the constable whispered in a tone barely audible the three words I had heard spoken so often before with the now familiar response given by my chaplain. The constable nodded his head slightly, indicating that we should be seated for our meal. Over dinner he invited us to stay in the castle's guest apartments that night.

Perhaps from my fatigue at all the riding we had done over the previous few days, or my concern over what had become of Sir Henry, before I fell into a deep slumber I experienced another vision that would stay present in my mind for the duration of our journey to St Davids.

The Lord came to me, telling me that I would soon know his purpose for me. He assured me that I must not fear what I would witness; that it was his love that I carried in my heart, and his grace and mercy that I must be prepared to shower on one of his fallen children whose mind was plagued by fears of great unworthiness. God told me that it was his desire that I provide this person with assurance of my love, and that, as such, I would help defeat the evils that filled his thoughts and caused him to bring harm upon himself and others.

The vision ended as suddenly as it had come to me; I opened my eyes, breathless and searching in the darkness of my room for anything on which I could fix my gaze to help allay my fears.

————

The next morning, we awoke early and set off for Margam Abbey, a distance of twenty-eight miles, again following the path taken by the scholar and historian Gerald. Like Tintern, Margam belonged to the Cistercian order and had been founded by monks from Clairvaux in France.

We arrived in time to be shown to our separate accommodation in the guest range before attending vespers. However, once I was seated in the abbey church, and I could properly take in my surroundings, I found a certain air of sadness about the place, as if its days of grandeur and magnificence had passed and it was in a period of decline.

Surveying the architectural details of the nave illuminated by candlelight, I could see where repairs to the walls and window tracery were urgently needed. Although the space was considerably longer than that of Tintern, it lacked the height and upper register of windows that would have created a sense of ethereal grandeur.

As we left the church after the service, I stopped to regard the façade. It was plain and unadorned. I wondered what was different in the history of the place to make it contrast so greatly with its sister abbey at Tintern. My questions were answered by our host, Prior Thomas, after we had finished dining in the abbey's refectory. The prior invited us to join him briefly in the chapter house before he led the monks in compline. Four of the brothers were already there, talking quietly in a group, when we arrived. We seated ourselves apart from them and listened intently as the prior described the financial affairs of the house before he changed the subject to the purpose for our travel.

"I must beg your pardon, My Lady. I have been so consumed with relating the dismal state our own affairs that I wholly ignored the reason behind your journey," Prior Thomas said, turning his attention to me.

"You are here to visit the place where Geraldus Cambrensis once stayed and about which he wrote in his *Itinerarium Kambriae*. His visit to our abbey in the late twelfth century was during the height of the abbey's affluence. Let me see, now... If I remember correctly, his entry for Margam Abbey included a charming anecdote about the loyalty of dogs to their masters. Did he not relate the story of a certain greyhound, belonging to a Welshman named Owain ap Iestin, who attacked his owner's assailants after they had killed Owain? I believe Gerald went on to describe how the loyal animal, marked with the wounds inflicted upon him as he had tried in vain to protect his master, was presented as a gift to King Henry II of England as an example of dogs' devotion to their owners. He also described a story by Saint Ambrose of a particular dog's ability to recognise his master's killer in a crowd of people. Dogs are indeed loyal beasts, are they not?"

"That is one of my favourite passages!" I exclaimed. "Père Charles and I spent many days analysing the text. I love all animals; indeed, I would say that horses, too, offer boundless loyalty to their owners."

"I do believe animals are a special gift from our Lord to all mankind; horses and dogs in particular," Prior Thomas concurred with a nod.

The evening soon drew to a close, and the three of us prepared to leave the chapter house.

"Just a moment, before you two go to your accommodation, there is something I must tell you, please follow me," Prior Thomas instructed.

We followed him in the direction of the guest range. Stepping into the deserted open space we were out of earshot of the monks in the chapter house.

"Your friend from Oxford, Father James Redding, has sent correspondence to me that arrived just before you did. He asked me to relay the news to you both, but only in safe quarters."

"What news has he then?" Père Charles asked.

"He says you must take extra precautions to guard against outlaws until you reach the safety of St Davids," Prior Thomas replied gravely.

"Outlaws? But we are already doing that, are we not? We do not stop unless we are in a clearing where no ambush can take place and we do not travel after dark," I asked with uncertainty.

"He does not go into detail, My Lady," Prior Thomas said. "He gave that instruction and he also mentioned the need to safeguard your treasure."

Père Charles and I exchanged concerned glances.

"We must not speak of this here, not even outside here," Père Charles said.

"What is the treasure he mentions?" I asked, confused.

"Never mind that for the moment," Père Charles said. "What is more important is our safety along the road."

"I agree," the prior nodded his head. "You must carry on in secret, the two of you. Know that I have sent word ahead and there will be reinforcements along the route who will watch you from a distance: you will not see them. Ride in safety knowing help is never far away. This Welsh guard are familiar with the roads and their topography far better than any Englishman."

"I am grateful, Thomas, thank you," Père Charles said.

"You are very welcome. I care for you and your friend. May you reach St Davids without incident," Prior Thomas stated.

"I shall pray for you, and for the future of Margam," I said sincerely.

"We welcome your prayers, My Lady. Richard, it is always a pleasure to see you. Please do pass along my greetings to your tutor James when you see him next."

"I shall. Come now, Lady Isabelle. Let us retire to our rooms, for the morning will soon be upon us."

———

We spent ten hours travelling to Kidwelly the next day, located to the north of Margam, along the coast. First crossing the two Gwendraeth streams on the edge of the town, at last we reached the town's fortified gate, bathed in long rays of sunshine. Once inside the town walls, we rode up an embankment before arriving at the castle's imposing gatehouse. The fortification's concentric design, its outer curtain wall punctuated with mural towers, perfectly suited its location, seated along the plateau of a steep ridge overlooking the River Gwendraeth below.

As we approached the barbican, a drawbridge was lowered for us. Père Charles dismounted and offered the porter our letters of introduction. After they had been examined, a pair of portcullises slowly lifted, allowing us entry into the outer ward of the castle.

The captain came forward with a groom, who bowed and took the reins from our hands.

"Good evening, Your Ladyship. Welcome back to Kidwelly, Richard, do follow me. Constable Perry awaits you in his privy hall for supper."

We followed the captain, entering the inner ward. I took in my surroundings, for never had I been in such a fortified castle. Not even Château Benauges was so heavily defended. As we climbed the stairs to the first-floor privy hall, I felt dwarfed by the four massive round corner towers, each rising to a height of three floors, the same height as the donjon where Margaret had been kept prisoner.

Glancing up at the tower before me as I stood upon the steps, I saw through an open window that the interior of the room was brightly illuminated by the late-afternoon sun. I felt my heart swell as I beheld the shimmer of a gilded cross placed on an altar covered with a white cloth in the chapel. An overwhelming sense of peace and comfort came over me after glimpsing the divine space.

We continued climbing the stairs until we reached the privy hall, where we stopped to wash our hands and faces in a laver at the entrance.

When he saw my guardian enter the hall, the constable rose from his seat and walked towards us, his arms outstretched in greeting.

"Welcome, Richard. You have come from afar." Constable Perry placed his arms around his friend and greeted him with a warm smile. "It has been well over ten years since we parted company when you left New College."

"Robert, friend, it is a pleasure to see you again as well. We thank you for your generous hospitality this evening. May I present Her Ladyship, Isabelle d'Albret Courteault. We are journeying to St Davids, following the path of Geraldus Cambrensis as part of Lady Isabelle's education."

"It is indeed a pleasure to make your acquaintance, Your Ladyship." Constable Perry bowed his head in deference to me as he took up my hand and kissed it. Smiling genuinely at me he continued, "Please, both of you, do come and join me at dinner."

Over supper the two men exchanged accounts of the intervening twelve years since they had been pupils together at New College. Both had been mentored by Father James, and it was clear that their bonds of friendship ran deep.

With our meal almost over, Constable Perry turned his attention to me and shared some startling news pertaining to my family.

"I am afraid that today, in anticipation of your arrival, I received a distressing message that affects you, My Lady. It was sent by Father James who knew how to get word to you safely. It has been reported that your aunt was recently in London under the assumption that she was to meet secretly with fellow members of the French King's Court who are on embassy in London and discuss what she knows of the English plans to protect Gascony. But the delegation who called her to meet them were not members of the French nobility; she was implicated by Edmund Somerset and other members of the Privy Council who believe that your aunt is a spy for her brother in the French army. It is rumoured that they wish to see her hang for treason. I am sorry to deliver such disturbing news, but I believe you must be made aware that you and your family are likely to fall under suspicion now. You are safe here in Wales with Richard as your guardian, but once you return to England you should take extreme caution until you are reunited. I have heard that in London there is a growing distrust of those from France and Gascony who reside in our country."

For several moments I sat in shock as I absorbed the news he had shared. In my mind, I recalled my vision at Rosete, the evening when we had returned with Margaret from Benauges. With horror, I realised that this was the first prophecy the Lord had sent me that had come true. My aunt was to be hanged for her treasonous sympathies! Certainly Father must know of his sister's fate. What would he say now to those concerns I had previously expressed about the document I possessed implicating my aunt? The Duke of Somerset was also the one responsible for telling Sir Henry about my chaplain's true identity. With dread, I worried for the safety of my family, and closed my eyes to say a quick prayer of mercy upon my aunt's soul.

"What you tell me is most alarming, Constable Perry. I fear for myself and my family, especially Sarah and Christophe, who are all now together in London. Père Charles, what will become of them?"

"We will have to wait for further news, I am afraid. In the meantime, as Constable Perry suggested, I shall do all in my ability to provide for your safety, you have my assurance of that. Let not your heart be troubled, Your Ladyship. You are secure with us tonight as I am sure your family is in London with those who are looking to protect them there."

Since our meal was now finished, my companions suggested we arrange our chairs before the fire. Constable Perry directed his attention upon me again, though this time the subjects under discussion were much lighter.

"Lady Isabelle, if my friend Richard is doing a proper job of tutoring you, then you are aware that the author of the *Itinerarium*

Kambriae and his fellow travellers spent the night in this very castle."

"Indeed, I believe that is why we have chosen to stay with you," I replied, the level of intimacy between the constable and my guardian having created an inclusive bond of friendship between the three of us.

"You must recall that Gerald related the history of a famous battle staged not far from here. Princess Gwenllian led an army of Welshmen against the forces of Englishman Maurice of London and Geoffrey, Constable of Roger. Her husband, Gruffydd ap Rhys, the Prince of South Wales, had gone to the north in search of military reinforcements. The fearless Gwenllian, whom Gerald likened to Penthesilea, Queen of the Amazons, rode into battle with two of her sons. Her son Morgan was killed, while her other son, Maelgwn, was taken prisoner by the English. The princess lost her life in a most violent manner, for she was beheaded. Many in her retinue suffered the same fate."

"I recall that passage well; I have often thought of the princess's courage in the face of overwhelming adversity. Comparing her with the queen killed during the siege of Troy is a fitting tribute to her remarkable heroism."

"I remember studying the text with Richard as we sat in James's room across the great quad from the college's chapel and hall. At the time I was unaware that I would one day be serving as constable in the very castle that lies adjacent to the place where the famous battle was fought. Those were such special days, were they not, my friend?" The constable's wistful tone marked his fondness for his time as a student and he cast his eyes upon his friend seated across the way.

"They were indeed. Lady Isabelle has been to New College and met our tutor."

"And was our college to your liking, Your Ladyship?" enquired Constable Perry.

"Oh yes, very much so. I only wish I were allowed to study in such a hallowed place; though I am blessed to have a fine tutor myself."

Père Charles caught my glance and our eyes locked.

"And what of the choir, Your Ladyship? Did you happen to hear their sung office?"

"We did arrive in time to attend morning prayer in chapel. I was pleased to recognise the words of the psalm in the sung offering, *Sicut cervus desiderat*; they hold a special place in my heart. We had a lesson in plainchant when we stayed in London with the monks of St Peter's Abbey. The piece we studied was composed by Johannes Ockeghem and the words were the very same."

"I see," Constable Perry said with a knowing smile. "And did your chaplain disclose to you that he has a most emotive voice and that he sang in the choir at New College? In fact, we both did, did we not, Richard?"

Constable Perry's tone hinted at the nostalgia he felt for the time the two men had spent in Oxford.

"Ah yes, so we did, Robert." Père Charles nodded his head slowly in agreement. "Though I think you exaggerate my vocal capabilities. Singing in the choir with you and the other young boys is one of my fondest recollections of life in college."

"One day, might I have the opportunity to hear you sing for me?" I asked my chaplain directly, catching him off guard. He immediately changed the subject without replying to my question.

"We had a long ride today, covering much difficult terrain. Tomorrow we shall continue on another long ride to Whitland Abbey."

"Then perhaps you should like to retire for the night. I shall summon my servant to show you to your rooms," Constable Perry offered, ringing a bell for assistance.

The constable then walked us to the door.

"Richard and Lady Isabelle, I bid you both a pleasant stay here tonight. You will recall, Richard, that our chapel is in the tower to your right as you leave this chamber. You may enter freely at any time. Rest well tonight, both of you. I shall take pleasure in seeing you off tomorrow morning."

———

I found I could not sleep that night out of concern for the fates of my aunt and family in London. I rose from my bed, silently leaving my bedchamber. Making my way across the inner ward to the steps leading to the privy hall, I sought the comfort of the sacred surroundings of the castle's chapel for prayer.

Upon walking up the stairs, I could see the light of several candles flickering gently through a partially opened door. Then I stopped. Two male voices could be heard coming from inside. As I turned to leave I was surprised to recognise my chaplain's voice. I inched closer in the shadows to hear and see more.

"I have heard no reports of such matters, Robert; not even James shared that information with me when I was in Oxford with him recently." Père Charles's normally calm voice was raised in alarm.

"It does not surprise me, Richard. Being in Oxford, James is far removed from the Brotherhood in Wales. But I can assure you, there is nothing for you to fear. We shall protect you. We shall *all* protect you."

"But I hear voices, Robert. I see phantoms in my sleep! I must do all I can to keep from either harming myself or others without being aware of it. I dare not tell anyone outside of the Brotherhood for fear of being charged with heresy for such actions. Only Lady Isabelle has witnessed their aftermath. By God's mercy she has told no one what she has seen and she has assured me of her devotion and friendship. I am so grateful for her kindness and love; without them I would surely have ended my life upon my return to England. I fear now as I complete this journey – a journey that will end in uncertainty, for me, for you, for all those involved – that I am no longer in control. I fear soon I shall lose my mind completely. I must have the demons exorcized, but now there is no time to do so."

I could tell from his weakened voice that he was close to tears. I longed to rush to his side and comfort him, but I remained, waiting to hear what would be said next.

"Come, my friend. Allow me to hold you."

I listened as the constable stepped forward to take my chaplain in his arms.

"We are your support: you are not in this alone. Do not forget that. Everyone is aware of your situation. Do not fear what is to be done. Keep your faith in the Lord as you always have, for he shall be with you to see you through and return you safely to us. And to Lady Isabelle."

"But you have told me that Sir Henry was freed by his men while he was being brought to jail in Oxford. What if this group is now following us? What if they come upon us as we ride to St Davids? I could never forgive myself if he attacks us; or even worse, if he takes the life of Lady Isabelle."

"You must put such thoughts from your mind. We have received no confirmation that Sir Henry is crossing over into Wales. Even if he does, there are members of the Brotherhood in the Welsh Guard who are prepared to do battle with him to the end. Take care of your lady friend. You are but two days from the safety of St Davids. The others with whom you will stay will keep you both safe. Remember what we learn from the gospel of John; *No one has greater love than this: to lay down one's life for one's friends,*" the constable's tone was reassuring.

Back in my room that night I asked God to put my chaplain's mind at rest, that he would know the love of Christ deep within his soul where his darkest fears lay. So great and unending was Christ's love for us that if he could suffer more of his Passion for our sin he would do so over and over; his love for us was unending and eternal. I asked God to plant the seed of his love deep in my chaplain's spirit, to grow as a protective vine shielding him from the demons in his mind that sought to destroy him.

XXXIII
Haverfordwest Castle

T he ride to Haverfordwest was unlike our recent journeys: the countryside had changed completely. In addition to there being far fewer rivers to cross, the dense forests of the east unfolded into vast areas of rolling hills, dotted with tiny farms to the west. We rode through some thickets, but nothing like the wooded acreage we had previously traversed. Few other carts and riders were evident on our journey.

It was early evening as we approached the hilltop castle. We passed a few townspeople who were making their way along the narrow paths that meandered at irregular points off the town's main, steep street. I was impressed by the castle's formidable position; it sat on the plateau of a craggy hill affording the garrison who were stationed there a clear view of the approach to the town from all sides.

To make our way to the castle's entrance above, we had to leave our horses below; we climbed on foot through a labyrinth of narrow passageways, their high walls open to the sky above our heads, our progress carefully observed from above by the sentinels stationed along the castle's parapet.

When we finally reached the top, it was clear that we would indeed be secure for the night; it was not possible to reach the castle ward undetected.

Following our dinner with the constable in his privy hall, one of the soldiers showed us to our accommodation in a building across the inner ward and isolated from the other ranges of the castle compound. We were the only visitors and I was pleased to find that we had rooms along the same corridor.

After being shown to his bedchamber, Père Charles immediately excused himself from my company, explaining that he had personal business to discuss with the constable in private.

Left to myself, I turned my attention to my journal, noting the events of the past few days. Following my prayers that evening, I extinguished my candle and climbed into bed, hoping to gain the rest I needed for the ride to St Davids in the morning.

Sometime later that night, I woke, startled by angry voices and what sounded like a brawl in the room next to mine. Worried for my chaplain's safety, I lit a candle and carried it out into the dark and empty passage. Approaching the door to Père Charles's room cautiously, I listened for the voices. But there was only silence.

I had decided to return to my room when I heard a man's voice shriek with agony. My heart pounding in fear, yet determined to see who was there, I rushed back to the door, slowly pushing it open, uncertain what or whom I would find on the other side. From the dark of the corridor, with only candlelight to illuminate the space, I could see nothing. With great trepidation I opened the door wider, still hearing and seeing nothing. As I stepped cautiously into the room, a hand reached out and grabbed my neck from behind.

In our struggle, the candle dropped from my hand and went out, plunging the space into complete darkness. I tried to scream but another hand covered my mouth and nose, preventing me from uttering a sound. The person dragged me to the bed as I tried to free myself, kicking and biting my adversary, but to no avail. I was trapped in the dark with no one to help me! Out of desperation I tried to pull his hands from my face but his strength overpowered me. Instantly I was struck with panic as images of my attack in the stable at Boarstall flooded my mind. My whole body became awash with the sweat of fear. I was certain I had been caught by Sir Henry! I began to shudder and cry, certain this time I would not survive whatever my assailant had planned for me.

And then the attacker moved his face closer to mine. As my eyes adjusted to the darkness that filled the shutterless room, I could finally make out who was there. It was Père Charles who was attempting to strangle me, not Sir Henry! His fair hair caught the reflection of the dim light and by his rough actions I could sense that a brutal change had come over him. The intensity of his facial expression had become one of burning anger and malice.

"No! Stop!" I attempted to scream, my voice weak, his grip around my throat so tight that I could barely make a sound. I struggled in vain to free myself. "Why are you hurting me? It is me, Lady Isabelle! Please don't kill me! Remember me? Isabelle? Your charge? Please, Père Charles, release me!" I pleaded, my voice no louder than a hoarse whisper. As I looked into his vacant eyes, I could see they were devoid of any acknowledgement of who I was.

At that moment I felt as though he was looking straight through me. Unable to make a sound, my breathing became shallow and constricted by the force of his grasp. Feeling light-headed, I was about to expire when suddenly he released me and dropped to his knees, hunching forward onto the floor. Rolling to his side, he curled himself into a ball. His whole body shook as he let out a deep and mournful wail.

I coughed roughly, trying to catch my breath, inhaling deeply to overcome my dizziness. In that moment, I witnessed a bright flash of light before my eyes as I heard the voice of the Lord directing me not to fear what I was witnessing.

Seeing my chaplain struggling with himself before me on the floor, so vulnerable, so clearly fighting against some unseen force within his soul, touched me deeply in my heart. With renewed compassion for the man I dearly loved, I hastened to be by his side, wishing to comfort him, choosing my words slowly and deliberately. On bended knees I reached over his recumbent body, laying my head upon his side. I placed my hands over his, gently alerting him to my presence, not wishing to shock him.

"Père Charles," I said calmly, my voice low and soft, barely louder than a whisper, "I am here now; you are safe with me. Can you hear me? I shall not leave you; do not fear, there is no one here but me."

I turned my body and sat next to him, leaning my back against the bed frame, taking his head and gently laying it in the folds of cloth from my dressing gown gathered about my waist. He remained unaware of my nearness. Gently stroking his face and head, I felt the cold, damp sweat of his body as it lingered on my fingertips.

The shock of the ordeal I had just experienced began to set in. I knew his madness was triggered by conditions beyond his control. I should have been afraid, I should have run away and left him, but instead I only felt pity for how he must be suffering in his mind with the demons of his past haunting him.

I continued to watch over him until eventually he awoke, as if from a dream. He turned his face and looked up at me, his head still nestled protectively against my lap. After what I had heard him admit to his friend in the chapel at Kidwelly, I knew what he needed most was to be exorcized of the devil that had hold of his soul.

"Lady Isabelle, what happened? Why are you here in my room? Why are we on the floor?" he enquired, the calm timbre of his voice once again the one I recognised as that of my friend and chaplain.

"Was I dreaming? Did I awaken you? I had such a terrible vision. I cannot tell whether what I experienced was only a dream or became something more. Did you see anything? Can you tell me what happened and how we came to be here together?"

Keeping my voice steady, I did as he asked of me.

"I awakened to the sound of voices and strange noises coming from your room. When I opened the door I could not see any-one inside. I proceeded to enter the room and that is when…" I paused, uncertain whether I should indeed tell him what he had done to me.

"Please, you must tell me, what happened next? Did I harm you? I can remember nothing of the incident. Please, tell me, did I raise a hand against you?"

I closed my eyes, for I could not immediately bring myself to admit the horror of feeling him nearly strangle me to death. Gently stroking his face to offer him assurance of my devotion, I described the moment he had seized me.

After my confession, he closed his eyes and lay silently weep-ing, initially unable to find the words to express his sorrow for his actions.

"There, there. I forgive you. I shall always forgive you. Is that not what our faith teaches us? The love of Jesus Christ and the fire of the Holy Spirit will protect you with their grace and mercy. They will defeat the evil that seeks to consume you in the moments when you feel your mind trapped by thoughts of great unworthiness. You had another one of your visions, did you not? Did someone in your vision tell you to hurt me?"

After some time, he regained his composure enough to respond.

"From what I can remember, I was asleep, and in my dream, or what I thought to be a dream, I heard someone knock at my door. I rose up and walked over to answer the call. Before I could even get there they jumped out at me from the corners of the room: four of them. There was nowhere I could hide. I thought that perhaps they could not see me in the dark of the room. I threw the chair at them, then the table. Next, I heard someone at my door. I lay in wait for him, prepared to jump on him as he entered and attack him from behind. When the door opened I sprang on him."

Père Charles paused and looked up at me, his sorrowful eyes full of concern.

"But that person was you! How could I have ever raised a hand against you?" He began to cry softly again. "I am so deeply sorry for what I have done. I shall never be able to forgive myself, for I have now brought you into the very depth of my madness. How can you ever bear to look at me or be alone in my company?"

In response to his honesty, I yearned to comfort him. I positioned myself on the floor with my chest against his back, enfolding my arms around him. Together we rested, with him cocooned in my arms, until he fell asleep again. At that moment I could sense his utter vulnerability. What he needed most was to feel the loving presence of his mother whom he had lost under the most terrible of circumstances.

I spent the remainder of the night enveloping him, my whole body and soul intent on trying to help ease the pain that nearly two decades of secrecy and hiding had inflicted upon his tortured soul.

When we awoke a few hours later, the dawn had yet to come. I broke the deep silence between us.

"You must understand that I know you as a kind and gentle man, one who cannot, and through the path of his vocation will not, raise a hand to strike another. What you did to me last night shall remain between us and us alone. I recognise now that you need me as much as I need you. The Lord has joined us on this path together, to remain steadfast and true to one another. It is not my place to stand in judgement of you, for I have not experienced the violent horrors of murder as you have. Take it upon your heart that I shall forever cherish you; even in your darkest moments, I shall always remain your friend. Do not ever forget that."

"After what I did to you last night, how can I ever trust myself not to harm you?" Père Charles took my hands in his as a sign of his sincere remorse. "Your grace and compassion are a testament to your faith and courage, Lady Isabelle, and your attentive love and friendship bring me such comfort. I pray I never do anything again to harm you or cause you to fear me."

We sat together, a comfortable silence between us, for in recognising the terror and pain of what we had endured that night, our honest exchange of feelings somehow consoled us, drawing us closer to one another through God's mercy. As we remained side by side, each of us lost in the silence of our own thoughts, the sound of birds calling out their predawn song roused us from our weary state and we parted from each other to get some rest before embarking on the final day of our journey.

———

Later that morning as we rode away from Haverfordwest, my mind filled with many conflicting images. I felt an overwhelming weariness after what I had witnessed the previous night. From his sombre expression I could sense that Père Charles was consumed with guilt over the sin he had committed against me.

We stopped to rest at midday near a small clearing in a copse, a short distance from the road. I spread out my woollen rug and we sat down together to share the food parcel the cook at Haverfordwest Castle had prepared for us.

I asked my chaplain the question that had weighed heavily upon my mind since experiencing his uncontrollable wrath being unleashed upon me.

"I am curious – what happened last night after we first parted? You went to speak privately to the constable. Are you at liberty to tell me what you two discussed? Perhaps something that was said to you triggered the episode that raised you from your sleep?"

Père Charles collected his thoughts before responding.

"We spent some time talking about the war in Gascony. From what he described, I am afraid the end of the duchy is near. Unless the Earl of Shrewsbury and his troops are able to defend Bordeaux until more troops can be mustered throughout England, Gascony will fall this summer. From what he has heard, there is little support amongst the Welsh populace and those who reside in the western counties of England for either King Henry or the war in France. I fear the duchy may well be lost very soon. It is fortunate that your family escaped when they did."

"I cannot believe that what you tell me is true; certainly the lives of our servants and the clergy in Bazas who have been caring for and guarding our estate are now in peril. And Rosete? What is to become of our castle and lands?"

I took in a deep breath, my heavy sigh an indication of the resignation I felt in my heart at the thought of never seeing Rosete again.

"It is too soon to know what the outcome will be, Lady Isabelle. We must keep strong in our faith and continue to pray for those who remain in the duchy. I am sorry to have to bear such a distressing report."

I could not bring myself to think any more about the loss of my childhood home; the thought of never returning there was unbearable. Instead, I wished to learn if anything else had been imparted during the conversation between the constable and my chaplain that could have resulted in the tragic events of the previous night.

"Is that all that was said? Such information about the fall of the duchy would not cause your mind to hear voices and see people who do not exist."

"That is not the only news he wished to divulge. I am sorry to tell you this, Your Ladyship, but I also learned that Sir Henry Lormont has left Oxfordshire. He evaded capture, as we feared he might. A messenger arrived last night with word of Sir Henry's latest movements as I met with the constable; he is following our trail and is now but one day behind us. I learned he is not travelling alone. He rides with several members of his garrison. From what the constable described, they are searching for me. Learning that they are pursuing me very likely had something to do with my waking dream and subsequent attack on you."

"What shall we do? Must we turn north to Harlech and Beaumaris and cross into Ireland to escape them?"

"The constable has assured me that he will arrest Sir Henry and his men should they pass through Haverfordwest. However, if they are riding along the outlying roads then it is possible they will continue undetected, even by the Welsh Guard. We have no way of determining their path. We must keep our trust in the Lord that he will see us safely to the end of our journey – the Bishop's Palace at St Davids."

"How far away from us were they last night?" I asked fearfully.

"The constable had word this morning that they arrived in Swansea yesterday evening. That would put them somewhere en route to Kidwelly this morning. Let us not linger here any longer. I am concerned for our safety and wish for us to arrive in St Davids by this afternoon."

"The thought that Sir Henry is riding with the men who wish to kill you means I, too, may fall victim to them! I pray they are intercepted well before they reach St Davids."

"As do I, Lady Isabelle, as do I."

Together we stood up and began to gather our belongings. Sir Henry Lormont and his retinue were indeed closing in fast upon us, determined to destroy the sole survivor of that fateful night outside Cambridge so many years earlier.

XXXIV
St Davids

As we took up the road from Haverfordwest to St Davids that ran along the windswept cliffs of St Brides Bay, Père Charles pointed out Ireland, a narrow strip on the horizon. To the other side of us lay the nearly barren rolling hills of Pembrokeshire. The landscape that surrounded us astounded me, for I had never visited such a desolate place.

We passed tiny farms with their solitary crops standing isolated amidst the deforested flatland. As I had learned in the course of our conversation over supper with the prior at Margam Abbey, the woods that once covered the Pembrokeshire coast had been cleared long ago, the timber being used to build the many towns and ports located along the southern coast of Wales.

At last we saw a welcoming sight in the distance. Rising up like a beacon to residents and pilgrims alike, the roof of the cathedral's central tower could be seen from outside the town walls of St Davids as we made our approach.

Nearing the eastern entrance to the cathedral, we came upon an imposing gate tower standing alongside an octagonal two-storey bell tower. At once we stopped, for positioned below, down a gently sloping hill, was the magnificent cathedral, her gracious stone façade like that of a glorious monarch reigning nobly over the serene setting that lay about her foundation. Before we could enter and gather a closer look, we needed to declare our business to the porter stationed at the gatehouse. He came out to greet us as we approached on horseback.

"Good afternoon, pilgrims," he said jovially. "That is, I assume you are pilgrims. Most visitors who arrive this time of day, coming from the east as you have, are here on pilgrimage. What may I do for you two?"

"Good afternoon. I am Father Richard Goodwyn. We are here to see His Lordship, Bishop Griffin Nicholas. May we continue to the Bishop's Palace? I have sent word in advance and he is expecting us."

"Certainly, I have been informed that you two might be arriving today, Father. Follow the road as it makes a sharp turn down the hill and over the River Alun. The Bishop's Palace is on the other side of the cathedral."

After giving us our directions, the porter stepped to one side, opening the gate and allowing us to enter the yard.

As we rode down a lane lined with prebendal houses, the towering presence of the cathedral in all her majesty lay directly before us. At that moment I fully appreciated why David, the son of the king of Ceredigion, had chosen the *Vallis Rosina* as the divine location to build the Celtic monastery called Menevia in the sixth century. Built upon the foundation of Menevia, the cathedral, surrounded by a peaceful churchyard, sat adjacent to the River Alun. The comparatively lush haven was completely different from the stark countryside through which we had just ridden.

The close was laid out in such a manner that all the buildings fell under the shadow of the cathedral and the palace. After passing the residences of the precentor and the archdeacon of Carmarthen, we crossed a tiny bridge over the slowly flowing Alun to reach the gatehouse of the Bishop's Palace. I was grateful to be at last in the place that Gerald had worked so hard to make a metropolitan see, the seat of the bishopric. Being on the threshold of the mighty residence offered a sense of protection and comfort from the threat of Sir Henry and his pursuit of us.

Arriving at the palace's gatehouse, we stopped as another porter approached us to enquire after our visit.

"Good afternoon. May I ask what business you have here?"

"Good afternoon to you. We have come to meet Bishop Nicholas. Please inform him that Father Richard Goodwyn and Lady Isabelle d'Albret Courteault have arrived."

"You may dismount here. I will have your horses put up for you. The bishop prefers not to have any riding inside the courtyard of the palace."

"But where will they put Peyriac?" I asked, casting a concerned glance at Père Charles.

Before my chaplain could respond, the porter interjected.

"Fear not, My Lady. The horses will be kept in the pasture and stables with the bishop's."

"Be of faith." Père Charles's gentle voice calmed me as he dismounted and came around to help me do the same. "I know you are concerned for Peyriac, but I can assure you, he will be well cared for here."

"Is it safe for you to give our names to this stranger?" I asked in alarm.

"Do not be alarmed; he can be trusted. We are in safe keeping here at the palace. The people you shall meet are companions and friends of Father James; they will do us no harm, I assure you."

I felt a rush of warmth as my chaplain placed his hands on my sides to help steady me as I dismounted. As my feet landed on the ground I feared my knees might buckle under me from my fatigue. Thankfully, the porter was too busy taking our horses away to notice my momentary lack of composure. However, it had not escaped Père Charles's attention. He cupped his hand under my elbow for support as he guided me through the gateway and into the palace courtyard just as a page hastened to greet us and ask that we follow him.

We made our way around the courtyard to a wide stone porch and stairway leading to the bishop's hall. Once inside, the page bade us to wait while he announced our arrival. He quickly returned and asked that we follow him to another adjoining room, the bishop's solar. Upon entering the smaller room, the page quietly retreated, closing the door behind him.

"At long last, Richard, we meet again," Bishop Nicholas said, rising from his seat and stepping forward as the two men greeted each other.

"It has indeed been a long absence, but what a welcome reunion this is," Père Charles said, before introducing me.

"Lady Isabelle, allow me to welcome you personally to my home," Bishop Nicholas said, taking up my hand to kiss it gently.

Something about the way the bishop reacted to my presence with my chaplain gave me cause for alarm. At that moment I could not tell yet if I trusted him.

"It is indeed a pleasure for me to see my friend Richard again after many years," the bishop continued, "and to make your acquaintance as well. Our academic hall here in St Davids is known for its scholarship and we send our men up to Oxford if they prove they are of the calibre to study at the university. I imagine you have met our mutual friend, Father James Redding, a fellow at the New College of St Mary?"

"I have, indeed. He has been most helpful to us in preparing us for our journey," I nodded my head in acknowledgement.

"I assure you, St Davids is truly a unique place. Perhaps it is owing to our remote location, or perhaps our rich and powerful diocese. Whatever the reason, you have chosen as your pilgrimage destination a place whose history I am certain will prove to be of interest."

"Why, thank you, Bishop Nicholas. I was not aware of your affiliation with the New College of St Mary in Oxford. This place is magnificent; I look forward to learning what you know of its past."

"Very good. Well, you two must need some rest after your lengthy travel. I shall summon the page to show you to your rooms. We shall meet again after the evening prayer service in my private chapel." He rang a small brass handbell that sat upon the table at his side.

Within seconds, the page entered the solar to escort us out, and I turned to follow him. We were crossing through the adjoining hall when I realised my chaplain was not with us. I turned around and saw him and Bishop Nicholas, their heads together, in a private conversation. They were speaking in low voices, too low to be heard clearly from where I stood. As I started to retreat into the room, Bishop Nicholas turned and saw me. The two men abruptly ended their discussion, their voices turning audible.

"Until this evening, Richard."

"Yes, we shall see you then."

Rushing to join us, Père Charles made no mention of the conversation I had just witnessed. But observing it had not lessened my distrust of the bishop.

The page beckoned us to follow him to our accommodation in the dormitory range across the courtyard. Walking through the open space, I noted the courtyard's design was unusual: in most palaces of such distinction it might be either entirely cobbled with paving stones or covered in a flower-and-herb garden. The central garden I observed was planted in grass; set within the lawn was some type of intricate stonework, with a pattern I did not recognise. Seen from ground level, the shape could not be discerned; it was too large and complex. I had little time to contemplate its meaning.

"Here we are. You will find your rooms at the top of the stairs. Father Richard, your room is on the landing to the right, and Lady Isabelle, yours is to the left. We have delivered your belongings for you. Please call upon me to assist you if there is anything you require while you stay with us."

I ascended the staircase and, once at the top, I waited for Père Charles on the landing.

"You exchanged words privately with Bishop Nicholas as we left his solar. Are you able to tell me what you two discussed?"

My question was a test; I was curious how my chaplain would respond.

"He and I have some unfinished business to attend to and we need to find some time when we can discuss it. Please, do not concern yourself with these private matters, Lady Isabelle. Do not be anxious, what we speak of does not relate to you."

"Very well, then. Let us take our rest this afternoon. Please knock on my door when you depart for the chapel."

"It is my pleasure to do so, Lady Isabelle," replied Père Charles.

Though disappointed and still believing there was something my chaplain was hiding from me, I decided against questioning him about it any further at that moment.

Entering my room, to my surprise it was comfortably furnished with a cot and a scribe's desk, replete with a blotter and fat tallow candle. From the unshuttered windows I took in the view across the courtyard towards the bishop's hall and solar, and the range housing the bishop's chapel. Beyond that in the distance, rising high above the palace walls, stood the cathedral's central square tower.

Then something drew my attention to the centre of the courtyard; to the lawn set with cobblestones. The details of the intricate and complex pattern had eluded me earlier and even from where I stood now they still were not clear. Something about the design was strangely familiar, as if I had seen it somewhere before, perhaps at Rosete.

It occurred to me that with no guests to entertain other than ourselves, the great hall would not be in use. Above the hall ran an arcaded parapet; along its façade a unique black-and-white checkerboard pattern spanned the rooftops of all the palace buildings. Being up that high would doubtless allow me the perfect vantage point from which to get a better view of the design. I decided I would search for access to the parapet after dinner when everyone was asleep.

Later that day, a quiet knock on my door alerted me that it was time to attend the evening service. I gathered my cape and psalter and joined my chaplain in the stairway.

After we had arrived and were seated in the private chapel, I noticed the remarkable level of detail in its interior design. Along the outer wall, three traceried lancet windows depicted scenes from the life of St David. The silhouette of the cathedral façade across the Alun was visible through a large pointed arch window above the altar. A series of carved heads formed the corbels that lay at the base of the springing supporting the ceiling's stone vaulting. Before the altar lay a woollen rug, woven with complex patterns in jewel-like tones of azure, emerald and amber. I could not immediately identify the symbol in the centre of the rug though it looked rather like a compass crossed with a square, instruments commonly used by stonemasons.

The bishop led the evening service with two other priests in attendance. When it had ended, we followed him out of the chapel and into his solar. He shed his outer vestments and then the three of us entered the adjoining private dining hall. It was an intimate space, with a welcoming fire that crackled softly in a corner fireplace. In the centre of the room a round wooden table was set with silver bowls and goblets. Two jugs were already on the table, one filled with mead and the other with ale. After we had taken our seats, three servants appeared carrying platters of cooked meat, boiled fish, stewed vegetables and bread. At the bishop's request they left the platters on the table for us to serve ourselves and retreated from the room.

"Tell me, Lady Isabelle, for I am curious to know, will you be comfortable in your guest chamber?" the bishop asked after giving his blessing over our meal.

"I shall be, thank you for making the room available to me," I replied. "And your private chapel as well."

"Normally, you see, I stay at the country estate associated with St Davids, at Lamphey, outside Pembroke. It is a smaller palace and one that suits my daily needs better. I do return here when I know we are expecting pilgrims, as well as for feasts and other special occasions. I came at once when I received word of your imminent arrival. I must admit, I do not know of any other member of your sex who has expressed an interest in architecture and history the way Richard informs me you do. Your visit is indeed a rare and special treat for me."

We continued our lively conversation over dinner when I recalled my curiosity about the floor covering I had seen earlier.

"Perhaps you can explain to me about the carpet in your chapel. What is the significance of the pattern?"

To my surprise it was Père Charles who responded.

"Lady Isabelle, the shape you noticed has significance to those who follow the teachings of Christ and believe in the Holy Trinity. One day I shall explain it to you."

I watched the bishop's expression change. He was clearly relieved that he did not have to give me an explanation. His response again gave cause for me to entertain doubts about his trustworthiness.

"Well, then, I hope that our dinner tonight has been to your liking. I pray you both enjoy a restful sleep. Tomorrow we shall have a full house. The students who will join us are the brightest scholars from New College. The tutors normally send us their cleverest students once a year to study for five weeks here with us. They will provide us with interesting stories and enlightened conversation, I have no doubt."

"It is wonderful to be together again, dear friend," Père Charles said, rising from the table.

I joined him in preparing to leave.

"It is indeed. I look forward to seeing you at matins tomorrow in the cathedral," the bishop replied.

We left the hall and walked to our rooms in silence. As we reached the landing at the top of the stairs, we turned to our separate doors. To my surprise, I felt an exhalation of warm breath on my neck.

"Please forgive me, Lady Isabelle," Père Charles whispered from behind me. "Please forgive me and never forget me."

XXXV
The Secret Symbols

"... Yet the keys of the Church are more dependable than the hearts of kings."

S. Augustine, Sermon 351, 12

Before I could turn around to respond, my chaplain was gone, the door to his room quietly closing behind him. His sudden departure stunned me but I decided to let it rest. I recalled what he had said on previous occasions when I had questioned his purpose. Even with his mysterious behaviour I felt more confused by the way in which the bishop behaved toward me. I could not escape the mounting level of distrust I felt about our purpose in journeying to St Davids. The only comfort I took that evening was knowing we were safe within the palace walls.

From my darkened bedroom I glanced out the window over the courtyard. The stones set in the centre grass still roused my curiosity. I wanted desperately to see what the pattern was.

I had not yet changed my clothes for sleep, and so I waited until I saw that all the candles had been extinguished in the bishop's hall and solar and then made my way back down the stairs and across the courtyard to the great hall. The other palace residents had long since retired for sleep. I could hear the voices of the cook and scullery boy in the kitchen next door, reminding me of happier times in the company of Jeanne and Pey back at Rosete. The two servants were still tidying up after our meal. Staying in the shadows while trying to avoid the moonlight spilling out from between the clouds, I made my way up the steps of the great-hall porch and entered the darkened interior.

Once safely inside with the door closed behind me, I gave my eyes time to adjust to the dimly lit room. With only glimpses of moonlight cascading through the ocular Catherine-wheel window and several large windows to guide me, I stepped into the dining hall. Looking down, I was surprised to find not a wooden floor covered in rushes and reeds, but one made of stone tiles, painted over with a small floral motif in the centre. Two long wooden tables were already set in preparation for the students who would arrive the following day, and the high table on a raised dais was laid out for Bishop Nicholas, Père Charles and me.

Even in the dark of the night I could just detect the outline of a floral design painted on the wooden beams overhead, mirroring that depicted beneath my feet. As I moved silently across the tiled floor I noticed that the room had no fireplaces in the corners or along the walls; instead, a hearth with a louvre overhead sat in the centre. Four large tapestries hung from the walls, adding a rich layer of texture and warmth to the room.

Continuing through the room, I looked for a stairway or some means of gaining access to the parapet above. In the wall behind the dais was a door. I opened it slowly and entered a great chamber with an archway tucked in a far corner that led to an annex. Upon entering the separate smaller chamber, I spotted a newel staircase in a corner turret. Climbing the stairs, I eventually reached the roof and wall walk behind the arcaded parapet. Stepping to the courtyard side, my feet froze in place. As I peered down over the edge to the garden below, I clearly saw the pattern that had eluded me before; it was a compass and square, the same symbols that I had seen in the centre of the carpet that lay on the floor of the bishop's chapel!

But why? I wondered. Why were the tools of builders and stonemasons depicted in the grass of the central quadrangle? Then I recalled where else I had previously seen the same symbols: on our visit to William of Wykeham's Broughton Castle. They were carved in one of the bosses over the arcade in the stairway connecting the corridor of the great hall with the chapel on the first floor. It was conceivable that the master of the works in both places had wished to commemorate the workmen responsible for creating the buildings with symbols of their craft. But how would that explain the same emblems in the chapel, woven into the carpet?

Just as I was about to step away from the edge of the parapet and return to my room, I noticed candlelight flickering through the window of the bishop's solar. Next, I heard footsteps on the cobblestones below. I peeked over the rim of the wall, curious to see who was there. At first I thought it was the page who had shown us to our rooms earlier, but when he turned I could just make out the deep scar on his face. It was Père Charles! I followed him with my eyes as he bounded up the porch steps to the bishop's hall and disappeared inside.

I felt compelled to pursue him, for with whom could he have a meeting at such a late hour under the cover of darkness, in the bishop's solar? I quickly retraced my steps back downstairs, through the great chamber and dining hall. Checking first to ensure that no one else was about, I cautiously ran across the courtyard and mounted the stairs of the bishop's hall porch as my chaplain had done only a few minutes earlier. I stopped and listened for any footsteps coming up behind me.

After catching my breath for a moment, I silently entered, carefully sliding my feet across the polished wooden floor to the door connecting the bishop's hall to the solar. I could just barely make out two men's voices – those of the bishop and Père Charles. With my ear pressed firmly against the door, I heard a third male voice. I knew I had heard it before, but at first I could not place where. I concentrated on trying to determine the identity of the third person when I heard my name mentioned in their conversation by the bishop.

"And what about Lady Isabelle? What shall become of her? Surely you cannot abandon a lady of her standing here in *my* care. Come now, Richard, you have more heart than that. I wondered why you decided to bring her on this journey when you know the dangers are so great against your life."

"I know it was a great risk, but you do not know Her Ladyship as I do." My chaplain's voice remained calm. "She is a woman of strong mind and determined will, and I felt entirely capable of caring for her *and* being cared for by her should something have happened to either of us – which, might I remind you, it did not. How was I to know that I would be called to complete my mission when we visited James in Oxford last week? I had to bring her with me. I had promised her long ago that I would one day accompany her to St Davids, following Gerald's path, even before we left Gascony. The timing of the mission coincided with our journey; I could not send her back to Boarstall unattended. Remember, I am fortunate that her father provided me with a safeguard both in leaving Bordeaux and establishing my residency with the family at Boarstall. I know what is expected of me and I fully accept the terms of the mission; I am simply asking for more time now, time to help her adjust to the changes that are about to occur in my absence."

"There is not time to worry about Lady Isabelle when Sir Henry Lormont and his gang are at this very moment crossing through Pembrokeshire in pursuit of Richard. His safety must be made a priority for us. He must leave St Davids before his assassins find him!"

The bishop's final statement sent a wave of panic coursing through my body, but I could not tear myself away. I had to learn more.

The unidentified voice interrupted the conversation.

"I say, Richard, it is too late. What is done is done. You will have to live with the consequences of your decision to bring Lady Isabelle here. But I am afraid we cannot allow you more time. The boat sails at dawn for France and you must be on it with the *Mandylion*. If you wish to write Her Ladyship a letter explaining your departure and absence, you can be assured I shall deliver it to her personally in the morning after you have left."

I let out a gasp as I finally recognised the voice. It belonged to Father James! But I could not imagine how he had arrived in St Davids so quickly unless he had ridden ahead of us when we stopped at Tintern Abbey. The news that my guardian was to be gone and in possession of the *Mandylion* before I arose in the morning caused my body to tremble as confusion gripped my mind. My chaplain was to be in possession of the shroud of Christ? Was this what Père Charles had meant with the words he had spoken earlier in the evening as we parted company? Did that mean he was a Knight Templar? But why, I wondered, had he kept that from me? Confusion and doubts crept through my mind as I recalled our private conversation on the *Salamanca*. I really did not know my chaplain after all. With a broken and fearful heart I knew I had no choice but to make my escape.

In great haste, I returned to my room, grabbing my surcoat and saddlebag, filling it with my journals, writing instruments and psalter, before racing back across the courtyard to the gatehouse. Tripping on one of the cobblestones, I fell flat on my belly. Rolling to the side, I let out a piercing shriek as my ankle wrenched hard under me. Afraid that someone might have heard me, I picked myself up and hobbled to the gateway.

After sliding open the heavy iron bar that secured the main gate, I pushed the cumbersome wooden door ajar and crossed the bridge over the river towards the cathedral close. Glancing about in the dark of the night, I tried to find the path leading to the stable yard. I had to get to Peyriac and ride away from St Davids – I feared what the men planned to do with me once my chaplain was gone.

XXXVI
The Mandylion

"Hortus conclusus soror mea, sponsa, hortus conclusus, fons signatus."

Song of Solomon 4:12

I finally found the path to the stable yard and called out to Peyriac upon entering the barn. He whinnied a greeting to me and came to the front of his stall. I limped to him and threw my arms around his neck. With my body still damp with the sweat of panic from rushing to find him in the dark, my horse could smell the apprehension I felt. My ankle was now swollen and throbbing where I had twisted it, yet I found great relief in holding on to Peyriac. Sensing my discomfort, he bent his head down, blowing warm air through his nostrils at me.

"Oh Peyriac, we should never have come here!" I cried as I took several moments to catch my breath. "We must leave this place and try to find our way home. We must leave at once before Sir Henry arrives!"

While excitedly talking to my horse and resting my tear-stained face against the silky pile of his coat, I had not heard the footsteps quietly approaching his stall. Suddenly two hands reached out and pulled me away. Shocked and fearing for my life, I fainted.

When I had revived and opened my eyes, I was surprised to find that I was resting in my chaplain's embrace. I pushed myself away from him, unable to look him in the face as I spoke.

"Why did you really bring me here? Why must you leave for France? Are you returning the *Mandylion* to Rome? What will happen when Sir Henry and his men arrive? They cannot be far away from us now – I demand that you tell me the truth!"

My chaplain took my hand and led me to a bench outside Peyriac's stall door.

"Lady Isabelle, worry not about Sir Henry. We are surrounded by the bishop, clergy and monks who have secretly trained as warriors. Under their cassocks and robes they carry hidden arms and they are prepared to fight to the death to protect us. I can only apologise to you for any anxiety and concern that I have caused. I think in order to quell any lingering doubts about why we are here in St Davids, you should first know more about the *Mandylion* and how it came to be hidden here in St Davids. Would you like to know the history?"

Though anxious about the looming threat of my attacker suddenly appearing and repeating his assault, I kept my voice steady as I silently meditated on the thought: *trust in the Lord always*.

"That would certainly help. I now have so many concerns about my purpose as your companion on this journey – and I am far away from my family and do not know the outcome of the affair with my aunt. If you are taken from me I do not how I will manage to return home," I admitted.

"I understand. I hope what I have to tell you will help bring you some peace of mind," Père Charles said before he began to relate the history that unlocked the final mystery surrounding his identity and mission.

"The shroud first came into the possession of the Knights Templar through someone of whom you have learned a great deal on our journey, Geraldus Cambrensis. After leaving the company of Pope Innocent III in Ferentino in Italy in the summer of 1203, Gerald travelled through France on his way back to England. The Pope had instructed him that he was to stop in Paris and meet John, the exiled Archbishop of Dublin, to pick up a sacred cloth held by the King of France that he had brought back from crusade. This directive was given with the utmost secrecy and, as such, it was not until Gerald returned here to St Davids that the members of the Brotherhood learned what His Holiness had asked him to carry out of France."

"Does this mean that the members of 'the Brotherhood' as you refer to them are also a part of the Knights Templar? And does the Brotherhood still play a role in safeguarding the shroud? Is that why it is kept here?" I asked, recalling the imagery of the square and compass I had discovered earlier in the evening.

"Yes. My friends and companions in the Brotherhood are linked through their ancestry to those who carried out the mission of the Knights Templar in protecting the sacred relics from being destroyed during the time of the Crusades. Because of the wars with France over the past two centuries, the shroud was kept here in this most remote place, St Davids. Though the crusading Knights Templar of old have long since disappeared, a separate branch was founded by a Frenchman during the reign of King Richard, your ancestor. He established the Brotherhood which is called the Order of the Passion; we are no longer warriors who wish to destroy other cultures and faiths but rather men who desire to preserve sacred relics from the time of Christ. Our mission is to bring all mankind together through knowing the love of God. The artefacts, in particular the *Mandylion*, are critical evidence of Jesus Christ's existence in Biblical times."

"I am surprised that this shroud has survived without being traced to or discovered in St Davids."

"A duplicate shroud was created to appease the King of France and provide a decoy relic to attract crowds of pilgrims. This proved to be fatal for two of our founding members. In 1314 our leader, the grand master of the Knights Templar in France, Jacques de Molay, and another member, Geoffrey de Charny, were put to death in Paris by King Philip IV of France for owning the counterfeit cloth, amongst other fabricated reasons. The king became angry when he learned that the authenticity of the relic he worshipped was false. He commanded that the organisation be disbanded and its members persecuted."

My eyes were wide in awe and expectation of what he would say next.

"At the time, the Holy See of Rome was forced to deny the legitimacy of the cloth that Grand Master Jacques and his associate Geoffrey held, which the Holy See could do knowing that the real one was in the safekeeping of the Templars at St Davids. In publicly accepting the cloth in France as a counterfeit one, the Holy See denounced the Templars in order to placate the French king, and the Church outwardly distanced itself from us.

"Following these tragic events, many of our noble brothers throughout France were imprisoned, tortured and put to death by order of the king for their membership of our secret fraternity. Some of our members who survived the persecution in France were forced into seclusion, while many others escaped to England, Scotland and Wales. Yet each subsequent Pope has privately recognised the validity of the Knights Templar, in particular those who reside here at St Davids, and our mission of guarding the one true shroud."

"But how does this concern you? Why must you sail at dawn for France?"

"When I was a young scholar it was decided by the Brotherhood that, because of my lineage and youth, I should be the one to convey the *Mandylion* back to Rome. I was not present at the gathering but it was agreed upon by the members that when I was older I would be made a Knight Templar in order that I could one day complete a quest assigned to my father. Upon my joining the fraternity, they informed me that there would come a time when I would be instructed to take action in a secret assignment."

"Then, you are *really* a Knight Templar?" I asked, as I felt a surge of devotion and pride for my chaplain rise in my chest.

"I am, Your Ladyship." Père Charles bowed his head deferentially as he took up my hand in his.

Suddenly my head was filled with many questions, all rushing to the forefront of my mind at once. One by one they came spilling forth.

"Does the urgency to return the shroud relate to the fall of Bordeaux and the end of English control of Gascony?"

"Yes, it does. The holy shroud has remained in safekeeping over the centuries here at St Davids. But those who oppose King Henry believe that the time has come for drastic change. They wish for England to establish her own Church, and reassert ten of the twelve original 'Conclusions' drafted by the Lollards and posted to the doors of Westminster Hall during the reign of King Richard. They are secretly dividing the peerage of Westminster into those who follow them, and desire a new reformed Church, and those who wish to remain loyal to Rome. Should this group of noblemen, headed by the Duke of Somerset and Sir Henry Lormont, seize the shroud of Christ, they would be wholly capable of establishing a new Church of England."

He paused briefly, allowing me to digest all he had told me thus far.

"Unlike my father, who was killed for maintaining silence on where the shroud was hidden, Father James Redding, as the leader of the Brotherhood, was able to evade the murderous threats posed by the Dukes of Somerset and their fellow noblemen by seeking out a simple academic life in the safety of the New College of St Mary in Oxford. Do you remember the heavily fortified entrance to the college? It was designed that way intentionally, to prevent members of our order from being openly ambushed and attacked by assassins as they entered or left the premises."

"But I thought you told me that the college was founded by Bishop William of Wykeham." The imagery that had alluded me earlier came to mind. "Is that why there was a square and compass carved in the stone overhead on the way to the chapel at Broughton Castle, and why the same shape appears in the carpet and quadrangle of the Bishop's Palace? Are they symbols of the Knights Templar?"

"Yes, you are correct. The bishop was a descendant of the Knights Templar and he had symbols of the order carved into special stones set in his buildings, including his residence at Broughton and the New College of St Mary in Oxford. We have never divulged that it was his money that has helped spare the monasteries and abbeys in England and Wales from ruin in recent times of famine or plague. Indeed, the coffers at St Davids are still well funded from the substantial amount secretly bequeathed by the bishop upon his death. The recent building works that you found so remarkable in the palace here would not have been undertaken if he had not left the diocese the financial means to carry them out. The priests of his Oxford college are members of the Brotherhood who seek refuge in the academic hall that was founded to protect them and their vocation. The three words of the college motto, Manners Makyth Man, when abridged and turned upside down form the three letters WWW. These letters abbreviate the phrase 'Who worketh wonders', the secret riddle our members use to identify themselves to one another. The answer to the riddle is our password, Immanuel, which means 'God with us' in Hebrew."

"I recall that you exchanged that greeting upon meeting several of your associates, but I was afraid to ask you at the time what the words signified."

"I had not previously met those men. Once we established that we were all descendant members of the Knights Templar, we knew that we were helping each other as members of the Brotherhood."

"What about the image in the carpet that I mentioned over supper tonight? I could see that neither you nor the bishop wished to tell me the truth about it. What is its real significance?"

"Just like the symbol in the courtyard, the carpet image is an emblem of our fraternal order. It refers to the building of King Solomon's Temple and the Holy Sepulchre in Jerusalem. The round Temple Church in London that is home to the Knights Templar Brotherhood was designed as a memorial to the ancient sacred chapel in the Holy Land that sits over the tomb where Christ once lay."

As the pieces of the puzzle came to settle in my mind I suddenly understood what all the details meant.

"So it was the *Mandylion* that the assassins were searching for the night your family was murdered?" I interjected, my mind settling on all the details of my chaplain's past.

"That is correct; it had been decreed by the Knights Templar that my father, who was both a descendant Templar Knight and a member of King Richard's Order of the Passion, would secretly return the shroud to Rome. The night they murdered my family, the Beaufort brothers and Sir Henry's father searched our home, thinking the shroud was hidden there."

Here Père Charles paused and turned away from me. I could see in his expression that he was searching for the right words before continuing. After several moments in silence, he turned back, looked at me and took my hands in his.

"From the time we were first introduced, your father offered me his wisdom and friendship. After some very personal confessions on his part, he felt he could entrust me with the knowledge that he, too, is a follower of the Order of the Passion."

As he spoke those last words, Père Charles gently squeezed my hands. Shocked by what he had said, I rose and stepped away from him, casting his hands away from my own. Had Margaret's release and annulment been the work of the Brotherhood? The months spent working in Bordeaux, the notion that my father was doing all he could to win favour with members of the English nobility so that he might hold a seat in Parliament in London – was that possibly related to his membership in the Order of the Passion?

I turned back to Père Charles and sat down by his side, taking his hand in mine.

"I don't know quite what to make of all you have told me," I began, my voice soft and distant. "I am afraid I don't even know how I should address you. Are you still Père Charles or Father Richard, or…?"

"Isa, please call me Richard from now on," he said as he gently kissed my forehead. "There is one more thing I must confess to you tonight, since I am clearing my conscience and revealing the truth of my family and my life. I no longer wish to live a lie and hide my feelings for you in the presence of our Lord."

Richard stopped speaking and looked at me directly. Taking up my hands, he kissed each one tenderly.

"I have fallen in love with you, Lady Isabelle. I felt it in my heart from the moment we arrived at Benauges to rescue your sister. It has become increasingly difficult for me to hide and ignore my affection for you in our daily lessons and outings. So many times I wanted to tell you about my family history in conjunction with the Brotherhood and to ask that if you could possibly wait for me to return from my mission, one day we might share a life together."

He pulled me close to him as he continued to declare his feelings.

"Along the ride out here, I had to resist the temptation to abandon my father's legacy with the Knights Templar and Order of the Passion. I only wished to protect you, Isabelle; I never knew where I could take you that would keep you safe from harm. You are a part of me now. I want us to experience our love openly and to no longer keep it hidden from your family and those with whom I associate. I am now prepared to leave the Brotherhood and the Church to give myself wholly to you."

I closed my eyes and at last felt the lingering tenderness of his kiss on my lips. Slowly pulling away from me, he removed his clerical cape from his shoulders and laid it open across a pile of straw next to us. Placing his hands about my shoulders, he sat me down and laid me back onto the woollen wrap. He protectively enveloped his legs around mine and I felt a longing mount in me as he lay down at my side, drawing his hands up my spine to the base of my head, untwisting my hair and setting it free. As he did so I responded by inclining my face around his neck until my lips found the lobe of his ear. Gently kissing it, exhaling warm breath as I did so, I felt his body shudder with desire. I became lost in him, for I had found my new home and I knew I never wanted to leave the intimacy of his embrace. Finally we allowed ourselves to express the deeply sacred love that had been guarded for so long.

———

Even now, decades later, the memory of the love we shared in the stable at St Davids on that night feeds my soul. I can still recall feeling an overwhelming sense of peace in the hours and days that followed the confession of Richard's secrets. Yet my greatest sorrow was yet to come. For you see, Gentle Reader, it was only a few hours later that my precious love left me in order to continue his mission and see it through, completing his father's quest.

To this day, given what I know of him and his moral character, I can think of no man greater than he. I can imagine that the temptation would be great to forgo one's destiny in pursuit of one's desire. Yet this was not so with Richard. He had made his promise to his brothers in Christ long before he met me.

At my advanced age, I have only the greatest respect for him and his decision. When I was younger, and living through the final hours leading up to his departure for France, it was a very different story. I now offer you the conclusion of our tale.

XXXVII
The Templar's Garden

O what simple joy I take,
To hold thy hand in mine,
And hear thee speak my name:
For thy attentive love will always remain.

Take my hand, and fear thee not,
Love's tender kiss will not be fought:
Come, follow me, cast thy doubts aside,
For in thy mighty fortress shall I abide.

17 June 1453, St Davids

In the final hours we shared before the break of dawn, the stable provided an intimate and private setting for us to express our mutual devotion to each other. In response to Richard's willingness to confess his love for me, I knew I must share my own feelings with him.

The early morning was slipping by and our time together was quickly coming to an end. We knew these were the last moments we would share for a long time, possibly forever. With one of my arms wrapped securely across his torso, he drew me close to his side.

"As I lay here with you now, I realise the sacrifice you have made in bestowing your love upon me. I wish you to know how it pains me that you must leave so suddenly, especially after all you have told me tonight. Now I must tell you how I feel; that you will know how I have come to love and cherish you over the past year."

I took a moment to collect my thoughts before I continued.

"I first began to recognise you were my intended when we travelled to Benauges to rescue Margaret. I had witnessed visions from God that indicated I would bestow my love upon someone who felt great unworthiness in the world. I knew not what that meant, but when as we crossed the river to Saint Macaire, I began to feel my heart yield to you. Your strength of character and lack of fear in the face of great adversity while at Benauges attracted me to you even more. When we returned to Rosete with Margaret and Johan, I felt a sense of overwhelming joy at the very thought of being in your company.

"With every devotion you have made you have led me to a greater understanding and love for the Holy Trinity that exists within us, bonding us in our love for each other through that of Jesus Christ and his Father. It is your faith that you poured into me, saving me in my darkest hours in the aftermath of my rape. You made me want to live, to continue with my writing, to ride again. Through it all I remained steadfast in my belief that you feel as deep a love for me as I do for you."

Upon hearing these words, Richard gently pulled me to him. Before I could continue, he took my face in his hands and kissed me, a deeply passionate kiss, full of his yearning and desire. It was several moments before I could pull myself away.

"Our trip here to St Davids has filled me with both anxiety and concern for you. This will not abate until I know we are never to be apart again. I can tell that something is not right with you, with your mind; I wish to be a part of your world, to help make you feel safe as you travel to places yet unknown. So deeply do I love you that I cannot begrudge what you have accepted to do in returning the *Mandylion* to the Pope in Rome. You are a gracious and honourable man to keep a promise made by your father. This is a legacy that you must fulfil. I fear for you, though, Richard – for the demons that haunt your mind; that what I witnessed at Haverfordwest Castle will not be the last episode of madness you shall experience."

I turned my head, locking my eyes on his as I revealed the truth of God's prophecy.

"Years ago, in my first vision, the Lord appeared to me and told me that I would one day impart his love on his devoted son. His message confused me, for at the time I knew not of what son he spoke, let alone what love. But over the past months I now understand that he was calling me to you in that vision, to care for you and to love you; to affirm Christ's mercy and forgiveness on your tortured soul. You see, you are forgiven; as I am with you and tell you now, you are a good and faithful servant of the Lord. He will always guard you and protect you, and when we are apart I shall still pray for you; that the grace of God and all the Saints in Heaven may surround you and keep you safe from any harm that might come from others, or that you might bring upon yourself."

I laid my head down against his chest and listened to the steady pulsing rhythm of his heart. My own heart already ached for him; ached for the loss that was only hours away.

My confession complete, at last fatigue overcame us and we fell asleep. Sometime later, when the peal of the cathedral bells announced the dawn of the new day, he gently awakened me with his kiss.

"It is time, Isa," he whispered in my ear.

"No, please, no. It cannot already be time for us to part." I looked at him, drawing my fingers across the well-defined features of his face and lips one more time, committing them to my memory forever.

"I am afraid it is, and I am already late. I must get on the boat before Sir Henry arrives. It is surely waiting for me, and I have yet to say farewell to Bishop Nicholas and James."

"But wait. What is to become of me? Who will protect me from Sir Henry? How shall I return to Boarstall without you?"

He helped me up and we brushed each other free of the debris that lingered on our clothes from lying in the straw.

"James has already seen to those arrangements. You will stay here with him under his care. Other members of the Knights Templar have been called upon to be your personal guard and defend you should you meet with Sir Henry and his retinue. In the meantime, James is prepared to accompany you as your guardian. You are within a few days' ride of the remaining places visited by Gerald of Wales, and you have a learned Oxford scholar to guide you."

"But I do not want to visit any of these places without you."

"There, there…" Richard embraced me from behind, kissing the back of my head reverently. Turning me around to face him, he continued.

"I know how unbearable this is. It is also so very difficult for me that I must leave you, that I may never see you again. As I stand before you now I commit myself to you. Our destiny, Isabelle, is not in our hands. You must rest your faith in the Lord our Father, that he will one day see us reunited, somewhere, somehow. I was once buried in my own loss and unworthiness before the Lord. But you have changed these feelings in me and I shall not rest until I have succeeded in my assignment; one day I will return to you."

He cupped my face in his hands. Gently lifting it, his lips met mine.

"Do not despair for me, dear Isa. Use this time while we are apart to continue your learning, your reading and, most importantly, your writing. I want you to ask James to share with you a written volume by a mystic, Julian of Norwich, for her profound visions of divine love described in her *Showing of Love* will bring you comfort and healing from the pain you are certain to face at our separation. James is familiar with her many texts on forgiveness and Christ's enduring passion and love for us; he can provide instruction on her writings. I am certain her words will prove calming to your soul. Remember that according to your vision we are blessed with sharing a divine love at the core of friendship. In my absence, take comfort knowing that our Father in Heaven is watching over both of us, that his love and mercy will support us both. I promise to do all in my power to survive and come home to you once more. And, when I do, I shall make you my wife, and together we shall live out our years."

He reached into the outer pocket of his clerical surcoat, pulled out a silk pouch and, opening it, took out a gold signet ring. "This ring belonged to my mother. My father commissioned it for her. It displays the Earl of Huntingdon crest. James kept it hidden all these years in case one day I should meet a lady whom I wished to marry. Upon meeting you for the first time, he knew you were the chosen one. That morning in New College, as we parted company, he gave me the document bearing instructions for the safeguard of the *Mandylion*. As I opened the document and read that I was being called into service, I found the pouch and ring inside. I knew in my heart that the decision I would make would be the right one, for now I can do this."

As he said these words he took my hands in his, slipping the ring upon my finger.

"I give this ring to thee, dear Isabelle. Wear it and never take it off. It is a symbol of my eternal love for you. Cherish it as a reminder of the divine love we share. Know that when I return to you, I shall have another ring, a marriage ring, to be blessed by the Pope, which will unite us forever as husband and wife."

"I shall wait for you, Lord Richard, you have my assurance of that. You are my one true love. I wish to be your wife and give myself wholly to you. Wherever you are, that is where I wish to be also."

He held me close as I buried my face in the folds of his cape. Neither of us moved until we heard the voice of Bishop Nicholas break the quiet stillness that hung in the air around us.

"Excuse me, may I interrupt you?" he began, hanging a little back and away from us to give us some privacy in our final moments together. "I am afraid it is time for Richard's departure. We have word that the winds on the coast have picked up and the Celtic Sea waters are likely to turn rough. Richard needs to board the ship moored in Caerfai Bay and sail for France as soon as possible. Of greater concern, we have received word that Sir Henry and his men spent the night outside Haverfordwest at Roch Castle, not far from here. We have packed your bags, Richard, and carried them to the stable yard for you. James is here, too. He wishes to say farewell. Can we be of help in getting your horse saddled?"

"No, that will not be necessary, Nicholas. Lady Isabelle can help me. We will be joining you shortly."

"Very well. I leave you to make your preparations." He then turned and departed.

"I should be most grateful if I might accompany you for one last ride before you sail. May I escort you to the dock?"

"Of course, Isa. Nothing would please me more."

We quickly saddled our horses and led them out of the stable into the chill of the early morning. The sun had yet to fully rise, and a cool breeze blew in off the waters of the Celtic Sea.

"Richard, dear friend," Father James called out when he saw us emerge. "Be assured, I shall look after and protect your Lady Isabelle. I shall ensure that she is safely returned to her family at Boarstall. Do be careful and send word only when it is safe to do so. Trust no one on the road. Anyone you meet could be a potential assassin."

"Thank you, James. It is difficult for me to leave all of you and most especially, Lady Isabelle, whom I have asked to be my wife. She has accepted my proposal, knowing full well what fate may befall me on this journey."

Father James and Bishop Nicholas looked jubilant as they stepped forward to congratulate us.

"Your Ladyship, Richard, congratulations!" they exclaimed, almost in unison, both men bowing their heads to me.

"What wonderful news to receive. Does she know about the order?"

"Yes, James, she may be trusted with our secrets."

"I am so very happy for you, my son," the bishop said, smiling. "You both will share a life full of attentive love together. It is a privilege that you proposed marriage here in St Davids. When you return, you must come back and visit me. We shall feast in your honour."

"Nicholas, you have been a true friend to me – I could ask for nothing more. We shall indeed return to you as man and wife and once again enjoy your gracious hospitality. These feelings we share for each other have developed over much time. Our decision to marry is not one we have made on impulse."

"I am certain that is so." The bishop pulled a worn leather pouch from inside his gown, where it had been hidden from sight. "Richard, here, take your parcel."

"What is that?" I asked, puzzled that a tattered old sack would require such concealment.

"It contains the *Mandylion*, Lady Isabelle, the shroud of Our Lord Jesus Christ, the most holy of holy relics. It must only be passed from the hands of one Templar to another," Bishop Nicholas replied, his hushed tone reverential.

Richard took the pouch and tied it around his waist, hiding it under his cape.

"Let us come together now and pray," the bishop instructed, and we bowed our heads in an attitude of prayer.

"Dear Heavenly Father, we ask you to watch over your son and guardian of the *Mandylion* as he travels to Rome to return the shroud to its rightful home in the sanctity of the Church of St Peter. Be with him on his journey; keep him safe and in good health and spirits. We pray that one day he will return to us so that he might enjoy the blessings of marriage to his betrothed Lady Isabelle. Keep her in your sight, O Lord, for she will need your strength in the coming days to keep her soul from bearing the pain of separation from her beloved. We commit these and all our concerns to you, our Father in Heaven," the bishop concluded, raising his hand in the air to make the sign of benediction over us. "In the name of the Father and of the Son and of the Holy Spirit. Amen."

"Richard, you may show Her Ladyship the way to the dock and ask one of the men down there to bring her back once you have sailed. These country roads can be daunting to someone not familiar with them. Safe journey and God be with you."

"Thank you, Nicholas. The peace of our Lord be with you, brother, and also with you, James. I look forward to the day when we can all once again enjoy a meal and each other's company."

"Godspeed, Richard. We shall continue to pray for your safe return to your home in England," said Father James, his voice solemn.

We mounted our horses, setting out through the tower gate and onto the road we had travelled the day before. I had been a mere student of history, on a trip with a man who was my guardian and chaplain, a member of the Knights Templar, and overnight I had become his betrothed. I was to marry the man whom I loved, a feeling that should have provided great comfort and elation, but instead I felt a sense of impending peril for both of us. I tried not to think of the dangers before him, and I offered a silent prayer for his safety. It was the first of innumerable devotions I would make in the months to come.

The sun was now rising above the horizon, its glorious morning rays illuminating the landscape around us. Presently we came upon a narrow path set in the coastal bluffs. Following its descent to the dock below, I could feel the breeze grow steadily stronger. In the distance, the mast of the ship that was to carry Richard to France swayed gently in the winds over the water.

"Good morning, Your Lordship," called out one of the sailors as we approached the dock.

As we rode up, the captain walked over and greeted us. "You must be Lord Richard of Huntingdon. I am Captain Stephen Dunsworth. It is best if we move along, Your Lordship. I can see that the winds are picking up and if we are to make the crossing safely and in good time, we must be setting sail. We are taking your horse, are we, My Lord?"

"Yes, thank you. My horse will accompany me on board."

Richard dismounted and handed the reins of his horse to a sailor waiting to board the animal and then turned to help me down from Peyriac.

"Let us make haste, Your Lordship. We must be on our way," the captain ordered before returning to his ship.

In our final moments together, Richard held me close to him, the breeze blowing through his fair hair, the sunlight casting a golden sheen upon his countenance. Tenderly he kissed my lips.

"Do not forget me, Isabelle, for I shall never forget you. It is for you that I shall survive this trip. I promise you, by the grace of God, we will see each other again and remain together as husband and wife."

With the rush of the sea breeze whipping up around us we stood a moment longer on the dock, our eyes locked on each other, neither of us wishing to pull away from the embrace we shared.

"I love you, Richard. I knew from the moment I felt the thrill of your first kiss many months ago. I could ask for nothing more than to feel, once again, the safety your presence brings to my life. I promise I shall love and honour only you. You are my salvation and I shall remain steadfast for you."

"Your Lordship, I am afraid we really must put out to sea!" Captain Dunsworth's voice called out from across the dock.

"Farewell, my sweet Isabelle," Richard uttered lovingly while raising his hand and affectionately stroking my face. He bent his head towards mine and our lips touched once more. With the greatest of difficulty we pulled away from one another and parted.

A sudden surge of abandonment came over me and I felt an emptiness in my heart, with no hint of how to survive my solitude. My eyes followed the shape of my beloved as he strode quickly toward the ship, finally jumping on board just as the ties were being let free. When he turned around, through his gaze I felt the penetrating flame of the Holy Spirit uniting our souls one last time.

The boat set out slowly from the inlet as the sailors hoisted the sails to catch the winds. Once out in the open waters and stronger winds, away from the protective shelter of the rocky cliffs around me, it picked up speed. I stood on the dock watching until it disappeared beyond the horizon.

In the coming months I would long to be with my Templar Knight – to hear the sound of his strong, clear voice; to be guided in my faith by him; to feel the intimacy of our love that had survived against all odds.

A voice came from behind me, reminding me that I was not alone. "My Lady? Excuse me, may I escort you back to St Davids now?"

"Of course. I am sorry; I did not hear you approach," I said, my voice low, wiping the tears from my eyes. "Yes, we should leave straight away."

I took one more glance out to sea and then mounted Peyriac for the ride back to the Bishop's Palace. My mind was still occupied with all that had occurred since arriving in St Davids. But now my love had truly departed, and the reality of what had happened filled my thoughts with great uncertainty, for I would have to rely solely on my own faith in God to see us reunited again. Though unknown to me at the time, what lay in store next for me was an even greater adventure than what I had already experienced in leaving Rosete to make a new life in England.

———

Gentle Reader,

Here I must take a moment to reflect on these events – I assure you there is much more to tell, if you will allow this elderly noblewoman time to collect her thoughts before continuing. As I watched my betrothed sail away from me that fine day in June, so many summers ago, I felt no desire to continue my journey in his absence. Yet God had another plan for me. I could never have imagined I might one day search for the Vitruvian wonders of ancient Rome, following the path of the Knights Templar. But now that I was Richard's betrothed, the course of my life was set. Very soon, I would find myself called to Italy. I would make my visit there along the route taken centuries before by Geraldus Cambrensis and countless other pilgrims on their way to St Peter's in Rome, the very seat of our faith.

PREVIEW

Queen of Heaven

The Maid of Gascony Series, Book 2

It is the end of the Hundred Years War. The House of Lancaster is on the brink of collapse, and with it, the King of England and those families who support him.

Young mystic Lady Isabelle d'Albret Courteault has discovered unsettling truths about her family and chaplain, ones that ultimately end in the deaths of her loved ones and destruction of her home at Boarstall.

During a time of mounting tensions and bloodshed across England and Wales, this is a tale of one woman's remarkable fight to protect those she loves and the faith she follows.

Coming soon

PREVIEW

The King's Treasure

The Maid of Gascony Series, Book 3

The madness of King Henry VI has tipped the balance of power at court in Westminster; the end of his reign is nigh.

Though still a mystic, Lady Isabelle d'Albret Courteault is no longer a maiden. She remains steadfast in her oath of loyalty to the English crown that she made in her youth, and she is committed to supporting the memory of the English King whose blood she carries.

At last, when she makes a startling discovery about her ancestor's icon, the purpose of her life begins to take shape. But will she survive long enough to complete the final journey to bring it home to England?

Coming soon

Glossary

Barbican – a heavily defended entrance to a castle or fortified place

Boss – a carved keystone often placed at the intersection of diagonally vaulted ribs in a ceiling

Cinquefoil window – a rounded window comprised of five leaf-like openings, radiating from a common centre

Corbel – a carved bracket supporting the springing of a ribbed vault

Crenellation – the open spaces of a parapet

Demesne – lands making up part of an estate belonging to a sovereign or manor house

Les filleules – a group of English held towns in Gascony located along the Garonne River

Inner ward – an open space within the walls of a castle

La Male Journade – 1 November 1450, the day Bordeaux was taken by the French, with hundreds of Gascon and English lives lost in the battle for control of the city

Lancet window – a type of narrow window opening culminating in an arch at the top

Latrine – a stone toilet set in a castle wall

Loophole – a narrow opening, often with a rounded centre, through which missiles are launched; can also be in the shape of a cross to accommodate a crossbow

Merlon – the filled spaces of a parapet

Mullion – a vertical bar between the panes of a window

Newel staircase – a winding staircase with a central pillar from which steps radiate

Parapet – also called a battlement, the low barrier running along the roofline of a castle roof

Portcullis – an iron grate used in a gateway to prevent access to a castle or fortified place

Postern – private, often rear, entrance opposite the main gate in a medieval castle

Quatrefoil window – a rounded window comprised of four leaf-like openings, radiating from a common centre

Refectory – medieval dining hall

Solar – private chamber in a medieval residence, usually placed outside the bedchamber

Springing – a collection of ribs formed at the base of a vaulted ceiling

Traceried roundel – a small round window ornamented with a delicate interlacing of ribs

Transom – a crossbar dividing a window horizontally

Acknowledgements

To Pete Duncan and the Duckworth team, my darling agent Andrew Hayward, Fanny Emily Lewis and the editors past and present: Joyce Thomas, Sally O-J, Louise Harnby and Elodie-Olson-Coons; you have infused the trilogy with the breath of life, unmasking Lady Isabelle so her voice can be heard and her story fully told.

To the many readers and friends who have supported me on this long journey I give deep and heartfelt gratitude, especially: Martin Kemp, Dillian Gordon, Jon and Linda Whiteley, Larissa Haskell, Ysenda Maxtone-Graham, Johanna Hall, Michael Stroup, Revd Annanda Barclay, Naomi Braun, Lyndlee Brown, Rani Fischer, Meijia Gao, Revd Bear Ride and Gina Williams.

To the priests at Church of the Advent in San Francisco: Fr Paul Allick, Fr Roderick Thompson, Fr Alex Martin, Fr John Porter and to the congregations and choirs there and in the churches and college chapels in Oxford, you are my touchstone. *Gratias vobis ago.*

About The Maid of Gascony Series

Set amidst the fall of the House of Lancaster and inception of the House of Tudor, the Maid of Gascony series follows the life and travels of young mystic Lady Isabelle d'Albret Courteault as she comes of age.

While the world around her is filled with bloodshed, revenge, and disease, she remains fearless in the face of her adversaries, relying on her steadfast faith and the love of her chaplain to survive.

Along the way she discovers a lost icon once possessed by her ancestor, King Richard II. Will its fourteenth-century origins finally be revealed?

Note from
the Publisher

To receive updates on new releases in the *Maid of Gascony* series –
plus special offers and news of other acclaimed historical fiction –
sign up now to the Duckworth historical fiction mailing list at
duckworthbooks.co.uk/maidofgascony-signup.